"Boy, you ever seen a lightning bug?"

The old man held out a glass cube. Frozen in its center was a heavy black beetle.

Cyrus closed his fingers around the glass.

"Careful, she's hot," the old man said.

Electricity shot up Cyrus's arm. He staggered backward and swung his arm down. Glass shattered on the asphalt as the beetle tumbled free. With a pop and a crackle, it launched, blue electric arcs trailing from its abdomen and flickering between its wings.

Cyrus's bare feet began to tingle. He spun, wet asphalt tearing at the balls of his feet as he scrambled toward the motel. Ten strides, and he'd reached the front door. He jerked it open.

Thunder knocked him forward.

Also by N. D. Wilson

ASHTOWN BURIALS
I: The Dragon's Tooth
II: The Drowned Vault

Leepike Ridge

THE BOOKS OF THE 100 CUPBOARDS

100 Cupboards
Dandelion Fire
The Chestnut King

✤ ASHTOWN BURIALS ✤
BOOK I

THE
DRAGON'S
TOOTH

N. D. WILSON

BLUEFIRE

Text copyright © 2011 by N. D. Wilson
Cover art copyright © 2012 by Jeff Nentrup
Map art copyright © 2011 by Aaron Becker

All rights reserved. Published in the United States by Bluefire, an imprint of Random House Children's Books, a division of Random House, Inc., New York. Originally published in hardcover in the United States by Random House Children's Books, New York, in 2011.

Bluefire and the B colophon are registered trademarks of Random House, Inc.

Visit us on the Web!
randomhouse.com/kids

AshtownBurials.com

Educators and librarians, for a variety of teaching tools,
visit us at randomhouse.com/teachers

The Library of Congress has cataloged the hardcover edition of this work as follows:
Wilson, Nathan D.
The dragon's tooth / N.D. Wilson. — 1st ed.
p. cm. — (Ashtown burials ; bk. 1)
Summary: When their parents' seedy old motel burns down on the same night they are visited by a strange man covered in skeleton tattoos, Cyrus, Antigone, and their brother Daniel are introduced to an ancient secret society, and discover that they have an important role in keeping it alive.
ISBN 978-0-375-86439-1 (trade) — ISBN 978-0-375-96439-8 (lib. bdg.) —
ISBN 978-0-375-89572-2 (ebook)
[1. Secret societies—Fiction. 2. Brothers and sisters—Fiction. 3. Apprentices—Fiction.
4. Magic—Fiction.] I. Title.
PZ7.W69744 Dr 2011 [Fic]—dc22 2009038651

ISBN 978-0-375-86396-7 (pbk.)

RL: 4.2

Printed in the United States of America
10 9 8 7 6 5 4 3 2 1
First Bluefire Edition 2012

Random House Children's Books supports
the First Amendment and celebrates the right to read.

❋

For James Kenneth Thomas III,
without whom, not a chance

❋

Please declare aloud: I hereby undertake to tread the world, to garden the wild, and to saddle the seas, as did my brother Brendan. I will not turn away from shades in fear, nor avert my eyes from light. I shall do as my Keeper requires, and keep no secret from a Sage. May the stars guide me and my strength preserve me. And I will not smoke in the library. Translation approved, 1946.

✳ one ✳

THE ARCHER

NORTH OF MEXICO, south of Canada, and not too far west of the freshwater sea called Lake Michigan, in a place where cows polka-dot hills and men are serious about cheese, there is a lady on a pole.

The Lady is an archer, pale and posing twenty feet in the air above a potholed parking lot. Her frozen bow is drawn with an arrow ready to fly, and her long, muscular legs glint in the late-afternoon sun. Behind her, dark clouds jostle on the horizon, and she quivers slightly in the warm breeze pushed ahead of the coming storm. She has been hanging in the air with her bow drawn since the summer of 1962, when the parking lot was black and fresh, and the Archer Motel had guests. In those days, the Lady hadn't been pale; she had been golden. And every night as the sun had set, her limbs had flickered and crackled with neon, and hundreds of slow cars and sputtering trucks had traveled her narrow road, passing beneath her glow. When young, she had aimed over the road, over the trees, toward Oconomowoc,

Wisconsin. Now, thanks to the nuzzling of a forgotten eighteen-wheeler, her glow has gone and she leans back, patiently cocking her arrow toward the sky, waiting to ambush the clouds.

The motel is nothing like its proud lady archer. While she stands tall, it sags, shedding yellow paint like an autumn maple casting off its leaves. The walkways are powdered orange with rust. The cracks in the small courtyard are thick with thistles. Behind the motel, a battered and split chain-link fence imprisons a swimming pool too small for a diving board even if its cracked bottom could have held water. Behind the pool and the fence, a thick and tangled barrier of brush and stunted plum trees protects the motel from sprawling unused pastures, murky streams, and the gray peaks of distant cattle barns.

To a traveler's eyes, the motel is dead and useless, a roadside tragedy, like the remains of some unfortunate animal in a ditch—glimpsed, mourned, and forgotten before the next bend in the road. But to the lean boy with the dark skin and the black hair struggling in the thick brush behind the pool, the motel is alive, and it is home.

Branches snapped as Cyrus Smith grunted, fighting the many fingers that held him in place. He had paths. He had tunnels through the hedge that he could follow doubled over with his eyes closed, hollows hidden from the outside world, floored with beaten earth and plum pits. To him, the hedge was no obstacle.

Unless he was carrying a tire. And today, he was carrying two.

Gritting his teeth, Cyrus surged forward. Wet rubber dug into each arm. Water sloshed out of the tires onto his sides. His schoolbag snagged on a branch behind him. He was close. The branch snapped and he was closer. Brittle wood clawed at him and gave way.

Cyrus lunged out of the hedge and let the tires fall from his arms. Panting, dripping, he leaned his back against the old rattling fence, braced his hands on his knees, and looked around. His hair was more than black. Wet with sweat, it glistened like obsidian—like his eyes. His legs and arms were smeared with mud. The tops of his shoes were hidden with silty muck from the bottom of the stream where he had found the tires. He kicked off his shoes and let his toes splay in the scraggly grass, breathing hard, listening to a team of cicadas electrocute the air from the brush behind him.

He didn't know what time it was. Dan and Antigone might be back. Might not. He didn't care how late he had been; they shouldn't have left him. Skipping out of school had thrown him off, and he'd gotten back to the motel just in time to watch the red station wagon disappear.

And then the front-desk phone had started ringing.

He shouldn't have answered it, but he'd been irritated. His days were always filled with shouldn'ts.

"Archer Theme Park and Resort," Cyrus had said. And then, though he wasn't sure why: "This is Dan."

A throat had cleared on the other end. "Cyrus?" The man's voice was low, his breath thick, like he was underneath a blanket.

"I'm Dan," Cyrus had said. He couldn't sound that different from his brother. He lowered his voice. "What can I do for you, sir?" Totally Dan. Nice. Patient. Groveling.

"Well . . . Cyrus Lawrence Smith . . . I need a room."

Cyrus had squirmed. "We're full," he'd said quickly. "But please try us again sometime." He should have hung up. Right then.

The man breathed in slowly. His rusty voice sharpened. "Listen up, kid. I'm just a few miles down the road, and tonight I'm sleeping in one-eleven. Not one-ten. Not two-eleven. Room one hundred and eleven. You understand? That's my room. Tonight. I don't care who's in it. Clear them out, or I will."

The line clicked dead.

"Whatever, old man." Cyrus had dropped the receiver and exhaled, trying to ignore the tightness in his throat, the sound of his own voice. Had the man watched Dan leave? Did some stranger really know his voice? He couldn't be scared. He wasn't that kid. He

4

survived school by not being scared. By not seeming scared, at least.

Still, he wasn't going to hang around alone. Instead, shouldering his schoolbag, he had locked the front door and tromped out into the pastures to burn daylight. Dan shouldn't have left him behind. Waiting around for psychos wasn't his job, and he wasn't about to clean a room. Not any room. Especially not 111.

Two tires. Blinking away sweat, Cyrus nudged them each with a toe. Not bad. He'd never managed two at once. He'd never even found two in the same week, let alone in the same muddy stretch of stream. He dragged his arm across his forehead. Had the kook already shown up? Why would anyone insist on a particular room at the Archer? It wasn't like any of them were mold-free or had Jacuzzi tubs or uncracked mirrors.

Cyrus pulled up the hem of his shirt and ground his face into it. The white cotton was already soaked with tire slosh, but it was better than nothing.

California had never been like this. Warm, sure. Sunny, always. Well, almost always. Not during the winter storms. But muggy? Never.

Cyrus closed his eyes and tried to picture the cliffs of Northern California falling away beneath him, the slow-rolling white lines of surf breaking off of the points, ruffling the kelp beds, tumbling the tourist surfers.

It didn't work. There would be a cool breeze coming in off the ocean. Sweat wouldn't stick to him like this. He'd been ten the last time he felt that breeze. Two years ago, and still his skin remembered.

Cyrus glanced up at the dropping sun. He'd been in the fields for a while. Dan and Antigone might be back. Sighing, he bounced slowly against the chain-link fence and then straightened. He needed a storm, something to break the heat's stranglehold on the day. There was supposed to be one, but he'd go crazy if it didn't break before dark. He bent over, grabbed the closest tire, heaved it to his shoulder, and launched it over the fence. It hopped on the concrete lip and flipped, scattering drops of filthy water, bouncing into the pool, where twelve other tires and two twisted bicycles waited. The pool was a mass grave for worn rubber. An open grave. Someday, when Dan wasn't around, he'd try to melt them all down. Maybe with a black rubber bottom, the pool would actually hold water. Or not. Things would find a way to go wrong.

The second tire followed. Fourteen.

Cyrus adjusted the strap of his bag, saluted the tires, and, leaving his shoes, walked barefoot around the side of the motel and into the parking lot. Empty. No strange man. No Dan. No Antigone. He walked to the peeling white door labeled 111 and checked the knob. Still locked. He slid his key into the dead bolt. Sticking knee-high out of the wall beside him, an air conditioner hiccuped. The knob turned and the door swung in.

Compared to the parking lot, the room was arctic. The lights were off, and Cyrus didn't turn them on. This was his space, and after two years, it no longer felt like a motel room. Maps—his father's—were tacked all over the walls. Tired shelves slept beneath his overcrowded collections—scavenged animal skulls, comic books, bones, license plates, oddly shaped or glistening rocks, and army relics that had been his grandfather's. In the corner by the bathroom, a plaid couch drooped with a broken backbone. Four skis stuck out from underneath it, mounted the previous winter. Dan had refused to pull it behind the station wagon. There was no television. Most of those had been sold. A three-legged record player sat on a dresser covered in dust. Six months ago, when Cyrus had found it in a ditch behind his school, he had intended to fix it. Now he had no intentions at all.

Cyrus threw his bag onto a rickety desk covered in pocketknife scrawlings and dropped onto his bed. When he'd skipped out of school at lunch, there had been stacks of papers in his bag—it was always that way on the last day. Grades. Accumulated math tests and quizzes. Science. Compositions. And they'd been good. Good enough. Not great. Better than his brother and sister would have guessed. Not that it mattered. After the red station wagon had disappeared without him, Cyrus had carried them into the fields for a somber ritual. They were all underwater now. Pinned beneath a heavy stone, never to be resurrected. Fish would learn the taste of math.

He would have shown his parents.

"That was different," Cyrus said out loud.

The air conditioner choked, struggled, and died. Cyrus didn't notice. Rolling onto his side, he shoved his hand under his mattress and pulled out two worn California drivers' licenses. Splaying them between his fingers, he studied the faded photos. His mother, known to the State of California as Catherine Smith, was described as 5'7" and 122 lbs. Her eyes were bright, even in the smudged photo on plastic. Cyrus had gotten her dark skin and black hair. So had his sister. Daniel was an early reproduction of their father. Straw-blond, at least when there had been California sun and salt water to keep it that way. Daniel's hair had been brown by their first Wisconsin Christmas.

Cyrus picked at a bent corner on his father's license. Lawrence Smith. 6'3" and 190 lbs. Smirking, not smiling. Cyrus had gotten the smirk. And the height.

Cyrus held his two grainy parents next to each other.

Twelve years ago, on a cliff overlooking the sea, he had startled these two people by being born. According to family legend, he had spent the rest of the day wrapped in a picnic blanket. For ten years, he'd heard his parents tell the story—he could hear them now, bantering in front of friends, his mother's accented voice assigning humorous blame to his father for the ill-timed hike, and finally, always together, delivering the closing line of his birth story with a pair of proud smiles: "That's Cyrus for you. He hasn't changed at all." And he wouldn't. Not ever.

But that story and its closing line were from another life and another time. Cyrus would never hear his father's voice again. And his mother breathed only the faintest whisper of whispers, trapped in her hospital sleep.

Cyrus exhaled, long and slow.

"Daniel!"

Thrusting the keepsakes under his mattress, Cyrus slid off the bed and jumped toward the door.

"Daniel Smith!"

Backing out into the parking lot and the sun, Cyrus looked up. At least the wind was moving now. The Pale Lady was wobbling and a black cloud range was chewing on the horizon. Old Mrs. Eldridge was perched on the walkway outside room 202. She was wearing her pink robe and a straw gardening hat. Last time he'd seen her, she'd been in 115. Before that, it had been 104, overlooking the empty pool. Three rooms in the past month, closer to a dozen switches on the year.

"Daniel Smith!" she yelled again. This time, she

cinched her robe tight and began to move toward the stairs.

"You're looking pink today, Mrs. Eldridge." Cyrus moved farther back, shifting bare feet on the hot asphalt. "Do you need something?"

Mrs. Eldridge stopped, covered her right eye, and leaned over the rail, squinting down at Cyrus. "What if I do?" she asked.

"Then I'll try to act like Dan," Cyrus said. "What do you need? But it better not be your toilet. I don't do toilets. You'll have to plunge it yourself."

The old woman straightened up and pointed down the stairs. "No one is answering the phone. Someone ought to answer. What if a guest had an emergency?"

"Daniel's gone, Mrs. Eldridge. He ditched earlier. And you're the only guest."

"Well, what if I had an emergency?"

Cyrus grinned up at her. "I'm here, aren't I?"

"Lotta good you'd do me." The woman scrunched her mouth. "I want the girl. Where's Antigone?"

"She's with Daniel in the city. Visiting Mom." Cyrus spread his arms wide. "I should be with them, but I'm not. It's me or nothing, Mrs. Eldridge. What'll it be? What's your emergency?"

The woman sniffed. "I want my waffle. Daniel knows I usually like it at six, but there's a storm coming and I want it now. I'm not going to miss my waffle for

10

any power outage, no sir." She squinted at Cyrus. "And scrub those hands before you make it. And change your shirt. You're filthy. Where are your shoes? You should eat something yourself. You look like you're made of broomsticks. Your poor mother would be ashamed."

Cyrus felt his body tighten and his toes clench at the pavement. His smile vanished. "Not like *your* mom, then?" He closed his mouth; he swallowed. His forehead was suddenly clammy, cool in the breeze. He shouldn't have said that. Another shouldn't. He liked Mrs. Eldridge.

"Sorry. I—" He bit the rest back. "Sorry."

The old woman in pink and the boy in bare feet stood in silence. Dust shuffled across the parking lot. The Pale Lady shook on her pole. Cyrus could feel guilt in his stomach, but he wasn't going to look away.

After a moment, Mrs. Eldridge turned slowly and began to walk back to her room. "Scrub your scrawny paws!" she yelled. "And you better not turn up at my door in that shirt. Not too doughy, and no crunchy bits either!"

The door slammed on 202, and Cyrus puffed out his cheeks. The sky above him was filling with dust, and the wet, warm air was growing heavier. It might rain mud. The day needed the storm. He needed the storm. And he hoped the station wagon roof leaked on Daniel and Antigone all the way home.

The original architect of the Archer Motel had blueprinted a full dining room and an enormous kitchen capable of producing three spectacular roadside buffets per day. Where the architect had dreamed his kitchen, the builders had put a broom closet. Where he had drawn his expansive dining room, they had put a small square with green carpet and fake wood paneling. There was enough space for one round table, one giggling refrigerator, and one pink Formica counter bolted to the wall. The counter held a chrome four-slot toaster and an oversize waffle iron built like an antique printing press.

Steam slipped out of the iron's sealed jaw, and a red light blinked lethargically on its back. Cyrus yawned and slapped his shorts, watching the dust slip away in clouds. He'd sprinkled chocolate chips in the batter as a sort of apology. He'd even washed his hands. At least he'd apologized. But crazy old lady or not, she shouldn't talk about his mother.

The dining nook rattled with the sound of a passing semi. Or the wash of distant thunder. It was hard to tell from inside the Archer. The walls could rattle if someone sneezed ten rooms away.

"C'mon," Cyrus said. He picked up a battered metal fork and rapped the waffle iron. "Seriously, how long does it take? Turn green already. It's just a waffle."

The light reddened slowly, and then faded to nothing, reddened again, and then drifted away, reddened—

"Fine," Cyrus said. "You're done." He popped the seal on the iron and lifted the lid. The waffle seemed solid enough, at least where it wasn't sloppy with chocolate bruises. Cyrus forked it loose, slapped it onto a plastic plate, and grabbed a stack of paper napkins. Whistling, he hurried out toward reception.

As far as Cyrus knew, no one had ever smoked in the reception area, but it still managed to smell like a cigarette graveyard turned full-time mold farm, like smoke had been stirred into the paint and stamped into the perpetually damp, fungal carpet. His sister, Antigone, swore that since their arrival two years ago, she hadn't once taken a breath in reception. Cyrus never managed to go for more than a month at a time. Eventually, he forgot and collected a noseful. Today, he remembered in time and his whistle died as he inflated his cheeks and caught his breath.

The paneled front desk was topped with pink to match the dining room counter. A huge mirror, flecked with gold and a little version of the Lady, hung behind it. Hustling past, Cyrus glimpsed himself. He slowed, and then stopped. He really did look terrible. His face was filthy, and his shirt could have been a mechanic's rag. Mrs. Eldridge had been right, but there was no way he was going all the way back to 111 for a clean shirt.

Still not breathing, Cyrus set the waffle on the front desk and grabbed his collar. Inside out, the shirt would be as good as new. He tugged the dirty cotton up around his puffed cheeks and over his head. As he did, the room rocked with thunder, and the walls shook like the sides of a kick drum. The mirror rattled, and Cyrus staggered backward, tangled in his shirt. Jerking his arms free, he dropped the shirt and looked around, his ears buzzing like two beehives. The lights flickered twice and died. Had the motel been struck? Blinking in the dim light, Cyrus picked up the waffle and wobbled toward the glass doors. Well, he was a hero now, wasn't he? The power was out, but the waffle was made. The Archer's service would not be compromised. He put his bare shoulder against the front door and pushed out into the court-yard. The air was cooler, the clouds had already choked out the sun, and Mrs. Eldridge was screaming.

Cyrus jumped into a jog. "Hold on!" he yelled. "I beat it! Waffle up!" Bare feet slapping on the sidewalk, he rounded the corner into the parking lot as the first bird's-egg raindrops spattered on the asphalt.

Mrs. Eldridge was once again perched on her second-story walkway, this time without her hat and robe. This time, she was holding a shotgun.

Cyrus froze. A long nightgown fluttered around Mrs. Eldridge's scrawny legs, and her thin gray curls feathered in the wind. The butt of the big gun was pressed against her shoulder. The two barrels were aimed across the parking lot at an old, round-nosed, macaroni-yellow pickup truck stopped beneath the Pale Lady.

While Cyrus watched, Mrs. Eldridge took careful aim at the truck, and she fired.

two

BILLY BONES

THE SHOTGUN KICKED and spat forked fire. Mrs. Eldridge staggered back against the wall and slid down onto the walkway.

Steam crept out of the yellow truck's dingy grille. The driver's door opened slowly.

"No!" Mrs. Eldridge yelled. "Don't make me do it, William Skelton! You know I will." Still sitting, she levered open the shotgun and forced in two more shells.

Heavy drops slapped onto Cyrus's bare shoulders as he looked from Mrs. Eldridge to the truck and back again. The sweet smell of rain on warm asphalt was mingling with the harsh taint of gunpowder. He took a step toward the stairs.

"Mrs. Eldridge!"

The old woman grabbed the rail and pulled herself up.

"Mrs. Eldridge?" Cyrus said again. One slow step at a time, he climbed up to the old woman's side, glancing back at the truck. "Hey," he said. "Maybe put down the gun. You're going to kill someone."

"Not that lucky," she said. "But I'll try."

A lean, white-haired man in an ancient leather jacket and gloves stepped out of the truck and into the rain. He was old, skeletal, and his weathered face looked too small for his skull. Cupping his gloves around his mouth, he lit a cigarette and stepped backward toward the Pale Lady's pole. Exhaling smoke into the rain, he leaned against the pole and dropped his hands to his hips.

"Eleanor Eldridge," he said. "What exactly are you trying to pull?"

Mrs. Eldridge snorted. "Get out of here, Billy. Move along. You're not wanted."

The old man grinned. "Can't keep me out, Eleanor, you old hen. But you know that already. Fire away."

Cyrus focused on the man's face. This was the guy. Room 111.

Electricity buzzed as long-dead neon chattered through forgotten veins. Above the old man, the Lady no longer slept on her pole. She was golden and dripping golden rain—her limbs, her bow, her arrow, all humming and flickering in front of the dark and drifting clouds. The Lady was alive.

The man patted the pole and stepped forward. "Let me on in, Eleanor. You know I'm not a body to fear."

The rain surged. Raindrops slapped down in crowds, and the wind broke into a run. Cyrus tore his eyes off the Lady, blinking away streams, shivering. He was directly beside Mrs. Eldridge now. He could grab her gun if he needed to.

Mrs. Eldridge shook her head. Gray strands of hair were rain-glued to her cheeks.

"I made a promise, William Skelton. I promised Katie. You remember. You did, too, but only one of us would care about a thing like that."

Cyrus glanced at Mrs. Eldridge. "Katie?" he asked. "Katie, like my mom, Katie?"

Eleanor Eldridge didn't look at him. She sniffed loudly, and then pushed her dripping hair back from her face.

The rain had doused the old man's cigarette. Flicking it away, he stepped forward. "That's right, boy—your mother. At least if you're one of the Smith mutts, and with that skin and that hair, I'm saying you are." He laughed. "I wouldn't be bragging about promise keeping, Eleanor, not with this Raggedy Andy beside you, shirtless and filthy in the rain. Maybe I'm here to keep a promise myself."

Cyrus squinted through the rain at the old man, at the truck, at the crackling Golden Lady. What was going on? None of this seemed real. But it was. The rain on his skin. The soggy waffle and drooping napkins. The smell of gunpowder.

Mrs. Eldridge coughed. "One more step, Skelton, and you'll get two barrels' worth of shot in the gut."

18

The man reached into his jacket and pulled out a thick, clear square of glass, holding it up between his gloved forefinger and thumb. Cyrus could see something dark and round in its center.

"You're bluffing!" Mrs. Eldridge yelled, but her voice wavered. "It's not real. We put them all in the collection!"

The old man's eyebrows climbed. "Go ahead and shoot me, Eleanor. But only if you want this place to burn." His white hair drooped on his spotted scalp. "Last call," he said. "Going, going, and already gone!"

William Skelton raised his arm to throw. Eleanor Eldridge cocked two hammers and braced herself.

"Hold on!" Cyrus yelled. "Hold on! I don't know what the fight is, but it doesn't matter." Still holding the waffle with one hand, he reached over and pushed the gun barrels to the side. "He can stay. It's fine." He turned to the old man. "You want a room, right? We can give you a room. Not a problem. Nobody needs to get shot, and nothing has to burn down."

The old man grinned. "Listen to the boy, Eleanor. Nobody needs to get shot."

"You've got no say here, Cyrus Smith." Mrs. Eldridge clamped her wrinkled jaw, but her eyes were worried. "I made a promise to your mother and that's that. Now get inside."

"I don't think he's leaving," Cyrus said. "And I own one-third of this motel, and I'm going to let him in."

The old man laughed and slid his glass cube back into his pocket.

Mrs. Eldridge didn't move. Potholes were overflowing now. The motel's gutters rattled. Cyrus looked down at the waffle in his hands. Half-sponge, half-dough, it was swamping on the plastic plate. Hooking one finger into its side to keep it from falling, Cyrus tipped the plate and dumped the water. Then he held it out to Mrs. Eldridge.

"Your waffle," he said. "It was done before the power went out."

The old woman lowered her gun and took the plate. She didn't look at it. Her veined eyes were searching Cyrus's. "Me or him?" she asked. "I told Katie I'd keep you safe. If he stays, I can't do that. Not from what's coming. I leave. No more protection. Not from anything."

"Protection?" Cyrus looked at the thin old woman, at her bone-white fingers on the black barrels of the shotgun. "No," he said. "No more protection. But you don't have to leave if you don't want to."

Mrs. Eldridge seemed to deflate. She looked at the plate in her hand, and her lips were tight. Scowling, she turned back into her room and slammed the door behind her.

Cyrus hurried down the stairs and moved slowly toward the man called William Skelton. He stopped a car's length away.

"How did you do that?" Cyrus pointed up at the

Golden Lady. The wet asphalt warped and spattered her reflected light.

"The sign?" The old man shrugged. "The lightning, maybe. I didn't do anything."

"It came on after you touched it."

William Skelton smiled. "Did it? Well, it wasn't me, exactly."

Cyrus licked rainwater off his lips and wiped it out of his eyes. "What was the glass thing?"

The old man blinked slowly. Up close, his skin was the color of caramel, freckled with patches of paper white and bone gray. He smiled, once again reaching into his jacket. "Boy, you ever seen a lightning bug?"

"Every summer," Cyrus said. "Why?"

"Not fireflies, son." The old man held out the glass square. "I'm talking lightning bugs." The glass was rippled and warped—homemade somehow. Frozen in its center, with six legs folded against its belly and black armor that glistened with blue, there was a heavy beetle. The glass was drip-free and dry. The rain didn't seem to touch it.

Cyrus stepped closer, squinting. "A beetle?" In glass. Like for a microscope. He wasn't sure what to say. What could be frightening about a beetle, even one the size of his big toe? But Mrs. Eldridge had definitely been scared, even with a shotgun.

Cyrus looked into Skelton's eyes and nodded at the Golden Lady. "This did that?"

The old man shook his head. "Nope. This didn't do anything. But you asked to see it."

Cyrus inched closer, watching the old man.

Water ran down around Skelton's eyes, dripping off sparse and antique lashes. He didn't blink. Instead, slowly, he looked down at Cyrus's bare shoulders, at his hands, at his feet.

The sky groaned, rolling thunder in its throat.

Cyrus reached for the old man's extended arm, his cracked glove, the glass square and its prisoner beetle.

"Careful, she's hot," Skelton said, and Cyrus closed his fingers around the glass.

Electricity shot up his arm, buzzing in his joints, tingling in his teeth. He staggered backward and swung his arm down, shaking himself loose from the current. Glass shattered on the asphalt at his feet, and the heavy beetle tumbled free.

Skelton hadn't moved. Hadn't flinched. Gasping, Cyrus watched the beetle right itself and lever up its wing casings. The wings beneath them were much too small to do anything, especially in the rain.

William Skelton whistled between his teeth. Blinking, Cyrus tore his eyes off the beetle and looked at the old man.

"If I were you," the man said, "and I wanted to stay alive, I'd get those bare feet off the wet ground and inside. Fast. She's ready to lay her eggs, and she's been waiting in that glass a long, long time."

Cyrus's feet began to tingle. With a pop and a crackle, the lightning bug launched and landed and launched again. Blue electric arcs trailed from its abdomen and flicked between its wings as it circled, bumblebee-heavy.

Cyrus spun away, asphalt tearing at the balls of his feet as he scrambled toward the motel. Four strides. Five, and he was in the courtyard. Ten, and he'd reached the front door. He jerked it open.

Thunder knocked him forward.

Antigone Smith yawned. She hated riding in the car. She hated it more than waffles. More than the Archer Motel and its wood paneling. More than the foul-smelling reception area. Of course, she only ever rode in the ancient red station wagon—the Red Baron—and she was sure that riding in the station wagon was less comfortable than riding in a wheelbarrow. It wasn't as bad when Cyrus came along. He always sat in the permanently reclining front passenger seat like it was some kind of throne. While Dan fretted over traffic or fuel or strange sounds behind the dash, Cyrus would cross his arms like a mummy and give cool commands, refusing to call Dan anything but Driver.

If it weren't for the mold on the seat belts, or the bloodred velveteen upholstery, Antigone wouldn't have minded the backseat. At least it wasn't angled like a dentist's chair. But Dan never let her sit in the back when it was just the two of them, and so she was stuck staring at the fabric bubbles on the ceiling, kinking her neck trying to watch the road, or perching on the front edge of the seat and crossing her arms on the dash with her face inches from the glass—which made her feel like a bobble-head. If she were just a couple of inches taller, as tall as her lanky little brother, she might have been able to lean back comfortably in the broken seat. But she wasn't tall by any standard, not for thirteen and a half, and feeling like a bobble-head was better than feeling like the seat was swallowing her whole.

Antigone sighed, adjusted the two worn camera cases that hung around her neck, ran her fingers through her cropped black hair, and then stretched her arms back until she touched the ceiling.

Rain chattered on the roof above her, and the station wagon's badly timed wipers flailed uselessly at the water on the windshield. She couldn't blame them. It was tough to wipe water off both sides of the glass. She dropped her hands into her lap and watched her older brother. His hands were tense on the wheel, and his jaw was grinding. Two years ago, he'd been a laid-back, sun-baked eighteen-year-old surfer thinking about college. Now he was thin and pale, eyes hollowed by stress, twenty going on forty.

"Dan?" Her brother didn't answer her. "Dan, relax. We'll be fine. We're close."

Lightning flickered silently in the distance. Dan twitched.

"Breathe, brother. Breathe," Antigone said.

Dan shot her a glance. "What will breathing do?"

A train of small drips fell from the roof, spotting Antigone's jeans. She watched the spots merge and grow. "Well," she said, pitching her voice up like she was talking to a sulky five-year-old, "breathing puts oxygen in your blood, enabling your brain to function. It keeps you alive. Which is a good thing, Daniel Smith."

"You know," Dan said, "sometimes you're worse than Cyrus."

Antigone smiled. "At no time in my life have I ever been worse than Cyrus. Maybe—*maybe*—when I fed him your goldfish family, but I was only four."

A heavy drip caught Dan's ear and he flinched, quickly grinding it dry on his shoulder. "Cy skipped out of school today, didn't he?"

Antigone scrunched her face and looked away.

"I should know," Dan continued. "If I were halfway good at my job, I already would. But we both know that I'm not, and I don't." He looked over at his sister. "Just tell me. Did Cyrus ditch? Why would anyone skip the last day of school?"

"You're not bad at your job," Antigone said quietly.

She knew she was deflecting, but it was true. "It's not even your job. You should be off at college, not stuck with us in a rotten motel."

Dan's jaw retightened. Antigone straightened, brushed back her hair, and popped open one of the cases around her neck. Carefully, like she was handling some fragile newborn creature, she pulled out her ancient silent-movie camera. The camera was small, mostly brown, and textured like leather. Three generations of Smiths had worn silver smooth finger tracks around its skin. Rotating the heavy little box in her hands, Antigone pinched a lever on the side and wound it tight. Then she leaned forward and pointed the small lens at her brother.

"Smile, Danny," she said. "I'm putting you at the end of the reel with Mom." She flipped another lever, and invisible gears chattered, spooling eight-millimeter film.

"You need a new camera," Dan said.

"You need a new car." Antigone slowly panned across the windshield. The wipers were so out of sync, they were bound to tangle soon. But it didn't matter. She knew the road, and they were in the final bend. One more corner and they'd see the Archer in the distance.

"Home again," Antigone said.

Blurry through the storm, she could just make out something bright and golden. Squinting, she leaned even closer to the windshield. It was the Lady on her pole, the Archer Motel squatting behind her.

Dan nearly drifted into the other lane. "What's going on? She's lit. Is that a truck? Someone's parked in the entrance. How is she lit?"

The front of the truck was yellow, but anything wet would have looked yellow beneath the glowing Lady. The truck's bed was dominated by an awkward wooden camper.

As the station wagon slowed, Antigone could just make out two shapes in the parking lot. One of them began hopping.

"Tell me that's not Cyrus," Dan said, stopping the car. "What's he doing out in this?"

Antigone pointed her camera toward her younger brother, shirtless in the rain. He was running. And something was sparking in the air behind him.

Antigone leaned forward. "Maybe he's—"

Snarled lightning ripped the world in half. Thunder shook the car. Deaf, blinking, Antigone slammed back into her door, banged her head against the window, and dropped her camera. Dan yelped, punching the gas and the brake at the same time. The station wagon rocked and smoked in the quivering air.

Rain drummed on the roof. Antigone's hands were shaking, and her eyes were seared with jagged white light. She could hear Dan breathing hard beside her.

The world came slowly back into focus. The two wipers had grabbed on to each other. Now they twitched in place. Through the distorting streams on the windshield, Antigone watched a blurry man in the parking lot pull a small bag out of the truck and walk slowly toward the motel.

Dan sat up. "Is Cyrus okay?"

Antigone squinted. "Don't know," she said. She cranked down her window. Cool rain spattered on her face, but she hardly noticed.

The old man looked back at the golden sign. He nodded. Then he waved at the station wagon and disappeared into the courtyard.

Antigone kicked open her door and stepped into the road.

Cyrus lay panting on his stomach just inside the motel's glass doors. Grit from the doormat was clinging to his skin, but he didn't care. The world was swirling.

Cyrus tried to lift his head, then dropped it back to the ground. He couldn't move, not just yet. Even lying on the floor, his body felt wobbly in the adrenaline aftermath of the lightning strike.

Slow, even breaths. In . . . out. His ears were ringing. Not ringing. More than that. They were crowded with a thousand screaming ants. He hadn't known how high-pitched an ant's screaming could be.

He shoved his knuckles into his ears. Opening and closing his jaw almost helped. False yawns.

Behind him, the front door opened. Footsteps, and a moment later, Cyrus was staring at a pair of very creased, very greased cowboy boots dotted with beads of water. One of them tapped his shoulder with its blunt toe.

"You dead or alive? I need the key to my room."

Cyrus tried to stand up but only managed to roll onto his back. He couldn't even bring himself to brush the clinging hair and gravel and poly fibers off his wet chest.

"Dead," he said. His voice was distant, slurring. "Pretty sure."

William Skelton grinned down at him. From the floor, the man's nostrils looked large enough to house bats. "I need my room." His voice was all breath, and his breath was all glass and grit.

Cyrus closed his eyes. He might throw up.

A bag dropped onto Cyrus's stomach. "Room one-eleven. Fetch the key, or I'll open the door myself."

Coughing, Cyrus shoved the bag onto the floor and elbowed himself up.

"What—" He swallowed. "What just happened? The bug...thing..." Cyrus stopped, blinking. He didn't even know what to ask.

The man slowly lowered himself into a crouch. Water beaded off his leather jacket and gloves. Cyrus cocked his head and squinted at him out of one eye, trying to focus. The man's skin had moved beyond the wrinkles of age, beyond scruff and widened pores and spider veins. His face was smooth and polished with use, like the seat of an old wooden stool. He smiled, and somehow his cheeks didn't crack.

"Kid," he said, and he reached out and squeezed Cyrus's shoulder. "You'll see stranger than that soon enough. Now, I didn't come this far and watch you burn a lightning bug to ask twice. Do you want this little roadside dive to come on down around your ears? Room one-eleven."

Cyrus knocked the man's hand off his shoulder, rolled onto his knees, and managed to stand. The room was spinning, but he squared his feet, crossed his arms, and tried to look stable.

"Taken," he said. "One-eleven is taken. I'd tell you to come back later, but it will be taken then, too. We have lots of rooms. Pick another one. My brother will make you a waffle in the morning."

"Your brother," the man said. "Daniel. The most like your father? The one I should have been talking to on the phone?"

Aluminum scraped and the front door let in the sound of slapping rain.

"Cy?" Antigone squeezed in. "You okay? What's going on?"

Dan slipped in behind her.

Cyrus looked at his sister. "You should have waited for me. I wasn't that late." He looked at Dan's dripping brown hair. "At least you're wet, too."

"Not as wet as you," Dan said. "Get a shirt on." He turned toward the old man and stuck out his hand. "Sorry about my brother," he said. "He gets primitive when we're not around. I'm Daniel. You need a room?"

The old man grinned as they shook hands. "Daniel Smith. We've met before."

Dan stood perfectly still, his eyes careening around the old man's face. "I'm sorry, I don't remember . . ." His voice cracked and trailed away.

The man shrugged. "You were young. Your father called me Bones; your mother called me Billy."

Cyrus watched his brother's Adam's apple bounce and his eyebrows crash together.

"What are you doing here?" Dan's voice had tightened. "What do you want?"

Billy or Bones or Billy Bones laughed. "Just a room. All I need is a room. One room in particular. Passing through and thought I'd say hello to the old place."

"It's my room, Dan." Cyrus pointed at his brother. "He wants my room. Don't give it to him."

While Dan moved awkwardly behind the desk, the old man turned to Cyrus. Digging a key ring from his pocket, he held up a long gold key between his fingers.

"I'll more than pay for the night. Park my truck. There's something for you on the seat."

The old man's face was pained but smiling. Once more, Cyrus stretched out his hand to take something from him. This time, Skelton seemed less willing. His eyes were hard and nervous. His breathing had stopped.

He dropped the keys onto Cyrus's palm, winked awkwardly, and turned away. The old man's back was suddenly more bowed. His skin had grown pale.

Dan nodded, and Cyrus moved slowly toward the door.

"I'll park the Baron," Antigone said. "The keys in it?"

Dan nodded again, all the while keeping nervous eyes on the old man.

Cyrus forced the door open and stepped to the side to let his sister through. He pointed at Dan. "Don't even think about giving him my room."

Turning away before his brother could answer, he shivered out into the rain.

"Where's your shirt, Tarzan?" Antigone asked. She wrapped the hem of her own shirt around her camera cases while they walked. The rain was fading.

Cyrus grunted.

"That lightning was crazy." Antigone pointed at a new pothole. "It melted a hole in the parking lot."

Cyrus didn't answer. He was staring at the Golden Lady. She looked better than he would have thought possible—glowing, buzzing, hunting the sky.

Antigone followed his eyes. "When did that happen?" she asked. "Was it the lightning?"

"No." Cyrus shook his head. "She came on when he leaned against her pole. Tigs, that lightning wasn't normal."

"Lightning never is. If it weren't still raining, I'd film the Lady." Antigone moved forward. "She looks amazing."

Cyrus wiped the rain off his nose. Antigone shifted into a jog. "Hurry up. I want to look in his truck."

Cyrus followed his sister, scanning the parking lot as he went. Lightning flickered silently behind distant clouds, and he felt his body tense. Everything had been moving so quickly, too quickly to understand. Mrs. Eldridge wasn't just a half-cracked guest; she was all the way cracked. William Skelton had known his parents.

And he'd had a beetle that could call down lightning.

Antigone reached the truck.

"I wouldn't open that!" Cyrus yelled.

She pulled open the door. "Why not?"

Cyrus caught up to his sister and stared into the cab. The seat was covered with old sheepskin, now worn down to flat wool. The passenger's side was crowded with grease-dotted paper bags, ripped and folded atlases, paper cups, and a large metallic box that was probably a cooler. In the center of the driver's seat, there was a small square of thick, rippled glass. Embedded inside, on its back with six legs folded in against its belly, there lay a single beetle.

"That's a fat beetle," Antigone said. "Is that what he meant? That's your tip?" She reached for it.

"Don't touch it!" Cyrus knocked away her arm.

Antigone faced him, raised her eyebrows, then reached up to flick her brother's ear.

"Seriously, Tigs," Cyrus said. "Don't." Antigone flicked, and Cyrus yelped, grabbing her wrist. "You don't know what happened. Just listen for a second and don't ask any questions. I have to get my head straight."

Antigone pulled back her arm. "Your head?"

"My ears are still ringing, and I'm not sure how to say . . . nothing seems true right now. You're not going to believe me."

"Mr. Mouth can't find his words," Antigone said. "Should I take a picture?"

"Promise you'll believe me," Cyrus said.

"Maybe I will," said Antigone. "There's a first for everything."

"Oh, shut up. You saw the lightning, right?"

"I did. Did you skip school today? And why were you late? I made Dan wait for half an hour."

"Come on!" Cyrus slapped both hands onto his

head, dragging them down his face. "Why now? I'm trying to tell you something."

"No," Antigone said. She pushed her short, wet hair straight back and then crossed her arms. "You're trying to get me to believe something. That's different. You want me to believe you? Hit me with the truth about school. And Mom. You never miss a Mom day."

"Fine," Cyrus said. "I skipped out of school today. Why wouldn't I? And then I lost my watch in a stream and got back late. You should have waited for me anyway. Now will you please listen?"

Antigone refolded her shirt over her camera. "Why would anyone skip the last day of school? That's what Dan wanted to know, and I think it's a good question. All we did was mess around in class and clean out our lockers."

"Exactly," said Cyrus. "I glued my locker shut three months ago, and I actually skipped out early this entire week. Mrs. Testy Teal called to talk to Dan about it a couple days ago, but she got me instead. Is that enough truth for you?"

Antigone blew rainwater off her lips. Cyrus knew how this went. A lecture was coming. He watched his older, smaller sister try to look angry. They only ever fought, really fought, when she tried to be his mother, which she seemed to think meant never believing a word he said and hugging him in public.

A pair of headlights approached, slowed, and looped out around the station wagon.

"Cyrus Lawrence Smith," Antigone began. Cyrus braced himself, but his sister's eyes had changed. Her wide smile took over. "I can't believe you glued your locker shut. Will they ever be able to get it open? They'll probably have to buy a new one. What kind of glue?"

"Not important," Cyrus said. It was hard not to smile, too. "I didn't use a lot. It'll pop open. Now listen to me, Tigs." He pointed at the glass on the seat. "That's a lightning bug. I swear it is. Not like a firefly. If you break the glass, it wakes up and then the lightning comes."

Antigone's hair fell forward. She brushed it back and scrunched her face. "You were right," she said. "I don't believe you. You're worrying me, Rus. Did you get struck? Seriously. And if you hadn't skipped school—"

"Seriously yourself," Cyrus said. "Don't start in on school again. And don't call me Rus." He watched his sister's face. "You have to believe me."

"No," Antigone said. "I don't. I don't even believe that *you* believe you. You're delusional. And shirtless. Probably concussed."

"Fine," Cyrus said. Leaning into the truck, he poked at the glass. No current. At least at first touch. Folding up a rag on the dashboard, he used it like a pot holder to pick up the glass. "Watch."

"Not yours, Cy. Put the poor dead thing back."

"It *is* mine. He said it was. It'll come alive when I break it open."

Antigone raised her eyebrows. "Like a cursed pharaoh?"

"Ha," Cyrus said. "Keep talking."

"Cy! Tigs!" Dan's yell came from the courtyard. "What are you doing? C'mon! The Baron should be out of the road!"

William Skelton stepped beside him. Cyrus whipped the rag behind his back.

"Careful there," the old man said. "Don't waste another perfectly good bug. It took your father weeks to catch it." He walked out into the parking lot and then down along the front of the motel, stopping at Cyrus's battered white door.

"When you've finished, bring that key ring back to one-eleven."

"No!" Cyrus yelled. "Dan! What? You gave him my room?"

Skelton opened the door. Saluting Cyrus with two fingers, he stepped inside and shut the door behind him.

⇥ three ⇤

THE LITTLE LAWYER

"I'm not giving the keys back," Cyrus said. "Not unless he gets out of my room." He was trying to pace, but there wasn't enough open floor. Instead, tossing the key ring from hand to hand, he turned in place between Antigone's two twin beds. The keys had a strange feel to them—almost a current, though vastly more subtle than the lightning bug. His skin cooled and itched wherever they touched.

Cyrus stuck his finger through the key ring and spun the bundle around his knuckle. His head felt extremely clear.

He was wearing his filthy shirt again, but inside out, with the grime against his skin. The glass-mummy lightning bug was propped up on the bedside table behind him, leaning against a lamp.

"Not a great idea," Antigone said. She lifted a black projector off a shelf and set it on a wobbly TV tray. "Someone like that, you don't steal their keys. You don't steal anything."

"Did Dan tell you more about him?"

Antigone shook her head. "Just what you heard. He thinks he remembers the guy at Christmas once, but he's not sure. And he thinks Dad chased him off when we were little."

"I should look through his camper."

"Worse idea." Antigone glanced up from her work. "Go give the man his keys and get some clean clothes. You're not staying in here until you've showered and changed."

"Whatever," Cyrus said. The key ring felt strangely light in his hands, and he couldn't stop himself from fiddling with it. There were only two keys hanging from their own smaller rings—the long gold one with a square head that he'd used to start the truck, and a shorter, round-headed silver key with a green tarnished head and a gleaming, polished shaft. More interesting than the keys were three large charms. Cyrus fingered each of them. A pearl, or something like one, moon white and gripped by a tiny silver claw. Beside it, a piece of reddish wood, worn smooth and polished with handling. And then the largest and heaviest of the three, the one that had looked at first glance like a silver animal tooth. On second glance and third handling, it had become more interesting. The silver tooth was actually a small sheath on a tiny hinge, hiding a real tooth within.

Cyrus popped it open one more time and ran his

thumb along the edge of what he assumed was a large, petrified shark tooth—black, smooth, and cold. It could have been stone.

His thumb tingled. It wasn't the keys, it was the tooth that chilled his skin.

Cyrus snapped the sheath shut, dropped onto a bed, and lobbed the keys up against the ceiling. A cloud of white paint powder and dust ghosted down, and the key ring bounced on the bed beside him. William Skelton. What did the old man with the yellow truck really want with his room? What was he doing in there? Room 111 was his, and it had been from the very beginning, ever since the world had ripped the three young Smiths up by their roots.

When Dan had finally pulled the Red Baron into the Archer's parking lot for the first time, Antigone had cried. It wasn't the California house. There were no cliffs. No sea. No father. And a mother in the hospital.

Ten years old, Cyrus had looked out his car window and seen three *1*s together on a door—111—a picture of what was left of his family. It had seemed like a safe number. It had been a safe number. A number not easily divided. And it held two years' worth of new roots—at least what he hadn't buried in the pastures and drowned in the streams. Antigone had insisted on taking the room beside him. When he was honest with himself—which didn't happen often—he was grateful that she had.

Cyrus looked over at his sister. Two years ago, she'd had long hair. Black glistening braids. It was all pixie cuts now, even though her short hair wouldn't stay tucked behind her ears and was always falling into her face. Antigone never seemed to do the easy thing. That was his job.

Cyrus yawned. "I'm starving."

"A pocket-size grilled cheese isn't enough for you?" Antigone had collected a blue collapsible tripod and movie screen from the corner. "Dan offered you waffles. Waffles are unlimited."

Cyrus groaned. "I think I'm made of waffles."

Room 110 was all Antigone. Like Cyrus, she had lined every bit of the open walls with shelves. Unlike Cyrus, she had actually painted the paneled walls first (pale blue), she actually dusted her shelves, and she actually vacuumed the golden-brown carpet. Cockroaches, ants, and spiders actually died in 110—111 was more like a wildlife preserve—and Antigone had found sheets for herself that were softer than the Archer's standard polyester surprise.

And her shelves were organized.

Most of the shelves held books—books that had belonged to their mother, their father, their grandparents, and a few that had belonged to people with "great" and "once removed" attached to the relationship. Three shelves sagged beneath photo albums entirely full of her own Polaroids. One sagged with old family albums, two sagged with circular tins full of film reels, and one held her cameras. She only had two—the eight-millimeter silent-movie camera that had belonged to their father's father, and an early bellows-style Polaroid that had been their mother's.

The only patch of wall that wasn't carrying shelves was just above her bed. There, nine picture frames hung in three rows of three. The top six were rotated out weekly, but the bottom three never changed. On the left, a young man with hair even blonder than Dan's had been in California was hanging upside down in a tree. On the right, a laughing woman with hair spun from midnight was reaching toward the camera, trying to block the shot. In the middle, a serious blond boy held hands with a very small dark-haired girl, and between them, seated and shirtless, a fat infant was eating dirt.

While Antigone adjusted the legs on her movie screen, Cyrus rolled up on his side and stared at the pictures.

"You'd've killed Dan if he put that guy in this room. You know you would."

"Yes," Antigone said. "I would. But I wouldn't steal the man's keys. And you can't blame Dan. I'm sure he's getting paid well, and we need it. You know he has it worse than we do."

Cyrus sat up. "Wait. You'd kill him, but you wouldn't blame him?"

"Right." Antigone stepped back to the projector and flipped it on. Empty wheels spun, and a misshapen square of light appeared on the screen.

"And he has it worse than us?"

"Right again," Antigone said. "I'm proud of you, Cyrus. You've learned to listen." She glanced up. "You and I don't have to deal with us. We are us. Dan *does* have to deal with us—you in particular. Now, here's the deal, Cy. You go give the man his keys, or you don't see today's reel." She shrugged. "I shot a lot of Mom, and I don't mind keeping it to myself."

"That's cheap. You shouldn't have left me behind in the first place." Cyrus stood. "You know, I don't even feel like today really happened."

"I feel that way about . . . everything." Antigone sighed and looked up, almost smiling. "Maybe tomorrow we'll find out that we're still four and five years old, I'm still taller than you, and everything around here has just been a very complicated daydream. Mom's fine, Dad's alive, we never moved, and Dan still knows how to smile."

Cyrus breathed slowly. Half a continent away, he could almost hear the ocean. "No waffles," he said. "No motel." He grinned. "But I was already taller than you when I was four."

Antigone spun her brother around, put both hands on his back, and pushed him toward the door. "Go," she said. "Movie when you're clean."

The door closed, and she was alone with a whirring projector.

Outside, Cyrus looked up at the night sky. The clouds had blown over, and the stars of early summer had crowded silently into place above the Golden Lady.

The yellow truck sat where he'd parked it, immediately in front of the two adjacent doors—110 and 111. Both rooms had curtains drawn over the windows, but both rooms still glowed. Dan's room was out of sight, by reception, opening on the courtyard. And no light trickled down through the walkway from Mrs. Eldridge's room. She had checked out two hours ago, showering Dan with a barrage of shouted warnings before dragging a single suitcase toward the road.

Cyrus took a long breath of the cool night and stepped over to his bedroom door. For a moment, he listened to the neon buzzing of the Lady, and then he knocked.

On impulse, he raised his thumb and covered the peephole. A mosquito drifted past his ear and settled on his extended arm. He slapped at it and waited. A few slow seconds ticked by, and he knocked again.

Muffled footsteps approached. A dead bolt slid. A chain rattled.

The door opened, and William Skelton, smoking, leaned against the frame.

Cyrus took a step backward. The man was wearing jeans and a tight, stained tank top. His face was pale and sickly, but his bare shoulders and arms could have belonged to a thirty-year-old lumberjack, a lumberjack with a taste for morbid tattoos. The man's skeleton had been crudely needle-etched onto every visible part of his body from the neck down. Scrawled collarbones stood out above a cage of blue ribs. Ink bones marched down his shoulders and arms. Even the backs of his hands and the tops of his bare feet were detailed with every joint and knuckle. Slanted notes and calligraphics filled in the remaining space on his arms and shoulders.

Cyrus couldn't help but trace every bit of ink with his eyes. He'd never seen anything like it. Fear was trying to crawl up his spine. He pushed it away. It was ink. Nothing but ink. Looking up into Skelton's sweating face, Cyrus dug into his pocket and pulled out the ring. "I brought back your keys. You know you can't smoke in here."

William Skelton turned and walked back to Cyrus's bed.

"Hey." Jingling the keys, Cyrus stepped into the doorway. His room had been destroyed. His shelves and their collections had been torn down off one wall and piled on the floor. The wall itself had been ripped open from end to end, revealing a row of hollow cavities and cast-iron plumbing. On the side of the bed, a small but bellied man was sitting with his legs primly crossed. He was wearing a gray suit, and half-moon glasses were perched on the end of his nose. Large sheets of yellowing paper were mounded around him.

"What?" Cyrus scanned the carnage of his room, his life. "You trashed my room." Fear was gone. He could feel his pulse in his fingertips as his mind scrambled for some kind of explanation. "You know what?" He kicked a shard of drywall at Skelton's legs. "I'm keeping your keys, old man. They're going to disappear. All of them."

The small, fat man clicked his tongue and cocked his head. "This is the boy?" he asked Skelton. "This is the best you could do?"

William Skelton nodded and pulled at his cigarette. He had chewed the end almost flat.

Cyrus glared at the man in the suit. "Who are you? Did you rip into my wall?"

Peering over his glasses, the little man examined Cyrus's shorts, his shirt, and finally his face.

"I was getting some clean clothes," Cyrus said. "It's been a long day. Why did you wreck my room?"

"You're sure about this, Billy?" the small man asked.

"About what?" Cyrus asked. The room was chilly with air-conditioning, but William Skelton wiped sweat from his forehead onto the back of his tattooed arm.

"Kid," he said quietly. "How do you feel about Death?"

"What?" Cyrus took a small step back.

"Death," Skelton said again. "Dying. How do you feel about it?"

"How do you think I feel about it?" Cyrus asked. "Death sucks. I don't like it. How do *you* feel about it?"

The old man stared at the end of his cigarette. "People say you can't run from Death." He shook his head. "People lie. Running's all you *can* do, kid. Run like Hell's on your heels, because it is. And if you're still running, well, then you're still alive."

Cyrus opened his mouth, but he had nothing to say. The little man was sorting through his wrinkled stacks of paper.

Skelton examined his tattooed hands. They were trembling, but his voice was calm. "You know what happens when you run too long?" He made a fist and looked into Cyrus's eyes. "Death becomes . . . a friend, a companion on the road, a destination. Home. Your own bed. The place where your friends are waiting. You stop being afraid. You stop running." He dropped the stub of his cigarette onto Cyrus's carpet. "Tonight," he said, grinding the butt out with his bare foot, "I stop running. Someone else is gonna start."

Cyrus blinked. Sweat dripped off the man's nose. His pale face was blotchy, like old dough. "You still look afraid," Cyrus said. "Your hands are shaking. What's going on?"

Skelton looked over at his small friend.

"A touch of spunk," the man said, nodding. "But only a touch. His odds are still terribly low."

"What does he have to sign?" Skelton asked.

"Him? Nothing." The small man raised a small selection of the papers. "You've signed the appointment already, and I've found the paperwork to demonstrate that you have the necessary relationship to do so, though leaving it with me in the first place would have been wiser than hiding all of this in the walls. I can supply the Order notary and testimony of fitness and volition. As a Keeper, I can witness the declaration." He reached into his breast pocket and pulled out a small, heavily creased paper card. Unfolding it, he extended it to Cyrus. "Read that aloud, please."

Cyrus looked down at the slip, and then back up at the strange scene in his room. "What's going on? Those papers were in my wall?"

"It was my wall first," Skelton said. "I gave this place to your parents years ago."

"Just read it," said the little man. "They haven't enforced the original oath in generations, but I'd like to cross all the *i*'s and dot all the *t*'s in this situation."

"It's the other way around," Cyrus said.

"We'll cross and dot both. Read it, please."

"No thanks," said Cyrus, backing toward the door. "I'm gonna go now." He tossed Skelton's keys onto the bed and felt for the doorknob behind him. "See ya."

The keys smacked into Cyrus's chest; Cyrus caught them at his waist. Skelton smiled and shook his head. "Those keys should have been your father's. It doesn't right old wrongs, but they're your burden now, Cyrus Smith. The race is yours. The world is yours. Run until Death's your friend, and then set those keys in another's hand. Not before then, hear me? Once you give them, you can't get them back. And not a soul should know that I'm setting them in yours. I've got more to give, but that's a start."

Cyrus looked at the little man on the bed, and then back into the empty eyes of Billy Bones.

"Don't worry about Horace here," Skelton said. "His family's kept more secrets than a dozen graveyards. And as for me, well, dead men tell no tales. At least, not usually."

Horace scraped the stack of papers off his lap, hopped to his feet, and slid the card into Cyrus's hand.

Skelton nodded. "Now read, boy. We're doing what we can to make sure you'll have the help you need."

Cyrus swallowed and looked at the keys. His hand closed around them, and for the first time, they felt cold and heavy. The old man was crazy, no question. "I don't want these."

"Don't you?" Skelton asked, creasing his forehead. "I've seen enough of you to know you're no coward. You want to walk away? You want to live a life without knowing what those unlock?"

Cyrus looked around his ruined room. He wanted the men to leave. He wanted his wall back.

Exhaling slowly and ignoring the old man's eyes, he dropped the keys into his pocket and moved quickly across the room toward the warped mirror door to his closet. He could always give the keys back in the morning. In the right kind of mood, he could even throw them into one of the pasture streams. He pulled out a pile of fresh clothes and turned around.

Antigone, wide-eyed, was standing in the doorway.

"What on Earth," she said, looking at the wall. She turned to the sweating old man, her eyes taking in the tattoos. "I hope Dan has your credit card."

"The girl, I assume?" The small man straightened his suit. "If both are present, only one needs to declare; the other can offer assent. Are you sure you want both included? You have the right to name two, but I can see definite benefits in selecting only one."

"Both," Skelton said. "They'll need each other."

"Who are you?" Antigone asked the little man. "What are we talking about?"

Cyrus slipped back to the door and held up the small card. "It's in another language," he said.

Antigone took the card from him and squinted at the printed letters. "No, it's not. 'Please declare aloud . . .' What is this?"

The little man stepped forward. "Excuse me, miss," he said. "If you don't mind, the Latin is actually preferable in the current situation. We're going above and beyond."

He plucked the card from Antigone's hands, flipped it over, and returned it.

"Pronunciation isn't important. Do your best."

Stepping back, he tucked his thumbs into his vest and waited.

Antigone stared at the words in front of her. "Are you serious? What is this supposed to be? I'm not saying it." She handed the card back to Cyrus.

Cyrus looked into the tired eyes of William Skelton.

"You really want us to read this?" he asked. The keys were heavier in his mind than in his pocket. Antigone didn't need to know that he was keeping them. Not yet.

The old man nodded.

"Okay," Cyrus said. "I'll read it if you answer our questions."

After a moment, the old man nodded again.

Cyrus handed his stack of clothes to Antigone. "How do you know Mrs. Eldridge?"

"We were schoolgirls together."

"Funny," Antigone said. "Har, har."

51

"It's close enough to the truth," said Skelton. "Met as kids. Hated each other since."

Cyrus swallowed. For some reason, his throat was tightening. He didn't really care about Mrs. Eldridge. "How did you know our parents?"

William Skelton sighed. "For a while, I was their teacher. For a while, I was their friend. I met them before they married. Helped them through some tough times. Made some tough times tougher." His eyes dropped to the carpet.

"And?" Antigone asked. "What happened?"

The little man coughed loudly.

Skelton nodded. "It's late," he said. "You can hear the whole story tomorrow." He pointed a tattooed finger at the card. "Do an old man a favor and read the paper. Soon enough, I won't be keeping any secrets."

Cyrus and Antigone looked at each other. Antigone nodded. Cyrus cleared his throat, raised his eyebrows, and began to read: "*Obsecro ut sequentia recites . . .*"

Pausing, he glanced up. William Skelton was staring at the ceiling.

Horace, the little man, was pursing his lips expectantly. "Go on."

At first, Cyrus read slowly, stumbling and tripping as his tongue attempted to string the odd syllables together. But after two lines, his voice found a rhythm, and he could almost believe that he understood his own strange chanting. He smeared words, blended, missed, and guessed at words, but he got through it, and when he did, he held the card out to the little suited man.

"Keep it with you," the man said. "Miss Smith, do you offer assent?"

"Um, sure," said Antigone. "I guess."

Hunching over the bed, the man checked his watch and made a note of the time on a large piece of paper. Then he signed the bottom with a flourish. "Billy Bones, that's all I need. Know that I am risking a great deal for you." He scraped all the papers into a pile, and then he shoveled the pile into an enormous leather folder. When he had finished, he shook hands with Billy, shook hands with Cyrus, bowed to Antigone, then picked a bowler hat up off the wreckage of Cyrus's shelves and popped it on his head. "Good luck and good night to you all," he said. And leaning to one side, he lugged the enormous folder out into the night.

Billy Bones slumped onto the end of the bed and put his head in his hands.

"Go now," he said quietly.

Cyrus and Antigone backed slowly through the doorway.

The old man looked up suddenly, and his face was gray and bloodless. "Wait. Music. Your record player. I couldn't get it to work."

"It's broken," Cyrus said. "Always has been."

"No, it's not," Skelton said. "Not for you. Not anymore. Turn it on for me."

Antigone's hand closed around her brother's wrist. Cyrus stared. The old man was getting stranger. Sleeping next door could be too close.

"Please," Skelton said. "Just flip the switch."

Cyrus walked to his dresser, glancing back at the man on the bed. He'd already put a record on. John Coltrane. Cyrus had never listened to it. He'd never had a record player that worked. Flexing his fingers, he reached down and slid the power switch with his thumb. A spark tickled its way up into his hand, and the vinyl disk began to spin slowly. The mechanical arm lifted off its rest and swung into place.

The voice of a smooth sax filled the room.

When the door to 111 had closed safely behind them, Cyrus turned to his sister. Antigone widened her eyes. "Can this get weirder?" she whispered.

"Yeah," Cyrus said. "I bet it can."

four

THE BEREAVED

CYRUS OPENED HIS eyes—there was no point in having them shut—and rolled up onto his side, clawing at his forearm. But that meant he couldn't scratch his calf. Splaying his toes, he put them to work, too.

The lights were off, and his sister's breathing was even. The curtains were glowing, backlit by the Golden Lady—he wondered if Dan even knew how to turn her off. The air-conditioning was humming, and the bed squealed every time he moved. He had kicked all his blankets onto the floor at least two hours ago.

They had only watched Antigone's movie four times, but he hadn't been able to stop replaying it in his head. His sister's movies were always odd. The clicking, flashing images made new things seem old and forgotten. They made his dark, smooth-skinned mother seem painted and imagined. Her sleeping face had somehow steadied the camera in Antigone's hands, and the picture had stopped bouncing and shifting and had become still. His mother's hair, almost invisibly white, had grown since their last visit, and Antigone had made an exception to her rule, as she always did on Mom days. She'd let Dan take the camera and had entered the frame herself, holding her mother's hand, brushing her mother's hair.

Cyrus should have been there, sitting on the other side of the bed.

And then the movie had cut to the car, to the flooding windshield, to Dan's stress, to the yellow truck, to Cyrus in the parking lot, to the rocking bolts of lightning.

Cyrus clawed at his calf and then sat up in bed, switching on the lamp between the beds. An old boxy phone with a tangled cord sat beside the lamp. The lightning bug glass stood on its side in front of it, catching the light. For a moment, Cyrus stared at his sister, breathing beneath a mound of blankets.

His dirty clothes were in a pile by the door. He stood up as quietly as the bed would let him and went over to fish in the pockets of his shorts. Out came the key ring. Out came the small paper card.

Antigone hadn't moved. "What are you doing?" she asked suddenly.

Cyrus sat back down on his bed. "You awake?"

"Take a guess."

"We never read the English," Cyrus said. "Do you want to hear it?"

Antigone didn't answer.

Cyrus fingered the key ring in the lamplight. He flipped open the silver sheath and rubbed his tingling thumb across the sharp, chilly tip of the tooth. The key ring had been in Skelton's pocket when the Lady had become golden. It had been in his own pocket when he'd touched the record player.

Antigone sighed loudly. "Tell me I'm not hearing keys. No. Don't tell me. Just turn off the light."

"Fine," Cyrus said. He dropped the keys on the bed. "But I'm reading the card first. Listen."

Antigone filled the room with a fake snore.

"'Please declare aloud: I hereby undertake to tread the world, to garden the wild, and to saddle the seas, as did my brother Brendan. I will not turn away from shades in fear, nor avert my eyes from light. I shall do as my Keeper requires, and keep no secret from a Sage. May the stars guide me and my strength preserve me. And I will not smoke in the library.'" Cyrus looked up. "'Translation approved, 1946.'"

Antigone flopped onto her face. "Now you've done it. No more smoking in the library." She pulled her blankets over her head. "Turn off the light."

Cyrus set down the card with the lightning bug, clicked the lamp off, and sat bouncing his knees in the dark.

"How can you sleep right now?" he asked.

"I can't," Antigone muttered.

Sighing, Cyrus rocked back onto his bed and stared at the dimly golden ceiling.

"Whatever it is you're tapping," Antigone said, "feel free to stop."

"What?" Cyrus asked. "I'm not tapping anything."

He held his breath and listened. Someone, something, *was* tapping. Faintly, beyond the window. Three taps. Scrape. Three more. Scrape.

Antigone sat up. "That's really not you?"

Cyrus shook his head. Both of them slipped out of their beds and crept toward the window. When they were on their knees, with noses above the sill, Cyrus hooked one finger in the curtain and peeled it back.

A large, dark shape was moving slowly through the parking lot, sweeping the white cane of a blind man in front of him. He reached the yellow truck, felt it with his hand, and then kept coming, finally stopping six feet from the pair of motel room doors. He was wearing an enormous coat and a heavy stocking cap pulled down snug around his scalp. Two large ears stuck out from the sides of his head like a pair of skin satellite dishes. His eyes weren't covered, but they were closed. He tapped the ground and turned his head from side to side, listening. Then he sniffed at the air with a flattened and crooked nose. His jaw was broad but uneven, visibly scarred even in the dim golden light. His long, slender cane was in his left hand, tip down, and he began bouncing it slowly beneath the weight of his arm.

"What's he doing?" Antigone whispered. "He's not really blind, is he?"

Cyrus put his finger to his lips.

"He can't be," Antigone said. "He walked right to Skelton's room." She nudged her brother. "Open the door. See what he wants."

Cyrus looked at her. "Yeah, right," he whispered. "You're crazy."

"He's blind. He might need help." Antigone tried to stand, but Cyrus grabbed on to her wrist. The blind man had pulled something out of his coat.

"Gun," Cyrus said. "Gun!" He forced Antigone back onto her knees. Four short, gaping barrels—two on top of two—all big enough to fire golf balls. Pistol-gripped. Black. Ruthless. An extra handle stuck out to the side of the bundle of barrels. A small cylindrical tank was screwed into the back of the gun above the man's grip.

Cyrus's mind was frozen. His nails were digging into his sister's arm. Should he yell? Should he warn Skelton?

The man tapped his rod on the ground three times. Six inches from Cyrus's face, a shape slid past the window toward room 111. And another.

Antigone was trying to shake her arm free. Cyrus let go. He wasn't breathing. He wasn't blinking.

The blind man stepped forward, raised a heavy arm, and cracked the butt of his gun against the door to 111.

"Bones!" the man yelled. "Friend Billy! Give it up. The good doctor doesn't take kindly to thieves."

Cyrus gasped, finally breathing. He pushed his sister away from the window. "Call the cops. Go!"

Antigone dropped to the carpet and crawled away.

Skelton's voice drifted through the wall. "That you, Pug? Maxi's letting you do the talking now? Come on in. I'll get the door."

The floor under Cyrus's knees shivered, a high-pitched whine vibrated the glass in front of him, and the door to 111 exploded off its hinges. The big man slammed into the nose of the truck before spinning up onto the roof of the wooden camper.

Smoke snaked out into the golden parking lot. For a moment, the world was still. The blind man's legs kicked slowly on the asphalt. His arms were draped on the old truck's bumper and his head lolled against its grille, blood dripping from his nose and lips. His hat was gone. His cane was shattered.

Turning his back to the window, Cyrus slid down beneath the sill.

"Yes," Antigone said. Her eyes were on him, peering up between the beds. "An explosion. And guns. That's what I said. The Archer Motel, room one-eleven. No, I won't hold."

She hung up. For a moment, Cyrus, breathless, stared into his sister's frightened eyes, and then William Skelton's voice roared through the wall.

"Come kill the killer!" he shouted. Something heavy crashed to the floor. "Betray the traitor. Rob the thief! Who wants to die with Billy Bones?"

Antigone dropped to the carpet beside Cyrus and lifted the curtain.

"Is he dead?" she asked. "Did Skelton kill him?" Her voice was low, but her body was shaking.

Cyrus swallowed. "I don't know," he said. His sister was hanging on to his leg. He could barely feel it. "I don't know," he said again. "Don't know." Stop it. He blinked, trying to clear his head. He couldn't be like this. This was how animals became roadkill. He had to do something. Wake up. Should they get under the beds? Should they run?

"Come on now, lads!" Skelton bellowed. "I know you can take more than that. Or can't the doctor's puppets kill an old man?"

Cyrus pulled himself back up to the windowsill. The blind man was on the ground beneath the yellow truck's bumper. He wasn't dead. His left arm still held a piece of his broken cane. His right hand still gripped his gun. He raised it slowly.

There was no sound of gunfire, no exploding black powder. Each of his barrels belched a burning white sphere, corkscrewing forward, braiding flame, tracing spirals in the air like racing sparklers.

Two tall shapes leapt into view, moving quickly, smoothly, more like animals than people. One vaulted easily over the truck. The other jumped onto the top of the camper, landing in a crouch. Both were wearing tinted goggles, both were hip-firing searing white flame. Another, shorter shape stepped out from behind the truck.

Four men, each with four barrels, filled the air with swirling magnesium and sulfur. Flaming spheres, infant meteors, exploded against the doorjamb, the wall, the window, and poured through the door into 111. White fire erupted into sizzling rings. The walls shook. The window in front of Cyrus warped and wobbled as pale rivers of flame raced across its surface.

Cyrus couldn't look away. He couldn't move. He couldn't breathe in the sudden heat. He didn't feel Antigone's hands. He didn't hear her screaming at him to get down. Not until she threw an arm around his neck and slammed him onto his back.

Blinking, he watched his sister sprawl across him, covering her head with her arms, trying to cover him with her body.

He watched the ceiling boil and crack. The walls surged and split, and Antigone's shelves avalanched to the ground. The first flames crept into the room.

A high-pitched whine was building somewhere—piercing, painful. Cyrus pushed his sister off, grabbed her wrist, and tried to crawl toward the bathroom. The bathtub. They needed water. His sister's books were burning. Her photo albums.

Boom.

The noise was simple enough, big enough, fundamental enough that all the other noises became part of it.

Cyrus felt his bones ripple like rubber as he fell. His gut twisted and flipped. The closet mirror ran down into the carpet. The glass in the big picture window liquefied and collapsed, splashing on the sill.

A moment's slice later, the sound was gone and the window had refrozen, paralyzed in its fountain before hitting the floor.

Cyrus lay gasping, gripping his sister's tense arms, watching fire dance on the wall, listening to distant sirens.

No more shouting. No more belching guns. He pulled, crawling for water.

Antigone pulled back.

"No!" she yelled. "Up, Cy! Out!" Reaching her feet, she dragged him toward the door.

"Your stuff," Cyrus said. He tore his hands free and stood, hunching in the smoke. "Get your stuff."

"I will, I will," she said. The top third of the wall was in flames. "We have to get Skelton out!"

Cyrus forced his sister away from the room's door and pressed his eye against the peephole. The glass had dripped out.

"Are they gone?" Antigone whispered.

"Maybe," Cyrus said.

"Just go," Antigone said. "Go!"

Wrapping his hand in the hem of his shirt, Cyrus jerked quickly on the sizzling doorknob, and the two of them staggered into charred air. The blind man—limbs impossibly bent—lay motionless beneath the truck's bumper. A second rag-dolled body drooped off the edge of the camper. A third was facedown behind the rear wheel.

Flames surrounded the doorway to 111 and were roaring on the walkway above. Inside 111, Cyrus's bed was on fire, the walls were scorched and flickering, and huge pieces of the ceiling had collapsed. Beneath one cracked slab of blackened drywall, they could see the bottoms of two cowboy boots.

Without saying anything, Cyrus and Antigone jumped through the doorway, kicked through the smoldering pile, and each grabbed a leg. The shins bent easily.

Billy Bones groaned in pain. "No," he said. "Don't pull."

Cyrus dropped the boot.

"Tigs, let go," he said. "His legs are broken."

"Not broken," Billy said. "Not—"

Both kids tore into the pile, quickly clearing the old man's body. He was wearing a burnt and smoking blue jumpsuit, and his face was soot-covered around a pair of flight goggles. The glass lenses had melted and were hanging from the bottom rims like icicles. Two canisters were strapped on his shoulders and pinned beneath him. A cracked silver tube laced with copper wire stuck out from under his arm like the barrel of a leaf blower. Oil oozed out of its mouth.

The old man licked his charcoal lips and smiled. His teeth were gone. "Killed Pug," he said. "The others? Maxi? Where's Maxi? He won't die."

The ceiling was crackling like pinecones. Antigone coughed and pulled her shirt collar up over her mouth and nose.

Billy Bones looked at her, and then at Cyrus. "Didn't break—" He paused to breathe, and his eyes shut. "Not every promise. Your father—"

Antigone slid her hands under the old man's shoulder. "We have to get you out of here. Cy, try gripping under his arms."

"No," the old man said. "No! Listen! I have no secrets." His voice was fading, drowned out by the popping of burning shelves, the loud breathing of flames. "Cyrus, my hands. To my neck. Hurry." Cyrus looked at his sister. Antigone nodded. Cyrus grabbed Skelton's wrists in the rubble. His arms were soft, boneless, like socks full of mud. As Cyrus lifted, the old man groaned, and then sobbed. Cyrus hesitated.

"Don't stop. Don't." With a final motion, Cyrus forced Skelton's hands to his throat. The old man's fingers moved, and in the darkness, Cyrus saw a thick necklace come free. It was glowing silver. "Yours now," Skelton said.

Cyrus blinked, confused. Antigone leaned in and took over.

She raised the old man's hands to her brother's neck. The necklace—the thing—suddenly moved, twisting between Skelton's hands. "Use her," Skelton said. "She was your father's once."

Heat seared against Cyrus's skin and slithered tight around his neck. Yelping, gasping, he reached for it.

"No!" Skelton yelled. "No! Defend what I give you. With your souls." His voice died. The thing around Cyrus's neck was only warm now, metallic but soft, scaled, as thick as a small rope.

"Cyrus," Antigone said, leaning close to the old man's face. "Cyrus."

William Skelton's voice sank below a whisper. "Smiths. Beekeepers. Trust. Nolan."

"Brother Bones. So dramatic in life, so he should be in death, yes?"

A man, slight, dressed in close-fitting black, stepped through the charred doorway. His accented voice was

66

smooth despite the smoke. A four-barreled gun dangled in his left hand. Flames from the wall licked his shoulder, but he didn't seem to notice.

"What does the dying man give to the little ones, eh?" he asked cheerfully. "William, what should their sweet souls be defending?" He cocked his head, listening. "Has he met with friend Death already?"

Grabbing Antigone, Cyrus slid away on his knees. The man moved toward them through the rubble as Cyrus scrambled to his feet. A bright smile full of very tiny teeth sparkled in the man's soot-covered face. His eyes were ringed with a pair of empty goggles. His hair, an ashen tangle, stood out around his small head.

"Children, please remain," he said. "I cannot find what I need. Can it be that the famous Billy Bones no longer holds it?" He pointed his gun at Skelton's body. "If he was still keeping his charm, I would not expect to see him in such condition."

A slab of ceiling collapsed onto Cyrus's bed, and flaming shards sprayed around the room. Smoke swallowed everything. Coughing, Cyrus tucked his face into his arms. His eyes were blinking acid.

The man hadn't moved. "What did old Skelton give the ducklings?" He raised his gun. "Tell your uncle Maxi."

Cyrus couldn't think in the smoke, without air. His brain was on fire. His lungs were bursting. Antigone squeezed his arm tight.

"Cy! Tigs! Where are you?" Dan, barefoot, wearing only a pair of sweatpants, appeared beside the truck.

Without looking, the man swung his gun over his shoulder and sent a pair of twisting fireballs spiraling through the smoke above the truck and into the trees across the road.

Spitting into his shirt, Cyrus pulled his sister. The gun didn't matter. Smoke mattered. Fire mattered. The two of them staggered toward the man, toward the crumbling doorway. Cyrus was ready for an impact. For a struggle. For a fireball in his stomach.

Instead, they shot through the doorway, careened into the truck, and tripped over the dead man's legs. Dan's arms wrapped around them and they were surrounded by cool, moving air. There were stars again. Lights were flashing. The world was full of sirens.

Bigger arms than Dan's picked Cyrus up and tore him free of his sister. He could hear her yelling. She wanted to go back in. But even louder voices were shouting orders and diesel engines were throbbing and red lights were whirling and someone was wrapping something cool and wet around Cyrus's face, pressing a mask over his mouth.

A fireman set Cyrus down on the hood of a police car. "Stay here! The paramedics will check you." And the man was gone.

Cyrus tore his mask off. A skyscraper of smoke was

rising from the Archer. The rooftop was an angry mob of bonfires. He slid down to unsteady feet, but the oxygen had cleared his head. Where was Tigs? Where was Dan?

Men with masks were carrying a body out of 111. Cyrus slapped at his pocket. No keys. Did he care? He tore off the thing around his neck, but it twisted in his hand, winding itself tight around his wrist. It didn't matter. The door to 110 was still open, and his sister's pictures were worth more than a dead old man's keys or charms. They were all going to burn—his father, his mother, every trace of another lifetime, another home in another world.

Cyrus was suddenly moving, tripping on hoses, pinballing through big men in helmets and yellow suits, running toward the roar of growing flames and a fading past.

Earth turned, twisting its shadowed back out of darkness, dragging a continent into dawn. The Archer Motel had changed. The potholes in the parking lot were brimming with water and skimmed with ash. In places, polyester curtains had melted into the asphalt. The second-story walkway had collapsed, and half of the second story had collapsed with it. Rooms were open to the morning air, missing their exterior walls like compartments in a scorched dollhouse, revealing burnt mattresses, blackened dressers, and the occasional melted television. Webs of yellow tape surrounded it all.

The Golden Lady, dim in the daylight, still glowed.

The sun was ready with summer heat, and the sky was clear. As the sun climbed, the motel's soaked ruin and the puddled parking lot began to steam, releasing the stink of burnt paint and carpet and curtains into the morning.

In the courtyard, a door was cracked open. Behind it, sprawling sideways across a queen bed, Cyrus and Antigone were sleeping.

Cyrus's hair was singed in places, and his skin glistened with a mixture of soot and sweat. A patterned ring of tiny blisters stood out around his neck.

Antigone slept with her filthy arms around a small mound of film tins and photo albums. Two cameras, both minus their glass lenses, were perched on top. Her projector, now little better than a pile of melted black plastic, sat on the floor beside the bed.

The door swung open. A little man with tired eyes, half-moon glasses, and a rumpled gray suit stepped into the room. He coughed loudly. "Excuse me. Pardon. Become wakeful!" He thumped his fist on the wall.

Cyrus stretched slowly, groaning. His eyes fluttered open and rested on the little man in the doorway. He blinked, slowly processing what he was seeing, and then he sat up quickly. He shouldn't have. Someone had inflated his head and filled his lungs with ashtrays. His eyebrows were going to explode, his eyes felt like they'd been replaced with steel wool, and his mouth was over-flowing with the taste of burnt tire.

"Sorry," the little man said. "My condolences on the motel. You were insured?"

Cyrus shoved his knuckles into his eyes and then grabbed on to his eyebrows to keep his forehead on. He snorted, he hacked, he roared, scraping at the smoked phlegm inside him. Dropping his hands, he spat on the carpet and opened his eyes. The walls bent and wobbled. Why was he in Dan's room? He shouldn't have spat. Not on the floor. Dan would yell. He looked around for a tissue. No tissue. No Dan. Just the little man from last night and Antigone curled up like a snail shell.

Last night.

The firemen had been angry with him. Dan had been angry. He couldn't remember how it had ended, but Antigone's arms were full of pictures. He must have made it into her room. Or she had. He dug his hand into his pockets. Key ring in one. A thick, misshapen square of glass in the other. The glass sent a buzz into his finger-tips. Lightning bug. The paper card was gone.

Squinting, Cyrus looked up. "Where's Dan?"

"Ah," said the little man. "I couldn't say. I'm here in my official capacity. In fact . . ." He tugged at his sleeves, adjusted his glasses, and pulled a sheet of paper out of his jacket. "I regret to inform you that a guest of this motel, one William Skelton, died early this morning, a fatality resulting from the conflagration."

Cyrus blinked. "Confla—? The fire? Yeah," he said. "I know. I was there."

"Mr. Skelton was pronounced dead shortly after his arrival at the hospital, may his soul find peace." He glanced at Cyrus over his glasses. "Though I wouldn't wager any large sums on that happening." Lowering his paper, the little man suddenly bent at the waist to examine Antigone's sleeping face. "Miss Antigone. Excuse me. It would be more ideal if you joined us."

Cyrus stood up, wobbling. Antigone opened her eyes and yawned.

"We spoke but were not formally introduced last night. I am John Horace Lawney the seventh, Mr. Skelton's solicitor," the little man said. He looked into Cyrus's eyes. "His lawyer."

"Yeah," said Cyrus. "I know."

"And what I have to say concerns you both."

"Oh, sick." Half coughing, half gagging, Antigone sat up and scratched at her matted black hair. "I feel like I ate a box of burnt crayons." She looked at the little lawyer and licked her teeth. "You're back? What are you doing here? Where's Dan?"

"Allow me to continue," the lawyer said. He straightened, sniffed, and looked back down at the paper in his hand. "Mr. William Skelton, Keeper in the Order of Brendan, is survived only by his goddaughter and godson, both recently declared as his chosen Acolytes, and, thereby, heirs to whatsoever of his estate and property may be deeded through said Order." He folded his paper, tucked it into his jacket, and sighed. "There. We've all had an eventful night, and I, for one, am glad to have survived it. I should, of course, be wearing black to deliver such news, but I haven't been out of this suit since we last met. And have I offered you, the bereaved, official condolences on the death of your godfather?"

Cyrus looked at his sister. She was blinking slowly, her mouth half-open.

"Heirs?" Antigone asked. "That's what that little card was about?"

Cyrus coughed up another shot of char. The skin around his neck felt badly sunburned. He touched it tenderly, tracing a band of tiny blisters all the way around, remembering the burning necklace from the night before.

John Horace Lawney VII pulled off his glasses and massaged the bridge of his nose. "Could I interest the two of you in breakfast? We have much to discuss and not much time for discussing."

Cyrus shook his head. "Thanks, but no. We have breakfast stuff here."

Antigone laughed. "Who wants waffles?" She turned to the little man. "Breakfast, like restaurant breakfast?"

"There's a little diner not far from here, if I understand correctly." The man raised his eyebrows. "I've heard it recommended by several discerning truckers."

"Dan!" Antigone yelled, and she limped toward the door. Cyrus followed her out into the puddled and ashen courtyard. Together, barefoot, they walked into the parking lot and stopped.

The blackened carcass of the Archer loomed in front of them.

Cyrus stared at it, his throat tightening, his already-singed tongue drying. This was bad. Where would they go? They didn't have any insurance. Antigone grabbed his hand. She was covering her mouth. Greasy, soot-clumped strands of hair were clinging to her forehead, and tears were piling up in her eyes. He couldn't do that. No crying. Not again. He'd been ten when they lost the California house. He could do better this time.

"Dan!" Antigone yelled. "Dan, where are you?"

✂ five ✂

HELLO, MAXI

CYRUS PEERED INTO the charred remains of his old room. Behind him, Antigone was still yelling for Dan. They had both lapped the motel and had looked inside the Red Baron and in every burnt and unburnt room that they could get into. Without the walkway, a lot of the second story wasn't an option.

Cyrus was dizzy with heat and hunger and nervousness. Dan wouldn't just go away. He could be with the police. It was possible. But he would have left a note.

Memories from the night before were jumbled, but clear enough when it came to Dan. He'd been there. Alive. Angry. And sorry. He'd even apologized for giving Cyrus's room to Skelton.

The image of a burnt body tucked beneath a slumping wall slid into Cyrus's mind, and he quickly forced it away. He shook his head. They wouldn't find a body because Dan wasn't dead. He hadn't been in the fire.

Cyrus stepped back from his doorway. Throwing up was a very real possibility, but stomach acid and ash were all he had inside him. Breathing slowly, trying to calm his gut, he turned around.

Horace was leaning against the yellow truck, checking his watch. "He's not here," the lawyer said. "I told you already. I made a thorough search before waking you. As he was your legal guardian, I had hoped to speak with him."

"Not was," Antigone said. "Is. He *is* our legal guardian." She was angry, flushed beneath the soot, which meant that she was worried. Cyrus watched his sister tuck back her hair and cross her arms. "We have to eat, Cy. He's probably talking to the police. Let's leave him a note and go."

Chewing his lip, Cyrus scanned the ruin. Unless they wanted to eat waffle batter and drink from puddles, they needed to go somewhere. The waffle batter wouldn't even be an option soon.

He turned back to the lawyer, pieces of the previous night shuffling in his head. "Did you know this was going to happen?"

Horace raised his brows. "No. I knew something was going to happen. I knew Skelton's old brotherhood was on his trail, and I knew that he intended to die. That is what I knew. I did not know that there would be a fire or such damage done to your property. As for what I know now, I know that Skelton has given you an object that some very dangerous gentlemen would like to possess for themselves, that we three are desperately hungry, and that there are legal matters that will require my—and your—attention immediately. Time, as I have already said, is short."

Cyrus spat a gray glop into the rubble.

Horace checked his watch again and tucked it back into his pocket. "And after speaking with police and hospital administrators early this morning, I know that there were three fatalities in addition to William Skelton, and none of them was your brother. I know what the thugs were after, but not how many of them there were or which ones were in attendance."

"I only saw four," Antigone said. "One was called Pug."

"Ah, yes," said Horace. "Pug. Thanks to his own terrible life choices, he has passed on. I wish I could pity him."

Cyrus looked at his sister. He could hear the first explosion and see the tongues of fire, the evaporating glass, the slender man who'd trapped them beside Skelton's body. "They talked about a doctor. And there was one called Maxi."

"Maxi?" Horace blinked slowly, looking from Cyrus to Antigone. "How much did Daniel know?"

Antigone shrugged. "What do you mean?"

"Did you tell him what Skelton had done? Did he know what you'd been given?"

Cyrus reached for his pocket. "You mean the keys? No. I don't think so."

Horace sighed. "Well, his ignorance may be some little protection."

Antigone looked at her brother, cocked her head, and turned back to Horace. "This is about keys? They burned down the motel and killed Skelton for a key ring?"

"Yes," Horace said. "They did. And for what is on that ring. Although I'm sure an overarching mean-spiritedness played into their motivation as well. And forgive me if I point out the terribly obvious, but as they didn't actually get the keys, we can expect them to make further efforts."

"Keys!" Antigone yelled. She walked toward her brother. "Cy! I told you to give them back. What were you thinking?"

Cyrus stepped backward, raising both hands. He didn't want his sister angry. Especially not now. "Hold on! I tried, Tigs. I did!"

Antigone stopped in front of him and raised a pair of vicious eyebrows.

"He didn't want them," Cyrus said. "He made me keep them."

Horace snorted loudly. "Mr. Cyrus, I may be a lawyer, but I was a witness to the event, and I know the truth." Again pulling out his watch, he flipped open its face and pressed down a small knob. "Mr. Skelton offered you the keys. He did not force them on you." The watch went back into his pocket. "And the gift was, if I recall—and I do—accompanied by a string of rather morbid admonitions and dark metaphysical threats." He glanced back at the road.

"Why didn't you take the keys?" Antigone asked the lawyer. "You knew they were dangerous, and you let a kid take them?"

Horace nodded. "Yes. Another reason why I am grateful to your brother for his rashness. I prefer this circumstance to that one."

He looked at Cyrus and smiled grimly.

"Now, I've called my car, and it's just around the corner. I have stretched and torn the boundaries of professional courtesy in this rather unusual situation, but I cannot remain in this place any longer than I have already. As Skelton's lawyer, I am an obvious target at this point, as I am bound to have information about the location of the keys. I must move to safer territory. You come with me to a brief explanatory breakfast, or you do not." Turning, he looked back at the road. "If you come, I can explain more to you about the nature of what you have been given, and who will be coming to collect it. If you do not, it is unlikely that we will ever see each other again, and I will consider your inheritance null and void."

A very low and extremely wide black sedan swooped around the corner and bounced into the parking lot.

Horace hurried toward it. "Leave a note if you like," he called. "But come now."

Antigone glared at Cyrus. "I'm leaving a note. Don't get in that car until I'm back. Got me?" She poked him in the chest and began jogging toward the courtyard.

Cyrus watched his sister leave. He watched a tall, lean driver in a black suit open the rear door for Horace and the stout little lawyer slide himself in. And he waited, leaning against the old wooden camper on the back of the yellow truck.

The camper.

Cyrus's heart skipped, and he straightened. The wooden planks ran horizontally above the truck's bed. Some sort of earwax-colored sealant was flaking off around the seams and above every knot in the wood. He'd seen the same stuff on old sailboats. There were no windows. Dragging his fingers down the side, Cyrus moved to the rear of the truck and stopped in front of a narrow door. A small T-shaped knob with a center keyhole had been snapped down and was dangling from a crushed spring.

Holding his breath, Cyrus tugged open the door and looked into the dim light of a dank and stale cave.

The floor and wheel wells were covered in a heavy carpet, which was in turn covered with filthy blankets, cardboard boxes, empty whiskey bottles, a cracked milk crate, tattered books, a stained pillow, and used tissues. Glass from a small skylight had melted out and rehardened in the carpet. The space smelled like wet dog.

He leaned in.

Photos lined one side of the camper. They were hung neatly, in two parallel rows of ten. Most of them were black-and-white. All of them were of faces, and over the top of each face, drawn crudely in blue ink, there was a skull. Just beneath the ceiling, the whole wall had been labeled with black sticker lettering:

GUILT

"Okay." Cyrus exhaled slowly. "This is creepy." He looked back over his shoulder. The black sedan was idling. Horace wasn't visible.

Cyrus climbed into the camper and knelt in front of the photos. Men. Women. Happy. Serious. Young. Old. All hidden behind skeletal scribbling. But there was a woman's face near the end of the second row with only half a blue skull. White hair spread out on a starched hospital pillow. Eyes were closed in sleep.

Catherine Smith.

"No." Cyrus tried to swallow, but his throat slammed shut. That was his mother's halo of hair. Those were her closed eyes. Gulping, he snatched the picture off the wall. He wanted to crumple it, but he couldn't do that to her. He looked up, eyes racing over the others. Top left. Second from the end. Blond hair in one of the few color shots. Eyes smiling behind a mask of ink, barely visible teeth and a prominent nose. The ocean and its cliffs were visible over his father's shoulder.

Antigone had the same picture in one of her albums.

Cyrus reached for it and stopped. Something else was tucked behind it, another photo. Pinching the white corner of a Polaroid, he slid it out.

The picture had been taken in the camper. Daniel's head was lolling against the bottom row of skull photos. Blood had dried on his forehead.

Slowly, stunned, Cyrus turned the image over in his hands. Someone had scrawled on the back.

Ashes, ashes, you all fall down.

"Cy!" Antigone's voice jerked at him. Tugging down his father's picture, he slid out of the dim camper and into the sunlight, eyes watering in the brightness. Antigone was storming toward him, fists clenched, mouth open.

"Jeepers, Cy!" Flustered, relieved, Antigone brushed back her hair and then hit Cyrus in the chest. "No disappearing!" Blinking, he stepped backward. He didn't know what to say or how to say it. "If you disappear, too, I'll take your scalp."

The sky seemed to slip out of place as Cyrus looked up, fighting to breathe, fighting to keep hot, angry eyes from overflowing. Fear, with all its enormous weight, pressed down on his chest and slid through his ribs, filling him, stifling his lungs. In his hands, the three photos felt as heavy as tombstones. His sister took them.

"What?" Antigone asked. "What are these supposed—" She stopped. Cyrus turned away, numb, unwilling to watch his sister's face. His legs somehow carried him to the waiting car.

The drive was hardly quiet. It was a big car, with two backseats facing each other. Even though the seats were wider than some couches, Antigone was right next to Cyrus and she couldn't hold still. She yelled at Horace. She demanded a phone. She demanded the police. But by the time the Archer had disappeared around a bend, Cyrus heard none of it and he ignored her thumping. His forehead was resting against his window, bouncing with the road. While his fingertips mindlessly tracked the blistered braille around his neck, his eyes were racing through the drainage ditch, skimming over gravel, faded soda cans, plastic jugs, and cattails and grass and scum-spotted puddles. Just like his life. He had no answers. He had no control. He couldn't make anything happen, and he couldn't stop anything from happening. And only one kind of anything ever happened. He was a paper cup in the surf, a bulb of kelp torn up and thrown onto the beach, thrown all the way to Wisconsin.

Dan was gone. Why? There were people who would happily kill for the keys in Cyrus's pocket. An old man—his godfather?—had been murdered for them in Cyrus's room. Did those killers think Dan had them? That he knew where they were?

Another home was gone.

Lifting his head slightly, Cyrus let his skull thump back against the window. He shouldn't have taken the keys. Skelton would be just as dead either way. The Archer would be just as burnt. But Dan would be stressing out about the motel and food and clothes and showers. He would be here, coming to breakfast.

Straightening his leg, Cyrus dug the key ring out of his pocket. Antigone grew quiet. Horace, perched on his broad leather seat with his back to the driver, adjusted his glasses.

Cyrus slid his finger through the center ring and let the weight dangle from his hand.

"If these are what they want, who do I give them to?" he asked. "The guy called Maxi? Do you know how to find him?"

Antigone looked at Horace. The little lawyer pursed his lips. The driver's eyes flitted up in the rearview mirror.

"Well?" Antigone said.

Horace cleared his throat. "No, thank God. I do not."

Antigone turned to her brother. Cyrus was expecting anger in his sister's eyes, but he didn't find it. Her eyes were like he remembered his mother's being whenever he'd gotten hurt—which had been often. She wasn't angry. She was in pain.

Blinking, Cyrus looked at the keys in his hand. "I'm sorry, Tigs. I didn't know. I couldn't."

"I know." Antigone tucked back her hair and leaned her head on his shoulder. "I would have kept them, too, Cy. You know I would have."

Horace slid forward, onto the edge of his seat. Reaching out, he set one hand on Cyrus's knee, and one hand on Antigone's. "I am going to say something that may initially be perceived as wildly insensitive." He coughed politely. "There are worse things in this world than your current circumstances. And an entire flock of those worse things—I do profoundly believe this to be the truth—would now be under way if the gentleman called Maxi was now in possession of what you, Mr. Cyrus, have been given. Worse for you, worse for all of us." He sat up. "Ah, breakfast. And well earned, too."

The car swung off the road, bouncing to a stop. Cyrus opened the heavy door and stepped out into a gravel parking lot and the sticky morning heat.

Antigone followed him, slamming the door behind her. Horace was already hurrying toward a low green-and-yellow building lined with murky windows. Behind it, tangles of brush were swallowing barbed-wire fencing, where a single cow was rubbing its shoulder against a sighing fence post. On top of the building, a large, flaking plywood sign spelled out PATS' in hand-painted letters.

Antigone kicked a rock and watched it bounce away. "I couldn't eat anything right now. Especially not here. Do you think they have a phone?"

"Who knows," said Cyrus. The two of them moved toward the door. "Do you think it's owned by someone named Pats? Or is there more than one Pat?"

Horace had stopped at the door. Pulling it open, he stepped to the side and smiled. "Mr. Cyrus, I wouldn't have thought that you would be one to notice—or care about—an apostrophe."

Cyrus glared at him.

"Right. Well, there are two Pats," Horace said. "And this place belongs to both of them."

Inside, Horace hustled all the way down to the far end of the long, dim dining room and squeezed into a corner booth.

Antigone looked around, irritated. "This place is a hole. Do you see a phone, Cy?"

Cyrus shook his head.

An enormous woman rocked toward them between two rows of yellow booths. "I don't know about 'hole,' honey." She winked. "Some people call it heaven." Turning to Cyrus, she pointed to the far end. "Go ahead and join your little friend in the corner. I'll be right back. Menus on the table." She nodded at Antigone. "Little lady can follow me if she needs a phone."

The woman made her way around a small counter lined with stools, and then back toward the sizzling grill. Antigone hurried after her.

Cyrus inhaled long and hard. The dining room was full of the sounds and smells of bacon frying and diced potatoes hopping in the grease. Only a few booths held customers, and they were all men, each of them alone with their newspapers and toothpicks and trucker hats and coffee cups and grease-stained knuckles. The photo of Dan had wiped away Cyrus's hunger, but the power of the smells brought it roaring back. His mouth was watering and his stomach was ringing hollow bells. Cyrus's body needed to eat, and that angered him. Dan was gone. Taken. He shouldn't eat. He shouldn't smell. He should be gone, too.

In his daze, Cyrus nodded at the other customers as he passed, but their return nods were better, more prac-ticed, exchanging respect with only the slightest lift of the head and a glance from unblinking eyes.

Cyrus slid into the corner booth beneath a low-hanging

lamp with a dead bulb. The key ring dug into one leg; the lightning bug glass dug into the other. His neck burned, and his wrist itched. From across the table, John Horace Lawney leaned forward, tenting his fingers. "What will you have?"

"Anything," Cyrus muttered. He grimaced and shifted uncomfortably in his seat, trying to adjust the contents of his pockets. "Dirt. I don't care."

The large woman was lumbering toward them with what looked like a pint of carrot juice. Horace flashed her a wide smile. She smiled back. According to the plastic rectangle on her shirt, her name was Pat.

"You dolls ready?" she asked. "What can I get ya? I can tell you right now that you've never had waffles as mean as what we sling. You'll be full till Christmas."

Cyrus's stomach seethed, and he groaned. He made himself look up. "Sorry," he said. "It's just that waffles . . ."

Pat shrugged. "Don't you worry about it. You're not a waffle kid. Well, you can't go wrong on this menu, no matter where you settle. And wherever you settle, it's gonna be on the house. This breakfast is on Pat and Pat. It's gotta be hard, your place burning down." She hesitated. "You are the Archer kids, aren't you?"

Cyrus looked at his sooty hands and then back up at the big woman. "Yeah. No water at the motel right now. No showers."

She patted Cyrus on the shoulder. "Well, you kids ever need to eat, tell Dan to bring you on by."

Cyrus nodded.

Horace rose to his feet. "Madam," he said. "Pat, we are ready to order." He handed her the menus. "Do you squeeze your own orange juice?"

"I stomp the oranges myself."

"Where are the oranges grown?"

"You know," Pat said. "I couldn't say. But they're orange, they're sweet, and they come with peels."

"Right." Horace rubbed his hands together thoughtfully. "We'll have a large pitcher of fresh-squeezed, a pot of coffee, two plates of links, one of patties, half a pound of bacon, eight eggs scrambled with your sharpest cheddar, diced ham, tomatoes, mushrooms, chopped—fresh, not frozen—spinach, black pepper, and a pinch of cayenne. Four fried eggs, not too runny, and half a loaf of wheat toast. And hashed browns. A pile of them. Oh, and with gratitude for your offer, I will be picking up the tab nonetheless."

He sat down, raised his eyebrows, and looked at Cyrus. "Will that do?" he asked.

Cyrus blinked. "I thought we were in a hurry."

"Oh, we were. We are. In part so that we could have time for this." Horace smiled. "Always breakfast like a man condemned. One never knows what a day may bring." He nodded at the waitress.

"Okay then," she said, tucking the menus under one arm while she scribbled notes on a tiny pad. "We are hungry, aren't we? Big Pat will be happy. He never likes an empty grill." Dropping the pad into her apron pocket, she turned and moseyed slowly away, the floor creaking beneath her.

Horace sipped his carrot juice, leaned back, and rubbed his jaw. Fine black-and-white stubble rasped against his palm.

Cyrus stared at him. "Tell me how to get Dan back."

Horace pursed his lips. "That's a difficult question."

"I have lots of questions," Cyrus said. "Not that you'll have any answers." He leaned forward. "What's so special about the keys? Who was Skelton? How do you know he was our godfather, and what exactly did he leave us besides a lot of trouble?"

Horace sighed. "Should we wait for your sister?"

"No," said Cyrus. "Start with the keys. What's the deal? They turn things on, don't they? Our sign never worked, not until Skelton touched it. And I had a broken record player, too. That's it, right? The keys turn things on." He looked at the dead lamp above him. Glancing at Horace, he reached up and wriggled the bulb. Nothing. He lowered his arm. Ridiculous. He was going crazy.

"Guess not," he muttered.

"Well . . . ," said Horace.

The lightbulb blinked and buzzed. But it wasn't

alone. Every booth in the diner had its own dangling lamp, and half of them—running down the length of the room—had been out. Now, in unison, they pulsed dimly, sputtered, and came to life.

"It appears," said the lawyer, "that you have your answer. But only part of it."

Cyrus frantically tugged the keys free of his pocket and dropped them loudly onto the table.

Horace groaned. "Without meaning to be paranoid, I cannot advise leaving them visible. Remember Skelton's warnings."

Cyrus swung a glance over the room. Antigone was coming. And none of the men in trucker hats seemed to have noticed a thing. He would be more nervous with the keys back in his pocket. He scratched at his itching wrist and looked down, surprised. He couldn't feel his nails, and his wrist seemed swollen. But it didn't look swollen. It looked soot-covered and grubby. He poked at it. His fingertip stopped short of his skin, but he was definitely touching something—something soft and very smooth.

"What is it?" Horace asked. "What are you doing?"

Cyrus didn't answer. He ran his hand over his blistered neck, remembering Skelton's liquid arms holding the glowing hot necklace in the dark. He'd torn it off. And then it had . . . he focused on his wrist. It was . . . he didn't know what it was. Carefully, he pinched his nails around the soft, invisible bulge, and he tugged.

Antigone slid into the booth next to Cyrus. "They said Dan didn't qualify as a missing person yet, but I told them about the picture and now they're sending someone right out. They'll come by here first, and then the motel. Cyrus! What is that?"

Every head in the diner turned, but Cyrus didn't notice. He was unwinding a snake—now visible—from around his wrist. Slender, silver, smooth, it twisted around his fingers and slid its own tail into its mouth. As it did, it disappeared.

Horace chuckled. "Little Patricia, I am very glad to see you. Or not, as the case may be."

"What's going on?" Antigone asked. "Cy, a snake? Is that what he put around your neck?"

Cyrus nodded, and he blindly pulled the snake free of its own tail. Visible again, he let it slither through his palms. After a moment, it wound itself tight around his fingers, ate its tail, and again disappeared. Pulling it free, Cyrus tilted his head to the side, exposing his neck. "And it burned me, Tigs. There are blisters."

Antigone leaned forward, squinting. "You have a little snake brand all the way around, Cy. A blister for every scale. Jeez. That could scar. I can even see the head on your collarbone." She looked at Horace. "What is this thing?"

Horace smiled. "She's a patrik, the one family of serpent permitted to roam free in Ireland. This is the only specimen I have ever seen. Skelton called her Patricia, and she must have been quite hot from the flames to have burned you. She will not eat or sleep, she can become invisible when she swallows her own tail, she will breed only once, and she will not die, though she is quite deadly."

Antigone slid away. Cyrus looked up, startled. The snake was now twisting around his forearm.

"Oh, not deadly to you, Mr. Cyrus," Horace said. "Or to anyone to whom you might give her. Deadly to the one who attempts to remove her from you. She is venomous and can become quite large in anger. If you were to die without passing her on to another—God forbid—she would remain with your bones until the end of the world."

"Patricia," Cyrus said quietly. "She doesn't like to be visible, does she?"

"How is this possible?" Antigone asked. "You seriously want us to believe that that snake won't die?"

"Trust your own eyes," Horace said. "Or don't. It doesn't matter to me what you believe, and we don't have time to marvel at natural or even transnatural wonders." He leaned forward. "Cyrus, please, slide her through the key ring and then place her around your neck. She will be quite useful to you."

Gently, Cyrus unwound the snake and tried to feed her through the ring. Without balking, she shot through and twisted quickly back, searching for her tail. Using both hands, Cyrus raised her to his neck and let her cool body slide around his blistered throat. The keys clicked high against his sternum.

"Wow." Antigone blinked. "They're invisible, too, Cy."

"Really?" Cyrus lifted the keys, trying to squint down his nose. "Do you think they're too heavy for her?"

Horace shook his head. "She's fine. And now, despite every distraction, please try to listen. It is, of course, good and proper that you have called the police about Daniel. But as your brother was taken by William Skelton's former comrades—people with distastefully inhuman abilities—I must tell you that the police haven't the faintest shred of a chance of finding him, alive or dead. Excuse my blunt insensitivity."

Cyrus clenched his fists. He'd seen the fireballs. He'd seen how the dark shapes had moved outside the motel—everything had been so quick and fluid and effortless, like cats. Wolves, maybe. One had even jumped over the truck. "We should trade," he said. "I don't care if we use the cops. Find the Maxi guy and tell him I don't want the keys. Tell him to let Dan go."

Horace leaned over the table, his voice sinking to a harsh whisper. "I am here to help you two. I am. Truly. But know this. I will have no part in any action that intentionally places"—he nodded toward Cyrus's throat—"*what you have* in their hands. You cannot understand the many ways the master of the men you saw has already worked to reinvent and mutilate humanity—humanness—itself. Give him what he wants, and . . . well, suggest it again, and I walk out the door."

Cyrus looked at his sister. She set her fists on the table. His own hands drifted to his neck and the cool body around it. Horace straightened and moved on.

"But I am not without suggestions. In fact, I believe I am able to solve all of your current problems. You are in desperate need of allies." He looked from Cyrus to Antigone and back again. "Skelton was an outlaw and a rogue, but he was also a member of an extremely private global community."

"It couldn't be a nice one if they let him in," said Cyrus.

Horace raised a finger. "Skelton's membership was by birth, and he was never successfully expelled—due mainly to my efforts—and several highly organized attempts were made. The Order of Brendan, as it is called, is—in its current vision—an international community of exploration. In reality, things are never quite so simple as a committee-approved vision statement, but that's not relevant at the moment. Once, the O of B was an empire. Now it could perhaps be best described as an extremely wealthy global chain of sovereign city-states called Estates. Members—citizens, if it helps to think of them that way—have access to resources that boggle and defy imagination. Your godfather, a member of sufficient rank in the O of B, knew that he was going to die. And for a number of reasons, it was his desire that the two of you stand as his heirs. But no member can pass inheritance to anyone outside the global membership of the Order. Thanks to my sleepless night, the necessary paperwork was filed before Skelton was declared dead by this county's noble and competent EMTs, and you two, Cyrus and Antigone Smith, were named as his Acolytes in the Order of Brendan."

"I don't know what that means," Antigone said. "And I'm not sure I care right now."

Horace raised his left hand. "It means that—should you appear and accept the appointment—you will be initiate members in the Order with the opportunity for advancement. That was Skelton's entire purpose in coming here. He has made you eligible to inherit the entirety of his estate, which, contrary to his personal appearance and style of life, is uniquely . . . valuable. In addition, the cost of your memberships, as well as the cost of all food, board, training, placement, and material supplies, will be paid by Mr. Skelton's estate, of which, of course, I am the executor." He raised his eyebrows. "This is a terrific opportunity for a pair of underprivileged siblings, one which will never come to you again. If you accept the appointment, your woes—your homelessness, your motel-lessness, your malnutrition, and your poverty—will all be over."

Cyrus opened his mouth, but Horace raised his hand and barged on. "Of course, of course, you don't care about money at the moment. Daniel's situation is your highest priority. The police are on their way. You have a photo and a nickname—Maxi—to provide as leads. But I can swear to you as solemnly as a judge—they will not find him. And if you run into police custody, then what does tomorrow bring you? Foster care? An orphanage? Of course, such care won't last long. Your brother is missing, taken by men you cannot begin to comprehend, and you two will be their next targets. You've got something they will kill for as soon as smile. Unlike the police, the Order knows these enemies of yours and has the tools to hunt them. They have real strength, real power, and they will go to the ends of the earth to protect their members.

"Accepting this appointment won't simply bring money. It's the best chance you have at keeping blood in your veins and in your brother's. It won't be easy. The Order has high standards for their members and, quite honestly, I'm not sure you can meet them. I do not know of a time when children of your station and education have ever been named as Acolytes. Of course, I am a lawyer—the best the Order's got—and it'll be my job to help you succeed, and short of that, to help the right people think that you have. In the end, it's often the same thing."

Cyrus picked up a knife and rapped it on the table. "Excuse me?"

"Finally," Horace said, ignoring Cyrus and inflating his lungs, "here is my last morsel of information to contribute: Your father was a member."

Cyrus stopped. "What?"

Horace nodded. "For a while."

"Our mother?" Antigone asked.

"No," Horace said. "She was not." He pursed his lips.

Cyrus shifted in his seat. "I don't care who was a member."

"Mr. Cyrus, I'm not sure you understand—" Horace began.

"I get it," said Cyrus. "The bad guys are going to come for us. When they do, I'll give them these." He tapped invisible keys. "And they'll give us Dan. We're not going anywhere until we get Dan. Talk to us then."

John Horace Lawney sighed. "Mr. Cyrus, you present yourselves as Skelton's successors now, today, and receive the help and protection and assets available to you, or not at all. Ever." Leaning forward, Horace groped for the keys with a thick finger. "The keys," he said quietly, "are valuable enough." He paused, having found what he wanted. "But this—" With the click of a small hinge, the black tooth appeared in the air, impervious to the snake's charm. It was darker than a shard of midnight, and its edge swallowed light. "Mr. Cyrus, how many ways can a living man be changed by someone with knives and drugs and the secret sorceries of flesh mixing—the words and chants that make ape ape and dog dog and man man? Do you know? How much vandalism can a victim withstand before Death finally frees him from his captor?" Horace paused, eyes sharpening, lips tight. Cyrus swallowed, unable to look away. The lawyer's voice sank into a whisper. "How many ways can a man be changed when death is no obstacle? No release. No escape. Cyrus Smith, this tooth can raise and rule the dead. And while you possess it, you cannot die. When Skelton placed it in your hand, he stepped into his grave. Better that you step into yours than trade it away—even for your brother." Horace straightened, sighed, sipped his carrot juice, and looked down the length of the diner. "Ah, breakfast," he said. "Pat comes bearing the wealth of plow and pasture."

Cyrus stared at the tooth. He didn't want to touch it, and he didn't want the sheath open. Antigone reached out and snapped it shut, locking eyes with Cyrus. The sheath, and with it the tooth, vanished.

The little lawyer leaned back in the booth. His attention was entirely focused on the large waitress with platter-lined arms.

Raise the dead? Cyrus didn't believe it. No way. But ice still crawled beneath his skin, and his feet felt cold and lifeless. What kind of dead? Fresh, unrotten dead? Lost at sea, swallowed by the salt water and all its creatures dead? His father dead?

"Pat, you are angelic." Horace grinned as plates of steaming food slid onto the table, followed by a pot of coffee and a chipped pitcher of orange juice.

"Enjoy, now," said Pat, drifting away. "Hoot and holler if you need anything else."

Cyrus reached for his neck, and his fingers found the tooth's cool sheath. Raise the dead? Not just record players and lightbulbs and neon signs. The dead.

Smiling, Mr. Lawney folded a stack of bacon into his cheek and pointed greasy fingers at Cyrus. "According to the laws likely to be applied in this situation, you have fourteen hours and forty-four minutes from the administration of the oath to present yourselves and be acknowledged as Acolytes and initiate members. And that," he added, "doesn't leave you much time." He tugged his fat silver watch out of his vest, slapped it onto the tabletop, and began to count, bobbing his head and chewing loudly as he did. "Boiling things down to the bone, that now leaves two hours and fifty-three minutes to present yourselves at Ashtown—the Order's nearest Estate."

Cyrus looked at his sister. He wanted her to say

something. His stomach banged out a muffled drumroll, and he stared at the sausages.

Breathing deeply, Antigone looked up, tucking back her hair. "Cy, as soon as we talk to the police, we should go. More help won't hurt. Money won't hurt, either. I don't know if that tooth does anything, but money does a lot." She turned to Horace. "How far is this place?"

"With my driver," Horace said, "we can be there in two hours."

Cyrus shook his head. "Tigs, I don't care about money. I care about Dan and Mom and . . . us."

"We don't have anything, Cyrus," Antigone said. "Nowhere to live, no way to pay Mom's bills. If Dan's hurt . . ."

"No," Cyrus said. "He's coming back."

Antigone bit her lip. "If Dan's hurt when he comes back, how are we going to take care of him? And Mom? And find a place to live? If they want a ransom for Dan, how will we pay it? If this Order means money and a place to stay and people to help find Dan, then we should go. It's not that far. Staying here, just waiting, trying to survive in the Archer, that would be selfish. It's time for *us* to do something, Cy. There's no one else."

Cyrus leaned his elbows onto the table, grinding his eyes against the heels of his hands. This wasn't happening. None of it. "Antigone, I can't. It's home." He looked up. "You go. You get the money and the help. I'll stay at the motel in case Dan comes back."

Antigone shook her head. "The cops would put you in a home."

"They wouldn't find me. Do you really think they could? There's an old camper in the woods just a couple miles from the motel. I could keep an eye on things from there. I could stay in barns."

"Cyrus," Antigone said quietly. "You're my brother. For now, we're it. The whole family. I'm not leaving you. We should go, but I won't unless you do. Now decide. If you stay, I'll stay. I'll camp in barns with you or sleep in the swimming pool with the tires. If the cops catch us and put us in a home, oh well. If we go to this place, Ashville, we go together."

"Ashtown," Horace said.

Antigone shrugged and finally took her first bite, turning slowly away from Cyrus. "Why fourteen hours and forty-four minutes?" she asked.

Horace smiled, scooping eggs onto his plate. "Because, on the Feast of St. Brendan the Navigator, that is exactly how long daylight falls on the spire of the Ashtown Galleria, from sunup to sundown. Less importantly, but significant nonetheless, 1444 is also the year the Order decided not to prevent new European exploration of the Americas."

Cyrus wasn't listening. He couldn't even see the table

in front of him. When he was nine, he'd fallen off a cliff and dropped twenty feet into a tide pool. Now, again, he could feel the ground sliding away beneath him, rock that he'd trusted pulling free and dropping with him. Familiar fear surged through him, throbbing in his teeth. Then, he'd known where he would land. Now, he had no idea. He only knew that he was falling and that grabbing at the cliff wasn't going to help.

"Okay." His own voice sounded distant. "Okay. We can go." He blinked, and Antigone swam into view. "We should get the money. And whatever help we can."

"You sure, Cy?" Antigone's eyes were wide, her face serious.

Cyrus nodded.

"Bravo," said Horace. "In that case, I recommend that you eat what you can. A long day awaits you. We'll be off in the next twenty minutes."

Cyrus ran his hand around his neck, tracing soft, invisible scales. His feet were bouncing. His fall had turned into a leap. He was diving toward who knew what, away from what he knew well. Fear wasn't fading.

"Who's Maxi?" he asked, and he could hear the waver in his own voice. "I want to know who's after us."

Footsteps rattled down the diner, and Cyrus looked up. A small man was approaching in an extremely baggy police uniform. Even without the soot and the goggles and the darkness, Cyrus recognized the small man's sharp face and his wide, smiling mouth.

His thick hair had been pushed straight back. High on his throat, against tight, pale skin, a thick scar completely encircled his neck. His tiny teeth were bleached white, but gapped and worn to nubs. The corners of his eyes were jaundiced, muddy with yellow around faded brown irises.

"My name is Maximilien Robespierre." His accented voice was smooth, childish. He winked at Antigone and bowed. "But we are all friends and comrades. Please to call me Maxi."

⚜ six ⚜

HAIL

HORACE WASN'T BREATHING. Antigone pushed herself into Cyrus, sliding him down the bench beneath the window.

Maxi smiled and sat down in the booth next to Horace. He commandeered Horace's cup of coffee and carefully picked out a single slice of bacon.

"So," Maxi said, chewing. "You ask about me. I am honored. But is now the time for stories? A brother has vanished. Perhaps can I assist you?"

"You can give him back," Antigone snarled. "You shouldn't have taken him in the first place."

"Shouldn't?" The small man picked up a piece of toast from Antigone's plate. "Little sweetness, *shouldn't, oughtn't, can't*—these are words I cannot be understanding. What do they mean? I have burned cities and killed kings while others were studying *shouldn't. Ma chérie*, if Maxi can, then Maxi should." He leaned his small, grinning face toward Antigone. "And Maxi always can."

Antigone slid back in the booth, and her hand dug into Cyrus's leg.

Cyrus picked up a table knife. "Where's Dan? What did you do to him?"

Maxi's gapped smile widened. "Can you cut me with that? I am not butter."

Horace managed to stand, sputtering anger. "Mr. Robespierre, you are a dog, a murderer, a demon, a poison. But know this, you will be struck down in the end. The Order will see your flesh rot in the soil like the rest of us."

Maxi gripped Horace's sleeve and tugged him back down. "The Order? The gaggling Brendan geese? Fat lawyer, I outlived all your wise men, your explorers, and I will be outliving you. Be silent." He turned to Cyrus. "Boy, what I need, you have, do you not? Give it to me. I will take you to your brother, and you shall never be separated again until the land is swallowed by the sea. You hear me swear it." Maxi wiped his mouth on his sleeve. "The tooth, the keys. What are they to you if your brother dies? Give them to me. What else can you be doing? You cannot leave. You cannot escape." He grinned. "Or . . . when Daniel is dead, I can cut you, too, so that you beg to give them to me. Can you stop me?" He pulled out a pair of long, slender knives. Both had smooth wooden handles black with age and needle blades worn with sharpening, glassy at the edge. He let them rest on the table. They looked like they'd been made for gutting fish. Or bigger things.

Cyrus felt Antigone's grip tighten on his leg. Pat was gone. The farmers were drinking their coffee. Horace was rigid with fear.

Cyrus breathed slowly, but his mind was racing. The keys didn't matter. But he wouldn't give Maxi the tooth. Not if it . . . He couldn't. And without the tooth, the keys would never be enough.

Cyrus set his hands on the table across from the knives and looked into Maxi's jaundiced eyes. They had to get out of the diner. He slid his legs back, tensing, bracing to launch.

"Well?" Maxi raised his eyebrows. "Choose your path, young Cyrus Smith. Will I love you, or will I be angry?"

Cyrus exploded forward onto the table, sweeping a storm of plates and sausage and eggs into Maxi's face. The two knives skittered to the floor, and Cyrus swung for Maxi's jaw. He didn't connect. Maxi slid to the side and a fist slammed into Cyrus's neck. Gasping, he rolled into the hash browns in front of Horace.

"Go!" Cyrus yelled, but there was nowhere to go. Maxi was on his feet, holding his knives. A huge, round man with a beard and apron came hurrying out of the kitchen, but stopped when he saw the uniform.

Maxi stepped forward, eyes on fire and tiny teeth grinding, knives held low. Orange juice and egg ran down his uniform. Cyrus slid back beneath the window, knocking over waters. Horace was standing. Antigone was crouching on her seat.

"Enough," the lawyer said. "Enough. Let the children go. I'll get you everything you need."

Maximilien laughed. The scar around his pale neck flushed red. "No," he said. "No. You cannot. The keys, Smith boy. Give them to me. Now. Before you die."

Cyrus felt a shadow move above him, and the window exploded with a roar.

Maxi staggered backward and fell. Glass rained down on Cyrus's face and neck and chest, bouncing like crystal hail on the table. Above him, Cyrus saw a long gun barrel fire again and again, spitting wide flame, but he heard nothing.

And then Horace dove over him and out the window. Antigone pulled him up and drove him out the gaping window hole. His knee caught the sill, singing with pain, and the two of them were falling together, tumbling onto an old bicycle, through tall grass, and onto gravel.

Cyrus climbed to his feet and staggered after his sister, around the building, toward the big black car. Horace was in front of them, diving into the backseat. The lean driver was holding the door for them, tall in his black suit, his big gun trained at the diner. There was a police car and two other men ducking behind it. The driver fired again. And again. Leaving the rear door open, he jumped in behind the wheel. Antigone dove inside, and then Cyrus followed, landing facedown on the car's strangely soft carpet. The car showered half an acre with gravel as it roared forward onto the road. The rear door slammed with the acceleration.

The heavy car rose and fell smoothly, gliding and shifting in time with the curves and dips of the road. It was an old car—Cyrus had known that at first glance—but it wasn't moving like one.

"I feel sick," Antigone muttered. "We should be dead right now. I could throw up."

Cyrus exhaled slowly. "Me too." He was holding the keys at his neck, clenching them too hard, digging metal teeth deep into his palm. Any harder and he would bleed, but he couldn't let go.

Antigone's leg was kangarooing in place. She had her eyes shut and was twisting her hair. Cyrus looked around the car and up at the glass divider. He wanted to see the driver. He wanted a good look at his face. The man with the big gun.

John Horace Lawney sat with his back to the driver and his head down, massaging his temples.

Outside the windows, bushes and pastures and signs and road reflectors snapped and flickered past like frames in one of Antigone's home movies.

Antigone looked up. "Maxi's dead, right?" She

nudged Horace with her toe, and the little lawyer looked up. "Please tell me he's dead."

Horace sighed, and the car bounced gently and banked hard around a curve.

He shook his head. "That . . . man . . . was born Sebastián de Benalcázar in Córdoba, Spain, more than five hundred years ago. As a conquistador, he traveled with Ponce de León into Florida—until Ponce had him shot. He escaped into South America and tried to set himself up as a governor, slaughtering Incas and his fellow Spaniards along the way. He was hung, stabbed, poisoned, and even keelhauled. But to no effect. The Order finally captured him when he tried to return to Europe. He was held without food or water for more than two centuries before some weak-minded fools released him. He reemerged in France under the name of Maximilien Robespierre. There, his taste for destruction reached revolutionary heights. More than thirty thousand French men and women were sent to the guillotine, including King Louis XVI, Marie Antoinette, and several of the Order's most notable French members. The Order did not capture him again until the mobs turned against him and he himself was beheaded—you saw the scar on his neck, did you not? It was a simpler matter when his head was in a basket and his body was in a cart. He was imprisoned again but escaped the Order's French Estate when it was destroyed during the Second World War."

Horace looked up at Cyrus, and then into Antigone's eyes. His brow was furrowed. "Unfortunately, the answer to your question is no. *Dead* is one thing that he certainly is not."

Cyrus swallowed. His throat had tightened and his serpent necklace felt suddenly heavy. He had nothing to say. He wanted to disbelieve, but he couldn't—not with everything he had already seen. He looked at his sister, and her dark eyes were worried.

The car surged forward and swooped around an RV. The Archer was visible in the distance. Cyrus leaned against his window. The Golden Lady was on her pole. But she wasn't golden. She was pale. Dead.

As the car approached, she began to glimmer. The tooth was returning.

"Who are they?" Antigone pointed at the motel. Three men were picking through the rubble. A fourth hopped out of Skelton's camper.

All four looked up as the big car screamed past. Two of them were tall and identical, pale green in the daylight. The other two were bare-shouldered. Tattooed. One bearded, one bald.

The driver ignored a double yellow line and passed two cars at once. Two minutes later, they were nearing town. And traffic lights. The first one was red.

"Um . . ." Cyrus sat up.

They shot through it.

Antigone looked around the interior of the car. They slowed slightly for traffic and ran the next light. She grabbed her brother and tugged him back in his seat. "Buckle, Cy. We're in trouble."

There weren't any seat belts.

The car accelerated and skimmed past a police car, nearly clipping its side mirror. Cyrus and Antigone wheeled around, watching the patrol car flick on its lights and then quickly miniaturize behind them. They were already through the small town. Fields and highway stretched ahead.

Horace cleared his throat. "Please don't worry yourselves. This car is a thing of beauty. She came off the line in 1938 and track-tested above three hundred feet per second. They won't catch up to us. Gunner up there isn't even pushing her yet, are you, Gunn?"

Cyrus turned back around, watching the tall driver's hands on the wheel. Something slammed into the roof above him.

A hole appeared in the leather ceiling and tiny feathers snowed down from the upholstery. Another. And another. Like hammer blows. Like piercing hail. Lead hail.

The car swerved. Glass shattered. Bullets rained down.

John Horace Lawney jerked and fell to his side.

The car jumped off the road, roared down a bank,

and sent a wire fence sprouting into the sky. Cyrus bounced against the ceiling and grabbed at the door. Antigone rattled on the floor with Horace.

"Hang on!" Gunner yelled, and he cranked the wheel. The car twisted sideways, sailing at airplane speeds through a pasture of sun-browned grass. Seed heads lashed and whistled at the doors, and a cloud of dust and chaff and splattered plant rose up around them.

On his knees, Cyrus stared out his window. Bellowing cows were running, cows that hadn't been meant to run, two-ton milk jugs, spotted black and white. One of them froze, panicked, unable to choose a route.

Cyrus braced himself, but the car swung in time, slamming his face against the glass. Antigone and a bleeding Horace tumbled up beside him.

Another fence flipped up the hood and off the roof, and they were heading downhill, past a barn, sliding by a farmhouse, through someone's garden and beneath a tree, thumping an ancient tire swing into orbit, jumping a ditch, and fishtailing onto a gravel road.

"Everyone okay?" Gunner glanced in his mirror. "We all alive?"

"No!" Antigone was stretching the lawyer onto his back between the seats. "Stop! Horace got hit in the shoulder, right by his neck."

"Can't stop." Gunner shook his head. "He breathing?"

"I think so!" Antigone yelled. She leaned her ear down to Horace's mouth as he coughed, misting her cheek with blood.

"Get some pressure on the wound!" Gunner yelled. "Cyrus, get your window down and squeeze on out. I need your eyes on the sky the next couple miles. And hang on! I don't want to lose you!"

Cyrus cranked his window down and immediately went deaf with the roar and rattle of gravel and wind. The driver lobbed back a pair of goggles.

"Pull 'em tight!" he yelled. "Tight!"

Antigone, white-faced, was crouched on the floor, pressing a wadded-up suit coat against the little man's shoulder. Looking into his sister's terrified eyes, Cyrus took a breath, pulled down his goggles, and fished himself out the window and into a hurricane.

Gripping the inside of the car, Cyrus eased his rear up onto the door, and his chin rose above the roof. The goggles shook, and his nose felt like it might disappear. The roof of the car was pocked with holes, and dust tornadoed on the road behind them. Gradually, gently, Cyrus looked up. At first, with his head shaking in the wind, he could only make out two contrails. And birds. Three of them. Maybe hawks or crows. High and circling.

Too big. Wrong wings. Kites? Hang gliders? The three shapes crossed paths and adjusted, forming a triangle. They were descending, following the car.

Cyrus turned his face forward, into the car's absurd speed, and the spatter of bugs stung his cheeks. In the distance, Lake Michigan, a smooth plane of perfect blue, stretched to the horizon. Beside it, the buildings of Milwaukee were clustered like a collection of models.

A minute later, gasping and wiping his face, Cyrus told the driver what he'd seen.

"We have to get to a hospital," Antigone said. "We have to call the police."

"We have to change routes," said the driver. "No more front gate for us. They'll be waiting. It'll push our time, but you can make it. And don't you worry about Johnny Horace. Not just yet. He's taken worse. He doesn't know how to die." The car accelerated even more. "Let's see how fast the old girl can run."

Cyrus and Antigone bounced on the floor of the car, popping like corn around the unconscious lawyer, taking turns pressing down on the man's bloody shoulder until Antigone began to be sick and Cyrus pushed her away.

"C'mon, Horace," he muttered, leaning all of his weight against the wound. But the car still bounced, and his hands bounced with it, releasing pressure. He had never seen so much blood; he'd never felt so much of it run between his fingers, fingers that were beginning to stick together with the clotting.

"His face," Antigone said behind him. She was breathing hard. "It's white. He's going to die, Cyrus."

"No." Cyrus wedged his legs against the door and pushed down harder through the bouncing.

Eventually, the car found asphalt, but the turns were no longer smooth, and Cyrus had to fight to keep from being thrown into his sister or against the doors.

Traffic grew, and soon, the car slowed. Buildings began to dance past the windows.

The turns grew harder. Full lefts and full rights. Squealing U-turns.

Antigone's face was gray and damp. Cyrus's arms were shaking as he adjusted the bloody ball of Horace's suit coat against the little man's neck. The flow had almost stopped. Might not be any more blood to bleed.

The car squealed to a stop beside a Dumpster. Gunner jumped out and jerked open the rear door.

"C'mon!" He grabbed Antigone's arms and pulled her out. Then he grabbed Horace by the ankles and dragged him through the door until he was sitting in a scum puddle on the asphalt.

Cyrus stepped out of the car and looked around. They were in a narrow, foul-smelling alley, but on top of the foul smell, blowing out of a big silver vent in the brick wall beside the Dumpster, he could smell pizza.

The driver scooped Horace up off the ground and staggered toward the alley mouth, his shoes clicking as he went.

Cyrus grabbed his sister, and the two of them

followed the tall black suit out of the alley and into a little square. There were people, but not many, and all of them stopped to watch the big man with the body.

Cyrus looked up, searching the sky. A single black shape was visible against the blue, almost motionless, hanging in place.

"Cyrus," Antigone said. "Why are we here?"

The big man, turning sideways, managed to force his way through a small glass door, a little brass bell ringing as he did. The name of the place was arched in gold letters on the front window.

"Milo's Pizza," Cyrus read. "I don't know, but we should go in."

It was early and the pizza place was empty. It wasn't even open. Two prep cooks were leaning out of the kitchen watching the driver and his load stagger through the dining room toward a door in the back. Black-and-white tiles checkered the floor, and rickety chairs were perched on the tables. An old Pac-Man arcade game chirped in the corner.

"Hey," Cyrus said.

"We're not open." One of the cooks raised a sauce-covered spoon. "You can't be in here."

"We'll just be a sec," said Antigone, and grabbing Cyrus by the wrist, she pulled him between the tables.

Gunner had opened the door in the back and was setting Horace down. He stepped to the side, holding the door open. Horace was hunched on an old toilet.

"What?" Antigone asked. "What are we doing?"

The driver beckoned them in, shut the door, and locked it.

It was a tiny bathroom, and there wasn't enough room for two people, let alone three and a man as tall as the door.

"This is one of the old entrances," the driver said. "It's been closed for I don't know how long. Might be blocked. Couldn't say when it was last used. Hold on to the sink."

A plastic air-freshener high on the wall spritzed essence of pine tree onto his cheek.

"Ack!" The driver grimaced and spat, blinking in pain, and then hunched over and lifted the lid off the toilet tank. Plunging his hand into the water, he began to feel around. The toilet flushed.

"What—" Cyrus didn't finish.

The floor shook and fell away.

Cyrus had only fallen downstairs once before, and they had been straight. These were spiral stairs, twisting down around an old cast-iron sewer line. And he was tumbling with his sister.

Gasping, yelping, crushed and crushing, the two of them rolled and flipped down the metal stairs and sprawled onto cold, wet stone. Nearby, water was running.

Antigone groaned.

Cyrus pushed her off and sat up, coughing in the darkness. In the ceiling above them, he could see the little well-lit and floorless bathroom. The toilet hung in the air, and Horace's legs dangled over the sides.

The big driver, with his legs spread, squinted down into the darkness. "You all right?" he asked. "I told you to hang on to the sink."

Heaving the little lawyer over his shoulder, he carefully descended the stairs.

At the bottom, he tugged a chain, and a strand of naked lightbulbs fluttered to life.

They were in a tunnel. The walls were made of brick, slimed green and black, arching into the ceiling above.

Cyrus stood up. The stone floor came to an end a few feet from where they had fallen. Beyond the edge, with a mounded back like a snake's, dark water raced past. Above it, a large basket hung on a heavy cable.

Cyrus glanced back at his sister. Wincing, she managed to stand. "Wow. What now?" She looked at the basket. "No," she said. "We're not getting in that."

"From here, it will be easy for you," the driver said. With Horace still over his shoulder, he wheeled a flight of stairs out of the darkness and pushed them to the water's edge. Kicking on a foot brake, he began to climb. The stairs squealed and bowed beneath him.

"No." Antigone shook her head and looked at her

brother. "We don't even know where we're going. I'm not getting in a moldy basket dangling over some sewage river in a pitch-black tunnel."

The driver heaved Horace into the basket and backed down the narrow stairs.

"We're just going to shoot off somewhere? What happens if the cable breaks? Why are we even doing what you say? We don't know you."

Cyrus scanned the tunnel. His head was throbbing and his world had shattered, but he knew what to do next. He knelt by the water, dipping his sticky hands in the cool current. "Not the time, Tigs," he said. "We're in it now."

"I'm Gunner Lawney," the driver said, and he wiped his forehead on his sleeve. "Johnny's nephew. Got into some trouble and came up from Texas ten years ago. Was supposed to be an Acolyte, but that didn't work out too well. But I found my niche." He smiled. "I can drive, and I can shoot. Beyond that, pretty useless." Gunner nodded at the basket. "Now get up in there. I gotta get back to the car and get it out of here."

"What makes you think we can do this alone?" Antigone asked.

"You have to," said Gunner. "Climb on up and I'll tell you what to do."

Cyrus splashed water onto his face and stood up. Antigone groaned, and then stepped behind her brother, pushing him toward the steep, rickety stairs. He climbed carefully, each narrow tread sighing in his hands, and when he reached the top he had to stretch for the edge of the basket. He pulled it toward himself, threw a leg in, and tumbled over the edge onto Horace.

The little lawyer moaned, and the basket swung.

Cyrus sat up and reached back for Antigone's hands. She grabbed his wrists and he grabbed hers.

Antigone's teeth were clenched, her eyes wide. "Cy, if you let go, I'm going to kill you."

Cyrus smiled. "If I let go, you're going to float away in a black river."

Antigone jumped, clipped her knee on the edge, and fell inside.

"Great!" Gunner yelled. "Cyrus, there should be a lever in the front of the basket. Pull it when I tell you."

Cyrus found the lever and waited. Powdered rust came off on his hands.

The basket jerked and the sound of grinding metal gears echoed in the tunnel.

He stood up and looked over the edge. Gunner was standing beside another lever in the wall. Two huge flaps had opened out of the sides of the river. Water was mounding over and around them, forcing them forward.

Something in the ceiling began to click like a roller coaster.

Cyrus looked up. The basket hung from a pulley,

straddling the grease-covered cable above the water. But two smaller cables were looped onto hooks on the pulley, and they ran up into the ceiling, where an enormous spring as thick as Cyrus's thigh was whining as it stretched.

"Oh, gosh." Biting his lip, Cyrus sat down on his sister's feet. She had Horace's head propped on her lap and was squinting at his shoulder.

"The bleeding stopped," she said. "At least on the outside."

The clicking in the ceiling slowed. A final metallic click. And then . . . nothing.

"Get yourselves to the Galleria!" Gunner's voice filled the tunnel. "Someone will take Horace to the hospitalers. Now hang on tight and flip the lever. I'll look you up in Ashtown."

Cyrus slid back beside his sister. "Hold on, Tigs. This is dumb. Really dumb. Are you ready?"

Antigone sniffed and tucked back her hair. "No," she said. "Not even close. Not even a little bit. Now do it."

Cyrus kicked the lever.

⚜ seven ⚜

ASHTOWN

CYRUS HAD NO way of knowing how far that first launch took them, only that it was far and fast and black. The basket bobbed and swung in the wind, occasionally grazing the walls where they narrowed, occasionally kissing the surface of the water, and at one point just missing another basket hurtling in the opposite direction.

Eleven times, the basket slowed and flipped some sort of switch. Naked lights sparked to life on the tunnel ceiling, hooks snagged the pulley, flaps opened in the river, and long-dormant springs uncoiled in the ceiling. Eleven times, they were launched, and the lights flickered off behind them. And then Cyrus stopped counting.

The tunnel changed. Brick became stone, and the bones of old arches dotted the walls and ceiling. At one launch, the ruins of another basket, rotten with moisture, dangled in a snarl of cable against the wall. At another, the river veered to the right while they continued on, straight through a much smaller, circular hole in the wall of the tunnel. By the time the next light tripped, the river—or another river—had joined them.

When the basket finally slowed and stopped for the last time, Antigone moaned.

"I was sick before this," she said. "Can you see, Cy? Are we slingshotting again? I can't do it."

Cyrus sat up. He could hear gears and splashing, but the sound was different. No clicking. No whining springs. He felt his way tentatively to his knees and glared at the darkness.

With a crack, two delayed lightbulbs surged to white. One exploded, dropping its glass into the river. The other sputtered and survived.

The current was turning a stone waterwheel. The wheel was powering two tarnished green gears. The gears were cranking a cable up into a hole in the ceiling and back down out of another. Small, hinged wire cages two feet across were rising and descending with the cable.

Beside the basket, a wire platform had been bolted to the stone. Cyrus gauged the distance. It would be easy enough to climb onto the platform and then lean out, grab the rising cable, and hop into one of the cages. At least if you weren't also trying to carry an unconscious lawyer.

"What do you think, Tigs?" he asked. "You first or me first? This is gonna be tough. He won't stay in one of those by himself."

He looked back at his sister. Antigone was huddled in a corner, as pale as Horace. Her eyes were squeezed shut, and she was forcing herself to breathe long, even breaths. It was her county-fair face—the face she made before losing her elephant ear and corn dog. It was the face that had thrown up in the front seat—and the backseat—of the Red Baron. And in the boat, out fishing with their dad. Many times.

"We're here," said Cyrus. "Tigs, you made it. Come on. See if you can stand up."

Antigone opened one eye, and then shut it quickly.

"Open your eyes." Cyrus grabbed her hands.

"You were moving," she said. "The basket is still rocking."

"Hardly," said Cyrus, and he pulled her up.

Both of Antigone's eyes opened wide and her head bobbed.

"No!" Cyrus yelled. "Turn! Point away!" He spun his sister around and leaned her over the rim of the basket. He couldn't hear it. He couldn't smell it. If he did, he'd be chucking, too. The county fair had seen it happen. Twice. The Red Baron hated it. "I'm not listening!" Cyrus began to hum an old car song his parents had used to distract them. His sister's back quaked beneath his hand. He looked up at the ceiling, breathing through his mouth.

Antigone straightened and turned back around slowly. "Worst ever," she said. "Seriously."

Cyrus raised his eyebrows. "Maybe in this state. What about Highway One, the windy one on all the cliffs?"

"Oh, gosh." Antigone shivered and raised her hand. "Don't even say that right now."

"And at least this time the river just takes it away. Sharing a bag is worse, and poor Dan sitting in between us, and Mom and Dad trying to sing us out of it."

"Shut up, Cyrus."

"I'm just saying . . ."

"Don't." Antigone bent over and got her hands under Horace's arms. "Help me. We have to get him to a doctor."

In the end, Antigone rode up first. Cyrus followed, his feet balancing on the outside of the wire cage, his hugging arms pinning Horace to the cable.

He had only begun to rise when the light clicked off, controlled by some kind of timer. The sound of the water faded beneath him. In the narrow shaft, the squeaking of the cages blended and echoed with the lawyer's rasping breath.

"Hold on, Horace," Cyrus whispered. "Wherever it is that we're going, we're getting closer. Hold on."

The cable bounced and shook. Above him, dimly silhouetted, Antigone's legs disappeared as she hopped out of her cage.

"Hey!" Her voice roared down the hole. "They turn quick, so you won't have much time."

Cyrus hooked his arms through the lawyer's armpits and flexed his legs, ready to lift.

His head rose into a musty room, lit only through cracks. He shoved the little lawyer at his sister, watched her stagger back into a wall, and then jumped, clipping his head on the ceiling before his cage vanished through the roof.

Antigone was coughing under the weight, sinking to the floor. Cyrus walked straight to the tallest crack of light, a seam between two doors. They were locked, but they were also thin and old, and they bent a little with pressure from his shoulder.

He backed up.

"Try one of Skelton's keys," said Antigone. "Is there a keyhole?"

"Nope." Cyrus threw himself against the doors. Wood popped, but he bounced back. "I can break it."

"You mean a rib? Maybe your shoulder?" Antigone adjusted her grip, propping Horace in front of her.

"There's just one little bolt," said Cyrus. "And it's set in old wood." He paused. What was he hearing? Voices. Shouting. "You hear that?" he asked.

Antigone nodded. "They don't sound happy."

This time, Cyrus used his foot. The wood splintered, and the two doors wobbled open onto a world of emerald and sunlight.

A butter-smooth lawn stretched away from the doorway. Dangling Horace between them, gripping his arms tight around their shoulders, Cyrus and Antigone staggered into the light and looked around.

They had emerged from a small building on one side of the lawn. In front of them, an enormous obelisk rose from a circular fountain. Well beyond that, the lawn ended in an iron fence. Beyond the fence, narrow roads were lined with gray stone buildings and townhouses.

Cyrus and Antigone were standing on a fine gravel path, separated from the grass with a clean, sharp cut in the turf. The path curved through the lawn until it met a much larger path and became stairs. The stairs grew into a looming forest of grooved columns guarding lean towers and railed balconies, porticoes and paned windows the size of the Archer's swimming pool, glistening in the sun. The place was a fluid behemoth of stone crowned with blue sky and a towering choir of statues. It was a museum, a palace—a hulking glory large enough to hold several of both. Two long mezzanined wings bent forward off the central structure, embracing the lawn on opposite sides.

Cyrus pulled his eyes away from the building. On one end of the lawn, a group of lean people were running in tight, synchronized formation, dressed in matching white shirts and very short shorts, changing stride and direction, accelerating and slowing as a man yelped orders from the front. But the real shouting was coming from the other end of the lawn.

Between the fountain and the stairs to the main building, a small group of adults stood with clipboards watching five sweating teenagers pedal furiously on a bizarre contraption of bicycles attached to five oversize spinning, umbrellalike propellers.

"It's like . . . ," Antigone began. "I don't know."

Cyrus didn't know, either. While he watched, the contraption inched off the ground and thumped back down. The adults made notes.

"Dig!" a pedaler shouted. "Dig, dig, dig!"

The five pedalers hunched over their handlebars, yelling, groaning, and whooping as they pumped frantically. The contraption shook. The big-bladed, wobbling propellers beat at the air, working to tear themselves free. And then, while Cyrus watched, the whole thing eased up off the ground. One foot at first, and then three. Yelling became laughter, and the elevation increased while adults ducked and the flying bicycle team slid sideways above the lawn. Ten feet. Twelve. Twenty.

"Cyrus!" Antigone said, tugging Horace. "Come on!"

Cyrus gaped. The design wasn't that complicated. It was just bikes and . . . He needed to learn how to weld.

"Cy!" Antigone pulled on her side of Horace, dragging Cyrus toward the grass.

"Tigs, aren't you watching this?"

Twenty feet up, one of the bikes snapped and dangled. A boy dropped, flapping and screaming, and then bounced in the grass and went limp. They were all screaming now. They were falling. The pedalers pedaled but only four propellers spun. The contraption slid down through the air, faster and faster, toward the fountain.

When the first propeller hit the obelisk, it tore free, whirring off in the direction of the synchronized runners. Another flipped through the grass, stopping at Cyrus's feet. Bikes and riders tumbled down the statues and into the water. The adults made notes on their clipboards.

"Cyrus, come on," said Antigone. "We have to find someone."

The two of them, with Horace's arms over their shoulders, stepped forward off the path and onto the grass.

A sharp whistle rolled down the steps from somewhere in the columns.

"Grass!" someone shouted, and a shape materialized, double-timing down the distant stairs, running with his toes pointed out. He was short, wearing a bowler hat and a suit, and he was blowing a whistle with each breath. At the bottom of the stairs, he broke into a rigid run, but he didn't come straight toward them across the lawn. He stayed on the footpaths.

"Hey," said Antigone as he finally approached. She shrugged Horace's arm farther up around her shoulders. "Where's the hospital? We have to get this guy a doctor right away."

The bowler hat staggered to a stop in front of them, straightened, tugged his coat, and blew his whistle one last time.

"You," he said, panting, "are on the grass."

Cyrus looked down at his feet. They were about eighteen inches from the edge of the path. He looked at the propeller, dug into the turf beside him, at the wreckage around the fountain and the distant team of runners. He looked back up at the man's face. But he wasn't a man. Too young and pimply.

"They're all on the grass, too, and you're just a kid," said Cyrus. "Now tell us where the hospital is or I'll stomp on the grass."

"I'm seventeen," the kid said. "And all contact with the grass is strictly prohibited without a usage permit, excluding sheep and gardeners."

Cyrus laughed, shifting his shoulder under Horace's arm. "You're not seventeen. You look ten."

"Sixteen," the boy said. "And I can write you up."

"Yeah, right," said Cyrus. "I'm taller than you."

"Excuse me!" Antigone gritted her teeth, flashing irritation at her brother. She was sweating. "This guy has been shot, and we need to get him to the hospital or a doctor or whatever you have here."

"Please, step off of the grass."

"No." Cyrus shook his head.

Antigone stepped back onto the gravel path, tugging Horace and Cyrus behind her.

For the first time, the boy examined the limp body's face. Even his pimples went pale. "That's Mr. Lawney. You shot Mr. Lawney?"

Antigone sputtered in frustration. "No, we didn't shoot him. He was bringing us here and got shot on the way." Struggling to hold up her side of the lawyer, she heaved Horace, adjusted her grip, and began to yell. "Tell us where the hospital is, you ten-year-old tick!"

"I'm fifteen," the boy said. "And don't yell. The hospitalers are gone right now anyway. Everyone not testing is in the Galleria." He pursed his lips, lofty and disdainful. "Even the other porters left their posts. The outlaw, William Skelton, named two Acolytes, and people said they were actually coming. I don't believe it. They'd have to be crazy. But they're too late anyway."

Antigone looked at her brother, and then back at Pimples. "How late?"

The boy turned and squinted at a clock tower on the building behind them. "Well, late enough, anyhow. They'd have to reach one of the gates and be granted clearance. That could take five minutes by itself—the guards won't exactly be helpful—and they have to present themselves at the Galleria in three." He looked back at Cyrus and Antigone. "At least if the other porters were telling the truth. They don't always. At least not to me."

"Grab his feet!" Cyrus said. "Quick!"

The kid blinked beneath his bowler hat.

Antigone nodded. "Please? Hurry! We can't be late."

Cyrus and Antigone turned, swiveling Horace's toes through the gravel toward the porter. The boy bent tentatively and gripped Horace by the ankles.

"Okay?" Cyrus glanced back over his shoulder. "Great. Is the Gallery in the big building?"

"The Galleria," the boy said. "And yes. Up the main stairs."

With Horace bouncing between them, Cyrus and Antigone steered straight across the grass, beelining for the stairs.

"Hey! Whoa! Stop!" the boy yelled. "I can't reach my whistle. My hat! My hat has fallen! In the grass! My hat is in the grass!"

Cyrus grinned at his sister. Breathing hard, Antigone managed to roll her eyes. Behind them, the boy jogged on tiptoe.

When they reached gravel and began climbing the stairs, the boy stopped yelping. Puffing, keeping his breath even, Cyrus concentrated on the steps. The treads were deep, but each step was short. He would have been able to skip a stair if he'd been running alone. He probably would have skipped two. But not now, trying to keep time with his sister and dragging a body.

"Come on," Antigone gasped. "We can do this, Cy. We're doing it. We'll make it."

They reached the top and rushed forward between two grooved columns. Huge wooden doors, taller than the Archer, were closed in front of them.

"Are you . . . ," the kid began, gasping. "Did you come . . . through the waterway? It's prohibited. Waterway's closed. Hazardous." He began coughing. "Use the wicket."

"What?" Balancing his part of Horace, Cyrus reached out with one hand and tugged on a dangling iron ring.

Horace's feet dropped, and the kid porter scrambled forward, pushing Cyrus aside. He grabbed a knob, and a small door swung open inside the large one.

"The wicket gate," the kid said, stepping out of the way.

A bell pealed loud and long, the sound ricocheting around the stone.

"Go. You have five rings. Follow the people. I have to stay here."

Antigone ducked through the door with Horace's arm and shoulder. Cyrus and the other shoulder followed. Inside, both of them froze. The huge corridor was crowded, and every face had turned toward them. High above the mob, the ceiling was vaulted, and each vault was frescoed with maps. An enormous reptilian skin was mounted on one wall, running around a corner and out of sight. In the center of the hallway, a large leather boat perched high on a stone pedestal.

The bell rang again.

"Um, hi," Antigone said. "Is there a doctor here?"

The crowd parted.

"Go!" someone yelled. "Hurry!"

Cyrus and Antigone Smith, caked with blood and soot, dragged their lawyer through the path in the crowd, his toes squealing on the marble floor. Whispers and murmuring swirled as the crowd closed behind them.

The bell rang again.

"This way!" A man's voice echoed through the hall. "Over here!"

"He lies!" a woman shouted. "Over here!"

Cyrus and Antigone stopped. The crowd pressed in, grabbing, pulling, pushing.

"Is that Horace?"

"Is he dead?"

The bell rang again.

Cyrus looked into the faces around him. Some were angry. Some were laughing. Some were worried.

"Cy! This way!" Antigone lowered her head and plowed into the crowd. A woman was leading her toward a tall open door. They were through, but still surrounded by the mob. "Don't ring it!" Antigone shouted. Her voice bounced through the vaults, and silence fell on the crowd. "We're here! We present ourselves! Or declare ourselves! Whatever! We're here! And we need a doctor!"

The bell rang again, and the echoes died slowly.

"Hello?" Antigone said, her head on a swivel. "A doctor, please? Our lawyer's been shot."

"Initiates, step forth!" The voice was deep—rumbling irritation.

The crowd pressed back to the sides of the enormous room, and Cyrus, regripping Horace, began to move toward the front.

"No!" Antigone pulled back. "Not until we have a doctor." She looked around the room. "He bled a lot!"

Two middle-aged, pale-faced women in white skirts edged nervously out of the crowd and then hurried forward. They took Horace and laid him gently on his back. One finger-checked his pulse.

Massaging her shoulder, Antigone nodded at her brother, and the two of them walked slowly toward the front of the huge room. Cyrus's eyes skidded through the crowd. White-haired men in safari jackets stared at him. A group of older girls in tall riding boots sneered. Behind them, deeper in the crowd, Cyrus spotted a small flock of starched nuns' hats. He moved on, past a cluster of fit, sweating boys in tall socks and the same short white shorts and shirts as the runners outside. They all stood with their arms crossed, each with a simple black medieval ship printed high on his cotton chest. Farther on, a young group of flushed, ponytailed girls in similar uniform whispered and giggled. Instead of a ship, each girl's shirt had a small snake curled in a ring, swallowing its own tail. Cyrus's hand went to his neck as women and men in pocketed shorts and trousers and jodhpurs scowled and stepped aside. A group of monks in brown robes with rope belts and sandals stepped backward, crossing themselves as Cyrus and his sister passed. Cyrus tore his eyes from theirs, from the crowd, and focused on the room.

Columns of different colors, scaled like fish, held crowded mezzanines on both sides, and light streamed down through large windows. In the front, a forest of enormous portraits collaged the wall with color. Men and women stood on ships, beside strange creatures, on mountains and beaches and walls. The paintings at the top, arranged beneath the high, black-beamed ceiling, were crude and simple. Below them, the canvases became more ornate, crowded and medieval, cluttered with red robes and dragons and sea creatures. Even farther down, the styles changed again and again, until, at the very bottom, a single abstract portrait hung— a boy's face, intense in its wide strokes, colored only with red and black. In front of the portrait, the same boy sat behind an ebony table. His face was freckled and sharp. His hair was brown and strawberry, and his loose linen shirt was open at the neck, revealing a heavy silver chain. A red cloth dangled over his shoulders, and a book the size of a small hay bale was open beside him.

At one end of the table, a tall black man stood behind a paper-covered lectern with his arms behind his back. His head was shaved almost to the skin, his strong jaw ended in a tight, pointed beard, and his eyes were as sharp as they were dark. At the other end of the table, sitting open on a low pedestal, there was a long wooden box. Inside, with tattooed hands crossed and eyes closed, lay the pale and charred corpse of William Skelton.

"Cyrus," Antigone whispered. "Cyrus . . ."

"Shhh," Cyrus whispered back. "I see it."

"Name yourselves," the bearded man commanded. His voice was accented, British.

Antigone coughed and cleared her throat. "I'm Antigone Elizabeth Smith, and this is my brother, Cyrus Lawrence Smith."

"Hi," said Cyrus.

"Do you present yourselves as the heirs of William Cyrus Skelton?"

Cyrus blinked. William Cyrus? "What?" he asked.

Antigone hit him with an elbow. "Yes, we do," she said. "And we're his apprentices or acolytes or whatever."

A thin man with a pencil mustache, wearing a cream suit and a skinny blue tie, stepped out of the crowd. He smiled at Cyrus and Antigone and then turned to the bearded man. "The Order challenges. With my colleague John Horace Lawney unfortunately injured, there is no longer a Keeper to confirm the children's identities. Without confirmation of identity, their presentation as Acolytes and claims to inheritance cannot be acknowledged."

The bearded man turned to the boy behind the table. The boy's eyes were down, but he nodded slightly.

"Will any Keeper stand up as witness?" The bearded man scanned the crowd.

The thin man winked at Cyrus.

"Hold on," Cyrus said. "Can't we wait till our lawyer wakes up?"

"You could have requested an emergency deferral."

The thin man smiled. "But you didn't. You presented and declared yourselves."

"Seeing no witness . . . ," the bearded man yelled.

"Wait a bit there, Rupert Greeves!" An old woman in a belted safari jacket forced herself forward. "Eleanor Elizabeth Eldridge will stand up. I watched them born, and I watched them grow."

Cyrus gaped.

"Mrs. Eldridge?" Antigone asked. "What are you doing here?"

"Identity has been confirmed," said the man called Rupert Greeves. Mrs. Eldridge nodded, and retreated to the rim of the crowd.

Stunned and confused, Cyrus watched her go. Then an old and very bald monk hustled forward, bowing to the boy as he came. "Perhaps," he said, bobbing, "I could remind the dais that William Skelton was duly excommunicated from the Order of Brendan on charges of theft, murder, and other gross misconducts. He was an outlaw with no standing to bring Acolytes into our Order."

The boy ignored him. Rupert Greeves cleared his throat. "Perhaps I could remind you, Gregory, that Brown Robes and Brendanites do not have the authority to expel anyone from this Order with your own declarations. Your charges were thrown out without a hearing."

"But our evidence," the monk said. "So much evidence."

"Visions, spectral testimony, and dreams are inadmissible," Rupert said. "You know this. Now step back."

Sniffing, the monk spun and retreated, glaring at Cyrus as he did.

The thin, cream-suited man jumped even farther forward. He was almost to the table. "The Order wishes to establish Passage."

The big, bearded man grimaced. "On what grounds, Cecil?"

The lawyer turned, smiling to the crowd. "These children stand before you, hoping to be established as Acolytes and heirs to one of the most notorious outlaws this community has ever seen. No, he was never successfully expelled, but his misdeeds have become a matter of record. If the community were to reclaim the entirety of the Skelton estate, it would be no injustice, and only the slightest step toward righting a lifetime of wrongs."

The crowd murmured its support, and the thin man turned, locking eyes with Cyrus. "In addition," he said, "twenty-one years ago, their father, Lawrence Smith, was himself expelled from this Order. Children to an outlaw, Acolytes to an outlaw? I have to wonder how committed these two would be to our ways and to the rule of our law. I have to wonder why we would want them at all." Again, he winked at Cyrus, and then turned to face the bearded man. "Their Acolyteship was filed literally minutes before the death of Mr. William Skelton—suspect already, to say the least—and their family has a questionable history with our Order. In fact, these two would become the only living members of the Order to have a known ancestor contained in the Burials. At a minimum, Passage as established in the case of Earhart, 1932, would seem an extremely reasonable request for the community to make before acknowledging such a substantial inheritance."

Rupert Greeves scratched his pointed beard and turned his dark eyes to Cyrus and Antigone. "Any response?" he asked.

Cyrus looked at his sister. Her brows were down over eyes that looked as confused as he felt. Turning back to the big man, he shrugged. His shoulders ached, and his head was spinning. "Honestly, I don't have a clue what's going on. But that guy is snaky."

"Our lawyer . . ." Antigone looked back over her shoulder. Horace was gone.

"If I may," the thin man continued. "The Order would like to suggest the achievement of Explorer for inheritance, and the . . ."

The boy behind the table shook his head. Whispers raced through the crowd as they strained to see.

"The Order would like to suggest the achievement of Journeyman, and the successful . . ."

The boy shook his head.

"The community would like to suggest the achievement of Journeyman?" The thin man's voice hooked up nervously.

The crowd waited. Rupert Greeves waited. Cyrus and Antigone, unsure of what they were waiting for, waited.

The boy at the table pursed his lips. For the first time, he looked at Cyrus, and then at Antigone. He nodded and dropped his eyes.

Chatter climbed the walls.

"Seal the records!" Rupert bellowed. "The estate of William Skelton, Keeper in the Order of Brendan, is declared dormant!"

Two men moved forward out of the crowd and closed the lid on Skelton's coffin.

"A final thought!" the thin man shouted, and the noise in the enormous room died. The boy looked up from the hay-bale book, where he had been writing. "According to Mr. Lawney's Acolyte filings, the oath—declared and assented to—was the Latin variation, last used by mandate on this continent in the year 1914. The Order would like to suggest that the Acolyte requirements correspond to the oath. Let the achievement of Journeyman be established according to the standards of that year."

Gasps of surprise were swallowed by laughter.

"That's ridiculous." Rupert Greeves shook his head. "Even for you, Cecil."

All eyes turned to the boy at the table. He shrugged, nodded, scribbled something in the enormous book, and rose. Turning his back, he walked toward a small door in the wall behind him.

Cyrus stood, surrounded by a wash of surprised voices while he watched the strange boy leave. He was hungry, he still had Horace's blood all over him, his throat was still phlegm-full of last night's smoke, and his feet ached. That much he knew. But he had no idea what had just happened.

"Cy," Antigone said. "I don't think that was good."

Before Cyrus could answer, the thin man stepped in front of them, clutching a folder, smiling, and scratching his mustache with a long finger. "Children," he said, nodding. "Lovely to meet you both. My name is Cecil T. Rhodes, and no, that wasn't good. At least not for you."

Cyrus glared at him. The man had a face like a mustached rabbit. "I don't like you," Cyrus said. "And I don't think I ever will."

"Ha," said Cecil. "Amusing."

The big, bearded man thumped on his lectern. "Rhodes, step back. Initiates!" His voice filled the crowded hall. "Approach the Book and place your hands upon the table."

Looking over his shoulder at the crowd, Cyrus moved cautiously forward. Most of the faces were smiling. But they weren't all happy, supportive smiles. Smirks. Giggles. Whispers. He knew the tone. He felt like he was being called forward in class after he'd fallen asleep and drooled on his desk.

Antigone's hands were already palms-down on the table, and she was studying the huge book. Cyrus made fists and pressed his knuckles against the smooth, waxy wood.

Rupert Greeves moved away from his lectern and stood behind the table, looming tall across from them.

"Kneel."

Antigone dropped quickly. Cyrus eased his knees down carefully onto the cool stone.

Greeves cleared his throat. "Do you renounce evil and all the powers of wickedness in this world and others?"

Cyrus glanced at his sister. "Yes?" they both said quietly.

Greeves leaned over the table. "I do renounce them," he whispered.

"I do renounce them," they said, almost in unison.

"Do you renounce all dark knowledge and sorceries which corrupt the body and destroy the soul?"

"I do renounce them," Antigone said.

"Yes," said Cyrus. "I mean, I do renounce them."

"Do you renounce all vile incantations, demonic snares, and dark communications with the dead?"

"I do renounce them." Cyrus twitched a smile at his sister. He'd nailed it that time. But what exactly were they worried he might do? Dark communications with the dead? How did you even try something like that? Suddenly, he could feel the weight of the key ring between and beneath his collarbones and his smile was gone. The room seemed colder. He tried to breathe slowly. With one quick pulse, nervousness had tightened his chest.

"Will you tread the world and tend the wilds? When the world whispers her secrets, will you keep them? Will you protect the weak and face your own end without fear?"

Cyrus swallowed. "Yes," he said.

"I will," said Antigone.

"Do you now honor and bind unto yourself the strength of heaven, the light of sun, the radiance of moon, the splendor of fire, the speed of lightning, the swiftness of wind, the firmness of earth, the will of stone?" Greeves leaned forward again. "I do honor and bind," he whispered.

"I do honor and bind," they said.

Rupert Greeves looked up at the crowd. "Do the assembled receive these among them, a brother and a sister to Brendan?"

A few laughed. Many muttered. But a cluster of loud voices announced their agreement.

"We do receive them."

Rupert Greeves nodded at Cyrus and Antigone, and they both quickly stood. Leaning across the table, Greeves gripped their shoulders. He spoke, and as he did, his dark eyes met Cyrus's. His accented voice softened. "May you be shielded from poison, from burning, from drowning, from wounding, from betrayal, from the rage of seas, the anger of mountains, and the plottings of men. May you be a strength to the Order, and the Order a strength to you." He turned to Antigone. "Miss Antigone Smith, Acolyte in the Order of Brendan, congratulations. Would you please sign the book?"

Greeves picked up a battered quill, dipped it in ink, and handed it to Antigone. Then, heaving pounds of dusty pages to one side, he found the appropriate place and set his finger above it.

Cyrus watched his sister sign her name in blobby ink, and then Rupert Greeves took back the quill and blotted her signature. The big man's pointed beard swung up, and his eyes were back on Cyrus. He redipped the quill. "Mr. Cyrus Smith, Acolyte in the Order of Brendan, congratulations. Would you please sign beneath your sister?"

While the crowd began to disperse behind him, Cyrus bent over the book, and the smell of dusty leather and ancient pages rose up to meet him. The paper was beyond yellow, aged to brown. He was signing in a long column of names, and all of their owners had better handwriting than he did. Biting his lip, he scratched his name as neatly as he could, but the lines thickened and bulged as he went. When he finished *Lawrence,* he began to breathe. And then he left out the "i" in Smith. Smth.

Greeves reached for the pen.

"Darn it," Cyrus said. "Hold on a sec." It was too tight to squeeze the letter in, but he added a large dot—more like a raindrop of ink. Straightening, he stared at what he'd done.

Smiling, Rupert took the pen and blotted the ink. "Come on, then. I'll show you each to your Acolyte quarters." Closing the book, he glanced up. The thin lawyer slid up beside Cyrus.

"The Polygon," said Cecil Rhodes. He giggled and then grew suddenly serious. "Show them to the Polygon, Mr. Greeves. The standards of 1914 have been applied. Don't go and disqualify them so soon."

Laughing, he hurried away.

Antigone sputtered her lips. "I really don't like him."

"Who cares about him?" Cyrus looked up at Rupert Greeves. "Hey, you know, we're actually in a lot of trouble. Horace said you would help us once we were members. And, well, a guy named Maxi killed Skelton and burned down our motel. Then he took our brother, Dan. He chased us here—probably shot Horace, too, him or one of his sidekicks."

"Maxi?" Rupert's jaw clenched beneath his beard. His eyes narrowed. "Why would a creature like Maximilien be after the two of you?"

"Ask him," Cyrus said.

Rupert shook his head and sighed. "You have brought trouble, haven't you? Maximilien wouldn't attack a member of the Order without reason. We are too large a threat to his appetites." He looked at Antigone and back at Skelton's coffin, and then he turned sharp eyes onto Cyrus. "You may have something his master wants."

"His master?" Antigone asked. "What kind of master are we talking about?"

"The kind of master capable of controlling a man like Maxi." Rupert inhaled slowly, inflating his broad chest. "He calls himself Dr. Phoenix," he said quietly. "And at times, Mr. Ashes. He is the stuff of nightmares, I will not say more. If Maxi took your brother, then he took him to Phoenix. I am very sorry."

Cyrus looked at his sister. Antigone tucked back her hair and crossed nervous arms. "Can't you . . . do anything?"

Rupert stepped between them. A few people were

still loitering by the big doors. One of them was an old woman in a safari jacket. Rupert whistled sharply.

"Eleanor Eldridge!" he yelled. "Can I beg some assistance?"

Cyrus watched the old woman approach, avoiding his eyes. When she got close enough, she began to chatter.

"Rupert Greeves," she said. "I don't care how big you think you are, and I don't care what you call yourself or what you think you can make me do. I knew you when you were as timid as a possum and as awkward as a young giraffe. I swore off these two ungratefuls. I washed my hands and shook the mud off my boots. I wouldn't tie their shoes if they lost their arms. I'll not be helping them."

Rupert almost smiled. "Something has come up. I'll need you to show them to the Polygon for me, Mrs. E." He turned back to Cyrus and Antigone, and for a moment, he simply stared, unblinking, breathing slowly. Cyrus squirmed, fighting to keep his hands from drifting up to his neck. The big man's face was worried, his eyes searching. When he spoke, his voice was low.

"Today, you two have become a brother and sister to me. Your brother by blood is now like my own, and I will do all that I can for him. I wish I could make you promises, but I cannot. Not when it comes to Maxi and Phoenix. For now, I will see what can be seen and hear what can be heard. When I know more, we will speak again. Soon." He smiled with tight lips. "I must hear more from the Order's outlaw Acolytes."

Turning, he strode toward the tall doors, the sound of his boots doubling and tripling in echo.

"Listen to Mrs. E!" he shouted, and he was through the doors and gone.

eight

LOST AND FOUND

CYRUS, FINDING HIMSELF wandering the halls outside the Galleria, progressed at a caterpillar pace. His own little shelves at the Archer loaded with ditch discoveries and thrift-store treasures were less than nothing compared to what surrounded him now. The walls were dotted with strange artifacts—tapestries, swords, axes, arrows, muskets, a pair of tarnished green cannons, certificates and charters, bones and teeth and skulls, paintings, maps, and fading photos of men and women in knee-high boots beside cloth-winged planes and sailboats and archaic trucks. Not one display was corralled with a velvet rope. Not one was guarded by a plastic sign commanding those with fingers to keep them to themselves.

And so Cyrus touched. And waited for Mrs. Eldridge to grumble before moving on.

While Cyrus browsed the walls, Antigone's eyes lurched between the ceiling and the floor.

The map frescoes on the ceilings glittered with gold

foil, and made no attempt at scale. These were maps where ships and sea creatures were larger than islands, and brightly painted birds and beasts floated in the air above forests.

The floor was a swirling mosaic of painted tiles, segmented into a different kind of map. When Antigone stared at her feet, she was looking down at tiny city streets, winding and twisting beneath her. Minuscule buildings, rivers and bridges, city squares and palaces were spread out in detail. A few steps later, they were gone, replaced by a crisp floor plan of some enormous structure, labeled in tiny Latin.

She scuffed at it with her foot. "Won't this stuff wear off with everyone walking on it?" She wasn't asking anyone in particular. Mrs. Eldridge had already refused to answer any of their questions.

Cyrus glanced over his shoulder, and then turned back to his examination of an oddly tusked skull. "It's probably lacquered or something. Tigs, what do you think this is? A mini-elephant? Maybe a warthog?" He reached out and brushed his hand over smooth, yellowed bone.

"No clue," said Antigone. "Ask one of them."

Four men wearing bulging canvas packs and wide belts heavy with hatchets, sheaths, and holsters hurried down the hall, followed by a boy with his arms full of rope. They split up to move around Antigone.

"Excuse me," Cyrus said. "Do any of you know what this is?"

The men managed to walk by without so much as seeing Cyrus or his sister. Four pairs of eyes twitched away, avoiding the soot- and bloodstained clothes and the questioning faces.

Only the boy turned around, smirking at Cyrus as he walked away. "Outlaw trash," he said. He grinned at Antigone. "Your mother was a savage." Shaking his head, the boy turned his back and hurried to catch up to the men.

"Wow," said Antigone.

Cyrus cupped his hands around his mouth. "Keep walking, you little snot! The outlaws are here!"

"Cyrus Smith!" Mrs. Eldridge came storming back down the hall, her thin white hair straggling in a tattered halo. "It's bad enough that you two can't keep up, and now you're shouting insults?" She crossed her arms and glared.

Cyrus shrugged. No smug kid got to say things about his mom.

"Did you hear what the brat said?" Antigone asked.

"I did," said Mrs. Eldridge. "And I can't say that I disagree. Look at you two, all filth and rudeness, goggling over the floors and touching everything. Do you belong here? No. No, you don't. And that's no insult. Here isn't always the nicest place to belong."

She spun on her heel and began to walk away. "Now stay with me this time, or I'll leave you to find your own way. And," she added, "you will never find your own way."

Cyrus sighed, and then yawned, trying to keep up the brisk pace. As much as he wanted to look at everything, as much as he wanted to be mad at the insulting boy and the rabbit-faced man, he was too hungry and too exhausted, and his head was still too full of smoke and thoughts of Dan. The mosaic floor looked like it would be cool against his skin, and he could easily stretch out beneath one of the long display tables against a wall.

Antigone tugged on his arm, forcing him to keep pace.

"You two should never have come," Mrs. Eldridge said, clicking quickly down the center of the hall. A group of six young girls wearing white snake shirts tucked into pocketed trousers tucked into boots, all carrying short rifles, moved by quickly in the opposite direction, eyes bouncing between Antigone and Cyrus. Three of them flashed friendly smiles. Around the next corner, four middle-aged men in full fencing gear, swords and wire masks tucked under their arms, leaned against the wall, laughing. Their laughter faded when they saw Cyrus and Antigone. Two faces hardened, but a short bald man and a tower with a beard both met Cyrus's eyes. Cyrus gave them his best diner nod, and then smiled when they nodded back.

"Good luck to you both," the beard said as they passed. "Your father was a good man."

"Cy," Antigone said when the men were well behind them. "This place is wild."

"I know," Cyrus said. He watched another row of animal skulls go by. "I kinda like it."

Antigone brushed back her hair and looked at Cyrus. "Yeah, but it's weird that Dad was here and he never said anything about it."

Cyrus shrugged.

Antigone looked away. "Those girls with the guns were even younger than you. Like that's safe."

Cyrus grinned. "Dad gave me a BB gun when I was six."

"And then took it away when you shot yourself in the forehead."

"Nope. Wrong. Try again. He took it away when I tried to shoot the neighbor's cat."

"And that's better?"

"And," Cyrus said, "he gave it back one month later. I didn't lose it until I fell off the cliff when I was nine."

Mrs. Eldridge's hand cold-clamped tight on the back of Cyrus's neck.

"Unkindest thing I ever did to Katie Smith was vouching for you with big Mr. Greeves. If I'd been smart enough to keep my trap shut, you'd have been bundled up and shuffled back where you belong. But you're here now, so come on." Letting go, Mrs. Eldridge snapped back around and clicked on. "Standing for Katie's kids." She shook her head, approaching a corner. "And as pups to Billy Bones, no less. You should never have let that old liar into the motel, Cyrus Smith."

They rounded the corner, and Cyrus stopped in his tracks.

"Oh my . . . ," said Antigone.

A two-story wall of windows overlooked green lawns running down to the unending blue of the Great Lake, perfect mirror to the sky, striped gold by the sun. A flock of brightly colored boats huddled safely inside a long stone jetty, while others, sails clinging to the wind, carved through distant water. Small buildings dotted the lawns, and on a long, flat stretch of grass, a pale-blue plane touched down.

"It's beautiful," said Antigone. "Let's go down to the water."

Cyrus watched the plane stop and its pilot jump out of his craft. Two men were walking quickly toward it. The pilot pulled off his helmet and shook out his—her—thick strawberry hair. And she couldn't be that old.

"Come on!" Mrs. Eldridge stamped her foot. "Now!"

Cyrus and Antigone followed Mrs. Eldridge through glistening clean halls and down crowded stairs. Door after door, room after room, they saw fewer and fewer people as they went, and the floors grew dustier all the time. Downstairs and downstairs and the rooms lost their windows. The doors they passed were rough and oily and sealed with heavy padlocks. The halls were cluttered with odd shapes, covered with filthy canvas sheets, and the few paintings still hanging on the dingy walls were muted with years of airborne accumulation.

Mrs. Eldridge brushed against a canvas tarp and sent up a small weather system of dust as she moved through an open arch.

Following her, Antigone began to sneeze.

Cyrus stopped. "Remind me why we have to stay all the way down here?" He sniffed. "What's that smell?"

"Get in here, Cy," Antigone said.

Cyrus moved through the arch into a broad room with an extremely low, blue glass ceiling propped up by intermittent stout pillars. Iron spiral stairs squatted in a corner.

Mrs. Eldridge was still moving.

Antigone looked back at her brother. "It's a pool, Cy. That's the smell. We're under a pool."

"Are you sure?" Cyrus asked. The water wasn't pale and bright like the pools he'd seen. And there were walls in the water, paths that twisted and turned and doubled back on themselves. It was an underwater maze.

While Cyrus watched, a blindfolded woman, barely bubbling, slid by in the dark water three feet above him, her hands tracing the walls at her sides.

"Wow," Cyrus said. "Tigs, how cool is that?"

Antigone shivered and grabbed Cyrus's arm. "It's freaky, Cy. Now c'mon. Mrs. E didn't stop this time."

Through another arch, and at the end of a long, curving corridor lit with naked bulbs, they found Mrs. Eldridge waiting beside a dark, empty mouth gaping in the wall. A thin metal pipe ran down the wall beside the doorway, ending in a small box with a rusty button. She pushed it, and a light turned on.

"Down these stairs, you will find the Polygon. Now maybe you'll go home. This is no place for you."

They were standing at the top of a stairwell, twisting down. The light Mrs. Eldridge had turned on was out of sight, but its glow rose up around the bend.

"Enjoy," Mrs. Eldridge said crisply. And she began to leave.

"Hey!" Antigone yelled. "That's it? You just drop us off at some dungeon stairs and leave? What are we supposed to do now?"

Mrs. Eldridge turned back, her lined face grim with shadow. "For the last two years, I kept my promise to your mother. I watched over you. I have no wealth, but I kept the lights on in the Archer. I paid for the waffle mix. And in the end, none of that mattered." Her face softened. "The Order has you now. It was always going to. It's in your bones."

"But what do we do?" Antigone asked.

"Do?" Mrs. Eldridge smiled. "You do what Acolytes have struggled to do for a thousand years—survive and achieve. But for now, try to rest. Someone from the staff will find you. With Skelton dead, Greeves will select you a new Keeper."

When Mrs. Eldridge was gone, Antigone looked at her brother. "Cy, we really need to find Horace, and we really need him to be alive."

"Well, we're here now," said Cyrus. "Let's go down."

Antigone shrugged, brushing back her hair. "As long as you're first."

Cyrus laughed. "Feeling brave?"

"Yeah," Antigone said. "If anything sneaks down after us, I'll protect you."

"Great," said Cyrus. "That's a relief."

He began his descent, dragging one hand on the stone wall. Antigone followed him down and around, down and around, passing only one lonely oversize lightbulb on the ceiling.

Antigone sneezed, and Cyrus glanced back. "Too dank for you? You could handle the Archer but not this?" His foot slapped on water and skidded off the stair. Flailing, he knocked his sister backward and landed on her legs.

"Ow." Antigone grimaced. "That hurt. Why so co-ordinated, Rus? That one was on you."

"Don't call me Rus, Tigger." Rubbing his right elbow,

Cyrus sat up and pointed at the wall. Water was oozing through the joints in the stone and trickling down the stairs. The steps were skim-coated with moisture, and tiny grooves had eroded into the stone where miniature waterfalls slid down from step to step.

"Oh, great," Antigone said. "We're supposed to sleep down here? We're going to wake up with mushrooms growing under our fingernails."

Cyrus levered himself back to vertical and began moving carefully down the wet stairs. "You know," he said, "I kind of get the feeling that some of these people don't want us around."

Antigone laughed. "What tipped you off? The insults or the dungeon?"

"Nobody offered us lunch."

Cyrus stopped and Antigone stepped down beside him.

"Ugh." Antigone grimaced. "Yuck."

Below the stairs, there was a small landing, a second lightbulb, and a large door. The landing was swirling with black scum-topped seepage. The walls were a forest of strange molds—orange rippling things that looked like they were part brain and part lettuce, long dangling things like spider legs, blue fuzz, white rings, brown everything else.

Bubbles slowly percolated in the scum pool.

"There must be some kind of floor drain, or the

stairs would be all full up." Cyrus crouched and looked at the water.

"Cy." Antigone tapped him with her foot. "Look at the door. It's locked. And it has an old flyer nailed to it."

Cyrus began unlacing his shoes.

"Oh, sick." Antigone laughed. "Are you really?"

"What else are we supposed to do?" Cyrus asked. "Go back up and cry to Rupert Greeves or Mrs. Eldridge or that kid from the hall? They're not getting rid of us now."

He stuffed his socks inside his shoes and dipped a calloused toe into the dark liquid.

"And?" Antigone asked.

Cyrus shrugged and stepped into the shin-deep water. In the middle, he bent and fished around with his hands.

"The door, Cy. I care more about the door."

"Then come on in and check it out," Cyrus said. "Yep. Floor drain." He tugged. "But somebody's . . . shoved . . . in . . . an . . . old . . ." His hands geysered up with a dripping black strip of cloth and oil. "Sock." He squinted at it, wiping his forehead on the back of his arm. "Orange stripes."

Antigone wrinkled her nose. Laughing, Cyrus threw the sock up onto the stairs.

"Cy, that is really one of the sickest things I've ever seen you do."

"You aren't around when I skip school and hit the creeks." Shoving his hand back into the water, Cyrus pulled up a long tangle of hair and drain scum hooked over his finger.

He held it out to his sister.

"No! Stop it, Cy!" The water was already bubbling quickly, glugging around Cyrus's ankles. He tossed the hair carcass against the wall and turned to face the door.

A single step rose up just beneath the heavy oak door. An iron strap had been bent around the handle and through a ring in the stone wall. An old lock reconnected the strap's two ends.

Antigone splattered through the last shallow water and wiped a coat of dust off the flyer on the door. The paper was old and soft with moisture. Two corners pulled free and curled.

"What's it say?" Cyrus asked.

"At the top it says 'Infestation Quarantine.'" She stood on her toes. "And it's stamped 'July 11, 1927.' There's something else written here, but I can't read it." Dropping back to her heels, she stepped away from the door. "You try."

Cyrus leaned forward and cocked his head. "Ulip Spitters? No. Whip Spitters? Whip Spiders!" He looked at his sister. "The place was infested with Whip Spiders?"

Antigone crossed her arms. "I am not going in

there. I don't know what a Whip Spider is, and I don't want to."

"Oh, please," Cyrus said. "This is from more than eighty years ago. And the door's locked anyway." He grabbed the iron strap and gave it a rattle. The ring in the stone wall shook. Dust dribbled to the wet floor. "Huh. Maybe . . ." Grabbing the door handle with one hand and the wall ring with the other, Cyrus tugged. The ring slid out so easily that Cyrus staggered back into the stairs as the door swung open. The hinges were silent. The motion was fluid.

Sucking air between her teeth, Antigone peered through the doorway.

"That was too easy." Cyrus picked himself up. "Careful, Tigs. Somebody wanted it to look locked."

"Which means what?" Antigone stepped into the dark. "There's something in here worth finding?"

She felt around the edges of the doorway until she found what she was looking for. A button clicked, and six more large lightbulbs buzzed and sputtered.

The room was sprawling. The ceiling was low but pocked with vaults. Squat columns were scattered throughout. All the stone had been painted white, but large portions dangled off in leprous flakes. The floor was dusty white linoleum, savagely peeling at the seams. White triple-stacked metal bunks were scattered against the many walls.

And there *were* many walls—angled out, angled in. Cyrus couldn't even guess at how many there were. A lot.

Strangest of all, a network of suspended plank pathways began just inside the door and ran throughout the room at least a foot above the floor. All of the planks were dangling from the ceiling by ropes and chains. None of them were dusty.

Cyrus tested the first plank with his foot. It swung slightly.

"What are they for?" Antigone asked.

"Walking?" Cyrus said. "I don't know."

Antigone looked down. Beneath the plank, painted in black on the linoleum, there was a triangle of lightning bolts around the same black stylized ship they'd seen on some of the boys' white shirts.

"Weird," she said.

Cyrus moved out onto the plank and it sagged gently. "There are all sorts of exercise posters on the walls, too. At least, I think that's what those are." He pointed. "The same two guys in short ties and high pants over and over again. Wrestling. Kicking each other in the head."

"Cyrus," said Antigone. "Cyrus . . ."

Cyrus reached a Y on his plank road. He went left.

"Cyrus! Turn around!"

Surprised, Cyrus turned. Just behind him, a strange-looking boy was standing at the first Y in the planks.

He was wearing a tight white tank top tucked into a pair of army-green, much-too-large, much-too-pocketed fatigues, cinched around his waist with a rope. His paper-pale arms were knotted with muscle and tied with blue popping veins. His short hair was the color of dust and unevenly cropped around his skull. His face was smooth and young and unsunned, but somehow it didn't match his eyes.

Cyrus stared into the boy's eyes, and the boy's eyes stared into his. What Cyrus saw, he didn't know. What he felt was layer upon layer of ancient. The boy's faint green irises looked like they had been beaten and polished more than the smoothest river rock, like they could see by nothing more than starlight—and they no longer cared to see at all.

Cyrus stepped forward and stuck out his hand. "I'm Cyrus."

The boy looked at his extended hand.

He took it, and Cyrus shivered at the chill in his grip.

"Nolan," the boy said, and he turned and swayed deeper into the room on the plank paths.

Cyrus looked back at his sister, questioning.

"Go," she mouthed silently, pointing after Nolan. She was already hurrying forward.

"I think he's the one Skelton was talking about when he was dying," Cyrus whispered.

The two of them stopped, watching Nolan disappear around a pillar.

Antigone looked at her brother. "What do you mean? Skelton just said something about beekeepers."

"Right. And then he said, 'Trust Nolan.'"

Antigone's eyebrows shot together. She tucked back her hair. "He did not. He said *no one*, not *Nolan*. And why would you trust anyone somebody named Billy Bones told you to trust." She shifted her weight, and the plank swung beneath them. Antigone scanned the pillared room. "I'm not trusting some weird kid who lives down here."

Nolan's voice drifted around the columns. "I knew Skelton. Perhaps he trusted me. I never trusted him."

Antigone blushed. Cyrus bit his lower lip.

"Come," Nolan said. "Voices move oddly in the Polygon."

Cyrus followed the planks deeper into the room, with Antigone close behind him.

"It's not that you don't look trustworthy," Antigone said loudly.

"I know how I look." Nolan's voice was quiet but all around them. "Stay to the right."

The suspended paths reached a large junction. Six routes splayed in different directions, winding around pillars and between rusty beds, disappearing around corners.

Cyrus paused. "Tigs, can you hear water?"

"Yes, you can," said Nolan. "Pass through the showers."

"Um, excuse me?" said Antigone. "Wouldn't this be faster if we just walked on the floor?"

"No," Nolan said. "The floor is not safe."

Cyrus and Antigone bounced forward into an area with no paint. The floor was still linoleum, at least where it hadn't been torn up, but the pillars and walls and ceiling were all dark, moist stone.

"What's not safe about it?" Cyrus asked. "What are we talking about?"

A chuckle reached them, doubling and tripling off the angled walls, and then reaching them again. "The Whip Spiders. Why do you think I have this place to myself?"

"They're still here?" Antigone scanned the floor. "That was over eighty years ago."

"It was," Nolan said. "Whip Spiders can hatch many young in eighty years. Stay on the paths."

The sound of water grew louder, until Cyrus and Antigone rounded a corner and stood looking at the showers.

Two miniature aqueducts ran from wall to wall above head height. Stone spouts lined both sides of both aqueducts, spilling water to the floor in four falling curtains. On the floor, the water collected in a central trough and drained through a hole in the wall. Where the plank path passed beneath the showers, the spouts had been plugged with wine corks.

Cyrus and Antigone moved carefully through, catching only a few drips on their shoulders as they did.

They had reached the end, or at least one of several ends, of the room. The plank pathway led straight into a dark, jagged hole in the wall.

Nolan leaned out of it, slowly stretching his arms against both sides. "Come in, if you're going to." He yawned and ducked back inside. "Or don't."

Cyrus hesitated, looking around. A leggy shape flashed out of a corner, clattering toward him across the grimy floor. Antigone grabbed his arm as the thing disappeared under the plank beneath them.

"Right," said Cyrus. "Well, we're not staying out here."

nine

WHIPS AND VISITS

Cyrus sat on cold stone. Beside him, Antigone was bouncing her leg nervously. Nolan's room was a bizarre assortment of elements. But, for a crowded crypt through a hole in the wall, it was surprisingly tidy and warm.

The room was circular and had clearly been intended for use as a tomb. Seven stone beds—for statues, hopefully; for corpses, maybe—had been set in arched and pillared alcoves all the way around. Oddly, all of the visible stone had been slathered with a thick coat of bright yellow paint. One of the alcove beds now held a vivid red cushion with tassels and a brown corduroy pillow. Another held a rickety, tightly packed bookshelf and two reading lamps with green shades. The third held an old pint-sized refrigerator, humming loudly, a hot plate, and a toaster oven old enough to match the Archer's waffle iron. Nolan had buried two pieces of bread beneath mayonnaise and cheddar from the fridge, and he was now crouching on the floor watching the mixture bubble in the toaster oven. The smell made breakfast seem like long, long ago, and Cyrus's stomach was humming audibly. The fourth alcove held neatly stacked wooden boxes full of odd-looking tools. The fifth held a stuffed two-headed eagle missing half of one flapping wing, and a square pile of mismatched blankets. The sixth was a nest of books, papers, a small lap desk, and a stack of tightly folded clothes. A similar load had been scraped out of the seventh, which now held an impatient Antigone and a curious Cyrus.

The floor was covered with a pair of Turkish rugs, one missing a burnt corner, the other boasting a large bleach spot near its center. A cluster of three ship lanterns hung from the middle of the yellow ceiling, and the decapitated head of a large grandfather clock, with pendulum and weights attached, was balanced on rough timber legs between two of the stone beds.

A tangle of electrical cords bound up with string ran out of the hole in the wall and up toward the ceiling.

Cyrus stared at the toaster. He hadn't actually eaten that much at breakfast before Maxi had arrived, and the previous night hadn't involved much sleep. He yawned, blinked slowly, and tried to ignore the hungry knife in his gut.

He passed his yawn on to his sister, and she stretched her arms above her head. "How long have you been sleeping in this tomb?" she asked.

The strange boy rubbed his smooth jaw. "Not a

tomb," he said quietly. "A Resurrection Room. They are different. In theory."

Antigone slapped the stone bed beneath her. "You're telling me there's not a body inside here?"

"Maybe once," Nolan said. "Not anymore. Not for a long time."

"You've checked?" Antigone asked. "You really pried up the lid?"

Nolan stared at the slowly melting cheese. "I was looking for a friend."

"In a coffin?" Antigone shivered. "That's crazy."

"My friend is dead," said Nolan. His voice was flat. "Where else would I look?"

Cyrus laughed. Antigone elbowed him. "And you're really okay if we stay in here with you?"

"No." Nolan leaned farther forward and peered into the toaster oven. "But I'm willing. For a time." He pointed out the room's rough entrance. "You wouldn't survive out there."

Cyrus looked through the hole at the plank paths. The Polygon was silent. Empty. He looked back. Nolan might be crazy, but it didn't matter. Right now, he was toasting cheesy bread.

Antigone tucked her feet up in front of her and pressed her back against the wall. "Are you part of the Order?" she asked.

Nolan smiled slightly. "I am a spider in a corner. I

watch. I listen. I live on what I find." He looked up. "On what finds me."

"Um." Cyrus glanced at his sister. She widened her eyes, and he turned back to Nolan. "Does Rupert Greeves know that you're down here?"

"Rupert Greeves." Nolan sighed. He sounded tired. "He can find a spider when he has need. He found you a nanny among the cobwebs, didn't he?" He looked at Cyrus and then back at the slowly toasting bread. "He is already lost in your troubles."

"What?" Antigone dropped her feet back to the floor and edged forward. "What do you mean?"

"Your brother was taken," Nolan said quietly. "I heard you speak with Greeves." He glanced at her surprised face. "I do not need to be seen to listen." The toaster oven sparked and its interior light flickered off. Sighing, Nolan thumped it lightly. Cyrus jumped forward, touched the toaster, and then sat back down. The light returned, along with the quiet hum of heat. Nolan's eyes narrowed as he looked at Cyrus. Cyrus blinked and said nothing.

"What else do you know?" Antigone asked.

Nolan inhaled slowly and turned his worn eyes away. "More than I care to. Maxi and his master are hyenas. Their pursuit will not end. But Greeves will stand or fall with you when the time comes. He's cut from old stone."

Antigone shivered, rubbing goose-bumping arms. "Greeves is the one in charge of this place?"

Nolan slid his stare onto her. "No. He's Ashtown's Blood Avenger. The Avengel. He protects and—when needed—he avenges."

Antigone dropped her brows. "I'm not sure I understand."

Nolan's mouth twitched into a small smile and then grew into another yawn. "If an Explorer from Ashtown freezes on Kilimanjaro or is burned in New Guinea or is imprisoned in France, Rupe sets out after the remains. If a member commits treason against the Order, Rupe's the one after him. If the Orbis—the circle of Sages—identifies a threat, Rupe hunts him—or her—or it—to ground. He is both hound and tiger." He slid a glance back over his shoulder, as if his own words wearied him. "And I am one who knows."

Crouching on the floor, Nolan flipped open the toaster oven, twisted a cloth around his hand, and pulled out the toasted bread. The cheese on top had browned and bubbled, and the edges were crisp. "Hot," Nolan said. "Careful." Banging the little glass door shut, he set the toast on the stone between Cyrus and Antigone. Cyrus breathed in slowly, letting the smell taunt his stomach.

"Thanks for this," Antigone said, and she poked an edge with her finger. Cyrus nodded in agreement.

Nolan moved across the small room and settled back into his low crouch, pale, gnarled arms wrapped tight around his knees. His smooth, river-rock eyes were on Cyrus and Antigone as they took their first tentative bites.

"So you think Rupert will find Dan?" Antigone asked.

Nolan ran a hand over the cobweb hairs on his jaw. After a moment, he shook his head slightly.

Cyrus stopped chewing. Antigone wiped her mouth.

Nolan shrugged. "But then Maxi Robes might not be running. He wants what he wants." He looked at Cyrus and his worn eyes flickered interest. Then, as it faded, he stood. "You have much to see and much to do if you ever want to move out of my Polygon. But you're tired." He stepped toward the door. "Sleep. I won't be gone long."

When Nolan had stepped through the hole and the sound of creaking planks had faded away, Cyrus looked at his sister.

"Tigs," he said. "We just ate cheesy bread in a crypt."

Antigone nodded. "I want to know how Horace is doing. What do you think happened to the driver?"

"Gunner?" Cyrus shrugged and moved across the room to Nolan's alcove. He squeezed in onto his back and propped his feet up on the painted yellow stone wall.

Gripping the keys at his neck, he hooked one finger

around his soft snake necklace and pulled her free. For a moment, Patricia's silver body was visible, lapping his fingers, but then she found her tail and was gone. It was hard to believe that she was real. He liked having her—another living thing in his life.

He held his hand flat, letting the weight of the invisible keys dangle from his palm. Feeling them with his other hand, he found the sheath and flipped it open. The tooth became visible, dangling in the glowing light of the ceiling lanterns, suspended in the air beneath his palm. Cyrus felt the now-familiar chill creep through him. What was this thing? What did it really do?

He glanced back at the toaster oven he had just resurrected. Shivering, he flipped the invisible sheath shut again, and the tooth disappeared. Closing his hand gently around Patricia's body and the invisible keys, he let his mind grind through the past two days. Normal life at the Archer—at least normal for him. And then a man in a yellow truck, and Mrs. Eldridge with her shotgun. Gunner and the fast car. Gunner. Guns. Guns that spat fire and bullets that fell from the sky. Maxi's smile full of worn teeth and Milo's Pizza. He wanted one of Milo's pizzas. He wanted all of Milo's pizzas. The river and darkness and cables and Antigone throwing up. Flying bicycles crashing into a fountain.

"Tigs?" he said quietly.

He turned his head. Antigone was curled up tight

on her side, arms around her legs, her chin against her knees. Her brows were down and her eyes were squeezed shut. Cyrus blinked slowly, and he didn't want the blink to end. Warm darkness.

He could see the big man named Rupert—Blood Avenger, Avengel. A towering wall of portraits and a pale boy beneath them. Nodding. Shaking his head. Nodding.

He and his sister were Acolytes in the Order of Brendan. Whatever that meant. The O of B. He'd signed the hay-bale book. Cyrus Lawrence Smth.

Dan was gone.

Asleep, lost in a tangle of darkness, lost in dark water, holding his breath, he swam through an underwater maze behind a blindfolded woman. The water faded, and he was moving toward the light of a too-familiar dream.

The California house had pale wood floors, polished to glistening. Cyrus was in the kitchen. He could smell his mother's lemon soap, and the counters were freshly cleaned. Antigone was in the living room, curled up on the couch, staring through the wall of quivering windows, watching distant spray jump the point on Elephant Island. Cyrus knew what was going to happen next. He waited for it. The kitchen door burst open, and his father slipped inside, smiling, brushing back wet hair, slapping his arms.

He handed Cyrus a note. "Give this to your mom for

me, will you, Cy?" He sounded like Dan, but unafraid. "I have to run a friend to the island. And tell her we might have an extra at dinner."

Antigone twisted around on the couch. "You're going out in this?"

"That I am," their father said. "But not for long. Back soon."

Cyrus took the note and nodded. His father's heavy wet hand slapped his shoulder and then ruffled his hair. "Look after Tigger for me." Then he fired a kiss across the room at Antigone and slid back out into the wind. The door didn't latch behind him, and the wind threw it open, banging it against the fridge. Cyrus slammed it.

That was it. His father was gone. Forever.

And then, for the first time in two years, the dream changed. Antigone didn't get up and pace the room in worry. She was frozen on the couch. Time didn't jump forward to his mother's panic and the cold food and the storm breaking and the light of a heartless moon. Instead, the door blew back open.

Cyrus slammed it. It blew open again, and he slammed it again. It blew open again, and he pressed his back against it, pushing with both legs until he heard the click of the latch.

It blew open again. How long this went on, the dream Cyrus couldn't say. Time had stopped. Antigone was frozen. Only he and the door and the storm moved on.

Finally, frustrated and confused, he stepped back and watched. Rain was whipping around the doorway, but not one drop entered the house or spattered on the floor.

Cyrus walked out the door and into the swarming, stinging rain. His father, enveloped in rubber rain gear, was frozen midjump into the passenger side of a truck. Suddenly, the dream moved in. His father landed on the seat and slammed the door. The truck began to pull away. The driver was big and . . . blurry. He wouldn't take shape. His profile should have been visible, but it was a smear of blankness. Cyrus squinted and cupped his hands around his eyes, but it wasn't a question of seeing. Somewhere in his mind, dusty, hidden deep beneath piles of the forgotten, stored with memories he never knew he'd collected—things said in third grade, the color of his first gum ball, his mother rocking him and singing in a strange language—there was an image of that driver. And something had stirred it. Something wanted to dig it back up and have a look.

The truck moved down the gravel drive, hopping in the puddles and potholes as it went. The dream disappeared with it.

"Cy!"

Cyrus opened his eyes and tried to stretch his arms above his head, cracking his knuckles—and a slender snake—against cool stone. His hand closed around sharp keys. Wincing, he sat up. He couldn't have been asleep for more than five minutes. Or an hour. Or two. He began to gently pull the snake loose from his fingers, but he stopped. Antigone was standing in the middle of the room, her cheek creased with sleep. Nolan was beside her, and his arms were full of ragged clothes.

Nolan set down his pile. "You shouldn't sleep any longer. I tried to find you a way into some normal showers. But you two aren't terribly popular, so you're left with mine." He nodded toward the hole in the wall. "Take turns outside. Stay on the planks. Not even a toe on the floor. I'll be back." He pointed at the grandfather clock. "Twenty minutes. I'll find you an actual list of the 1914 standards."

Tugging a stiffly folded towel and a brown brick of something soapish out of one of the alcoves, he handed them both to Antigone. Then he ducked through the hole and walked quickly down the bouncing planks.

Antigone opened her mouth to object, but the objections didn't come. She was filthy. Horace's blood was still caked between her fingers, and her hair looked like it had spent some time in a deep fryer. Even Cyrus had showered more recently than she had.

She stepped to the hole.

"You're going to do it?" Cyrus shook his head. "I'm not. No way. Not out in the middle of a room, standing beneath a cold drip."

"Yes, you are," Antigone said. "If I do it, you're

doing it, too. And I'm doing it, Rus. Scoot around the corner and look in the coffins or something."

Standing on a wobbly plank beneath a corked spout on an ancient mini-aqueduct carrying who knew what kind of water, Antigone hesitated. But not for long. Holding her breath, she reached up and tugged out the cork. Frigid water tumbled down, tightening skin and panicking nerves. Gasping, Antigone bounced in place.

"Sounds cold!" Cyrus yelled.

Antigone chattered.

"Tigs," Cyrus said. "You remember when Dad went out to the island, you know, the last time?"

She said nothing. He knew she did. Cyrus continued. "Did you get a look at the guy he went with? The guy in the truck? I dreamed it again, but this time I could almost see . . ." His voice drifted off.

"No," Antigone managed. "Just the back of the truck. Two heads." Scrubbing the soap brick at the blood on her arms and hands, she looked around the cold cavern, shifting her feet on the plank. Why did Nolan live here? Why was she here? Because nobody wanted the two Smith kids around. These people wanted her to fail, maybe even die. Why else would they send her off to live in an infestation? They'd hated Skelton and now they hated her. She wasn't used to being hated.

A crowd of feelings jostled around inside Antigone's

cold skull. She was shivering. She was confused. She was hungry and worried and more than a little creeped out. But louder than all of those things, she was curious. And irritated. Mad, actually. Angry. And anger made her feel a little stronger. She needed to feel strong right now. It would be too easy to curl up in a corner and cry about the burnt motel and her sleeping mother and missing brother. Who did these people think she was? She wiped cold water from her cheeks. She was a Smith. Her father never backed down. Her mother didn't, either.

"Cyrus," she said. "We're going to get Dan back, and we're going to beat these stupid people."

Cyrus laughed. "Fine with me."

When Nolan returned, he was carrying a huge nest of pillows and blankets and had a creased booklet clamped in his teeth. Cyrus and Antigone, both shivering awkwardly in new clean clothes, were looking through his books.

Antigone was wearing ripped brown pants that almost fit tucked into tall, extremely worn caramel riding boots. She had slicked her hair straight back. Cyrus's hair had been rough-toweled in every direction, and he'd cuffed his pocketed and tattered pants at the bottom to shorten the legs. Patricia's cool body was back around his blistered neck and the keys dangled high on his chest. The canvas shoes Nolan had brought had been too small, so his feet were back in the pair he'd stolen from Dan's room that morning. Both of them were wearing overly pocketed linen safari shirts with sleeves that rolled up and buttoned in place, but the color was badly faded and blotchy. Cyrus's collar was torn, and two of Antigone's pockets had threadbare holes. But at least the clothes were blood- and soot-free.

Nolan dropped his pillow pile and held out the booklet.

Cyrus took it and read the title. "*Order of Brendan, Guidelines for Acolytes, Ashtown Estate, 1910–1914.* Are they much different from the guidelines now?"

Nolan scratched his chin and turned away. "'Lytes now wouldn't survive the 1914 kitchens."

"Well, that's encouraging." Antigone gestured at her battered boots. "Who did you take the clothes from?"

Nolan twisted back around, his eyes suddenly alive, his already-pale face whitening. "You think I'm a thief?"

Antigone glanced around at the room's odd assortment and then looked at her brother. She shrugged and raised her eyebrows. "Um . . ."

"Out!" Nolan yelled. "Out!" He grabbed Antigone by the shoulders, driving her toward the hole.

Twisting, kicking, punching, Antigone pummeled the lean boy, but his grip only tightened. An arm slid around her ribs and she was off the ground.

"Stop!" Cyrus yelled. "Put her down!" Grabbing a thick book, he jumped forward and swung with both hands, driving the corner of the spine into Nolan's ear. Dropping Antigone halfway out of the hole, Nolan turned.

"If you touch her again . . . ," Cyrus said. "If you touch her again, I will seriously try to kill you."

Nolan's white-hot face cracked with laughter. "Kill me? Yes, please," he said. "Especially with a book." Rubbing his ear, he looked down at Antigone, her head and shoulders lying on the plank pathway. Turning, she reached down to push off the linoleum floor.

"No!" Nolan jumped forward, kicking her arm as a gray shape flicked out from beneath the plank toward her hand.

Tripping over Antigone, Nolan staggered down and out onto the dusty white floor. A swarm of clattering shapes suddenly swirled around him.

While Cyrus watched with wide eyes, Nolan spun, jumping, cursing, stamping, crunching something with every step, slapping at his legs, and then his hips, and then his stomach and back. Reaching the showers, he jumped and grabbed on with one hand. With his other hand, he kept slapping, grabbing, and throwing.

"Meat, eggs, anything!" he yelled at Cyrus. "From the fridge!"

Cyrus rushed to the little fridge and jerked open the

door. Rank eggs. Fuzzy cheese. Green meat. He grabbed two fistfuls, turned, and lobbed it all out the hole.

A moment later, the scene changed.

Nolan knocked the last clambering shapes to the floor and monkey-barred his way back to the plank path.

The Whip Spiders had found a new focus, and more and more of them were tap-dancing in from around the room, clicking and swarming on the food.

Breathing hard, Nolan looked at Cyrus and Antigone. His right arm was dotted with large red welts all the way up to his bare shoulder and onto the side of his neck.

"Um," said Antigone, pointing. "Your pocket's moving."

The pocket on Nolan's right hip bulged, and then a leg emerged. Nolan made a fist and slammed the spider against his leg. Then he shoved his hand into his pocket and pulled out the stunned creature.

He held it on his palm. Five inches long, its back was hinged with armor like a tailless scorpion. Two slender crab claws on arms longer than the body extended forward. Behind those, two long, barbed whips curled and groped slowly. The remaining six legs dangled off the sides of Nolan's hands. The creature seemed to be naturally brown, but its color shifted and lightened, approaching the shade of Nolan's skin.

"Were they pinching you?" Antigone asked.

"Stinging," said Nolan. "The whips have stings to bring down prey. Then they strip it with their pincers." The Whip Spider on his hand quickened and its legs tensed. Nolan dropped it on the plank, crushed it with his heel, and kicked the limp remainder into the seething mass on the floor. "They hunt in packs, change color like octopi, and, given their preferences, would camouflage themselves on the ceiling, dropping onto whatever passed below. In this circumstance, they make do lurking beneath my planks."

The three of them turned, staring down at the melee of creatures polishing the floor. The food was virtually gone, and dozens of spiders were already scurrying sideways back beneath the paths.

Cyrus looked around the room. "Can't they climb these walls?"

"Oh, they could." Nolan smiled. "If I hadn't rubbed down the base of every surface and pillar with oil. I did that before I hung the planks. And got a share of stings to show for it."

"Your arm looks terrible," Antigone said, grimacing. "Should you put something on it?"

"I'll be fine in the morning."

"I thought you were done for," Cyrus said. "That many scorpions would have killed you. At least these aren't fatal."

"They are," said Nolan. His tired eyes emptied, and he sighed. "For you. One whip strike would stun a man. Two could bring death. Three would kill a draft horse."

Cyrus eyed Nolan. The lean boy was rubbing his sting-blotched arm and staring glassily at the floor. "You almost killed my sister."

"Yes," Nolan said quietly. "But I did not kill her. And I regret my anger." He looked up at Antigone. "I do not care to be called a thief."

Cyrus snorted. "Do you care to be called a murderer?"

"No." Nolan's shoulders sagged. His worn eyes held no argument. "Forgive me."

Cyrus looked at his sister. Antigone was pale with anger and shock, and her short hair was reaching for everywhere. She pressed it flat, shivered, and crossed her arms.

"Nolan," she said. "If you ever . . . just don't, okay? Don't ever do anything like that again. Don't ever touch me, don't ever freak out like that, and for the record, now I really think you stole the clothes. Especially since you went so nuts about it."

Nolan took a long, slow breath and his head drooped. He looked young and old at the same time. "I'm sorry," he said. "I had no intention . . . I . . . Skelton asked me to help you. I gave him my word. I give it to you now."

His river-rock eyes rose from the floor. They were wet. "Those clothes were being thrown away. You'll get your own soon enough." He looked from Antigone to Cyrus. "I'm sorry. You *can* trust me. I will make this up to you."

Cyrus looked at his sister. Antigone inhaled slowly, tense, her eyes searching the strange boy's face. And then she exhaled, tension vanishing, and her eyes settled on the stings. "You really should put something on those welts."

Nolan looked down at his dotted, lumpy arm. Moving quickly, he jerked a long-sleeved red shirt out of one of his piles and stepped out onto the planks, tugging it on. "I'm fine. And my penance starts now. I will introduce you to *my* Ashtown. Bring the *Guidelines*—there's a map in the front."

Antigone looked at Cyrus. Cyrus shrugged. A moment later, the two of them were balancing carefully on the bouncing planks, passing peeling posters and bunk beds as they tried to catch up. Nolan was already out of sight.

Somewhere in Nolan's stuff, Antigone had discovered a long red string, and Cyrus watched her use it like a headband, tying back her damp black hair while she walked. She didn't seem too worried about her balance. Or about Nolan.

Cyrus tugged on his sister's shirt and leaned forward

to whisper, "You want me to go first? He did try to kill you."

"I'm fine," Antigone said, pulling free.

"Right," Cyrus said. "I forgot that girls love moody guys."

"Don't be a moron, Cy. It's not a good time."

Cyrus grinned, following his sister. "When is a good time to be a moron? You should get me on some kind of schedule."

"You know what I want to know?" Antigone asked. She twisted back, whispering over her shoulder. "Why didn't the spiders kill him?"

Cyrus shrugged. "Maybe he built up some kind of immunity or he drinks their milk or something."

"Drinks their milk? What did I just say about morons?"

"You two do not learn quickly." Nolan's voice echoed off the walls. He had stopped at the door, waiting. "Sound behaves oddly in this room."

"So which is it?" Cyrus yelled. "Are you immune, or do you drink spiders' milk?"

"I am immune to many things." He pushed the big door open and stepped back in surprise. He'd knocked someone back onto the stairs.

"Excuse me," a boy's voice said. "Apologies. We're looking for Cyrus and Antigone Smith. Is this the Polygon?"

Cyrus and Antigone bounced up to Nolan. The

pimply porter stood beside a pretty girl with green eyes and curly brown hair pulled tight in the front and exploding in the back. She was clutching a clipboard to her chest and fidgeting nervously.

"Hey!" said Cyrus. "It's the ten-year-old from earlier. Thanks for your help, by the way. We wouldn't have made it if you hadn't grabbed his legs."

"I'm fourteen," the porter said. "And my name is Dennis Gilly. You're welcome." He nodded at the girl beside him. "This is Hillary Drake. She failed the Acolyte exam when I did, but she was placed in Accounts." He inflated his chest. "When she heard that I was the one who found the outlaws and helped carry Mr. Lawney's corpse, well, she knew she could ask me to help."

He smiled at the girl beside him. Her wide green eyes were bouncing from Nolan to Cyrus.

"Corpse?" Antigone asked. "Horace is dead?"

"No. Well, I don't know," said Dennis. "Maybe. Maybe not. Anyhow, Hillary asked me if I would bring her to you. I'm on break, and she has questions for you. For her forms. And well, what with inheriting from Billy Bones, and him being murdered, and people saying that you probably killed him and Horace and maybe Gunner, too, and you being all the way down here, she was a little scared to meet you alone. And the infestation notice was disturbing, too." He looked at Hillary, and his pimples practically glowed with pride. "Not to me, though."

Dennis stuck his thumbs in his waistband and waggled his eyebrows. But then he looked up into Nolan's eyes. The porter's brows froze and then drooped slowly.

"Which dining plan, please?" Head down, Hillary coughed the question out all at once.

"What?" Cyrus asked. He looked at his sister.

"What's normal?" Antigone asked.

"Full access, dining hall only, breakfast only, lunch only, supper only, Monday-Wednesday-Friday only, Tuesday-Thursday only—"

"Hold on!" said Cyrus. "Didn't Horace set us up with something? Mr. Lawney? He didn't talk to you all about what we would do? He said the Skelton estate would cover all our costs."

"Um." Hillary slowly raised her eyes. They were very wide, very green, and clearly as curious as they were nervous. "He tried. But the forms were, um, voided. Mr. Rhodes says you don't have access to the estate. Not while you're still Acolytes. The Order established Passage."

"They don't need anything," Nolan said. His voice was stony-certain. "No dining plan."

Antigone caught Cyrus's eye. Her brother shrugged.

Hillary had already ticked a box. "Maid service?"

"No," said Nolan.

She ticked another box. "Access to local and/or global community aircraft and nautical vessels?"

"No," said Nolan.

"Wait." Cyrus leaned forward. "How much is that? What would it cost if I said yes?"

Hillary's big eyes bounced up to his and then back down to her clipboard. "Global or local?" she asked.

"Let's just say local."

"Ten thousand American dollars, per Acolyte, per nine-month Acolyteship period, with a twenty-five percent deposit due immediately."

"Wowza." Cyrus laughed. "Can we defer payment until Horace wakes up?"

Hillary coughed, confused, and she stared at her clipboard. "Due immediately."

"Right," said Cyrus. "Let's stick with the 'no,' then."

"How many aircraft and vessels will you be bringing?"

"Um . . ." Antigone looked at her brother, and then at Nolan. "None?"

"I don't understand." Hillary tested a small smile. "You have to bring your own or you register to use the Order's. Most people just bring their own."

"Why?" Cyrus asked. "What if we don't want to sail or fly a plane?"

Hillary cocked her head to one side.

Dennis laughed. "Mr. Smith, you're Acolytes. You have to."

Antigone squinted at him. "We have to fly a plane?"

Nolan sighed loudly. "Give me the book." He snatched the *Guidelines* out of Cyrus's hands and faced the girl with the clipboard. "Miss Hillary Drake, the whole package—room, board, usage fees, hangar and harbor fees, weaponry fees, tutorial fees, maids, tailors, insurance, everything—how much?"

"I just, it would . . ." She flipped two pages. "Fifty-five thousand, four hundred and fifty American dollars."

"Each?" Nolan asked.

Hillary nodded. "Per nine-month Acolyteship period. Twenty-five percent due upon arrival."

Nolan sighed. "Were you in the Galleria today when these two presented themselves?"

"Yes. I thought Mr. Rhodes was unkind. Even if they are outlaws." She smiled at Cyrus.

"He was," said Nolan. "But he was kind in another way. What Acolyte standards were applied?"

"Nineteen-fourteen!" Hillary said, flushing angrily. "And that's impossible. No one thinks they can do it. Nobody could."

Nolan flipped open the booklet and turned to the back. He cleared his throat. " 'Fees for Acolytes: Room and Board, one hundred fifty dollars; Light, Fuel, Craft Usage, Harbor and Hangar Fees: one hundred fifty dollars; Tailoring, Tutoring, Weaponry, Library: fifty-five dollars. Acolytes must place a fifteen-dollar deposit against their fees upon arrival.'" He snapped the booklet shut. "They'll have the full package. Everything." He pointed at the clipboard. "Write it down. Make a note. Make sure they get on every list tonight—dining, library, haberdashery, everything." He dug a cigar of crumpled bills out of his pocket. "Here's a twenty, and here's a ten. Thirty dollars for the two of them. That's the deposit paid in full. Check all the boxes." He grabbed the big door and began pulling it closed.

"Wait!" Hillary shoved a piece of paper into Nolan's hand, but her eyes were on Cyrus. "Here's the list of available Keepers."

"Thanks," said Cyrus, but the door had already boomed shut. Cyrus, Antigone, and Nolan all stood quietly on the same sagging plank. Antigone took the paper from Nolan's hand.

"Ancient Language. Modern Language. Navigation? Flight? The Occult?"

A spider's whip curled up over the lowered edge of the plank, and Nolan crunched it quickly with his toe.

"No languages for me, thank you," Cyrus whispered. "Are they gone?"

Someone knocked loudly on the door. Nolan rolled his eyes and pushed it open.

"Excuse me," said Dennis. "But are there really Whip Spiders in there?" Hillary peeked out from behind him.

Nolan tugged up his sleeve, revealing his sting-tumored arm.

Dennis froze in the doorway, his mouth open.

"Oh, go on," Antigone said. She folded her paper and tucked it into her pocket. "I'd like to get out of here."

Pushing Nolan into Dennis, she shoveled them both through the doorway and onto the damp stone landing.

Dennis grabbed the door and slammed it shut. Standing on tiptoe, he chalked the door in large letters.

DANGER NO ENTRY STAY OUT

Beneath that, he drew a convincing skull and crossbones. Finally, he added his initials and the date.

Cyrus felt a hand on his arm. Hillary's wide green eyes were looking up at him through long lashes. She smiled. "I would love to show you the dining hall."

"No thanks," said Cyrus. "Nolan's going to show us around."

Antigone pushed forward, bathing Hillary in an enormously false smile. "Dennis," she said through her teeth. "Would you please get Hillary safely back to wherever Hillary belongs?"

"Absolutely." Dennis held out his arm like an usher at a wedding. Hillary took it, and the two of them climbed the stairs.

"Nonsense," Nolan muttered. "Fees. Why do they need fees?"

"Thanks for that, by the way," Cyrus said. "We owe you thirty bucks."

Nolan picked the foul sock plug up off the stairs and crammed it back down into the floor drain. "The water discourages people," he said. "Not many just splash in and dig around for a plug." He stood up, wiping his hands on his pants. Then he slapped at his stung arm, rubbing it briskly. His breath had quickened, and his eyes were bright and alive. For the first time, he looked entirely like a boy. "The venom just reached my heart." He grinned and then exhaled and bit his lip. His whole body shivered slightly. "Pain. For a little while, it will make me feel alive. Come." Surprised, Cyrus watched Nolan turn and begin moving up the stairs. "The map's in the front. Find the dining hall. The unmarked space beside it is where we begin. It's known—at least to people who actually set foot inside it—as the kitchen. You slept for a while, but we will still beat the dinner rush."

Antigone and Cyrus began quickstepping to keep up with him.

"From there, we visit the place marked Upper Quarters and move into the library and a section the map calls No Access." He shot a smile over his shoulder. "If Skelton were here, you could see the zoo. 'Zoological Collection: Keeper Escort Required' on the map."

"Why if Skelton were here?" Antigone asked.

Nolan disappeared into the hallway. When they reached the top, he was already out of sight. "Because," his voice tumbled back down the hall, "some locks can't be picked."

Cyrus and Antigone jogged around the first corner and almost ran into him. He was standing in the center of the hall, holding up one end of a large, decorative iron grate—the cover for a bulky heating vent.

"Skelton," Nolan said, "was a man with keys for any lock. Rhodes will have them now—taken off of Horace by the hospitalers. Or Maxi Robes has them. Or . . . well"—his eyes sparkled—"maybe some runtling Acolytes got their hands on them." He nodded at the vent in the floor. "Climb down. There are rungs tight to the side."

Cyrus slid his hand up to his neck. Antigone looked at her brother, eyes wide, and she shook her head. She knew what he was thinking.

Nolan misunderstood Antigone's look. "If you're bothered by tight places, don't worry, it opens up."

Cyrus gritted his teeth. What had Skelton said? Trust no one? Trust Nolan. He'd heard what he'd heard.

"What if I did have them?" he asked. "Skelton's keys. What then? What would I do with them?"

"Mirror, mirror on the wall," Antigone said, "who is the dumbest of them all?"

She took two frustrated steps down into the vent and then dropped to the bottom.

Nolan's polished eyes locked into Cyrus's. His breath was still oddly quick and short. His hands were twitching and his pulse fluttered visibly on the side of his neck. His lips quaked into a smile.

"With you? Here? Now?"

Cyrus sighed. "Maybe."

In the dining hall, in the library, and in the Galleria, Antigone's voice rose up from the vents in the floor and poured out of the walls. "Oh, queen, 'tis true that you are dumb. But Cyrus Lawrence Smith is dumber than a pile of cow patties."

✣ ten ✣

TOURISTS AND TRESPASSERS

THE HEAT TUNNELS were not quite six feet tall, and about as wide as a sidewalk. Dusty, cloth-wrapped pipes criss-crossed the floor and ceiling or ran in bundles along the wall. Tunnels intersected. They shifted and turned, almost always at hard angles. They dead-ended into vertical shafts, both up and down, and old wooden ladders had been propped in place.

The train of three had climbed up and down, they had turned left and right, and Cyrus knew that he would never be able to find his way back.

He stopped beneath a floor vent, squinting at the map in the booklet. "Where are we now?" he whispered.

"Almost there," Nolan whispered back.

"These tunnels connect everything?" Antigone asked.

Nolan nodded. "Almost. They run through every large building and beneath every external footpath. In the winter, the tunnels keep the paths clear of snow. When the furnace pits are stoked beneath the Galleria, you could roast in here. One more turn."

Cyrus closed the booklet and tailed Nolan into dwindling light. Antigone followed, grabbing on to the back of her brother's shirt.

"Cyrus," Nolan whispered. "Many would kill for those keys."

Antigone's grip tightened.

"Maxi and Phoenix would kill for anything," Nolan continued. "But especially for those keys."

"Okay," Antigone said. "Who is Phoenix? I get that he's nasty and mean and he's the one who sent people to kill Skelton, but who is he?"

Nolan turned and pressed his finger to his lips. "Whispers," he said. "Whispers. I'll tell you everything in a minute."

"And I want to talk to Greeves again," Antigone continued. "And we definitely have to see Horace. Where's the hospital?"

Nolan glared back at her. Cyrus smiled and stepped on his sister's foot. She hit him.

They had stopped in front of a large grate mounted on a wall. Through the decorative iron, plates clattered. Singing mingled with laughter and the occasional shout.

Nolan pushed the grate up, ducked out, and held it open.

Cyrus and Antigone stepped into the largest kitchen they had ever seen.

A wall of windows faced the enormous ocean of a lake. Beneath them, a small army of aprons and caps were chopping and dicing and grating and rolling and mixing on a row of tables. Another wall held a dangling mountain of copper pots ranging from dollhouse small to boil-a-whale big. The center of the room was an island of flame. Fire spurting up through grills, fire roaring beneath spitted meat, fire licking pots and gobbling every sizzling slop. Men and women with flushed and sweating faces scrambled toward ovens with mittened hands and prodded meat with long-handled prongs still too short for safety.

"Nolan!" a voice boomed across the room. "You missed my lunch! Don't tell me you're here for an early supper. Back to your tunnels!"

Nolan ignored the voice and moved casually into the kitchen.

Cyrus shifted nervously. Antigone stood beside him.

Nolan stopped. Beyond the island of fire, Cyrus could see a big man moving toward them. His black-and-silver hair was tied down with a handkerchief, knot forward, and each of the cooks jumped out of his way as he eased down the line, dipping his finger in sauces and sneering at meat. He was dressed all in white, and his heavy black beard was bagged in a net. Small gold bells dangled from his ears, jingling like Christmas when he bent to sniff a pot or sip from a spoon, and as he finally moved completely into view, Cyrus felt his sister squeeze his arm in surprise.

The man had no legs.

Of course he has legs, Cyrus thought. They're just . . . metal.

Below his apron, two thin, bending black rods ran down into a rubber-coated ball joint of an ankle. Beneath each of those, a small triangle hoof of rubber made contact with the ground. Cyrus tried not to stare. It was like seeing an elephant with antelope legs.

Standing in front of them, the big man put two hairy fists onto his wide hips, and he glared.

"You bring guests," he said. "Invaders." He raised his eyebrows and smiled. "Outlaws. And at this mad hour, too."

Nolan didn't seem put off. "This is Big Ben Sterling, lord of the one-acre kitchen. Ben, behold the last two Smiths of Ashtown—Cyrus and Antigone."

"Nice to meet you," Antigone said, elbowing Cyrus. She held out her hand. Ben Sterling swallowed it with his.

"I know all about you two." He winked. "Oh, the chatter today. Billy Bones picked himself quite a pair. Your ancestors were living outside the law before Skelton's great-granddad had his first thieving thought. Rogues to the bone, you are. Bones's new rogues."

Cyrus opened his mouth, confused, but Sterling waved him off. "Oh, don't fret yourselves. Be it true or false, the kitchen hears everything, the kitchen knows everything, and I . . . am the kitchen." Slapping Cyrus on the back, he whistled sharply between his teeth. "Make a hole at the rail! Three stools!"

Immediately, the lineup at the windows compressed, and a man who had been shaking potato peels into a can scurried off after stools.

Bells ringing, Sterling walked them toward the newly empty space. "I'll stop and chat as chat can," he said. "But your tour guide chooses the devil's worst moment."

Three stools were shoved in place. Sterling pulled one out for Antigone and stepped aside for Cyrus. "I have a rule for you two," he said, eyeing them both. He rubbed his netted beard and then leaned down, lowering his voice. "If there's a light on in my kitchen, you come in and make free. If there's not, well, you come in and make free. Night or day, you two duck in. My breakfast crew will catch the crumbs. And don't feel as if you have to use the tunnels, like some I could mention."

He grinned and straightened.

Cyrus laughed. The man's eyes were sharp and knowing. His teeth were gapped but brilliant white. His netted beard was thicker than a bundle of black hay. But no matter where Cyrus looked, his eyes snapped back to the man's bouncing earrings, catching and spraying the chaos of kitchen light, chiming with every step, breath, and smile.

"Thanks," said Cyrus. He wasn't sure what else to say.

Nodding, the cook turned away. "Melton!" he bellowed. "Look to your sauce, man!"

A woman in white slid three bowls of fine noodles onto the rail, followed by a platter mounded with well-sauced skewers of grilled beef.

Cyrus inhaled slowly.

Antigone looked at her brother and smiled. "I'm surprised I'm this hungry," she said. "You probably aren't surprised at all."

Cyrus shook his head. Nolan was scraping beef onto his noodles. "Is he for real?" Cyrus asked. "We can come in any time we want?"

Nolan nodded. "But don't make enemies on his staff. Always clean up after yourself."

A chuckle came from the man chopping vegetables next to them.

"How did he lose his legs?" Antigone asked.

"Lake shark," Nolan said. "Midair collision. Motorcycle racing. Or he lost them to Thai pirates. Or he cut them off and cooked them for a cannibal chieftain. Depends on the day and on how much wine is in him when you ask."

Cyrus shoveled in a large first bite, and the flavors swam together—soy and cayenne and peanut sauce. His eyebrows climbed in surprise. It was a combination he hadn't tasted in more than two years—his mother's combination.

Antigone set her fork down, swallowing. She looked at him with wide eyes. "It's exactly the same." She looked at Nolan. "It was our dad's—" Her eyes flooded. Tucking back her hair, she looked up, breathing evenly. "This is stupid. I'm just tired and hungry."

Cyrus cranked around on his stool. Ben Sterling was hugging a tall, smiling, ponytailed girl who had just pushed through a swinging door into the kitchen. But the big cook was looking back over his shoulder as he did. He flashed Cyrus half a grin and winked. The girl tugged his netted beard to get his attention.

Cyrus turned back around. "It's not like he could have known."

Nolan rubbed his welted neck, chewing. "Oh, he knew. Your father *was* here. The kitchen knows everything."

"Dan should be here," Cyrus said. "That's the only thing that could make this taste better."

Antigone winced, knuckling the corners of her eyes. "Don't, Cy. Please. I'm trying not to cry. I already feel like a puffy-eyed moron."

Cyrus twisted up a mass of noodles and wedged it into his mouth.

"These are the new ones? You're letting 'Lytes into the kitchen?"

Cyrus and Antigone spun around on their stools.

The ponytailed girl was standing immediately behind them, wearing glistening, oiled boots, trousers, and a white linen shirt almost identical to Antigone's—although she was a year or two older, inches taller, and hers was spotless and fit perfectly. Her hair couldn't decide if it was red or brown or gold, and her tan face and arms were sun-freckled. Her sharp eyes were bright blue at the rim, but her pupils were haloed with brown. The big cook loomed behind her. It was the girl from the plane. Cyrus knew it was. The girl pilot.

Cyrus felt sweat forming on his forehead, and he almost choked, gulping down his load of noodles. Peanut sauce dribbled out the corner of his mouth. He wiped it quickly, but more kept coming.

"Are they Acolytes?" Ben Sterling asked. "How's a cook supposed to know a thing like that?" Shaking his head and smiling, he retreated to Fire Island.

The girl scowled, but then she saw Antigone's worried face. "Oh, I'm sorry," she said, her eyes widening. "I was only joking. It must have been a long day, and I've heard Cecil Rhodes has been a prat. The Rhodeses always are. But you'll be fine. I grew up thinking Smiths could do anything. Sorry I wasn't there for your presenting, or I would have yelled something rude about Cecil's mustache. I'm just getting back from a longish trek. Do you mind?" She snagged a piece of beef off Antigone's plate and popped it into her mouth.

She turned to Cyrus. He managed another swallow, wiped his mouth, and straightened.

"Already heard a story about you," she said. "My cousin says he thrashed you in the hall after you tripped him."

Cyrus blinked.

The girl laughed. "Don't worry. I heard the real story, too. You actually called him a snot?"

"Um," said Cyrus. "Yeah. I think so. He was your cousin?"

"Everyone is my cousin. And you were right. He is a snot. Well, I have to run to get some stitches out." She tugged down the collar of her shirt, revealing a jagged and crudely sewn-up gash at the base of her neck. Cyrus stopped chewing. "A little run-in with a cave owl, and I'm not much of a seamstress." She backed away. "Best of luck and all that. I hope you make it. Don't always eat in the kitchen!" She strode toward the swinging kitchen door, ponytail bouncing as she went. One hand jumped, flicking Ben Sterling's left ear bell as she passed.

"Who was that?" asked Cyrus when the door swung behind her.

"That," said Nolan, "was Diana Boone. Youngest-ever woman in the O of B to achieve Explorer. She's not even seventeen yet. Beat Amelia Earhart by one month."

"I'm not sure about her," said Antigone. "Wait. Amelia Earhart? You're serious?"

"Who's Amelia Earhart?" Cyrus asked.

Antigone slapped him without looking. She sighed. "I'm really confused. Cyrus might not mind. Confusion is one of his best friends. But I hate it. Acolytes and Keepers and Explorers? There should be some sort of, I don't know, orientation."

Nolan leaned over and tugged the *Guidelines* out of Cyrus's pocket. "Everything you need is in here." He folded back the front cover.

Still glancing at the kitchen door, Cyrus returned to twirling his noodles.

"Five ranks in the O of B." Nolan's breathing had leveled and his hands were barely twitching. The food had helped. "Acolyte, Journeyman, Explorer, Keeper, Sage. Each has its own privileges and chores. This morning, you would have just been accepted as Skelton's heirs by becoming Acolytes. But Rhodes challenged, so now you have to become Journeymen before you inherit. If you don't inherit, the Order gets everything." He smiled at Cyrus. "Including those lovely keys. Rhodes made it even harder by applying 1914 standards—"

"Yeah, yeah," said Antigone. "We know."

Cyrus looked at his sister, and then at Nolan. "Is that when the Order started? 1914? Wow. I guess Horace did say it was old."

Nolan stared at him, his eyes searching. And then, for the first time, he laughed. And he was clearly out of practice. He wheezed. He sputtered. His paper skin flushed, and he grabbed at his welted neck in pain.

"What?" Cyrus muttered. "I mean, I know I'm hilarious and everything. . . ."

Nolan leaned forward, wiping tears from his cheeks. "The Order *is* old," he said. "And not just by your American standards. Its seed was planted fifteen centuries ago, and like anything else that has survived for so long, it has seen some dark times."

Cyrus's chewing slowed.

Nolan shrugged. "There has been light, too, and plenty of heroes to the world's benefit. But a fair share of villains as well. Through the centuries, the people of the Order have called themselves many foolish things— Knights of the Navigator, the League of Brother Explorers, and on and on. But only two names matter now. This is the Order of Brendan, and within the Order, there is *Custodis Orbis*—the Guardian Circle. Those are the people who oversee the Order and, at times, have overseen the world."

"People like Rhodes," Cyrus said.

"No," said Nolan. "Nothing at all like Rhodes. Much wiser or much more foolish than Rhodes." He winced and closed his eyes, rubbing his arm. Exhaling through gritted teeth, he collected himself.

Antigone winced with him. "Are you sure you're okay?"

Nolan nodded, and his legs began to bounce. "I'll back up. Sometime in the sixth century, Brendan the Navigator set out from Ireland in a big leather boat. He and sixty others reached this continent and sailed up what is now called the Hudson River, finally stopping here. They built some of the first—very small—structures of the Order right where we are now. Leaving some men behind, they sailed on for another seven years. Those sixty were the first *Custodis Orbis*.

"The Order of Brendan maintained harbors and holdings on every continent. Ashtown was one of the measliest, designed as a grim penal colony—a prison. The Order, in all their explorations, had begun to encounter things they could never defeat and could only hope to contain. At the far reaches of the known world, Ashtown was a dungeon for the most dangerous of those things. Here, the Sages explored death and how to bring it to the undying. Here, they collected and burned legions of vile relics—and, in some of the more foolish centuries, some of the greatest treasures man could ever hope to find. That is when Ashtown earned its name. Civilization has grown up around it, but Ashtown remains. And it still houses the most dangerous collections.

"The Order saw its boom before World War I—global membership was above one hundred thousand. Since the close of the Second World War, it has been well below ten. But the O of B still explores, discovers, and preserves as it sees fit. And if you know where to look, it can still tell you the world's secrets—to historians, the worst kind of myths and legends; to scientists, rumors, impossibilities, and even nightmares."

Leaning forward, Cyrus raised his eyebrows. "You're saying a guy named Brendan discovered America?"

Nolan groaned. "Is that all you heard? No. There were entire civilizations here long before the arrival of Brendan's sixty." Nolan turned all the way around on his stool, propping his elbows against the table, watching the kitchen bustle. His fingers began to twitch. He clenched them into fists. "Of course, for many people here, the great mysteries are as normal as Sunday's nap. The origin of the first pyramid, the death of the moon, the fire eyes of the leviathan, how to confine an incubus—they know these things like you know of Pilgrims and butterflies and baseball. They have always known them. Their parents and grandparents and one-eyed uncles are hanging in pictures on all the walls." He half-smiled at the two of them. "Just like yours."

A sharp whistle rang through the kitchen. Ben Sterling jerked his head toward the wall with the heat tunnel. The kitchen door banged open, and Cecil Rhodes stepped through, sharp nostrils flaring above his tiny mustache.

Nolan hopped off his stool. "Leave the food. Stand straight. Don't run. Stay behind me."

Cyrus and Antigone followed Nolan as he wove slowly through the traffic of cooks. Rhodes was tracking Sterling in the opposite direction, occasionally glancing around him.

Nolan reached the wall, lifted the grate, and turned around.

Antigone ducked in.

Cyrus ducked in.

Nolan and the grate followed. He pushed past them. "Keep up. We have to be quick."

"Why?" Antigone asked.

"Because as long as Cecil Rhodes is in the kitchen, he can't catch you anywhere else. Acolytes aren't allowed in the hospital. Now you see Horace."

The tunnel, long and straight at first, had become busy with noise. Fingers of golden light spread around the iron flowers on a dozen decorative grates. The dining hall was rowdy with silverware and laughter and conversation.

Cyrus squinted through the first grate. The hall was partitioned into sections with huge tapestried walls on wheels. He could see tuxedos and waiters. He could see a man in a jumpsuit dotted with oil stains. He saw Diana Boone throwing a roll at a boy at another table. Probably a cousin.

"Up," Nolan's voice echoed. "Let's go, Cyrus. Climb."

Straightening, Cyrus looked around for Nolan

and his sister. He was alone in the tunnel, but a silent blizzard of dust was descending through the golden grate-sliced light.

Iron rungs stuck out of the wall. He couldn't see anything above him, but he could hear breathing, and the occasional squeal and groan of metal.

He began to climb.

Ten feet up, he sneezed for the first time. Twenty feet up, he ducked his head and held his breath. Thirty feet up, he rammed his head into the back of Antigone's legs and clutched the ladder while he fought a sneezing fit.

"Quiet, Rus-Rus," she whispered. "Down, boy. Nolan said to wait here. He's checking something."

Cyrus sneezed again and one foot slipped free.

"Cyrus," Antigone said. "Just hang on, okay?"

He snorted out his nose and ground the runoff onto his shirt shoulder. His eyes were streaming. "You try hanging on down here. It's like a dust volcano. A dust bath. No. You know what it's like, Tigs? It's like climbing straight up a long shaft with more dust than the moon while your sister climbs above you, kicking it in your face. That's what it's like." He sniffed hard, cleared his throat loudly, and then leaned back off the ladder, spitting between his feet at the tiny light square beneath him.

"Did you just spit?" Antigone asked. "You're hawking loogies inside?"

"My sinuses are solid snot clods," Cyrus said. "And I think my lungs each have two inches of mud."

"Okay, come on up," Nolan whispered. "Cyrus, I could hear you two rooms away. And if I could hear you, so could anyone near any vent in this entire wing."

"If you could hear me"—Cyrus sniffed—"then you know what I was doing."

He followed Antigone up. At the top, Nolan grabbed his wrists and pulled him to his feet in another horizontal tunnel.

Wheezing, Cyrus grabbed his sister. "Can I borrow your shirt? I need to blow my nose."

Antigone shrugged him off, and the two of them hurried after Nolan. He had stopped beneath a dark grate in the ceiling. Little constellations of pinprick light dotted his scalp. Stepping onto a rickety, old library stool, Nolan pushed up.

The grate rose on one side, and white light flooded in along with the lemony smell of cleaning fluid. Wedging it open, Nolan dropped back down.

"Go ahead," he said to Antigone. "I'll boost you."

Antigone stepped up onto the stool, and then onto Nolan's cupped hands. She hopped, he pushed, and she wormed through onto the floor above.

Cyrus jumped and managed to wriggle his way up. With a shove from behind, he hooked his waist on the lip. Antigone grabbed the back of his shirt and dragged him forward out of the hole.

Cyrus rolled onto his back. "I could have done that by myself," he said. "I would have been far more grace-ful."

Antigone smirked. "That's you, Cy. Mr. Graceful. Now stand up."

From his back, Cyrus looked around. They were in a hall. The walls were white stone, the floor was covered with oddly interlacing glistening white tiles, and frosted skylights in the white ceiling were glowing orange with the evening light. White doors with white glass win-dows and black numbers lined both walls. Cyrus sat up. Voices trickled down the hallway around them.

"Nolan," he whispered. "You coming up?"

Nolan's face appeared in the hole. "No. I wait here." He scraped the grate closed behind them. "Good luck."

Antigone stood and grabbed Cyrus by the hand, pulling him to his feet.

"Where do we start?" Cyrus whispered.

His sister stepped to the closest door, cracked it open, and stuck her head inside. "Nobody. You do that side, and we'll work our way down."

Cyrus glanced back down the hall. "I'm not sure about this. We're going to get in trouble."

"Do you care?" Antigone asked.

Cyrus shrugged. "Not really. What can they do?"

He opened his first door and peered in. The room was small and, not surprisingly, almost entirely white. A kid with a broken leg suspended from the ceiling was eating noodles and beef off a tray. He looked up.

"Sorry," said Cyrus. "Enjoy your dinner."

"Wait!" The boy bounced in place, nearly toppling his tray. "Hold on. Talk to me. I've been stuck in here for a week, and all sorts of things have been happening. Nothing ever happens around here, but now it is, and no one will talk to me. But you will, right? Tell me what's going on."

Cyrus pulled back, checking the hall. Antigone was apologizing to someone and shutting a door quickly. He stuck his head back into the room. "Tell you what?"

"I heard the nurses talking about Billy Bones. My mom used to tell me he wasn't even real. Was he really murdered? Did Greeves really have his corpse in the Galleria? Did you see him?"

Cyrus nodded.

"Was his whole skeleton tattooed onto his body? Even his face?"

"Yeah," Cyrus said. "But not his face."

The boy nodded, processing this. "And his 'Lytes? Were they tattooed?"

"No." Cyrus smiled. "Not that I know."

"Oh." The boy was disappointed, but not for long. "I can't believe they came at all. Can you imagine? Not me. I'd stay away. And they're Smiths, too. I heard that much, but I wish I knew more about them. Have they killed people? They have to be crazy. And with an ancestor in the Burials, too? It would freak me out. I wouldn't be able to sleep at night." Suddenly, his eyes widened. "Are they with the other Acolytes? Where do they sleep?"

"Down in the Polygon," Cyrus said. "With the Whip Spiders. I really have to go. Good luck with the leg."

"Wait! The Polygon? Is that real, too? I never know what to believe around here. Whip Spiders?"

Cyrus smiled again. Being notorious could work. He winked at the kid in the bed. "You'll meet them soon enough."

"Cyrus Lawrence Smith!" A cold hand clamped onto Cyrus's ear, twisting his head around and forcing his skull against the doorjamb. Mrs. Eldridge's face leaned in close to his, her breath more dill than pickles. He grabbed at her wrist, at the hand twisting his ear, but he couldn't fight it. She bent him lower. "What do you think you're doing here?" she asked quietly. "Where's your sister?"

Cyrus's eyes rolled around the hall. Had Tigs left him? "You're tearing my ear off. Let go!" He bit his lip. His eyes were watering with pain. He tried to find her legs with his feet.

"Smith?" The boy's voice was almost a squeak.

"He's one of them? He could have killed me. What does he want?"

Ignoring the kid, Mrs. Eldridge released Cyrus into the hall and shut the door.

Breathing hard, Cyrus massaged his ear and examined his fingers for blood. How could his ear not be bleeding? How was it still attached?

Mrs. Eldridge crossed her arms, examining him.

"You're nuts," Cyrus said. "Did you have to do that?"

"Boys need hard lines," said Mrs. Eldridge. "Sneaking into the hospital." She shook her head. "The Polygon's not rough enough for you already? If I'm to be responsible for you around here, I'll do what needs done to keep that empty head on your shoulders. Where's Antigone? I always thought you were the dimmest Smith bulb, but you never know with families."

Near the end of the hall, behind Mrs. Eldridge, a door cracked open. "Cyrus!" Antigone whispered. "Get in here! He doesn't look good."

Mrs. Eldridge smacked her lips. "Well, I have my answer then, don't I?" She turned around. "Miss Antigone!"

The door widened, and Cyrus watched his shocked sister step out into the hall.

"Mrs. E?" Antigone asked. Cyrus blinked. His sister sounded relieved to see the woman who'd just tried to souvenir his ear. "Horace doesn't look good. He's gray and barely breathing and hooked up to all sorts of stuff."

Mrs. Eldridge, arms crossed and angry, deflated a little. "I know, doll. I know. He doesn't look good 'cause he isn't. He's the opposite of good. They put all new blood in him twice over—that bullet was a big one, and it spread out and splattered. Now come on. Let's get you two out of here and back to where you belong. I know what I said, and I know what I swore, and if it were up to me, I think I'd shut you two out and stick to it. But with Skelton dead and Horace dying, Rupert didn't give me a choice. I'm your Keeper now, and that's that." She glared at Cyrus. "And you'll be doing as I say, starting now. In the morning, we'll get you proper clothes of your own and get you working. You two have got an impossible lot to learn."

"Yes, ma'am," Antigone said.

"Just tell me how you like your waffles," Cyrus muttered.

eleven

BED

WHEN MRS. ELDRIDGE finally rereleased Cyrus and Antigone into the Polygon—she actually stood at the top of the dank stairwell, tsking them all the way down—and the two of them had made their cautious way across the network of planks, through the corked gap in the showers, and through the hole, they found Nolan tucked awkwardly onto a stone bed. His teeth were chattering, his shirt was off, and sweat dripped from swollen mountain ranges of Whip Spider welts. His right arm was twice as thick as his left, and his neck had expanded out past his jaw.

Wheezing, Nolan opened his eyes. "I'm fine," he whispered. "Happened too many times to count. Need to sleep."

Antigone looked at her brother. "We should call someone."

"No." Nolan shook his head, and then managed to point to a thick envelope on the floor. "Was on the door. For you." He squeezed his eyes shut.

"What now?" Cyrus asked, watching Nolan breathe.

Antigone picked up the envelope, ripped it open, and sat down on one of the other stone beds.

Cyrus watched his sister pull out the three defaced photos he'd found in Skelton's camper. Then she tugged out a rectangle of misshapen glass. His beetle.

"Ow!" Shaking her fingers, she dropped the glass, kicked it off her foot, and sent it tumbling across the carpet. A small note fluttered out of the envelope and settled on the floor.

"It shocked me," Antigone said, popping her fingers into her mouth. "Who's it from?"

Looking back at Nolan, Cyrus pinched the glass and dropped it into his pocket before he picked up the note. "'U left these in the car. Creeps. Made it back. Couple stitches but fine. Heard about you. Sorry. Horace is deliryous. Check in later. Gunner.'" Cyrus looked up. "I'm glad he made it. I wonder what he heard about us."

Antigone laughed. "Maybe that we got stuck in the Polygon. Tomorrow I absolutely need a toothbrush. And a hairbrush." She looked around the room. "And a mirror. And someone who can tell us what's going on with Dan." She shivered, pulling her knees up to her chest. Her eyes settled on Nolan's dripping face. "I really don't want to sleep in here, and I feel like I'm going to cry."

"Well, don't," said Cyrus. "Think of me. How much worse would it be for me if you were crying?"

"It's not like I'm planning on crying. It's just that, well, here we are. And Mrs. Eldridge is the only person we know, and it's not like she's excited to help us. Dan's gone and we don't know if anyone is doing anything about it. Mom's back at the hospital—when will we get another Mom day? Are we even allowed to leave? And we're sleeping in a room with a boy we just met who looks like he's dying, and there are Whip Spiders, and the motel is burned, and who knows what's going to happen tomorrow? This place was supposed to help us." She scrunched her face.

"I think you *are* planning on crying," said Cyrus. "It's like you're trying to talk yourself into it."

"Dork."

"Girl."

"Oh, shut up." Antigone raised her head. "If you think making me mad is going to keep me from crying, you're dumber than I thought, and you haven't been paying any attention to girls for pretty much your entire life."

"Just trying to make you laugh."

Antigone dropped her forehead onto her arms. "I don't want to laugh right now, Cy. I can't. Honestly, this has been the most traumatic forty-eight hours of my life. Tell me *that's* not true."

Cyrus pulled in a long, slow breath, and his mind jumped back in time—he couldn't stop it—and an old

222

ache, forever fresh, broke out of its cage inside him. His lungs compressed, his heart tightened, and his ears began to ring. In a shattered second, the temperature of his soul had dropped ten degrees.

"Tigs," he said, breathing carefully. "That's not true."

Nolan sputtered. The grandfather clock on its lumber stilts tocked. The lights of the Polygon buzzed. The little refrigerator hummed. Together, Cyrus and Antigone were far away.

Antigone lifted her head. "You're right," she said. "This is nothing like as awful as that." She sniffed. "This is just another part of that."

The two of them sat, seeing and hearing invisible things, sharing silence.

"I miss Dan," Antigone said.

Cyrus nodded. He missed too many things. His mom's smile. Her laugh. The blackness of her hair. His father's heavy hands and thigh-thick arms that had so easily popped his ten-year-old ribs. The smell of his wind-salted skin.

Dan. Their mother might never look in Cyrus's eyes again, and his father's smile was at the bottom of the sea, but Dan would be back. He had to be. Dan gone for good would be too much. More pressure than Cyrus's lungs could fight.

He didn't want to think about it. He didn't want to care. Caring hurt. But not caring would be worse. And then his mind arrived where it always did when the deep ache got out of its cage. Death was real. It was waiting. For him and for everyone he loved and needed. In the end—in one year or in ninety—he would be alone in a cold box, silent, breathless, bloodless, listening to the slow groping of tree roots.

Stupid. He shook his head, wishing he could dig the thoughts out of his ears with his little fingers. He wondered if Antigone thought the same way he did, but he wasn't about to ask. Not ever. She cried, but she always ended with a smile. If she thought things would get better, he should keep his own sour thoughts to himself. He could put the ache back on its leash and drag it behind the old bars. He could renumb the raw, if only for a while.

Across the little room, Antigone sniffed and wiped her eyes. And she smiled.

"We'll get Dan back," she said. "Somehow."

Tight-lipped, Cyrus returned her smile. And then out in the Polygon, the door squealed open and heavy feet found the planks.

"Sir," a girl whispered. "I'd really rather not."

"Fine," a man said. The voice was Rupert's. "Just give them to me and go." The door closed. "Hello? Anyone here?"

Cyrus looked at his sister. She shrugged. "All the way back!" he yelled.

When Rupert Greeves ducked beneath the showers, his arms were stacked with folded blankets and towels, capped with three bulbous pillows. He stopped at the hole and leaned in.

"May I?" he asked Antigone.

She nodded.

He stepped inside, filling what was left of the small yellow space. He was wearing a loose linen shirt with rolled-up sleeves. The neck was unbuttoned low enough that a cluster of bulging old scars were visible on his dark chest. His brows flickered when he saw Nolan, but he focused on Cyrus and Antigone. "I brought you some things, though I see you've found some for yourselves already. Your deposit is listed as paid, but the maid service didn't want to come down. So here I am. Special delivery." He set the pile on the floor.

Antigone smiled. "Thanks."

Cyrus said nothing.

The big man eyed him, scratched his pointed beard, and then twisted his head, looking at the skull-inked photos still dangling from Antigone's fingers.

"Cy found these in Skelton's truck," she said. "Pretty sick. Take them."

Antigone handed over the pictures and watched Greeves thumb through them. He focused on each image without any reaction and then fanned all three out. Cyrus stared at the calloused and battered hands holding the photos. One of Rupert's fingernails was black with old blood.

"There were more," Cyrus said. "Other people. I only took those three."

Rupert nodded. "Unpleasant. I'll have someone collect the others."

"Unpleasant?" Cyrus snorted. "I don't know. I love having a picture of my mom with a skull drawn on her face. And the one of Dan bleeding has a nice note on the back, too."

Antigone slid to her feet. "Ignore him," she said. "It's been a rough day."

"Rough?" Cyrus asked. He wanted to be angry at Greeves, at someone, but he didn't feel up to the effort. He sighed. "That's one way to put it."

Antigone collected herself. "I have a question. Two, if that's all right. Maybe three."

"Maybe twelve," Cyrus muttered.

"Ask," said Rupert. His eyes were on Cyrus. His accented voice had grown an edge.

Antigone looked at Nolan. "You think he's going to be okay?"

Rupert nodded. "Yes. Nolan is always okay."

"Dan," Cyrus said. He had to keep his voice calm. "What are you doing to find our brother? What's happening? Where is he? What do you know?"

The big man straightened, his head nearly grazing

the ceiling. "I'm sorry I don't have better news," he said. "Maxi sent him to Phoenix, his handler. They used a small grass airstrip not far from your motel, and I have a description of their plane. But where Phoenix is right now, I cannot say. In the last ten years, I have flushed him out of dens in Paris, Miami, and Quebec. I've even put a bullet in him. He's not immortal—nor even transmortaled, I suspect—but he has some vile charm about him. Tonight, I have people and"—he paused, rubbing his jaw—"things searching for where he might be. In a few hours, I will be joining them." He raised his eyebrows, turning from Cyrus to Antigone. "What might Daniel have that Phoenix wants? Does he have any particular gifts, strengths, abilities?"

Cyrus shook his head slowly. Greeves continued. "Did Skelton give him anything before he died? The doctor always has a twisted reason for what he does. He's after something."

Antigone swung meaningful eyes onto her brother. "What's he after, Rus?"

Rupert waited. Cyrus chewed his lip. "I want to come."

Greeves crossed his thick arms. "I beg your pardon?"

"You said you were going to be looking for this Phoenix guy tonight." Cyrus cleared his throat. "I want to come. I can't stay here, sleeping in this . . . basement. I have to do something. Let me come."

Rupert Greeves leaned forward slowly until he was eye to eye with Cyrus. For a moment, the man simply stared, and Cyrus struggled not to squirm, not to blink or shuffle or look away. When Greeves finally spoke, his voice was soft. "Rightly or wrongly, you feel some guilt for this. Now, do you want to make yourself *feel* as if you are helping me find your brother, or do you want to truly help?" He didn't wait for an answer. "What does Phoenix want? Why take Daniel?"

Cyrus exhaled. "I don't even know who Phoenix is. How should I know what he wants?"

"Who is he?" Antigone blurted. "And don't say we don't need to know."

"Right," Greeves said. He ran a hand over his tightly shorn head. "Phoenix is someone I hope you never meet. In his own mind, he is the greatest of all altruists, philanthropist to the natural order, god to new races, savior to the world. In reality, he is a soul-crippled, subhuman devil of a man, part scientist, part sorcerer. He was expelled from the Order when I was young. He should be an old man now, but he still appears relatively young. I have no doubt that he robbed the collections of Ashtown before his expulsion, but there is very little order to them, and the darkest collections are sealed. Few people would miss anything. If I knew what he took, I might understand his weaknesses better. Then again, I might not. There may not be any weaknesses."

"What did he do to get kicked out?" Antigone asked.

The big man's jaw rippled, clenching. He pulled at his pointed beard. "The truth will not be reassuring. Phoenix began by secretly conducting experiments—as cruel as can be imagined—on animals in the Order's zoo. He moved quickly to working on Acolytes, staff, and poor ignorant wretches he and his friends collected from the surrounding population—pulled from farmhouses, bus stops, schools. . . ."

Rupert's scarred chest inflated. His eyes lost their focus. He was looking straight through the stone wall and into memory, seeing old horror. Cyrus glanced at his sister. Her eyes were wide, worried.

"Ten years ago," Rupert said quietly, "I found the . . . remains . . . of seven Acolytes hidden in the floor of his old rooms. I dug graves for them myself. Among the murdered was my elder brother, missing from my childhood. Also among them"—Rupert's eyes found Cyrus's, and they were heavy, glistening—"were the bodies of Harriet and Circe Smith." He turned to Antigone. "Your father's sisters."

Antigone blinked.

"What?" Cyrus said. "What? Our dad didn't have . . . How do you know?"

"Because Phoenix labeled them." Rupert's voice was cold and level, his face undisturbed. "Phoenix is why I strove to become the Avengel, and I am why he lurks in shadow, afraid to show himself. The blood of the Order that he spilled is mine to avenge. And so help me God, I will leave his lifeless body to the birds so that he might be spattered across the land. But if, through witchcraft and devilry, he now numbers among the transmortaled, I will prepare for him a place in the Burials of Ashtown, deeper in anguish than any before him."

Cyrus swallowed. Antigone slid to the back of her bench. The big man's dark eyes had become stone.

"Keys," Cyrus said quietly, and he looked down at his own toes. Rupert's eyes were too uncomfortable to meet. "Skelton gave me his keys before he died. He told me to keep them safe."

The big man breathed in slowly and turned his face up to the ceiling. "And have you?" he asked.

Cyrus was confused. "Have I what?"

"Kept the keys safe."

Cyrus nodded. "Yeah. Well, I still have them."

"And whom have you told?" Rupert asked. "Who else may know what you're carrying?"

"Just Nolan," Cyrus said. "He's the only one."

"And there were two keys?" Rupert's eyes grew even darker.

"Yeah." Cyrus nodded. "Normal-looking. Old, I guess. One is small and silver, one's longer and gold, but the gold one was just to his truck."

"Mother Mary." Rupert breathed deep and shook

his head. "Too many Skelton rumors prove to be true. No, Cyrus, the gold one was not just to his truck." He became suddenly worried. "He placed these keys in your hand? He gave them to you? You did not take them?"

Cyrus nodded.

Greeves seemed relieved. "Then Skelton has already given you more than you can imagine." He stepped toward Cyrus, blocking the ceiling lanterns with his shoulder. "With these two keys, was there anything else? Did Skelton speak to you about a tooth? Not a whole tooth. A shard? It would have been black. He might have called it a dragon's tooth."

Cyrus blinked. His neck was suddenly quite heavy.

"Reaper's Blade? Resurrection Stone? Anything like that?"

Cyrus glanced at his sister. Her eyes were wide, nervous, waiting for his decision. He looked back up at Rupert, and then he shook his head.

"Skelton didn't say anything." He swallowed. It wasn't really a lie. Skelton had been dead. Horace had done all the tooth talking.

Rupert's brows slid slowly down, and his eyes disappeared in shadow.

"Are you going to take the keys from me?" Cyrus asked quickly.

Greeves blinked, and the shadows on his face slid away in surprise. "Take them? Is that what you think of me? Cyrus, I am not a bullying thief. And if I were, Solomon Keys protect themselves. If I did force them from you, those keys would be deadly for me. For any mortal. They do not take kindly to theft. And if you gave them to me freely, they could never be returned to you. They are ancient, they are powerful, and no man living can know or understand the charms woven into them."

Cyrus burst out laughing.

Antigone, surprised, blinked daggers at him.

"I'm sorry," he said. "It's just that, well, we're talking about different keys. These are just regular old keys. They're not ancient at all."

"Where are they?" Rupert asked. He sat in the alcove across from Cyrus and leaned forward onto his knees. Seeing Cyrus hesitate, he quickly waved off his own question. "I understand your caution. The Order has not yet been kind to you. But when I am gone, test the keys and see if I am wrong. Soak them in water or try any lock you can find. Between one or the other of those keys, no door will remain closed to you." He grew suddenly stern. "But use them honestly, Cyrus Smith. Solomon Keys have made thieves of many good men, and having made them thieves, it is never long before those keys unlock a door that leads only to death."

Patricia adjusted herself invisibly on Cyrus's neck. Her cool body tickled.

Cyrus swallowed, tucking his hands beneath his legs

to keep them down. The big man's dark eyes were still on him, reading Cyrus's face.

Greeves began to stand. "I will leave you now."

"No!" Antigone yelped. "No, no!" She stopped and collected herself. "Could you tell us more about our father first, about our family? Please. We didn't even know that he had sisters. Did you know them?"

Greeves eased himself back down.

With nervous fingers, Antigone tucked her hair behind her ears. "And the guy with the tiny mustache said our dad got kicked out of this place. Why? What did he do?"

Patricia moved again, and Cyrus grabbed at her while Greeves watched his sister. For a moment, her silver body twisted in the air, and then she was gone, wrapped tightly around Cyrus's hand. The keys rested in his palm. With his free hand, he scratched at his itching neck. Tiny blisters broke beneath his nails.

Rupert glanced at him and turned back to Antigone. "Your father was expelled, yes. And yes, I knew him. And I knew his sisters."

Rupert's eyes emptied, and he stared out of the hole at the Polygon's plank pathways. His deep, accented voice rolled up quietly from his chest.

"We met when we were eight. I had just come from England for my first time. We often competed, as had our fathers and our grandfathers. We were rivals, but only until I realized that *we* were not." Greeves almost smiled. "Lawrence was not unhappy if I beat him—not if the sun shone on the waves, and the wind was kissing the water. In mood, I was a shark, he was a dolphin. And the dolphin overpowered me.

"By the age of ten, we were brothers in soul. Our families contracted the same tutors, but as we could not both be the best of the Acolytes at everything, we chose to alternate victories. He at fencing, I at shooting, he at diving, I at flying, and so on. Our tutors would have been furious if they'd known.

"When my brother and Lawrence's sisters disappeared, our bond grew even stronger. When his older brother was killed in the Congo, again we grew closer. My own parents died in a plane crash in Ethiopia. His parents died of slow grief, mourning his siblings. In a few short years, he was the beginning and end of my family, and I of his. Together, we became Journeymen and then Explorers. We walked the world searching out the deepest shadows, the darkest evils. Though we never spoke of it, I knew we were both searching for death.

"But then, more than twenty years ago, on the verge of rising to Keeper, we trekked into the mountain jungles of Guiana in northern Brazil. We barely escaped."

Cyrus watched Rupert's calloused hand reach for the open collar of his shirt and the tangled scars on his chest.

"But we did escape, and we returned to Ashtown

with many strange things. The strangest of all was your mother."

"What?" Cyrus sat up. "What do you mean?"

"Her name was Cataan—the name of her people. She became Katie to us, and bringing her back to Ashtown was a direct violation of modern Order policies. To make things worse, your father wanted to marry her. The Sages were amenable, but the Keepers absolutely refused to sanction the union. For the first time, your father and I grew apart. Lawrence defied the Order, and was befriended by other defiant elements as a result— Skelton became his confidant. He married Katie and lost everything. After centuries, the Smiths were gone from the Order. Until now."

"You're telling the truth?" Antigone asked. "This is real?"

"It is," said Greeves.

"We knew Mom was Brazilian." Antigone looked at her brother. "But I thought they met when she was a student."

"Oh, she was a student. But she's not Brazilian." Rupert rose to his feet. "She is Cataan—one of the daughters of an ancient and forgotten people. Look at your hair. Look at your skin. They are her gifts to you." He smiled and stepped toward the hole. "Good night."

"Wait," Antigone said. "Don't just leave. Can't you tell us the whole story?"

Greeves stopped, and for a moment, his pointed beard hung beneath a wide grin. "Good night," he said again, and the smile was gone. "I have a hunt to join."

Antigone jumped to her feet. "You said our dad had an older brother, too. What was his name?"

"Daniel," Rupert said. "Your uncle's name was Daniel." Ducking his shorn head out the hole, Greeves disappeared. Planks rattled beneath his weight.

"Cyrus..." Antigone turned slowly to face her brother. Her eyes were wide.

"What do you want me to say?" Cyrus asked. "No wonder that kid in the hall called us primitives."

"Should I douse the lights?" Rupert's voice echoed through the hole.

"No!" Antigone sat back down and her legs began bouncing.

"Go ahead!" Cyrus yelled.

"Fine!" Antigone yelled. "Thanks for the blankets."

The lights throughout the Polygon punched off. Only the little lanterns in the center of the small crypt remained, glowing dull orange.

The big door boomed shut.

Antigone stood and tucked a fresh pillow beneath Nolan's sweat-soaked head. Then, grabbing Cyrus by the arm, she pulled him to his feet.

Together, wordless, minds chewing, they emptied two of the other alcoves as completely and as neatly as they could. Blankets were folded. Blankets were spread. Pillows were placed, and two new beds were born. With the piles of pillows from Greeves and Nolan, cold stone became comfortable. Antigone turned off two of Nolan's three lanterns.

Out in the darkness, Whip Spiders roamed free, clicking as they crept, clattering as they fell from oiled walls. Beneath his blanket, Cyrus stared at the ceiling.

"Cy," Antigone said quietly. "We're not from California." She rolled up onto her side, facing her brother across the room. "We're from here."

Cyrus felt anger surge through him, but he clamped his mouth shut. He wanted to be tired. He didn't want to think.

"Cyrus? Seriously, two aunts, an uncle, grandparents? This is where we're supposed to be."

Cyrus forced his jaw to relax. "Night, Tigs," he said, and he turned his face to the wall.

"Cyrus, you are not going to sleep right now, and you *are* going to talk about this. This isn't a math test that you won't show me, or an English paper that—for some absurd reason—you feel the need to sink in a creek."

Nolan snored. Cyrus heard Antigone sit back up. A shoe bounced off Cyrus's shoulder blades. He didn't move.

"Will you sit up and stop acting like you do at school,

please? This is me, not some grief counselor. All this stuff . . . Cy, it changes who we are."

Cyrus pressed his forehead against the stone and let the cold tighten his skin. "No, it doesn't, Tigs. I am who I am. I'm not changing, and I'm not talking about it."

His sister sputtered and her blankets rustled. She was giving up.

"You shouldn't have lied to Greeves about the tooth. Do you even want it? What good's it going to do?"

She was right. Why did he need the tooth? For a trade? No. He'd passed on that already. Did he want to raise the dead? No. Yes. But he didn't know how he would even start. His father had been lost at sea. Beneath his blanket, he gripped the keys against his wrist. The metal sheath was warm. He clicked it open and closed his hand around the tooth. A cold current shot up through his arm. Frozen bone.

"I'll tell him," he said quietly. "Okay?"

"When?"

Cyrus inhaled slowly. "Tomorrow. Next time I see him. Good enough?"

"Tonight would have been better."

"Want me to go after him now?"

"Yeah." Antigone exhaled and began to yawn. "You do that. Fix everything. In the dark. With spiders."

She was relaxing. Her breathing evened out, blending with Nolan's.

"Night, Tigs."

"Night, Cy. Russell."

"Tigger."

He waited for the counter, but it didn't come. Antigone groaned softly. The crippled clock counted off five minutes, and then ten. Cyrus listened to its beat mingle with Nolan's painful moanings and his sister's muddled whispers. He listened to the click of spider whips and distant echoes through the stone. He slept. And he woke. And he slept again. He turned and he rolled and he tangled his feet in his blankets.

Dan was gone. Gone. And he, Cyrus, was doing nothing.

He sat up, swinging his bare feet down to the tassels of a Turkish rug.

In the dim orange light, he could see that Antigone was still. Nolan was stirring. Cyrus held his breath and waited. The boy's red welts had almost disappeared, replaced with empty blisters of scaly skin. Cyrus unwound Patricia from his wrist, and she looked at him with bright emerald eyes. In the low light, her silver body actually glowed. He stroked her head with his thumb, and she slid forward, rubbing her whole body against it.

He eased the key ring down to her tail. Solomon Keys dropped into his hand.

❧ twelve ❧

BURIAL

CYRUS DUCKED OUT of the door. Inching along the shadowy planks, he stopped at the showers. The faint glow from Nolan's lantern barely reached his feet, giving him just enough light to see what he was doing. Gripping the three charms and the key ring tight, he stuck the shafts of the two keys into the nearest falling stream of water. He could see nothing in the splashing, but his arm grew suddenly heavy. Breathing hard, he slid back from the edge and looked at the keys in his hand.

Greeves hadn't lied.

One gold, one silver, but shaped like no keys he had ever seen, and heavier than they had any right to be. The gold one had a hollow triangle at its head, a square in its center, and a circle at its end. Smooth teeth lined its shaft on every side. The silver one was thin and bent like an elongated and slightly corkscrewing crescent moon. Some kind of writing, shaped like Arabic, had been etched into its surface, but Cyrus wasn't going back to the light for a closer look.

Dropping the heavy keys into his pocket, he made his way into the deep blackness of the Polygon.

Once Cyrus had managed to open the door and hop barefoot over the flooded threshold, he had enough nervous energy to rush the stairs, skipping slippery steps as he went. The hallway above was dimly lit, and he found his way quickly back into the big blue-glowing room beneath the water maze. From there, rather than trying to retrace Mrs. Eldridge's route, he headed for the iron spiral stairs he'd seen earlier, cobwebbed into a dark corner. His bare feet scuffed through heavy dust on the cold stone floor and found the metal stairs. The treads were rough with rust blisters, and Cyrus climbed slowly, his heart pounding against his molars.

He wound his way above the thick glass ceiling and into a tall shaft. Two of the walls were glass, with views into the maze, and the higher Cyrus climbed, the more terrifying the maze became. It was as tall as it had been wide—a full cube—with underwater tunnels tangled in an impossible three-dimensional knot of drowning potential.

Cyrus reached the top and stepped out into a high-ceilinged room with a single dangling light in its center, glowing like the moon. The floor was tiled around the edges, but the entire center was glass, sealing the water maze in all but two small open hatches in opposite corners—an entrance and an exit, with a whole lot of wet death in between.

Cyrus moved toward the closer one, trying to imagine what it would be like to drop in and swim into total confusion. The water rippled slightly at his feet, and his chest tightened. What would it feel like to have panicked lungs fill with water? His father knew.

Something moved beneath the glass. A quick shadow. And then water erupted at Cyrus's feet, and arms slapped at the tiled edge. Cyrus yelled, jumped backward, slipped, and sat down. Puddles raced toward him, and he scrambled up onto his feet.

Gasping, Diana Boone pulled herself up out of the maze and rolled onto her back. She was wearing a black suit with leggings that reached her ankles, but her tan arms and freckled shoulders were bare. The stitches were gone from the gash at the base of her neck. Spitting to the side, she reached up and pulled her hair loose from its ponytail.

"You okay?" Cyrus asked.

Startled, Diana twisted around, and then sat up. Still panting, she smiled and nodded. "What are you doing here?"

Cyrus shrugged. "Just looking around."

Diana stood up and began wringing her hair out over her shoulder. "Well, be careful. Rupe has beefed up security. Acolytes are supposed to be in quarters, but especially you."

"What? Why?"

Diana's eyes widened. "You have to know. Rupe

242

called a big meeting, Keepers and Explorers together." She paused, and her voice softened. "He said that Phoenix is after you and that he already has your older brother. I'm really sorry."

Cyrus swallowed and then nodded. He wasn't sure what to say.

Diana stepped toward him. "Rupe even tried to put us on gun-ready—sidearms at all times. He thinks Maxi might try to drop in. Cecil put a stop to that, but a lot of people will still be carrying. I would if I were you. And not just because of Maxi. Some of the Keepers are possum-scared and some are hornet-mad. They'd throw anyone overboard if it kept Phoenix away."

She rubbed her wound, thinking. "Keep a special eye on the guardsmen and groundskeepers. They're all working off demotions or debts—by far the surliest." She looked at Cyrus's bare feet in the puddle she'd made, and then back up at his face. "I need to go, and so should you. I'm in on a few flights tonight."

Cyrus watched Diana collect a small bundle of clothes along with a large, holstered revolver. She looked back at him when she reached a swinging locker room door.

"You're not heading back to your room, are you?"

Cyrus shook his head.

Diana laughed. "You really are a Smith. You know, my dad knew yours. I've heard the stories."

The door swung, and Diana Boone was gone.

Cyrus looked around. The room held what looked like another locker room door and then two big wooden doors set into arches on opposite ends. He hurried for the closer one and tugged it open on quiet hinges. Stone stairs led straight up, and he jogged them quickly while the door closed behind him. At the top, he followed a hallway around two corners and then paused. He'd reached a covered stone sky bridge lined with windows on both sides. Out one side, he could see the great lawn, the lit fountain, and a small group of men moving around with rifles. Out the other side, a half-moon hung between jutting statues on the high roofline of the main building, a chewed pearl stuck in some monstrous jaw.

Cyrus hurried across the bridge and banged into a locked door hidden in shadow.

"Darn it." He turned around. Back to the water maze? The heavy keys were pressing against his hip. Digging them out quickly, he faced the door.

"Don't worry," Cyrus said quietly. Antigone was asleep and nowhere near, but he could still hear her worry in his head. "I'm not going to steal anything."

Behind Cyrus, moonlight sprayed through the windows, but in front of him the door was in total shadow. He felt for a keyhole, but he couldn't even find a knob.

Cyrus tucked the key ring into his mouth. Then he

unwound Patricia and held her next to the door, her silver body pooling light on the dark wood. The keyhole was set exactly in the middle, but Patricia quickly ate her own tail and disappeared.

"C'mon." Cyrus unwound Patricia again. Her emerald eyes stared at him. Her mouth opened, and her tail flicked up.

"Uh-uh," Cyrus said. Before he could think, he popped the tip of his forefinger into her mouth. She hesitated, looking at him, and then she slid herself up past his first knuckle and wrapped her body tight around his fingers.

Cyrus laughed, spitting the keys down into his free palm. "I hope you come off just as easy." He held his snaked hand up to the door and looked at the keyhole. It wasn't small. He slid the gold key in easily and felt the metal change in his hand. He turned the key. Inside the door, a latch clicked. Cyrus pulled what was now a plain gold skeleton key out of the hole, glanced at it, dropped it into his pocket, and pushed open the door.

Holding Patricia up in front of him, Cyrus moved into a narrow arched hallway. Small doors pocked the walls. Stone faces, part bust, part gargoyle, looked down at him from the ceiling. Light glowed beneath one of the doors, and he could hear the low mumble of voices.

Cyrus hurried forward. Beside a large tapestry of a woman decapitating a unicorn, the hallway ended in a tight stone spiral stair. Up or down? Cyrus went down, moving in Patricia's faint silver light.

At the bottom, he entered an undecorated hallway. The ceiling was higher and the hall was longer, but there were only two facing doors. Both were black riveted steel. One had been left open.

Listening to his drumming pulse, Cyrus stared at it. He could hear footsteps. He saw flashlights. Tugging his finger out of Patricia's mouth, he jumped backward into the shadow of the spiral stairs.

Exhaling and biting his tongue, Cyrus leaned his head into the hallway. Two men, nothing but shapes behind their flashlights, stood at the open door.

"I don't care," one of them said. "He can't make us open it. We checked the lock and that's that. If Rupe wants to check the inside of a Burial, he can do it himself. I might be stuck as a watchman for the next two months, but I'm not the bloody Avengel."

The other man spoke, but his voice was too low to make out, swallowed by whispering echoes. Cyrus slid forward.

"Can't see the fuss of it all," the first one said. "Double guards and Burial checking? Does he think old Rasputin's gonna up and walk away? And what exactly am I gonna do if he does? Or Tamerlane? I'd like to see the two of us put that one back to bed."

The black door boomed shut behind them, and

flashlights flicked in both directions. "Who's Rupe protecting anyhow? Skelton's mutts? And for what? They'll be twice the trouble he was—there being two of them—and it's Billy's own outlaw friends that have Rupe sweating." The man snorted and then shivered loudly. "Truth? Run me into that nightmare Maxi, and I'd hand those two Smiths right over—with Parmesan, too, and an offer to grind the pepper. And Phoenix is worse than worse. Will you be dying for those two?"

"No, sir," said the second man. "Leave the dying to Rupe."

The men had turned and were walking away, voices fading with their footsteps.

Cyrus stepped into the dark hallway. When it was as silent as it was dark, he found Patricia's head and popped his finger back in her mouth. She didn't even seem surprised, sliding all the way up to the second knuckle. Holding his coiled silver light above his head, Cyrus moved slowly to the big black door. He slid his hand over the cold, rivet-puckered steel and found a single star-shaped keyhole beneath a heavy ring.

He looked around. Why not? Rupert had basically told him to test the keys. He breathed slowly, trying to quiet his pulse. His muscles were tightening—he felt just like he had before he'd climbed onto the roof of his school with a bucket of water balloons. Antigone would hate this. Dan would yell at him. He had no endgame at all. The principal would ask him exactly what he had been thinking, and there would be no answer. But still . . . he dug out his keys. The gold one was too big. The silver one slid in easily, became a starred shaft, and turned.

Beneath his hand, Cyrus felt a quiet series of shafts sliding and tumblers tumbling. And then, nothing. He removed the key, and the heavy iron ring on the door sighed when Cyrus lifted it. The door swung in. Cold breath crawled out of the darkness and into Cyrus's lungs.

Cyrus stepped forward. The floor was colder beneath his bare feet, and his faint silver light didn't seem to penetrate the darkness beyond the door. He moved all the way in.

The room was an empty cube, entirely lined with the same black riveted steel as the door. Cyrus stretched his lit hand from side to side, to the ceiling, to the floor, straining his eyes. The floor in the center of the room was patterned—a small circle surrounded by a large ring of flat steel petals, like a black armored sunburst. In the very center, there was a keyhole. Cyrus moved toward it, easing his bare feet onto the broad steel petals. They were the source of the cold, and for a moment, he thought his feet would freeze in place. He knelt and inched forward on his knees, breathing hard.

"What do you think, Patricia?" Cyrus whispered. He

was already pulling out his keys. His legs were frozen, his hands were almost pale. The gold key slid down into the floor. But he didn't turn it. He looked over his shoulder at the door and listened for footsteps. Nothing. He should go back. But retreating now would only mean coming back again later. Tomorrow. Next week. He wouldn't be able to leave it alone. Not for long.

Cyrus shivered. He was here now. . . .

Bracing himself, Cyrus turned the key, and the floor began to fall away beneath him. Jerking the key back out, he dove onto his side, rolling clear of the growing hole. Steel whispered to steel as the petals dropped to form another spiral stair. Cyrus scrambled to his feet. Frigid air rolled across the floor, and pale-blue light flickered on the ceiling above the shaft.

"Right," Cyrus said, and he moved to the stairs. Patricia tightened on his fingers. He knew what he was doing. Maybe. This had to be one of the Burials. There could be a dead body at the bottom—maybe a frozen body. Maybe two. But whatever it was, he was going to see it. He was going to go down even if it froze his feet off.

Why? He could hear Antigone's frantic, absent objection. *You can't. You shouldn't. Don't!*

Cyrus bit his lip and inched forward. Why? Why had he gone through every room in the Archer, opening every drawer, every closet, and lifting every mattress?

Why had he pulled tires from streams and wormed beneath the floorboards of barns and climbed into the ceiling of his mother's hospital room?

Because he needed to.

As he descended into the cold blue light, Cyrus clutched Patricia's body as tightly as she clutched him. Green mixed with blue, flickering like fire. But it couldn't be fire. The colors were wrong. And it was cold.

Around each step, Cyrus expected to see the source of the light. But around each step, he found only more steps. The steel ran out and became stone. Another slow turn and his feet splashed into moving water. Cyrus didn't even notice.

In front of him, a large room was full of fast water, swirling in a whirlpool that reached every wall. Down in the whirlpool's mouth, before it became a throat, there was a nest of icy blue-and-green flame. In the center of that nest, a black stone column ran down out of sight. On top of the column, a man sat with his legs crossed. Cyrus could see the thick iron bands that clamped his crossed legs to the stone. But he could not see the man's arms. Fifty feet—at least—of brown beard and hair had tangled around his shoulders and arms and was stretched out in the swirling water like seaweed, even reaching the walls. The man's face was oddly peaceful, even noble. He looked like he was lost in some distant, slow-moving dream, or was savoring the warm crawl of a summer breeze on his face—as if his surroundings, the water, the stone, the cold fire and iron bands, were all illusion. His eyes were closed, and his skin was translucent white. In the center of his forehead, there was a brutal hole the size of a bullet.

While Cyrus stared, the flames between him and the man receded slightly. Something liquid, something warm and alive, reached into him. He could feel it racing in his veins. His jaw locked, and every hair on his body stood up and screamed.

Kill me.

He heard the voice, but the man on the column had not moved. His eyes were still closed.

The Reaper's Blade. Come. Cut me loose from this flesh.

Cyrus's right foot slid forward and down a step, deeper into the rushing water. What was he doing? He tried to jerk his foot back. He tried to pull himself away. His other foot was moving forward. The flames shrunk further.

I can live in you—

In a rush, the flames rebounded, roaring to the ceiling. The voice was gone, ripped from Cyrus like his own gut. Gulping, gasping for breath, Cyrus fell backward onto the stairs.

As the flames receded to their original height, the bearded man raised his head slowly, opened his eyes, and looked into Cyrus's.

Crab-crawling frantically, Cyrus made it up around the first bend and out of sight. Coughing, still fighting for breath, he rolled onto his knees, scrambled to his feet, raced up the stairs, and tumbled out onto the steel floor. Then he crawled back to the keyhole, slid in the gold key with a shaking hand, and managed to twist before he dropped onto his face. The stairs rose slowly back up into the floor.

His hands were twitching. His stomach, knotted in fear, was loosening into nausea. His face, pressed against the icy steel floor, still dripped with sweat. Patricia stared at him from around his finger. She'd loosened her grip, but his finger was stinging. She might have bitten him.

"I'm sorry," Cyrus mumbled. "I'll listen to you next time."

He forced himself up. He needed to get out. Now.

He managed to pull the big door closed quietly, and made sure that it had locked. Then he staggered for his little spiral stairs and the long trek home.

He stopped. Voices. Laughter rolled out of the stairwell. Flashlights.

No. Cyrus spun around. No, no, no.

He ran down the length of the hallway on boiled legs, rounded a corner, sprinted another length, and dead-ended at a door. Not locked. He didn't need the keys. Dropping them into his pocket, he slipped carefully through onto a cold marble floor. Another hallway, this one with sconces on crowded walls, burning low enough that the paintings and maps were mere shapes in shadow. He popped the still-glowing Patricia off his finger and raised her to his neck.

Beneath his bare feet, the floor became rough with mosaic.

A final corner and he knew where he was. He had reached the main hallway—big leather boat, reptilian skin, fresco-mapped ceilings and mosaic-mapped floors, all sleeping in shadow. He slowed down. Two chatting watchmen disappeared through a distant door.

Cyrus could see the entrance to the Galleria. Another fifty yards and he would be at the dining hall. Through the dining hall and he would reach the kitchen.

Food. At the suggestion, his body roared to life with complaints. He needed something to settle his stomach and refill his veins, something to take the wobble out of his legs and the panic out of his mind. He needed something to make him stop shivering and shaking. Then he could start his trek back.

Battling to keep his breathing low and his feet from slapping, he jogged close to the wall around statues and tables and tusked skulls.

He reached the dining hall and ducked out of dimness, through swinging doors, and into black nothing. He had only ever seen the space from behind a heating grate, not well enough to pass through it blind, but he didn't bother Patricia again. Pausing inside the doors, his wide eyes strained for the faintest dusting of light. His pulse thundered, his ears rang, and the dim outline of a door appeared in the distance.

A plane passed overhead.

Cyrus felt his way through a graveyard of tables, burdened with upside-down chairs, bumping and adjusting his course until he finally reached the kitchen door and pushed it open on tired hinges.

Fire Island was dormant. The wall of copper kettles, pots, and skillets was fully armored. Beyond the wall of windows, a swollen half-moon skunk-striped the black lake. Harbored boats rocked naked masts. Flashlights and colored wands bobbed around the airfield. A plane, twin engines whining, passed by the windows, eased itself away from the earth, and disappeared.

In the kitchen, only one small, elbowed lamp was lit beside a large pot—a copper vat—squatting on a low-flame burner near the windows. Spices, bottles, and a tub of molasses were scattered around it.

Cyrus rounded the island and approached the light. Steam was rising from the pot, and so was a smell to melt his heart. Barbecue sauce. It had to be. And stronger than most. Cyrus's mouth was suddenly liquid. Dan had tried to barbecue at first, but only ever with bottles of store sauce, and not for a while. Meat was expensive.

This simmering joy was different. This would be sauce like his father's had been—or better.

Inhaling slowly, Cyrus rose onto his toes and examined the thick brown surface inside the pot. A slow bubble grew and burst, releasing spiced breath from the depths. He couldn't resist. Cyrus tapped the side of the pot, testing for heat, and then dipped his finger. Hot. Perfect. He raised it to his mouth.

A hairy fist clamped onto his wrist and spun him around. Big Ben Sterling loomed above him.

"What thief is this?" the cook asked.

"I—I'm sorry," Cyrus stammered. "I—You said—"

"Cyrus Smith, is it?" The cook scratched his unnetted beard. The very tip was tied tight with a small pink ribbon. Sterling grinned. "Ben did tell you to help yourself, didn't he? Well, not to this." He looked at the pot. "This needs testing, and that's a job for the vice-cook."

Grabbing a rag, he swabbed Cyrus's finger clean.

"I'm sorry," Cyrus said again. "It smells really good."

"That it does, lad," Sterling said. "But smell is only the beginning." Releasing Cyrus's wrist, he stepped back, and his thin metal legs were invisible in the darkness. He looked like a huge man levitating on his knees. The bells were missing from his ears. "Now tell me why Cyrus Smith is out wandering the night's middle while the Keepers are all in a beer froth about his safety?"

Another plane rattled the windows. Cyrus looked

back over his shoulder, watching its wing lights disappear. He felt dizzy, and his legs were weak.

"I just . . ." He paused. "I couldn't sleep."

Sterling tugged on his beard and lowered his brows. "And you look to have had a fright, too. Well, frights are easy things to find in Ashtown." He slapped Cyrus on the shoulder and winked. "Lad, if it's your brother you're frettin' about, Rupert Greeves is the bloodiest of bloodhounds. He gets his man, don't you worry about that." He nodded out the window. "He'll be running planes till the sun rises, no matter who's complaining. You rest easy. He'll find what's there to be found."

"What are they looking for?" Cyrus asked. "What can you see from a plane at night?"

"Oh, they're not looking out the windows," Sterling said. "Rupert will have his hunters out."

"Hunters?" Cyrus looked out the window. "Hunters, like people, or like . . . things?"

Sterling laughed. "Things. The planes just follow along like horses behind the hounds. Hold on now, lad."

The cook bounced slowly toward a pantry and returned with a cloth napkin. He held it out to Cyrus. A hunk of cold chicken sat in its center, coated with a skin of spiced molasses.

Laughter wandered into the kitchen. Sterling slapped the chicken into Cyrus's hand, grabbed his shoulders, and pointed him toward the dining hall.

"Get on now, quick. I don't want to be explaining you to the watchmen, not in the mood they're in. Back through the dining hall, and quietly, too."

Cyrus hurried to the door. The laughter was growing louder. "Thanks," he whispered, and the legless cook saluted.

Thirty-two minutes later, a relieved Cyrus stepped into orange light and the sound of two breathing sleepers beside a tocking grandfather clock. He'd been lost and found and lost again, but he'd found his way in the end, and without getting caught. And he'd be able to do it again.

With chicken in his teeth and the sound of airplanes in his ears, he slid beneath his blankets. Sleep was waiting for him, soft and swift.

Cyrus flew in his dreams. He flew all the way back to the sea, back in time, back to a cold night on the north coast of California with the moon sliding low beneath broken clouds. He flew down beneath the cliffs, above thundering winter surf and into a red station wagon sitting on the sand. There he shivered with his sister and his brother while his mother stammered quick prayers in a language he didn't understand. He watched distant rocks and the lights on the small boat when they disappeared forever. He watched his mother plunge into the midnight water and strike out into the surf. He heard Dan yelling, calling for her. Splashing. Searching.

• • •

Daniel Smith opened his eyes. His throat was desert-dry and desert-hot. He blinked, and the world hardened a little, regrowing its edges. He squeezed his eyes tight and tried opening them again. This time, he could see a blue curtain partitioning his bed from the rest of the room. Was he in a hospital? What had happened? The fire? The smoke? He remembered the fire trucks leaving before dawn. He remembered Cyrus and Antigone unconscious across his bed.

He had been standing in the parking lot, alone with the Golden Lady, staring at the ruins of his life. And there had been . . . a man. With very worn teeth. And knives.

He tried to sit up. An invisible weight on his chest crushed the breath out of him, pinning him down.

Cold fingers stroked his cheek. Dan flinched, twisting his head to the side.

An extremely thin man seated next to Dan's bed withdrew his hand. He was wearing a jarringly white suit and vest beneath what looked like a tattered and stained lab coat. His thick black hair was slicked into heavy curls at the back and shone like polished wax. His needle-sharp eyes were as pale as blue pearls.

The man smiled slowly, folding long, tight lines into his cheeks. His teeth were whiter than his suit, and a large gap in the front punctuated his smile like an exclamation mark. "Mr. Smith," the man said, his voice crawling out slowly in a musical drawl. "Welcome to my home. I apologize for your unconsciousness, and for any pain you may have been caused. My name is Dr. Edwin Phoenix, and I do hope we can be friends. There's just so much I can do for you and for yours."

He leaned forward and turned Daniel's head to the right.

"If we're friendly, that is."

Another bed was just beside Dan's. His mother, breathing softly, as peacefully unconscious as she had been for the past two years, was propped up on pillows.

Phoenix sat back, his smile shrinking. "Are you my friend, Daniel Smith? Do please say yes."

Dan tried to kick but only managed to wiggle his toes. He tried to roll, but his shoulders wouldn't come off the mattress. Sweat beaded on his forehead and dripped into his eyes. The man stood and leaned his thin body over the bed, eyes locked on Dan's.

"Don't rush your answer, now." He pressed cold lips against Dan's forehead, then straightened and turned away.

Anger and panic inflated Dan's veins. A roar filled his lungs, but it rose from his chest as silent as a breath.

Cyrus Smith jerked, opening his sleep-clouded eyes. He blinked, his mind still half-dreaming. In the doorway, Nolan was writhing, jerking at his skin, scraping his naked body with a knife, peeling off translucent sheets, stepping out of his legs like reptilian socks. The skin, empty and weightless, floated out to the clattering spiders.

Cyrus closed his eyes, and he was running through deep, cool sand toward two unconscious bodies stretched out on the beach—his brother beside his mother.

⇒ζ thirteen ζ⇐

TOOTH TALES

YAWNING, CYRUS KICKED his blankets to the floor as he stretched. His legs flexed and shook. His hands pressed against cold stone. Stone? In the Archer?

Cyrus sat bolt upright.

Antigone was facing him, sitting stiffly on her own stone bed. She tapped the bridge of her nose.

"You have some goop."

Cyrus slapped at his face and then ground his knuckles into his eyes.

The lights were on in the Polygon, and Nolan was missing. His blanket was folded neatly and his pillow was perched on top of it. Antigone's black hair was freshly wet and pulled back tight. Her eyes were tired. She already had on her riding boots, and her ragged safari shirt was tucked in. A piece of paper and the *Order of Brendan, Guidelines for Acolytes, Ashtown Estate, 1910–1914* sat open beside her.

"We're done for, Rusty," she said. "Listen to this."

Cyrus yawned again. His sister picked up the booklet.

"Are you listening?"

Cyrus nodded.

"'In order to achieve the rank of Journeyman, Acolytes must be tested in the following areas before the end of the year in which they were presented: Linguistic: Competency in one ancient language and one modern (in addition to their mother tongue) is required. Celestial Navigation: Acolytes must complete a three-day open-sea voyage without instruments (may be tested in pairs). Weaponry: Acolytes must achieve the rank of Free Scholar with dagger, foil, and saber, and the rank of Marksman with small-caliber pistol and rifle. Aerocraft: Acolytes must complete pilot qualification in the Bristol Scout biplane or comparable (to include advanced maneuvers and solo flight). Medicinal: Acolytes must be competent in the diagnosis and herbal treatment of infectious disease, the resuscitation of the drowned, the setting of bones, and the amputation of limbs.'"

Antigone looked up at her brother. His eyes and mouth were wide. "Yeah," Antigone said, nodding. "The amputation of limbs. And that's not all. 'Physical Fitness: Apart from specific exclusions granted by the community of Keepers, Acolytes must be capable of running a grass-track mile in under six and one-half minutes, submerging for a duration greater than two and one-quarter minutes, and free diving to a depth of ninety feet. Zoology: Acolytes must show themselves capable of handling creatures of at least five distinct and deadly species. The Occult: Acolytes must demonstrate themselves to be impervious to hypnosis and intrusive telepathy.'"

Antigone sighed and spread the open booklet over her knee. "Should we go home now or wait until they kick us out?"

Cyrus tried to clear his sinuses and ran a hand through his matted hair. "Look on the bright side, Tigs."

"What bright side would that be, Brother Optimist? I have to learn how to amputate a limb. And shoot a gun. And they want us to fly a plane? That has to be illegal. So please, share with me the sunny bright side."

"No math," Cyrus yawned. "As long as there's no math, I'm fine."

Antigone burst out laughing. "Cyrus Lawrence Smith! How deluded can a kid be?"

"Who's the kid? And I can be as deluded as I need to be. Everything gets harder if you start going on and on about how hard it is. This will be tough enough without you giving up beforehand."

"Cyrus," Antigone said. "You've always hated school."

"Yeah," said Cyrus. "What's your point? This isn't school. We decided to come here for a reason, Tigs. Because we came here, Rupert Greeves is trying to find Dan. He *will* find Dan. And after Dan comes back, we're going to stay here until we learn how to do all those things you just read, and then we get Skelton's estate, and then we're going to buy a big house in California right on the cliffs, and we're going to move back to the ocean and not worry about money and never eat waffles again." He smiled. "Plus, you have to admit it would be pretty cool if we could actually do all those things. Flying planes? We'd be like, I don't know . . ."

"Journeymen in the Order of Brendan?"

"I was going to say ninjas. But you're right. And we'd be the hardcore 1914 version, the kind that live in the Polygon—the Polygoners."

"You really think we can do this?" Antigone's eyebrows reached maximum arch. "We're going to learn languages and fencing and free diving and flying?"

Cyrus flopped back onto his bed. "And we'll amputate limbs. I wonder how you practice that? And we have until New Year's. That's practically forever."

"Right." Antigone puffed her cheeks. "Practically."

Cyrus laughed. "And maybe Christmas will distract everyone and they won't notice that we haven't learned anything. And if that doesn't work, we can always be squatters down here with Nolan. Where *is* Nolan?"

Antigone stood up. "I don't know. But I want breakfast and a toothbrush and a bathroom, and I want some different clothes, and I want to know where the laundry is. And I want to know what Rupert found out about Dan. And I want to find out when we can visit Mom."

She tucked the tutor list and the *Guidelines* into her pocket, and walked out into the big room.

"Come on, Cy. You're dressed already."

When they finally reached the great hallway outside the Galleria, Cyrus stopped, yawning desperately and rubbing his head. His hair was sticking straight out in back like the feathers on a duck's butt, and it felt just as oily and water-resistant. But he didn't care. He just wanted to curl up against a wall and go to sleep. Antigone tugged on his arm and kept him moving.

He watched the mapped ceilings go by, bumping into people and muttering apologies, but when they passed the leather boat on its pedestal, his eyes drifted to the corridor that he knew led to another hallway and two big black doors and a man on a column with a hole in his head. The whole thing felt like a strange dream, and for a moment, he wondered if he should tell his sister about what he'd seen. But only for a moment.

The hallway was crowded, and Antigone was moving slowly in front of him. Most of the people were heading in the same direction—toward the dining hall. But a fair number were leaving—women chewing muffins and carrying fencing sabers, men in flight suits munching bacon, teams of boys and girls in white.

Everywhere, Cyrus saw guns on hips. All the passing people looked at Cyrus, at his face and his hair, and all of them smiled.

From down the hall, small bells began to ring, echoing from every wall. The river of people paused and separated. Antigone saw her chance.

Dropping her shoulder, she forced her way into the opening channel in the middle of the hall. With Cyrus jogging behind her, she hurried around the corner and straight toward the dining hall doors. Thirty feet away, a line of monks was coming in the other direction. Ten men in brown rope-belted robes paced in time, chanting something in a strange language. The second man in line was ringing the small bells. A bald, fat-faced man in the very front held a long, thick green bamboo rod, using it to slap at any feet or hands or thighs that encroached into the monks' center path. Looking up, he saw Cyrus and Antigone, and his small eyes lit up.

"C'mon!" Antigone grabbed her brother's arm and raced toward the door.

Spitting unintelligible wrath, the thick monk hustle-shuffled to beat them.

Antigone reached the doors and blasted through. The monk, shouting, jumped after her, knocking Cyrus away. The clatter and chatter in the dining hall died as every head turned.

The monk grabbed Antigone by the back of the

shirt, raised his bamboo rod, and lashed it down across her neck.

Cyrus saw the first blow, he saw his sister drop to her knees, and the last vapor of sleep steamed out of him.

"*Porca spurca!*" the monk screamed, and he raised his rod again, but Cyrus was already above his sister. He took the next blow across his raised forearm, feeling nothing but the heat of his own anger. The monk struck again, this time at his ribs.

The bamboo bounced off his side, and Cyrus kicked hard for the monk's groin, sinking his foot deep into a low-hanging belly instead.

The monk gasped, doubling over, breathless.

Cyrus jumped for the bamboo, wrenching it free with both hands. As shocked monks peered through the doors and hundreds of breakfasters watched in openmouthed silence, Cyrus raised the bamboo rod like a baseball bat. The wheezing monk's head bobbed in front of him like a piñata. Cyrus hesitated. Then, sliding his hands apart, he brought the rod down over his own knee.

It snapped easily. Two feet of green bamboo jumped free, spinning across the room, clattering onto a platter of sausage.

The monk dropped to the floor.

Cyrus, seething, teeth clenched, stepped over the whimpering monk with what remained of his bamboo club raised.

"You don't ever touch my sister," he said. "Ever."

He looked at the rest of the monks and then threw the broken rod at their feet.

"Cy, c'mon." Antigone was on her feet, one hand on her neck, tugging her brother from behind.

Cyrus turned. Hundreds of eyes were on him. Some had jumped from their seats, but the fight had been over too quickly for them to intervene. Now they sat slowly.

Standing by the kitchen door in a white suit, Cecil Rhodes grinned and mock-applauded.

Antigone steered Cyrus toward the buffet line. A chubby man in front, wearing a too-small leather flight jacket, stepped away to let them in, staring at the ceiling the whole time, refusing eye contact.

Flustered, Antigone handed Cyrus a plate and grabbed one for herself. A long red welt stood out on her neck. Cyrus eyed the crowd, beginning to eat again.

"We came to eat, Cy, and we're going to eat. I don't care what they think." She knocked the bamboo out of the sausage and shoveled a pile onto Cyrus's plate. "Thanks, though." She smiled and lowered her voice to a whisper. "You just beat down on a monk."

Cyrus set down his plate and rubbed his forearm. The anger was fading, replaced with pain. He grinned at his sister. "That wasn't me. I'm not a morning person. There's another person inside me that does all the morning things."

"No," said Antigone. "The scary part is, I think the morning you is the real you. The older you get, the more that will be you all the time."

"Oh, gosh," said Cyrus. "I hope not. The morning me is always either angry or tired."

With loaded plates, they turned to find a table. The nearest one, surrounded by girls in white workout wear, immediately emptied.

Antigone and Cyrus sat down.

Working on his first sausage, Cyrus looked around the room. The monks were back, and they'd brought Rupert. They were pointing at him.

Rupert Greeves moved toward them with long strides. He didn't look happy.

"And . . . darn it," said Cyrus. "Tigs."

Antigone looked up as Greeves reached them. With two big hands, he pulled them up to their feet and leaned his head down between theirs. His whisper was thick and smelled of breakfast.

"That, Cyrus, is not exactly how I want these things dealt with in future. And, Antigone, please do not race the monks unless you intend to lose. You have both made my job more difficult. Leave your plates. Go into the kitchen and eat something there. I'll feel better when you're out of this room."

He straightened and slapped their backs. "Kitchen duty," he said loudly. While smiles spread and whispers were passed from table to table, he turned and hurried back out of the dining hall.

Cyrus looked at Antigone. She shrugged, and together, they made their way to the swinging door and walked into the sounds of a kitchen waging war on a thousand eggs.

Big Ben Sterling whistled at them, wiping floured hands on his apron. Behind him, on the other side of the wall of windows, clouds were building towers while wind frothed the lake. Sterling waved them toward two empty stools near their spot from the night before, and he lumbered to meet them.

Before they'd reached the stools, his heavy hands gripped their shoulders and his netted beard slid down between their heads. A gold bell grazed Cyrus's cheek, jingling in his ear. Springs creaked in metal legs.

"Good to see you're still alive," he said. His breath was sweet. "But you'll need food if you're to survive a second day in Ashtown."

The big cook forced them onto stools while young men and women in white rushed by with trays. Sterling stopped a girl, robbed her of two plates, and slapped them down on the table in front of Cyrus and Antigone. Fried eggs. Ham. Toast.

Cyrus dug in happily. Antigone buttered a piece of toast.

"Strange times for you two," Sterling said. "And

for the rest of us. Keep your strength up, and no more fiddling about with monks. Choose your battles while you still can. Soon enough, they'll be choosing you."

Sterling leaned onto the table beside them. He lowered his voice. "Big Ben Sterling isn't having a laugh now. Last night, the vice-cook was killed by an intruder. Greeves found him drowndead in the harbor. He's spent the morning storming about like the world's largest wet wasp." He nodded back at the dining hall. "There are plenty in there that think you're not worth the trouble."

He eyed them both. Cyrus stopped chewing. Antigone dropped her toast. "But you are worth it, aren't you? The kitchen knows you are." His voice sank even lower. "Hear this, Smithlings: People say old Bones carried a pair of keys on a ring. People are wondering where those keys might be. And they're thinking, well, Skelton was killed in your motel—God rest his dirty soul. John Horace Lawney caught himself a bullet getting the pair of you here. You two are candles lit for trouble's moths, and the kitchen knows why."

He smiled and raised his thick eyebrows above friendly eyes. "Phoenix hasn't got the keys, nor has that bone-chewing stooge, Maxi. If he did, he wouldn't care one wormed apple for you two. But you see, I know it's more than just keys that's lighting this fire. Before his death, whisper was that Bones was holding a set of triplets—relics rarer than a butcher's fresh cut." Reaching up, he tapped the bell on his right ear. "A tidal pearl, I heard." He tapped his left ear. "Bark of a truth tree." He leaned all the way forward and his eyes bounced between them. "A Resurrection Stone."

"What?" Antigone asked. "Are we supposed to know what that is?"

Big Ben Sterling curled back his lips and clicked his jaw. "The Soul Knife. The Reaper's Blade. Old Draco's Crown—the Dragon's Tooth. In the chapel, you'll find brass plates scratched with the names of the O of B's dead from each of the World Wars. You'll find newer plates listing the thousands lost at sea, lost on land, and fallen from the sky just in my own lifetime. Those lists run long and sorrowful, but another plate could hang just as long, etched with the names of those who died questing and feuding for that Dragon's Tooth.

"Keepers and Explorers have died for it, murdered for it, betrayed for it, sold their souls and been damned to the Burials for it." He paused. "Billy Bones found it. Or so the little birds began whispering two years back. This world has a nest of secrets, but there can't be many that Phoenix wants his claw hands on more than that little chip of death. If I were a betting man, and I am, I'd put my vice-cook's name right on that brass list of dead, just beneath William Skelton's. And those keys, well, I might have just heard some Keepers whispering about doors being opened in the night that should have been closed."

Antigone glanced at her brother. Cyrus swallowed. His hand floated up toward his neck and stopped. He could feel Patricia, but the weight of the keys was gone. His hand dropped. He'd slept with them in his pocket, but he couldn't feel them against his leg. Sterling's eyes were on him. He couldn't reach for his pocket now. Scooping up eggs, he loaded his cheeks.

"Mr. Cyrus," said the cook. "Miss Antigone. You can trust Ben Sterling. I was a friend to your father and he to me. I even taught your mother a few of the kitchen's ways, and that's not something that's happened for another. Time may come when you two need a friend who can keep a secret. If you do, Ben Sterling will be standing there, just like he always was for your father."

Cyrus slid his hand down to his leg and looked at his sister. He could feel chilly sweat beading on his forehead. He groped his legs, but the only lump was a little square that he knew was holding a beetle. Antigone was staring at him, her eyes widening.

"Something wrong, Mr. Cyrus? Egg too slippy?"

"No." Cyrus was forcing himself to breathe slowly. "No."

Antigone spun back to the cook. "What is that thing, the tooth, even supposed to do?" Her voice was pitched too high. She knew something was wrong.

Cyrus shoved his hand into his pocket, but he already knew the keys were gone. The lightning bug glass buzzed his fingers as he searched around it.

Ben Sterling turned back to Antigone, scratching his beard. "I couldn't say—not being a wizard, an angel, a demon, or a man of science. I'm just a cook missing his legs and making do with a pair of delicate ears."

Hesitating, Sterling twisted around, scanning his kitchen. "Susanna!" he yelled. "Watch the line."

Cyrus pulled a small piece of paper from his pocket where the keys had been. A short message had been written in hurried black letters.

You couldn't give them and ever get them back. And taking them can't hurt me—I'm a cursed thief already. TRUST NOLAN

Inflating his cheeks, Cyrus rolled the paper into a tight ball and dropped it back into his pocket. Trust Nolan? He'd been robbed. He felt insulted. Moronic. Was Nolan taunting him? He looked down at his breakfast, his appetite fading.

"The tooth," Sterling said. "In tales older than the oceans, from when the moon was young and green, the tooth is always said to have the power of Death. But any sharp stick can kill you, I'm not meaning that. I mean Death's own power. Death as men imagine him to be, carrying that long-bladed scythe, harvesting souls like corn. The tooth is like the Reaper's Blade."

Sterling breathed in deep. When he spoke again, his voice had found a different rhythm. The swirl and bustle of the kitchen was forgotten. His story had dropped into a rocking chair beside some quiet fire.

"When Man was first tilling ground and tending gardens, before he thought to wall his cities, Draco the Devourer came on down from his stars. He hated Man for his body and soul, joined together in one creature, and he meant to rip the two apart forever—Man would be mere flesh, or mere soul, but never both. Old Draco fashioned himself a monstrous scaly body and a set of charmed teeth with edges to them that could slice a soul's hair sideways.

"But things just didn't go as planned—they never do for dragons. Raging, Draco spread his wings and dropped through the sky's floor. Cities burned, and everywhere he went, souls withered, sliced and uprooted from their flesh. But one boy picked up a stone, and while men fled screaming, he threw it into the demon's mouth and knocked out just one tooth as long as the boy's own arm. He picked it up by the root, and with it, he slew the dragon body. Draco retreated into the stars, but he left behind that tooth."

The cook smiled. "And if you listen to an old cook, that's where the tooth came from."

"You're joking, right?" Antigone asked.

"Am I?" asked Sterling.

Antigone ran her hands over her hair and looked at him sideways. "Well, you don't believe that. A star dragon?"

Sterling straightened. "Come with me," he said, and springs squealed in his steel legs as he strode away. Cyrus and Antigone followed him across the kitchen to a side door.

"I'll tell you this much," the cook said over his shoulder. "Jason used that tooth to fetch the Golden Fleece. Called up immortal warriors with it from sown Dragon's Teeth, and it was the only blade he could use to cut them down. Cadmus used that blade to call warriors from bone when he founded Thebes. It can call the dead to life—though not as they were—and shatter the undying. Alexander used it to raze the world and only failed when it was stolen. Julius, Hannibal, Attila, Charlemagne, Napoleon, Hitler—all of them sought it, and some of them found it. For a time."

The cook lumbered down the corridor in front of them, bells jingling, flour drifting off him in slow curls. He was leading them back toward the Galleria, toward the leather boat on its pedestal. Before they reached it, he stopped and pointed up at the wall, where an enormous reptilian skin ran along above the floor.

"Is that real?" he asked.

Cyrus scanned it. "Is it from a huge snake?"

"Not a snake, lad. Follow it around the corner." The cook turned down a side hall, and Cyrus and Antigone followed him. The skin ran with them. And then it splayed into the fingers of a claw—three forward and one back, each of them longer than Cyrus was tall.

"Not a snake, lad," Sterling said again. He walked to the end of the hallway and turned into another passage. Cyrus, in a daze, staggered along beside his sister, not paying any attention to where they were going. Whatever the tooth did, it was gone now. Probably forever. He should be relieved. He tried to be. But all that he felt was lead-bellied failure.

Sterling stopped and gripped the handle of a black door.

"Well, it doesn't have to be a star dragon," Antigone said. "It could be a dinosaur."

"Could be," Sterling said. "But if I was eye to eye with a flying reptile the size of a house and with a mind to eat me, I wouldn't use the word *dinosaur*."

He forced the door open with a pop and stepped to the side. "After you, Miss Antigone."

Antigone stepped into darkness. Cyrus followed her, dust and decay trickling into his lungs. He sneezed. The door boomed closed and they were left with only four senses—ears straining, skin tingling, the smell of fur and formaldehyde, the taste of old, undisturbed air.

The cook's bells jingled. "This is one of six African collections, though Celtic and Asian is a bit mixed up in everything."

He punched a switch and electricity crackled overhead. After a moment, an army of dangling lanterns fluttered to life beneath the high, beamed ceiling.

Row after row of shelves and collection cases, full to overflowing, teetered up beneath the lights. Tiny, cluttered spaces, no more than two feet wide, ran between each row. A backbone the size of a large tree hung above it all, dangling from anchor chains.

Cyrus's eyes widened, his failure forgotten for the moment. "What is all this stuff?" he asked. "Why is it here?"

"These shelves hold the maps, journals, treasures, samples, and artifacts of every Journeyman, Explorer, Keeper, and Sage to have wandered the African continent on behalf of this Order." The cook waved big arms at the shelves. "Most of this here is from Ashtown explorations, but some of the collections were brought over from the Order's European Estates before the French Revolution.

"In here, if you know where to look, you'll find pieces collected by old Marco Polo, including the rhinoceros horn that sent him into months of black dog funk." Sterling laughed. "He thought the rhino was his long-sought unicorn, and sadly, it was nothing like he'd hoped a unicorn would be.

"You'll find skins and photos of various things shot by Theodore Roosevelt—he was a little quick with the trigger when the bushes moved, but those were the times.

"You'll find charts drawn by Magellan's steady hand, photographs of Solomon's diamond mines, and a Phoenician sphere—a true map of the world etched in a globe of silver. That little beauty was recovered from a shipwreck off the coast of Mauritius." He clicked his teeth. "The Phoenicians are always good for a surprise. The map includes Florida, the Mississippi River, and Tenochtitlán—Mexico City these days. But none of that's why I brought you here. Turn around."

Cyrus and Antigone both turned.

"Oh . . . ," said Cyrus.

Antigone jumped back and covered her mouth.

A huge human skull was sitting on a red cushion beside the door. The jaw, four inches off the ground, was as wide as a horse's chest. The smooth cranium was waist-high. The eyeholes were larger than cantaloupes, and gold had been plated in halos around them.

"This here is one of the sons of the gods," Sterling said. "An immortal—not a transmortal, mind you— who chose Ethiopia for his kingdom and fashioned Stonehenge for his bathing circle."

The cook patted the enormous head.

"That was before the stones were stolen by the Irish."

"The Irish?" Cyrus laughed. "Stonehenge is in England."

"Truth," said Sterling. "But only because Uther Pendragon, Arthur's padre, stole it again with a few cheater's tips from the weasel Merlin." He laughed. "And so it has always gone for the Irish."

Antigone opened her mouth, but Big Ben Sterling shook his jingling head. "Don't say a word, Miss Antigone, not about the Once and Future King. I won't hear it."

He looked back to the skull. "Well, this lad here, like most immortals, didn't understand people. He cooked 'em, ate 'em raw, slaughtered 'em for sport, demanded their worship, and then still stewed 'em with apples for their troubles. But one day a young Ethiopian girl stole a sword from a priest, and so much for immortality. Do I need to tell you which sword it was, or are you two sharp enough to fill in my blanks?"

"Couldn't it have just been a . . . big guy?" asked Antigone helplessly. "A pituitary problem?"

"Tigs," Cyrus said quietly. "You're a total hypocrite. My whole life, you've been telling me that dragons and unicorns and giants were real. I never believed you."

"I never believed me," said Antigone.

Cyrus pointed at the skull. "What's the gold for?"

"A touch of religious decoration," Sterling said. "The skull was idolized in a human sacrificial cult for more than a century. You can hear the thing breathe if you make it angry enough. The demon soul huffs and it puffs, but it can't find its way back in. There are others—"

"Hold on," Antigone said, raising her hands. "Stop! The skull gets mad?"

"Miss Antigone," Sterling said. "Take me or leave me. You'll sleep better if you disbelieve. It isn't the skull that gets angry—it's nothing but bone and gold. It's what used to live in the skull, unable to leave—that's all immortality is, drifting around, with nothing better to do than linger.

"This one's been dealt with, and by a girl like you. But I'm sure he still thinks he was badly treated. I would, too, if I were a hellish big immortal, overfeeding on the villagers, seeing no end of myself in sight. Getting sliced by a wisp of a girl with a sharp tooth would be startling on a warm Ethiopian morning. A mortal would have coped better. We all expect a bit of death at the end."

Cyrus backed away. He had already seen things in Ashtown that he didn't want to believe. He stopped and crouched down until he was shorter than the skull. "What makes it mad?" he asked.

"Cyrus," Antigone said, shivering. "Don't even ask. I don't want to know."

"Ah, she's a believer now," said Sterling. He stepped back beside Cyrus. "Don't you worry about Sir Roger here. There's only one or two things to anger him. Most of the time I don't think the big lad even knows he's here."

Sterling looked down at Cyrus. "If you whisper the name of the little girl who did him in, the demon finds a memory. And, of course, if either of you happened to be carrying that tooth with you, he'd be more than a little upset."

Antigone looked at her brother, confused. Cyrus turned away from her, staring at the skull instead. She thought he still had the tooth. That's why Sterling brought them here? To see if he really had the tooth? Well, he didn't. He was an idiot, and he'd let it get stolen.

"What happens when he's mad?" Cyrus asked. He hoped his voice sounded normal.

"Oh, he does a bit of heavy breathing—absorbs some of the room's light. Years ago, the Journeymen named him Sir Roger, and they got a fair bit of use out of him when it came to hazing the Acolytes."

Cyrus shifted his weight. "Say the name."

"No. Stop. I'm leaving," Antigone said. "Seriously, this is dumber than poking a rattlesnake."

Sterling sighed. "I'm sorry, Mr. Cyrus. But I couldn't do that to your poor sister. But I'll spell it so you can test my word when you're alone sometime—it takes a bit more courage alone. S-E-L-A-M. The name means 'peaceful,' a lovely spice of irony."

Putting his hands on his hips, the big cook scanned the room. "There are other skulls like Sir Roger in the Order's collections in Europe and Africa—a pair in Istanbul have only a single eye—but this one required the Dragon's Tooth for the harvest. Like the lads we keep in the Burials."

Cyrus stood up. *Kill me.* The whisper ran through his head. The man with the bullet hole and the beard had known he was carrying the tooth.

Edgy nerves were all over Antigone's face. "What do you mean? About the Burials?"

Ben Sterling jingled to the first row of shelves. He was at least a foot too wide to fit between them.

"Well," he said. "I'm not saying it's pretty, but what options do you have when an immortal or transmortal takes to . . . misunderstanding people? The Sages collect names. Make lists. Do their best to monitor behavior. And it's up to the Explorers to collect more than names. Before and after everything else, Ashtown is a prison, and don't you forget it. Beginning and end, start and stop."

"Wait a sec," said Cyrus. "Are any of the people in the Burials dead?"

"Not always people," Sterling said. "Never dead. They sleep."

"For how long?" Antigone asked.

Sterling shrugged. "Forever. Or, like Maxi, until

they are wakened, roused, released, or busted loose. In the beginning, the Burials were all neat and orderly—a polished little dungeon. But there were too many incidents, too many revivals and escapes. Now each Burial is hidden. A guard might know one or two, but only the Avengel keeps a full map. But I'm scaring you now. There hasn't been a transmortal put down in nearly a century."

"You know," said Cyrus, "I saw the thing on Skelton's keys. It was small—like a petrified shark tooth. I don't see how it could be the tooth you're talking about."

Antigone shot him a warning glance.

Cyrus shrugged. "I saw it. So what?"

Sterling's face spread into a wide smile. "Did you touch it? Did you handle it?"

"I don't know," Cyrus said. "I guess. He had me park his truck. It was just a little black point—not a sword big enough to take off a giant's head."

The cook sighed happily, tugged his beard, and then crossed his arms. "Billy Bones, you had the point," he said quietly. "You old dog."

He looked back at Cyrus. "The tooth was shattered centuries ago by monks who didn't want it used as a weapon. They scattered pieces around the world to be used in healing—they said—but the truth was rank grisly. To them, the shards were Resurrection Stones, and they used them to raise the dead. After certain . . .

questionable rites, the gravely ill and mortally wounded would be sealed in chambers with the shards.

"Resurrection rooms, they called them, though nothing appealing ever resurrected. If you're with Nolan, you sleep in one of those rooms now."

Antigone grimaced.

Ben Sterling tucked his hands into the pockets of his apron and shifted his weight, leg springs sighing. "Look around in here if you like, but I hear the kitchen calling."

He tugged the door open, jingled through, paused, and leaned back into the room.

"Cyrus, you said you parked old Skelton's truck?"

Cyrus nodded.

"And he just gave you his keys?"

"Yeah, why?"

Sterling's eyes sparked above his smile. "No reason." The door shut behind him.

Antigone looked at her brother, irritated. "Cy, now he knows you have them."

Cyrus moved to the nearest shelf. "I don't have the keys, Tigs." He fished the little paper ball out of his pocket and tossed it to his sister. "That's what was in there this morning."

Antigone unrolled it. "Trust Nolan?" She looked up. "We should tell Greeves. You said you were going to tell him about the tooth today anyway. He needs to know that Nolan has it."

"I don't want to tell Greeves."

"Why? You want to hunt for Nolan yourself?"

"I just don't want to tell him. It's embarrassing. And I don't want to hunt for Nolan. We have enough other things to do, but mostly I don't think we could find him."

"We should find Mrs. E." Antigone tugged on her brother's shirt. "She said she would help us this morning. C'mon, we should go."

"I want to look around first." Cyrus scanned the shelves.

"Cy, I'm not gonna hang out in here with you and Sir Roger."

Cyrus grinned. "I think you are. If you head for the door, my mouth might just sort of slip." ·

He walked toward the skull.

"Cyrus . . ." Antigone sighed. "If you want to play games, find a new friend."

"I'm not playing," Cyrus said. He tapped a gold-plated eye socket.

"Cyrus Lawrence Smith," Antigone said, raising her eyebrows. "Stop acting your age. Do you think *I'm* scared? You wet your pants the first time we watched *Chitty Chitty Bang Bang*."

"Seriously, Tigs?" Cyrus said. "Who has more nightmares? And this won't be a nightmare. This will be real."

"Little brother . . ." Puffing frustration, Antigone

smoothed her hair, gritted her teeth, and pointed at the skull. "Selam."

Cyrus jumped, staggering into his sister. The two of them crashed back into the shelves and down into a row.

Antigone felt her brother's fist in her stomach and the hard floor against her shoulder blades. A box landed above her head. Glass broke. Paper rained down.

Water slapped into her hair.

Above them, the lights dimmed.

✦ fourteen ✦

QUICK WATER

CYRUS COULDN'T ROLL to either side. And he didn't want to scoot backward toward the skull. So he crawled forward, over the top of his sister, carefully sliding his hands through paper, glass, and some kind of puddling liquid.

"Get off!" Antigone slapped at him.

"There's glass," Cyrus said. "Hold on."

Antigone pushed his hips up into the air, got her boots braced on his legs, and then heaved him into a somersault.

Cyrus slammed awkwardly to the floor.

"Ow." He groaned. "Tigs, you just ruptured my kidney."

Antigone sat up. "My apologies. Now shut up. I'm trying to listen."

She leaned forward, staring at the skull.

Cyrus scraped himself up. "I think my hand is bleeding."

"Shhh." Antigone grabbed a shelf, thought better of it, and then pushed herself up off the floor. Water dribbled down from her hair and slapped onto her boot. "Nothing," Antigone said. "Absolutely nothing."

"The lights dimmed," Cyrus said. "I know they did."

"How would you know?" Antigone asked. "You were busy tackling me while screaming and sucking your thumb."

"First," Cyrus said, standing up, "I didn't scream. Second, that was *your* thumb in my mouth."

"Selam," Antigone said, stepping forward. "Selam."

Dust trickled across the floor. The lanterns dimmed and swung on the ceiling. For a moment, the temperature wobbled, and a long sucking sound, like a breath pulled through teeth, filled the room.

And it was gone.

The dust stopped.

The light grew.

"Hmm," said Cyrus. "We've seen it. It happened. Now let's agree not to do that again."

Antigone laughed. "Really, Cyrus? Who was just pretending to be the brave one?"

"I wouldn't have done it. I'm not dumb, Tigs. You're just funny when you're scared."

"Yeah, right. Can we go now, or do you need to change your pants?"

"Why? Oh. Aren't *you* hilarious. No. I didn't wet myself, Brave Sister. But only because you inspire me. What's all over the floor? It's on your boot, too."

Tiny drops of clear liquid were rolling through yellowing pages and ancient envelopes. Cyrus thumped to his knees. The drops were seeking each other, growing larger as they tumbled over shards of glass, through bunnied dust, and around Antigone's boots.

A ball slopped off Antigone's toe, swallowing a whole flock of drops, and gathered around her sole.

"I wouldn't touch it," Antigone said.

Cyrus extended a finger. "It looks like water."

"It's not acting like water. It's acting like mercury."

"I've never seen how mercury acts." Cyrus poked it. The ball quivered and slid slowly away on its flat belly.

"*That's* how it acts," Antigone said. "But it's silver, and it doesn't go looking for itself."

More tiny droplets tumbled past to join the ball. The bigger it got, the faster the smaller drops moved toward it.

Cupping his hands, Cyrus picked it up.

"Mercury is poisonous," Antigone said. "In chemistry, Mr. Sampson said it can soak through your skin and kill you."

"But this isn't mercury," said Cyrus. "This is water. Should I taste it?"

"You've been a little hard to deal with lately, so yeah, go ahead."

Cyrus held the ball up to the light. Antigone pressed up beside him to get a look. Tiny particles of dirt and splinters of wood were floating inside it, but as they watched, all of the impurities rose to the top of the sphere, then slid down around the outside until they reached Cyrus's skin.

It was cleaning itself.

"Wow," said Cyrus. "Tigs, try something. Cup your hands beneath mine."

Antigone held out her hands beneath her brother's, and then Cyrus spread his fingers.

The liquid immediately slopped through and bounced into Antigone's cupped palms.

Cyrus examined his fingers. "It feels just like water, but my skin's dry. All the gunk is left, though." He brushed off his hands and began scanning the rubble on the floor. A rectangular box lay open on its side. Glass was scattered around it.

Cyrus picked up the box. Inside, it was lined with red velvet and looked like the inside of an egg carton. A dozen baseball-size indents were set in two rows. One of them held half a hollow glass sphere. The rest were empty. A small, lined piece of paper had been tacked inside the lid.

"This is really weird, Cyrus," said Antigone. "Look what happens when you break it in half."

Cyrus glanced at his sister. She was cupping an egg-size ball of the water in each hand.

"They're two feet apart," Antigone said. "But they pull like serious magnets."

Her hands slapped together, and a single large ball dropped to the floor and bounced like a doomed water balloon.

Antigone scrambled after it as Cyrus looked back at the list. Eleven names had been handwritten in a column labeled MEMBER. They had written their ranks in the next column, and the "date of withdrawal" in the next. The "date of return" column was completely empty. The last "date of withdrawal" was 1932.

"They need some librarians around here," Cyrus said. "Some curators. Something. Somebody should be collecting late fees. Tigs, we can take stuff out of here. You just write your name down." He closed the lid and looked at the top of the box. A typed label had been filled out with a sloppy fountain pen and then glued down.

Fungus: (Supra) Tremella Hydrozoa
Common Names: Quick Water, Demon Jelly,
Jelly Eye, Witch's Spy
Toxicity: None
Origin: Congolese
Collected by: P. Jonathan Smith, Explorer

"Tigs, it's a fungus," Cyrus said. He held out the box. "And it was collected by a Smith. That makes it practically ours."

Slopping the ball from hand to hand, Antigone read

the label. "Let's go with Quick Water. The other ones sound evil."

"Quick Water it is," said Cyrus. "Give me half."

Antigone splashed half her blob into her brother's hands. He held it back up to the light.

It was clearer than any water he had ever seen. Clearer than air. And it did strange things with the light, like a fish-eye camera lens. Looking into it was like looking into a different room, a different world, spread out, bent, curving, but perfectly sharp. He raised it all the way up to his eye and tried to look through it. Shelves warped up toward the ceiling around . . . his sister?

Antigone screamed, and Cyrus jumped backward, tripped, and nearly fell again.

"Cyrus!" she said, covering her water. "We have to put them back. I saw an eye. The whole thing was magnifying an eye—an eyeball just sitting in my hand."

"It spooked me, too," Cyrus said, "but mine was looking at you. You were in mine."

"What are you saying?" Antigone asked. "I was in yours? How?"

"I was looking at you. I looked into the water, and the room was all bent, and at first I didn't notice that it wasn't the right part of the room, but then I was looking up at you."

"I don't get it," Antigone said. "More importantly, I don't like it. We're putting them back."

"I was looking into mine and out of yours!" Cyrus said. "I mean, I'm guessing that's what happened. That was my eye. Hopefully. Look again."

Cyrus held his water up—farther from his face this time—and he grinned. His wobbling ball was dark. But then Antigone opened her hands. When her water's quivering had settled down, there was her brother, smiling up out of her sphere like a bizarre cartoon—enormous-nosed and pencil-necked.

"Tigs," said the cartoon Cyrus. "This is the coolest thing ever, and we're taking it with us."

The door banged open, and Cyrus and Antigone jumped.

Eleanor Eldridge glared at them. She was wearing a straw hat and had a heavy book bag slung over her shoulder.

"What do you two think you're doing?"

Antigone slipped her water into Cyrus's hand and jumped forward. "Sterling said we could look around."

"Sterling," Mrs. Eldridge muttered. "Don't you go listening to Benjamin Sterling—he's a man with a dirty soul, though he did tell me where to find you."

She turned around. "Come along, then. It's time we talked about your tutors."

"Oh, we have the list," Antigone said.

The old woman laughed. "Throw it away. You two may be the most unpopular Acolytes Ashtown has ever seen. Nobody wants to share a room with you, let alone share a lesson. And the club masters with their little white uniforms wouldn't go near you for a triple fee."

She glanced back at Cyrus and snorted around a half smile. "You surely won't be getting any language help from the monks. But I've done my best and you should be grateful. Hop to, hop to! I'm not waiting."

She hurried back through the door. Tucking balls of Quick Water into their pockets, Cyrus and Antigone jogged after her.

"Now," she said when they'd reached the main hallway, "you're on the list as having paid all dues—though I'm not sure how—so we'll start with proper clothes. Keep up, keep up. I'll explain things on the way."

Mrs. Eldridge led them out the main doors and into the muggy summer morning. Dennis Gilly, sweating under his bowler hat, grinned at them as they passed. The far side of the lawn was busy with white-uniformed grapplers taking turns throwing and bouncing each other in the grass. On the gravel path directly at the bottom of the stairs, two boys were each working on a single bicycle with its own large umbrella propeller.

But Cyrus's eyes were in the air.

He stopped and Antigone stopped with him. No more than fifty feet off the ground, six small, football-shaped hot-air balloons were engaged in a battle. Three of the balloons were white and three were red, but each was painted with a different symbol—Cyrus saw the ship, the snake, and something that looked like a bear.

The baskets were tiny, barely big enough for one person but each holding two. On the back of each basket there was a large fan, like something off a swamp boat. Mounted on the front, there was a small cannon.

From one of the baskets, two people had fallen and were dangling at the end of long ropes tied around their waists. A third person, a girl, had taken over their balloon. She was running the fan and the cannon by herself.

Mrs. Eldridge stopped at the bottom of the stairs and looked back up at Cyrus and Antigone. She clicked her tongue and snapped her fingers. Cyrus didn't hear. The balloons were circling each other, ramming each other, and firing brown lumps at each other that tumbled down to the ground.

One of the lumps bounced off a balloon and spun through the air toward Cyrus, thumping onto the stairs not six feet from where they were standing. It looked like a compressed loaf of bread.

"What are they doing?" Antigone asked.

"Nothing productive," Mrs. Eldridge said. "It's quite childish, though Journeymen have been doing it as long as I can remember. It's a game of conquest. Board an opponent's balloon and hurl him from the basket. They're only supposed to fire stale bread at each other, though

Sterling's kitchen tends to provide it fresh. Now come on, and watch your heads."

Cyrus and Antigone stumbled down the stairs. While they watched, two balloons collided. Bread and shouted threats were exchanged from point-blank range, and then the boarding struggle began, with fan-driven baskets spinning.

Antigone yelped as two bodies fell, bounced, and dangled—one from each balloon. The war above them raged on.

Cyrus and Antigone reached Mrs. Eldridge.

"No Keeper would agree to give you flight lessons," she said. "But there aren't many I would trust in a 1914 canvas and wood plane anyhow. Diana Boone has agreed to teach you both, but Rupe had her flying all night and she's sleeping at the moment. Your first lesson will have to wait."

Cyrus could feel Antigone looking at him. He bit his lip and fought back a smile. He was going to fly. The path began to circle the broad lawn.

"As for weaponry," Mrs. Eldridge said, "well, that was worse. The best I could do was Gunner for your shooting, and he's an Order washout—hardly ideal. But he can shoot, and no one will argue with that. Rupert Greeves will handle your fencing himself. He's a master's master, but good luck with scheduling, especially with all the trouble you've brought to his life. James Axelrotter,

'Jax' whenever he's actually seen, might help you with zoology, though those requirements are ludicrous and infeasible—I intend to speak with Mr. Rhodes about it."

"Where are we going?" Cyrus asked. They were lapping the lawn, heading for an iron gate. Beyond it, gray buildings hugged narrow streets.

"Outfitters," Mrs. Eldridge said. "As I've already told you. I have yet to find anyone willing to give you occult or medical training—particularly when it comes to instruction in amputation—and you'll have to depend on Greeves again for your fitness. Your choices are very limited in free diving, and I recommend Llewellyn Douglas—a sour old carcass of a man. You'll find him on the jetty most days. I absolutely refuse to speak to him for you. I haven't yet looked into your navigational options."

She pushed through the gate and led them out. The gravel path widened.

"What about languages?" Antigone asked. Cyrus glared at her.

"I'm afraid that you'll be stuck with me and I with you." Mrs. Eldridge glanced back at them. "Which means it'll be French and Latin. They'll be the easiest. I know others, but I don't feel up to trying to communicate them to you. It will be hard enough listening to you desecrate French."

She had led them to a tall, narrow stone building.

Now she pulled open the door. Cyrus and Antigone stepped into low light; cool, humming air-conditioning; and the smell of leather and oil and mold. The place was intensely cluttered. Shelves overloaded with boots, jackets, trousers, scarves, belts, and bags climbed twenty feet to the cobwebbed and vented ceiling. Dusty ladders leaned against the loads at odd angles. An old man was snoring in the center of the room, his feet propped up on a pile of leather jackets, a dead cigarette dangling from his lower lip.

Mrs. Eldridge whistled sharply and the man jerked upright, spitting his cigarette across the room.

"Two Acolytes to be outfitted," Mrs. Eldridge said. "Smith, Miss, and Smith, Mr. Everything typical 1914 or older."

The man scratched a stubbled cheek and squinted at Cyrus and Antigone. He was a man with eyebrows, or maybe they were eyebrows with a man. Ownership would have been hard to establish, and Cyrus couldn't focus on anything else—the two fur hedges looked like they were trying to escape his face.

"Not possible," the man muttered, shaking his head. "Heard about them two, but not possible."

"Make it possible," Mrs. Eldridge said. "I know you never throw anything away, Donald. Now get to it. They have a Latin lesson waiting."

The man stood slowly, put his hand over his right

eye, and looked the two Smiths up and down. Sighing, he turned and trudged away through piles of clothes. "Twenty minutes," he said, "and you'll get what I got."

What the man got turned out to be a rather large mound of antique clothing. Mrs. Eldridge nodded and snorted her way through the pile until she'd cut it in half, sending up a storm cloud of dust as she worked. Finally, she pulled out two small bundles and handed one to Cyrus and one to Antigone.

"Get changed," she said, and turned to the man with the eyebrows. "Have the rest pressed and baled and delivered to the stairway above the Polygon."

The eyebrows bobbed. The man grunted. Mrs. Eldridge jerked open the door and stepped outside.

Hiding in a cluttered aisle, Cyrus kicked off his shoes and pulled on his new, very old pair of pants. They were brown faded to tan with large vertical flap pockets on the hips and horizontal flaps on the seat. And they fit.

Cyrus transferred his Quick Water and lightning bug out of his old pants and into his new ones, and then he moved on. He didn't like the look of the boots. They were awkwardly tall, but they fit well once they were on, and they felt lighter than he'd expected. Two leather tongues and buckles cinched them tight against his calves. The faded and wrinkled shirt was collared, buttoned, and extremely pocketed. He left it untucked and examined his jacket.

Leather. Ancient. Oiled almost to the point of dripping. Creased and worn. It was hard not to love, especially with the patches stitched on the shoulders. On the left shoulder there was a simple round tricolor. The right held a yellow shield around a black boxing monkey. Cyrus smiled, tracing the embroidered animal with his fingers—this was his symbol. He'd stick it on everything if he could. He turned the jacket over. On the lower back, part of the leather had blackened in some decades-old brush with fire. Between the shoulder blades, Cyrus's fingers found three holes. Bullet holes. Inside, the pale-blue quilted lining was stained red-brown.

"Cyrus! C'mon."

Cyrus swung the jacket on—he didn't care if it was hot outside—and hurried toward the door. Antigone was waiting for him, wearing improved boots and a jacket of her own—darker and longer than his and belted at the waist.

She smiled and put her hands on her hips. "Cool, right?"

Cyrus laughed. "Mine's cooler. I think someone died in this one."

He looked back at Eyebrows.

The old man was working on a toothpick now. He shrugged. "Good jacket to die in."

Antigone grimaced, Cyrus grinned, and the two of them barreled out the door and into the heat.

Dan's eyes sprung open. Sunlight was glowing through his blue curtain. He hadn't been asleep. He knew he hadn't. But his mind had stopped. Someone had stopped it. He could barely move his head, and the back of his skull felt open to the air. Rolling his eyes around the room, he could just see Phoenix in the chair near his feet. Today, the suit beneath his stained and yellowing lab coat was as black as his hair. His face was furrowed with thought, and he was drumming long fingernails on the arms of his chair.

His pale eyes drifted up into Dan's.

"A very good morning to you, Daniel Smith." His drawl was slow and flat, and he yawned into the back of his hand. "Forgive me." He straightened in his chair, and then leaned forward. "I must also apologize for entering your mind without a formal invitation. You were sleeping, and as I believed we were friends, I thought it unkind to wake you for something so trivial as permission. But Daniel Smith, I'm afraid our friendship is already in danger. Friends help each other, and you seem to know absolutely"—his hands became clenched, bloodless fists; his voice sank and hardened its edge— "absolutely nothing about that which I need."

Sighing, he massaged his eyelids slowly. "And now, unfortunately, I must befriend your siblings as well. Though I'm told that they, too, may not have what I need." He lowered his hands and inhaled slowly. His face was full of regret. "If that proves to be the case, Daniel Smith, I'm rather worried that I may take off this lab coat. And when I take off this coat—I won't tell a lie—things are liable to become heated."

Daniel tried to twist, to see if his mother was still in the room. He tried to open his mouth, to lick his cracked lips, to speak. But his jaw was locked and his tongue was trapped inside his teeth. Where were Cyrus and Antigone? What had happened to them?

Phoenix grimaced, and then answered Dan's thoughts. "Regrettably, they have been taken in by some rather unsavory characters. But I wouldn't worry yourself about them. I've taken steps."

Dr. Phoenix smiled—his almost pupilless blue eyes were looking directly into Daniel's. He stood up slowly from his chair, his long, thin body towering over the bed.

"On a more scientific note, I must say that it is both remarkable and unfortunate how precisely your mind is cut from the Smith mold. I did once have the opportunity to study two of your aunties—terrifyingly dull examples of the same simple mental organization and total lack of imagination that you manifest, forgive me for saying. So much potential in Smith blood and Smith bones, but never realized."

He paused, licking thin lips. His brow furrowed. "Would you expect your brother and sister to be more . . .

intriguing? Do say yes. After all, they seem to have far more of your feral mother in them than do you. And your mother's mind is truly a remarkable maze of striking images and animal desires—as one would expect, of course, from a woman raised as she was."

The doctor looked at Dan, at his feet, his legs, his arms and chest, and his sharp nostrils flared. "You are still my friend, Daniel Smith. And your mind is rotten with worry. Your body is malnourished and weak from pitiful sacrifice. I cannot allow this, this *you*, to exist any longer." He leaned forward and cracked his long knuckles. "When you wake again, you will have been renovated. Remade." He waved his fingers, studying them as he did. "As a friend, I will find you a more interesting way . . . to be alive." Daniel twitched as a long fingernail traced his bare rib cage. "More interesting than *you* being *you* as *you* are currently being. But don't feel badly about yourself. Traditional humanity is all so . . . dull."

"Dr. Phoenix?" The voice was male. The speaker was out of Daniel's view.

Cocking his head, Phoenix stroked Daniel's cheek with the back of his cold, damp hand. Dan's body managed a shiver.

"Yes," Phoenix said. "What is it?"

"Word from Ashtown," said the voice. "Maxi's inside."

"Lovely," said Dr. Phoenix. "Dear little Maximilien should keep them busy. The twins and I will join him tomorrow. They're the only company I'll be needing." He leaned farther forward, his empty eyes pulling at Daniel's. Close, closer, and Dan's eyes watered out of focus. Tears leaked down into his ears.

"The Smiths are in need of a reunion," Phoenix whispered.

His moist breath was tinged with cinnamon. Daniel blinked it away, but reality softened and faded. His heart slowed, and darkness swallowed him.

Cyrus's first Latin lesson had consisted of being shut in a small second-story, one-window, stone-walled room with his sister and a stack of yellowed and flaking books, and then having his head slapped repeatedly by an old woman.

Mrs. Eldridge had thumped him, flicked him, kicked him, and pulled on his ears. Antigone had gotten one mild cheek pat, but then she had actually been trying to make sense of the material in front of her. Cyrus had been more interested in the windows, the planes that occasionally floated past, and thoughts of hot-air balloon wars and flying bicycles and keys and a cold black shard of tooth.

And then, finally, Mrs. Eldridge had moved to the door. "If I'm not back in thirty minutes, you may as well try and find old Llewellyn Douglas. He's usually at the harbor."

"Where are you going?" Antigone asked.

Cyrus wanted to kick his sister. Who cared where Mrs. Eldridge was going so long as she went?

"To speak with Mr. Cecil Rhodes about the two of you."

That had been an hour ago.

Now Cyrus was lying on his back on a small table, his feet resting on the sill of the open window and his new jacket mounded beneath his head. He could still hear his sister turning pages.

His eyes were on green treetops, shuffling slowly, straining for the small grazing clouds above them.

Today was a day to go looking for tires—to distract himself from thinking, to hunt, collect, and explore. But that wasn't possible, and his mind was beyond distracting.

Was Dan dead? Was there blood? Had there been pain? What did he look like right now? Would Rupert find him? Would they ever get to see his body? Would there be a goodbye, or would it be like that older loss, the loss that began all of their losing—a smiling face and a door closing against the rain? That was the only goodbye. Goodbye to a father and then a mother and then a house and then an ocean. And to something inside him—he didn't know what, but something important.

Cyrus's throat tightened. The familiar ache started

behind his ribs, his stomach flipped slowly, and he shut his eyes like someone fighting motion sickness. The air from the window was warm, but his skin went cold. Moisture beaded up on his nose and forehead.

He wanted to break something, to smash his knuckles into a wall and trade pain for pain. But he'd done that too many times before, and it didn't work. Still, his fists clenched, and his toes curled in his boots.

Breathing slowly, he forced his body to relax, to liquefy. His pulse slowed, and his stomach calmed. He didn't want to open his eyes. He might even sleep. Maybe he'd dream again, and this time, he'd get a look at the man in the truck, leaving with his father.

"Hey, boy genius," Antigone said above him. "Wake up. I don't think she's coming back. Let's go."

Cyrus blinked. "Go where?"

"You pick," Antigone said. "I'm tired, and I think my brain pulled a muscle. We can look for Nolan or Greeves or that Llewellyn Douglas guy."

"I'm hungry," Cyrus said.

Antigone snorted. "Good luck with that."

Cyrus sat up. He wanted to find Nolan, but that didn't seem likely—not if Nolan didn't want to be found. They should look for Rupert. Or Diana Boone. A flight lesson would be fun.

Antigone grabbed his wrist. "C'mon. I want to talk to Rupert."

"I thought I was picking."

"Yeah," Antigone said. "But then you didn't, and I did."

She pulled open the door and dragged him outside into the humid air. Dotted with doorways, the covered stone walkway overlooked the sprawling green courtyard. Three doors behind them, a stairwell would take them down to the lawn.

"What about the books?" Cyrus asked.

"Leave them," said Antigone. "We don't know where they go."

They reached the stairs and clipped down. At the bottom, they stopped. In the main building, bells had begun to ring.

Cyrus looked at his sister. This was not the slow tolling that kept time. And it wasn't celebration. This was panic. The hot-air balloons, beginning another battle, cut their fans and hung motionless. All around the courtyard, people had stopped and were looking back at the main building.

Three stories up, above a bank of sleeping gargoyles, a tall window erupted and a black shape dove to the grass below in a storm of falling glass. Tucking into a ball, the shape bounced, rolled, and found its feet.

❧ fifteen ❧

AN END

WHISTLES SCREAMED. Porters ran. White-uniformed runners and grapplers scattered. The black shape began moving across the grass. It—he—wasn't running. He was walking coolly, and he was walking straight toward Cyrus and Antigone.

Antigone squinted, trying to make out the distant face. "Who is it?"

Cyrus grabbed her by the shoulders, pulling her back into the shaded stairwell. His eyes were better. He could make out the small man's shape, his frazzled, haloing hair, his lean limbs dressed in tight black, and the heavily loaded belt around his waist.

"Maxi," he said.

The bells roiled the air, and doors all around the courtyard were flying open. Maxi drew two guns and emptied them while he walked. A porter tumbled onto his face and the others retreated. He threw the guns down and drew two heavier, four-barreled monsters—the kind that spat fire, the kind that could burn motels. People shouted. Doors slammed.

"Up, Tigs!" Cyrus said. "Go! Go!" He hadn't needed to say it twice. Antigone was already scrambling back up the stairs on all fours, keeping below the solid railing. From around the courtyard, adults and training teens and porters had drawn sidearms and were returning fire. Cyrus snuck a look above the rail and watched corkscrewing flame explode first one and then another hot-air balloon. Baskets dropped while people screamed.

Maxi, laughing, focused both his flaming guns on the main building. One, two, three white-hot spiraling spheres splattered on the steps, erupting toward the doors. A tall shape tumbled through the flame and down the stairs, rolling back to his feet—Rupert Greeves. He was carrying a gun longer than he was tall, what looked like a wooden-stocked musket but with a massive black ammunition drum above the trigger.

"Maximilien!" Rupert bellowed. "Stand and fight!"

Cyrus inched up.

Maxi was less than fifty yards away, heavy guns dangling from his hands. "Are we hunting elephants, Monsieur Greeves? The Avengels I've tilled into earth must weep for you."

Greeves raised his long gun. Still laughing, Maxi ducked and began running, zigzagging toward the stairs.

The gun roared and green turf exploded. Again, and again, and two more craters emptied themselves into the sky. Again, and Maxi's running legs were swept out from under him.

Giggling, coughing, wheezing like a child tickled sick, Maxi staggered to his feet. Rupert was aiming while jogging. A pair of fireballs spiraled back toward him.

"Cyrus!" Antigone barked. She was still on her hands and knees. "Where do we go?"

The walkway was lined with doors, but Cyrus didn't know if any of them had exits. Windows. They'd have to jump and hope for the best. He glanced back into the courtyard as Rupert dove into a somersault, a sunburst of white fire licking at his heels. Once more, the huge gun rose to his shoulder. Behind him, just visible through the hazing smoke, another, smaller shape dove from the high, broken window. A bounce, a roll, and it raced to the side of the courtyard.

"Into the room!" Cyrus said, crawling forward. The elephant gun fired, but he didn't look back again.

Inside, he jumped to his feet, slammed the door, and tried to wedge a chair beneath the knob. It didn't work.

Antigone was already at the window, leaning out and looking down. "There's a tree, maybe close enough if we were squirrels and if this window opened wider. It's high, Cy, and the ground looks pretty rough. I don't think we can jump."

Cyrus dropped the chair and ran to the casement. Pushing Antigone to the side, he jumped onto the table and kicked at the window's hinges. His boots were solid. Aluminum bent and warped and popped. Finally, the window swung wide, slammed against the outside wall, and tore free, dangling awkwardly.

Antigone was right. A straight leap out was their only chance, and it wasn't a good one. "You first, Tigs," he said. "Roll when you land."

The door to the room banged open and Cyrus spun around, grabbing a chair, not sure what he would do with it.

Breathing hard but evenly, Nolan shut the door behind him. His bare arms and white tank top were covered with dust. His eyes were empty. His voice was strangely calm. "Maxi's up the stairs. Eldridge is dead. Greeves is burning. You should jump."

The wall shook, and fingers of flame curled in and fisted around the door behind him, tearing it from its frame. Nolan, the door, and blazing heat tumbled across the room.

As Latin books crackled, Maxi stepped into the doorway.

Antigone lunged for the window, but Cyrus pulled her to the floor as Maxi fired again. Searing magnesium flame swirled out the window and into the tree, exploding through the branches.

"No window this time," the man said, licking his worn smile. "Not again, *ma chérie. Mi florita.*"

Nolan rolled out from beneath the door and stood. Cold, rigid, he stepped in front of Cyrus and Antigone. His dirty skin was striped with angry veins, and a piece of glass stuck out from the back of his neck.

"Children," Maxi said. "There is something you are very much wishing to give me."

A bullet whistled into the room and ceiling plaster shattered. Pumping fireballs over his shoulder, Maxi stepped to the side, leaning his back against the blackened wall. Antigone's fingers were digging into Cyrus's arm. She was trying to pull him up. Together, they stood.

"If you do not give it to me"—Maxi shrugged, showing them his tiny teeth—"then there will be much dying. Your brother, your mother, the two of you." He pointed his four-barreled gun at Nolan. "And this one."

Nolan took a small step forward. His voice was low, unruffled. "Fight with me, Maximilien. You think you cannot die? Fight with me." His fists pulsed. Clenched in Nolan's right hand, Cyrus glimpsed the keys, the unsheathed black tooth protruding between his knuckles.

"Ah . . ." Maxi's eyebrows shot up. He brushed back his hair, and his smile grew.

Cyrus's eyes drifted down from Maxi's miniature teeth to the thick scar that encircled the man's neck.

"You are Nikales," Maxi said. "The little serpent,

oldest and most cursed of thieves. I can free you from your curse."

Without looking, he blasted fire out the door beside him, swiveling his gun around the walkway. Shouts. A scream.

Then he drew a long, slender knife from the small of his back.

Nolan took another step, tense as a coiled snake. "I can kill you, Maxi. I will be the one to pluck the life from your flesh—as easily as picking some low, worm-riddled fruit."

"Can you?" Maxi asked. "Are you then greater than God, little thief?"

Nolan exploded forward. Latin ashes tumbled and sparked.

Cyrus watched Nolan spit himself on Maxi's knife. He saw Maxi's gun rise and Nolan's toothed fist flash forward. The gun fired too soon. Swallowed in flame, Nolan tumbled across the room, slamming into the wall.

The blast knocked Cyrus to the ground, Antigone gasping beneath him. Singed, hair smoking, Cyrus clattered toward Nolan. The keys were dangling from his limp hand, and his shirt and the skin from his chest and stomach had burned away.

Maxi fired again out the doorway, and then moved forward through the rubble.

"Cy!"

Cyrus heard Maxi step behind him, and he hunched farther forward, trying to hide what he was doing. The key ring was around Nolan's finger, and it had been crushed in place. Frantic, gritting his teeth and pinning Nolan's wrist down with his knee, he tugged harder. The knuckle popped, and the key ring slid free.

"Give them to me." Maxi jerked Cyrus around and clamped his hot hand tight around Cyrus's neck, crushing veins, nails digging deep into skin. Cyrus tried to twist, he tried to breathe, he heard Antigone scream, and then he felt Patricia grow.

The silver snake, suddenly as thick as his arm, struck straight for Maxi's face. Shocked, releasing Cyrus, Maxi staggered back, knocking the first strike away. But the snake was still growing. Patricia slid down Cyrus to the ground and reared up after Maxi, chest height, hissing like a monstrous silver cobra, emerald eyes sparkling with wrath. Maxi raised his gun and fired as Patricia struck the barrel, taking the fireball down her wide throat. The snake's thick body bulged, glowing orange, and then a pillar of fire exploded back out of her mouth and up Maxi's arm.

Heart racing, Cyrus slid the tooth out between his knuckles as Nolan had done, clenching his fist around it. Selam. *Kill me.* He knew what had to be done. Maxi's gun was on the ground and his back was against the wall. With one hand, he was gripping Patricia just beneath the head as she spat and fang-groped for his forearm. With the other, he raised a knife.

Muscles taut with drumming adrenaline, Cyrus threw himself forward, fist raised, focusing on the man's temple as he swung. He saw Maxi's eyes turn toward him, surprised. He saw the knife flick through the air, but he didn't feel the blade graze his scalp and nick his ear. He didn't hear himself yelling.

Bone crunched.

A cold, jarring shiver ran up Cyrus's arm and into his skull. He staggered backward and sat down in smoking rubble. Patricia, her head now the size of a football, retreated to him, slowly winding her heavy body around his waist. She was shrinking quickly.

Maxi still stood, back against the wall, arms hanging limp at his sides. The keys and the charms hung from the tooth in his head, brushing against his cheekbone as he began to sway. His eyes, no longer surprised, rolled slowly toward Cyrus. His lips twitched into a final smile.

"*Merci . . .* ," he said quietly.

Cyrus scrambled to his feet. Patricia was barely a belt now, and she'd found her tail.

"Where's Dan?" Cyrus yelled. "Where's my brother?"

Keys jingling, Maxi fell forward.

Cyrus caught him. The man was bird-light. Rolling him onto his back, he stared into empty eyes that had seen centuries of murder and massacre and revolution, that had struck fear into the hearts of kings and chieftains and mobs. Now they were glassy and false— their secrets gone—like the eyes of some huge and horrifying doll. Grimacing, Cyrus tugged the keys from the man's skull, ignoring the gore, and shoved them quickly into his hip pocket.

Antigone dropped to the ground beside Nolan's smoking body. His eyes were closed, but somehow he was still breathing. The long knife stood out from his chest.

"He alive?" Cyrus asked.

Antigone nodded. "For now."

With his huge gun raised, Rupert Greeves crashed into the room. Parts of his safari jacket were missing and the rest was smoking. He had burns on his forehead and jaw. Half of his pointed beard was gone.

Lowering his gun, he nudged Maxi with his foot and then crouched to feel for a pulse. His eyes settled on the black oozing wound in Maxi's temple. Again, he checked for a pulse.

"Sebastián de Benalcázar," he said quietly, "Maximilien Robespierre, you have been hung, shot, stabbed, keelhauled, and decapitated by guillotine, but now you are dead."

Rupert looked at Cyrus and raised a long finger. "Cyrus Smith, I will give you only this one moment to speak the truth to me about what you have done and what you are carrying. Decide now if you want me for a friend."

Nolan groaned.

"I'm sorry," Cyrus said. "I was going to tell you today. Seriously. Antigone made me promise." He pulled the key ring from his pocket and held up the sticky tooth. Hooking his finger through the ring, he then unwound an extremely slender Patricia from his waist.

Rupert's eyes widened. "And a patrik?"

Cyrus nodded. "Skelton gave her to me. She and Nolan are the ones who really did the fighting. I just punched him once."

While Greeves watched, Cyrus wiped the tooth on his pants and clicked the sheath closed. Patricia was winding around his wrist. Rupert blinked when she found her tail and vanished.

"Now you know everything," Cyrus said.

Rupert sighed. "I know that in all the Estates of the Order, in every villain's den and necromancer's lair, from the hidden alleys of New Orleans to the witch doctors' lanes of Sierra Leone, men and women will hear that Maxi Robes is dead. They will hear the name of Cyrus Smith, Acolyte of Ashtown, and they will know that he carries the Reaper's Blade."

He looked into Cyrus's eyes. His voice was low but furious. "They will know that once more the immortal can die, and the dead can be raised. Cyrus, I cannot protect you from what will come, but I must protect Ashtown. Give me the tooth."

Cyrus swallowed, looking at the key ring in his hand. Then he looked up into Rupert's eyes and shook his head. "Skelton told me not to give it up. Not ever."

"Rupe?" A nervous voice trickled in through the door. "You all right in there?" A head peered in around the corner.

"A moment!" Rupert yelled. His eyes hadn't left Cyrus's. The head withdrew.

"They got him!" the voice yelled. "Maxi's dead!"

"Cyrus," Rupert said. "It's too dangerous."

Outside, the murmur and chatter of a crowd began to grow. Three more faces peeked in the doorway.

"Go!" Rupert yelled, and they pulled away.

"Listen, um, Mr. Greeves," Antigone said. "Could we be mad at Cyrus later? Nolan really needs help."

Rupert ignored her. He held out his hand to Cyrus. "Let me keep it safe for you. It's what your father would have done."

In the corner, while Antigone winced and turned away, Nolan whimpered and raised his arm. He slowly pulled the knife out of his chest and dropped it in the rubble.

Sighing, Cyrus began to twist the charm off the key ring. "My father," he said, "was kicked out of this place." He reached out to drop the silver sheath in

Rupert's broad palm. He felt weak, like all his adrenaline was falling through the floor. "You don't know what he would have done," he said quietly.

Rupert suddenly closed his empty fist, looking at the silver sheath still in Cyrus's hand. "Good. I can trust you, Cyrus Smith." He looked up. "Do you trust me?"

Cyrus nodded.

Rupert leaned down eye to eye with Cyrus. "When I ask for it again, you must give it to me. Without question." Cyrus nodded again, closing his fingers tight around the sheath. The bones in his arm tingled. Greeves continued. "The tooth stays on the patrik. Tell everyone that I took it. If they think the Avengel of Ashtown carries it, those who come will come after me."

Antigone grimaced, listening to Nolan's spastic breaths start and stop, and then she raised her voice. "Nolan should really be in a hospital right now!"

Rupert shook his head. "No . . . Nolan should be in a grave. But he will not be, no matter how hard he tries. The little thief has been cursed with life."

Nolan's eyes opened, sparking. His breath fluttered, and they closed again.

Rupert hoisted Maxi's corpse easily to his shoulder and picked up his enormous gun. He looked at Nolan. "Take the thief where you will. Tell no one—*no one*—what you still carry." He began to turn toward the doorway.

"Wait!" Antigone yelped. "Mrs. Eldridge? Nolan said . . ."

Rupert paused, and then nodded. "She's gone. Bravely. No doubt trying to protect you." Turning quickly, he left the room.

Antigone stood up. "What?" she yelled. "Really? You're just going?" She looked back down at Nolan and inhaled slowly. "Cy, come here."

Cyrus turned away from the door and began twisting the tooth back onto the misshapen key ring as quickly as he could. Then he unwound Patricia, fed her through the ring, and raised her to his neck while he moved to help Antigone.

Gripping Nolan's arms, they pulled him to his feet, and then each slid under a shoulder.

Nolan muttered something in another language.

Outside, the courtyard and walkway were crowded. Armed guards, porters, young runners and bicyclists and balloonists, men and women with guns in hand were all parting as Rupert Greeves strode through them with a corpse on his shoulder. As Cyrus and Antigone emerged with Nolan, the sea of shocked and gaping faces swung back to them.

The stairs were crowded.

A tall boy in white workout clothes with a tattoo of a hieroglyphic eye on his neck stepped out of the crowd. "Who killed Maxi?" he asked.

Cyrus gritted his teeth and ignored the question as they moved down the stairs to the path below.

"Cy did," Antigone said. She looked at her brother. "With some . . . black bone blade from Skelton. Greeves took it."

A rumble rippled through the mob as the people in front passed the news to the back.

"Hey!" Diana Boone tore herself free of the crowd and hurried forward. Antigone was struggling. Diana relieved her, ducking a shoulder beneath one of Nolan's arms and grabbing on tight to his waist. She nodded at Cyrus. "Come on."

Cyrus imitated her on the other side, his arm crossing Diana's on Nolan's back. She didn't seem to notice the oozing burns and tarring blood, or care that she was pressing up against it.

"Grab his belt and lift," she said.

Antigone jumped around front and drove herself like a wedge into the crowd, pushing, shoving, shouldering a path into existence. People began to move before her elbows reached them. Cyrus, Diana, and Nolan followed.

"Nice, Tigs," Cyrus grunted.

"What's the fastest way to the hospital?" Antigone asked.

"Not hospital," Nolan mumbled.

When they reached the bottom of the main stairs,

Diana shrugged Nolan off, hooked him onto Antigone, and wiped her wet face on her arm. "The fastest way is to find some nurses. Get him up the steps and wait there."

She skipped quickly up the stairs and disappeared. Cyrus watched her run. Antigone watched Cyrus watch.

"Come on, Cy." The two of them lumbered forward. "Don't forget that you're not even thirteen. She's sixteen."

"What?" Cyrus asked. "What are you talking about?"

"You know what I'm talking about."

Suddenly, Nolan tore himself free and fell onto the stairs. Cyrus and Antigone dropped beside him.

His eyes fluttered open and found Cyrus's. "Used the keys. I know Phoenix"—he swallowed, writhing—"stole the cloak. His coat. Phoenix's coat."

Nolan's nostrils were flaring, and the veins on his neck flickered above his burnt chest. His eyes sharpened with desperate pain. "The tooth. Like Maxi. Kill me."

"Nolan, stop it!" Antigone yelled. She leaned over him, holding his face. Nolan began to cry.

"Nikales," he sobbed. "The thief." Spreading his arms and legs, he leaned back, gritted his teeth, and closed his eyes.

Diana Boone and two nurses crested the stairs.

· · ·

Daniel Smith opened his eyes. He didn't recognize the room. He didn't know how long he'd been asleep. He didn't know if he *had* been asleep.

He sat up.

Two metallic rods slid out of his nose. Curly cords rattled as he moved. They were taped all over him. He tugged thin receptors out from beneath his fingernails. He reached for his eyelids and peeled off four small pieces of tape. Tiny shaved patches dotted his scalp— each with its own coiling cord dangling down through a grid in the low ceiling. Wincing, he ripped them off in fistfuls.

Working slowly down his body, he freed himself. And then he stood.

He was a lot taller. His arms were longer, and his legs were thicker. His heart was beating slowly. Very slowly. And his eyes—he could see the fibers in the threads in the window curtain as he pulled it back. The sun, low above the water, seemed larger, and its aura clear.

Something, someone was pulling at him from somewhere. He was supposed to leave the room.

Dan turned and walked around his bed to the doorway. His hand twisted the knob and his ears caught the smooth, oily click and slide of the hidden metal tongue.

The hallway was long and the floor was as green as

a horsefly's eyes, tiled with thin rectangular pieces in a herringbone pattern.

Someone needed to be seen.

Dan walked down the hall. He chose a door, and he entered. Dr. Phoenix looked up from behind an enormous desk. Half of his mouth smiled.

"Daniel Smith," said Phoenix. "Well, don't you look splendid. And our relationship is beginning to find its proper footing." His smile grew. "You came when called." He pushed his thin body up from his chair. His lab coat was as dingy as ever. Beneath it, he was back in his white suit. "You do feel well, I hope? You're so much improved already. Not all that you will soon be, mind you, but it is a start."

Something tripped in Daniel's cotton-candy mind. Anger bubbled up in his chest and overflowed, roaring through him. A white marble bust of a bald man with a large beard rested on a wooden pedestal beside the door. Daniel's right hand found the back of its stone neck. He lifted it easily, and he threw it.

The bust spun through the air. Dr. Phoenix slipped to one side, and the heavy head crashed onto his desk.

Wood splintered. Papers flew, and glass vials shattered. The head bounced to the floor without its beard, cracked tiles, and split in half.

Breathing evenly, Daniel stared into Dr. Phoenix's pale, dilating eyes.

"Where's my mother?"

Dr. Phoenix eyed the rubble on the floor, and another small smile creased his face. "A certain amount of aggression is to be expected after even minor animalian modification, but I must say, you've been rather unkind to poor Mr. Darwin, don't you think? Do please remember that I am your friend."

"I could kill you right now," Daniel said. His voice was cold and even. Somewhere deep inside himself, he was surprised. "Take me to her."

"No, sir, and no, sir," said Dr. Phoenix. His smile vanished. "You could not kill me, and I will not take you to her." He looked Daniel up and down.

Clarity wavered. Something was changing.

The white-coated doctor eased back into his chair, and then pointed a long finger across his damaged desk to a chair on the other side.

"Mr. Daniel Smith," he said. "Such a short time, and I have already made you magnificent. Imagine what I could do in a year." He sighed. "Look at those legs of yours—thighs swollen with strength, calves of a kangaroo. Envy overwhelms me, my friend. Please, do sit down."

Daniel stepped behind the chair. He didn't sit. He was struggling to find his mind. His normal mind. The mind he had been using for twenty years. It was angry, but his anger was . . . useless, erased, buried deep with unremembered dreams, taped in a cardboard box and forgotten. He shut his eyes, chasing the feeling, not wanting the rage to leave him. Why? Why should he want anger? He didn't. Not anymore.

"Sit," Dr. Phoenix said again.

Daniel sat.

The doctor grinned, picking thoughtfully at the gap in his teeth. "People repress themselves," he said. "They repress their strengths, their potential, their dreams. They close doors. I hate closed doors, Daniel. I open doors. I am an opener of doors, a realizer of potentials, a philanthropianist of human obtainments, a composer of goodnesses and judgments." He paused. "And I am your friend. Are you mine? I have given you new strengths, Daniel Smith. Will you use them for me? Will you fight for your friend?"

Daniel blinked. The man wasn't making sense.

"Yes, I am," said Phoenix.

Yes, he is, thought Daniel. Now I understand. His mind suddenly focused. His image of the thin man in the coat grew bright, as sharp and crisp as ice crystals after fog. He saw intellect. Sacrifice. Love.

"Good," said Phoenix. "Indeed, I am all of those things." He smoothed the lapels of his coat. "But every god has a devil. Anger me, disobey me, betray the gifts of my friendship, and you will meet with a storm of wrath greater than any sea can hurl up at the cliffs. In anger, the Phoenix burns. I am Dr. Phoenix. I can become Mr. Ashes."

He leaned forward, his pale eyes bright. "Soon there will be a funeral with very few guests and very many boxes. You will help me to fill them. Ashes for Mr. Ashes, and then the Phoenix will rise. Our real work will begin."

No part of Daniel Smith's mind was listening. Phoenix had mentioned the sea. And cliffs. And anger. Insuppressible memories welled up. Cold, pounding waves. His father's boat chewed and swallowed by distant rocks. His mother's unconscious body—

Dr. Phoenix ground his teeth. "Daniel Smith," he said. "Where have you gone? Leave her. She will never wake up. Come back to me."

Daniel blinked. He was staring at the strange man who had taunted him and threatened him and climbed inside his head. The man who had kidnapped his mother.

Lunging across the desk, Daniel clamped his hands around the man's thin throat. They crashed backward in the desk chair and rolled onto the floor.

Daniel sat up and put his knee into the man's chest. "Where is she?" He clenched his teeth and squeezed.

Four large hands grabbed his shoulders from behind, picked him up, and threw him against the wall.

Gasping, Daniel slid to the floor.

The two men were identical—tall, lean for their strength, eyes bloody gold, features sharp, skin more green than tan. A row of skin slits fluttered on both sides of their necks. They helped Dr. Phoenix to his feet and stood behind him as he stepped toward Daniel.

Daniel coughed, swallowed blood, and tried to stand.

"Daniel Smith," said Phoenix, rubbing his throat. His eyes were sparking, and clumps of his black hair had fallen forward. He brushed them back. "These, Daniel, are my firstborn. Twins—my Romulus and Remus. They have a human mother, a wolf mother, a mother from among the great orange apes, and a mother devouring tuna in the sea. I am their father, and in them I am well pleased. You could have been their brother."

He extended his thin arms out from his sides. Behind him, the two gilled men stepped forward and began removing his coat.

Phoenix pulled his arms free of the stained sleeves and crouched in front of Daniel. His black hair began to lighten to white. His pale eyes muddied. His teeth lengthened, and a growl rumbled in his throat. "Now you must meet Mr. Ashes."

Rocking forward, Daniel slammed his fist into the man's face.

❧ sixteen ❧

CONFESSION

CYRUS SHRUGGED HIS blankets farther up around his shoulders. He had been awake for a while, but the blankets were warm, the stone bed was cushioned perfectly to his shape, and the night had been long, too much of it spent in the hospital wing watching Nolan writhe. But Horace was doing better—the nurses thought he might even wake soon. And Gunner had been there, watching his uncle breathe and gloating over Maxi's death.

Cyrus's sleep had been full of dreams, full of his fist swinging and bones crunching and Patricia swallowing people whole. But all dreams led to the one dream, and eventually, he'd ended up back in the kitchen of the California house. But this time, he'd been holding the tooth in one hand and the keys in the other. This time, he'd walked all the way outside into the rain, and his memory-vision had been clear.

He'd seen the man in the truck.

There was no way to tell what time it was without rolling over and checking the stilted clock. For the past hour, rolling over had seemed like way too much effort. It still did. His mind was too busy chewing.

Antigone's breathing was steady—slow, out of sync with the ticking clock. She sniffed. No. The sniff was wrong. A throat cleared.

Cyrus whipped over and sat up. Antigone was sleeping, virtually invisible in her nest of blankets. Seated one alcove over, Rupert Greeves was reading a book. At least, he had been reading. Now his eyes were on Cyrus. His forehead and jaw were bandaged. So was his left hand.

"What are you doing here?" Cyrus asked.

Rupert smiled. "Waiting for you to wake up. You earned your sleep yesterday." He raised his eyebrows, scrunching the bandage above them. "And down here, I do not have so many Keepers demanding access to a certain shard of tooth for their research or the monks asserting ownership and demanding that I immediately execute all the occupants of the Burials. Even some of the Sages have heard the news and wandered out from their rooms. Where is it?"

Cyrus slid Patricia off his neck and held up her silver body. The keys clinked against the tooth as she slowly squirmed, rubbing against Cyrus's skin. Cyrus had liked her already. He could have spent an entire day just watching her move. But after yesterday, he loved her.

Rupert nodded. "Good. Put it back on."

"Her," Cyrus said. "She's named Patricia." She went back around his neck. "Why did you let me keep the tooth?"

"Because that is something not one of my enemies would expect me to do. And because I felt that I should."

Cyrus inhaled slowly, gathering courage. He looked straight into Rupert's eyes.

"It was you," he said quietly. "In the truck. The day our dad died. I remember your beard."

Yawning, Antigone pushed back her blankets. She blinked, looked at Rupert, at Cyrus, and sat up. "What's going on?"

Rupert Greeves set his book down and cleared his throat. Cyrus watched the man's big hands clench, and his dark skin glistened with moisture. He tugged at what remained of his short, pointed beard and then scratched the nest of old scars high on his chest.

Cyrus shifted on his seat. Antigone glanced at her brother, eyebrows up, eyes wide.

Rupert sighed and ran his bandaged hand across his scalp. "Two years ago, I was contacted by Skelton. He was insulting, but he was also warning me. Phoenix was quite near to recovering the last remaining shard of the Dragon's Tooth." He looked up. "I should tell you what the tooth is."

"We know," said Cyrus. "We've heard the story."

Greeves nodded. "Of course. Then you know that

it was supposed to be destroyed—even the shards. Well-meaning fools did some horrible things with the Resurrection Stones." He looked around the little room. "Skelton told me that Phoenix knew where the last shard was—in a place where your father and I had once searched for it. Skelton and others were being sent to collect it, but he wanted me to get there first. He did not want Phoenix to have it. The man was becoming too vile—even for Billy Bones."

Rupert looked into Cyrus's eyes, and then turned to Antigone. "There weren't many people I could trust, and I was in a hurry. Your family had moved to Northern California, quite close to where I needed to be. I knew your father could help me, and I arrived at your house a few hours later—right before a storm. I saw you both then. Briefly. I did not know if you had seen me."

Antigone sat up like she'd been shocked. "What? You said two years ago. Two years ago when?"

Cyrus couldn't find words. Blinking, he could see his father smiling, the kitchen door closing, and the back of two heads as the truck bounced away.

Antigone tucked back her hair and stood up. "You were the one! How? You're supposed to be dead. Were you in the boat? What were you doing? Dad called you Rupe, didn't he? When Mom got home, she totally lost it. She put us in the Red Baron and we drove down onto the beach and just stared at the island until dark and, and . . ."

Rupert coughed.

Cyrus tried to breathe slowly. The itch in his memory was gone, but it felt much worse. He didn't want Rupert to tell the story. He didn't want to hear what had happened. He was falling again, he was tumbling toward something unknown but awful. He was going to hear something that could never, ever be changed.

His heart kicked hard against his ribs.

Antigone shoved her fingernails between her teeth to keep from talking.

"I was on the island—"

"Elephant Island," she said. "With all the elephant seals. The sharks live around it. It's illegal to go on it."

"Yes."

"With the ruined mansion," she added. "And the smashed lighthouse and the tidal caves."

"Tigs!" Cyrus yelped. He couldn't have looked away from Rupert's face if he'd wanted. He needed this over.

"All those things, yes," Rupert said. "May I go on?"

Antigone nodded, chewing.

"We anchored the boat beneath a small cliff, and the sun was setting by the time we reached the ruined mansion. It was impossible to hear anything with the barking and bellowing seals, and they hated our flashlights. The animals were in every room of the house—

upstairs and down—except the one Skelton had told us to search. That room was full of Phoenix's men. Skelton was with them. They'd gotten there too soon, and we hadn't seen their boat anchored in a tidal cave.

"We ran. We ran down through that rickety ruin of a mansion, tripping over seals and slipping in their scum. And then we ran out across the rocks. They were shooting at us before we reached the water—bullets, not fire. One of them hit me in the shoulder. I fell on the rocks and was knocked unconscious.

"Your father must have carried me, because when I came to, I was washing around in the bottom of our sinking boat—the frigid water had stopped my bleeding. The waves were pounding us through the jagged boneyard just off the cape, and the hull was cracked and cracking further. Cold water was rushing in. Your father was slumped over the wheel. He'd been shot in the back. More than once.

"I tried to reach him, but the hull was splitting fast, and the swell was towering. Before I reached him, we rolled beneath one final monstrous wave, the boat shattered, and I was left clinging to flotsam. Your father was gone.

"The boat flipped and sank not far from the cliff. The wash of the next wave slammed me up on the rocks, and I managed to grab on. Then I climbed.

"That night, while we were being chased, Skelton

palmed the tooth. The next morning, knowing Phoenix would uncover his betrayal, he went on the run. If I had died, he would have felt no grief, no guilt at all. But your father, he loved. And that is the reason why you were there when his running ended, the reason why he made you his Acolytes and tried to leave you everything, the reason why he placed that tooth in your hands, Cyrus Smith. Your father died for it. And I will not be the one to take it from you."

Cyrus bit his lip. His eyes were blurry. His hand was at his throat, gripping the sheath. Antigone's thumbnail was bleeding. She still chewed, staring at the big man, the man who had taken her father to his death.

"He didn't drown?" she asked quietly. "I always pictured him drowning, shivering in the water. I had dreams."

Rupert shook his head. "He did not drown."

Cyrus shut his eyes. He felt cold and sick in his stomach, hot and angry in his head. His pulse drummed in his temples.

"My mom," Antigone said quietly. "She tried to swim out. In freezing water."

Rupert lowered his head. "I know."

"Dan pulled her out. She never woke up."

Rupert nodded.

Cyrus jumped to his feet, wiping hot tears from his face, stepping forward. "You did nothing for us! Our dad saved your life. Two years and you never said anything! You never even told us what happened."

"I did several things," Rupert said quietly, "none of which make up for what you lost. I was the one who bought your California house. That money has kept you alive these two years."

"Why didn't you buy the motel?" Antigone said. "We hated the motel. That's what we wanted to get rid of. We all cried when Dan sold the house."

"It was better that you be closer to Ashtown. In violation of a number of protocols, I sent Eleanor Eldridge to inhabit the Archer Motel and protect you."

"That didn't work," Antigone said coldly. "Now she's dead, too."

"Yes. And these hands will bury her." Rupert's jaw pumped. "I thought the Archer could provide for you. When it didn't, I left what money I could for Daniel to find."

"You came into the Archer?" Cyrus asked.

Rupert nodded. "It had belonged to Skelton—he used it as a club for his more rebellious understudies and recruits. He gave the motel to your parents when your father was first expelled. It was all they had. Your father gave me a key. Because of your mother, I had never used it."

Antigone sat down. "Why didn't you just tell us everything?"

"Your father wanted you to know nothing about

337

the O of B, and to have nothing to do with it. When I became a Keeper, I offered to bring Daniel in as my Acolyte. Lawrence nearly threw me through a window. Katie, your mother, hated me, too. To her, I was a traitor. I represented all that had been stolen from her husband as a result of his love for her. It was difficult for me to accept, but I honored it."

"That's really dumb," Antigone muttered. "Our dad was dead, our mom was in a coma, and poor Dan, trying to take care of us. Forget what they wanted, you should have just done what you thought was best."

Rupert Greeves met her eyes. "Miss Smith," he said calmly. "That is exactly what I did. But now you are here, and many things have changed."

Cyrus swallowed hard. "Why don't you just take the tooth? I don't want it."

Rupert sighed and shook his head. "Maximilien is dead. Later, I will take you to the Brendan. He can decide the tooth's fate."

"The Brendan?" Cyrus asked. "Who is he? Where is he?"

"You will know soon enough." He glanced at Antigone. "Today, the two of you should meet with tutors. Without Mrs. Eldridge, I am now your Keeper. I will train you both, but not in every field—I know too little myself. Nolan—when he shows his face again—is more than capable with languages."

"Shows his face?" Cyrus asked. "What do you mean? How bad was he burned?"

Rupert smiled. "Nolan is fine. He peels quickly. But he hates hospitals and doctors, and he disappeared last night. I asked him to go on the run for a while—act like he stole something important." He turned to Antigone. "Did Eleanor, Mrs. Eldridge, mention any available tutors?"

Antigone nodded. "Diana Boone, Llewellyn Douglas, somebody called Jax, you, and some others I don't remember." She looked at her brother, and then at the few retrieved papers and semicharred Latin books beside Cyrus's jacket on the floor.

"That's good enough for a start," Rupert said, standing. He stiffened and cleared his throat. "Acolytes, your Keeper, Eleanor Elizabeth Eldridge, lies in the chapel, awaiting burial. We shall not all die, but we shall all be changed." Stepping forward, he gripped Cyrus's shoulder with one hand and Antigone's with the other. Surprised, Cyrus began to twitch against the strong grip, but stopped himself when he saw the man's face. Rupert's eyes were soft with grief, his voice was a chant.

"Who brought us to birth? In whose arms shall we die? He that keeps us neither slumbers nor sleeps. He is the Keeper of souls."

Rupert exhaled and looked from Cyrus to Antigone. "I owe a debt to your father. I will repay that debt to you."

Dropping his hands, he ducked through the hole in the wall. The planks sighed beneath him as he left.

Cyrus looked at his sister. For the first time, he knew exactly how his father had died, and it made him feel raw, peeled like an orange. In his head, he could see Rupert Greeves in the truck. The last man to see his father smile? To hear his laugh? To see him move? No. That would be the men who'd shot him—the killers. Had any of them died in the Archer's parking lot? He hoped so. And Mrs. Eldridge . . . she was really dead. All the way dead. Not coming back. Gone. He hadn't liked her enough, hadn't been kind enough to her, and that made it worse.

Antigone tucked back her short hair and squinted at him out of one eye. She obviously didn't want to cry. He didn't want her to cry.

"Should we go to the chapel?" he asked.

She nodded.

"Okay," he said. "And then food. And then we'll find that Douglas guy."

Dennis Gilly sat on a thirteen-inch stone ledge, with his knees tucked tight beneath his chin. When the other porters were on break, they played cards in one of the porters' closets. When Dennis was on break, he perched above the kitchen's garbage stoop, staring at the lake.

The first time he had climbed up onto the ledge, it

had taken him half an hour. Now, a mere four minutes into his break, he could be up, breathing easily, his eyes on the water and his mouth around an apple filched from the kitchen. He didn't know that he oughtn't take apples from the kitchen, just like he didn't know that he oughtn't climb up onto the ledge above the garbage stoop. Some rules had yet to be written. Nobody had ever said anything about it, one way or another. But he still felt a little guilty, and that made enforcing all the rules he did know about even more important.

Despite the growing wind, Dennis was wearing his bowler hat, tied on with a ribbon beneath his chin. Despite the heat, he was already wearing his black waterproof cape in anticipation of the rain he could see on the horizon.

Dennis loved storms. He loved wind. He loved the sound of snapping sails and the creaking of decks and the splash of the bow in rough water. Watching the colors in the harbor and the rise and fall of the small boats in their slips and the larger ones tugging at their anchors, Dennis ached. And he took a bite of apple.

Yesterday had been a bad day. Three porters were in the hospital, two with burns and one with a bullet wound. Judging from the bullet hole in his cape, he had nearly been killed himself—and by one of the nightmare transmortaled, too. But Cyrus and Antigone had put an end to him. Imagine an Acolyte having a weapon like that. Of course, Rupert had taken it away. He had to. The Order was buzzing. And the monks had been shouting at Rupert during breakfast. Why would anyone want something like that? Unless, of course, they were trying to kill someone like Maximilien Robespierre.

Dennis shivered. Today, of all days, he needed water. He needed wind. He needed to race in front of the growing storm on the Great Lake's hackling back. Then worry would disappear. Loneliness would vanish.

But he couldn't sail anymore. He couldn't walk down to the harbor and hop into the Order's little number thirteen and let the wind drive him out onto the lake.

He was a porter. Not an Acolyte. His parents were dead. Dues had gone unpaid. But at least he was still here, still able to wedge himself onto a ledge and watch the water. He filled his mouth with crisp, starch apple.

Beneath him, the door on the garbage stoop opened. And then it slammed.

Dennis leaned forward. Cecil Rhodes was fidgeting nervously, turning in place beside the trash bins, picking at his mustache. He was talking. Muttering quietly. Not to himself. Someone else was with him, out of sight beneath the ledge.

Dennis Gilly heard the jingle of small bells and the sound of a lighter flicking. Pipe smoke rose up around Dennis's toes before a gust from the lake swept it away.

"I'm not useless," Rhodes said. "Sterling, I've done everything, everything he's asked. And more."

"Having Eldridge tortured in your office was a lovely bit of planning," Sterling said. "You could have just asked where the whelps were; I've been keeping tabs. And Rupe's more than just a touch curious what Maxi was up to in your rooms, isn't he now? *And* he has the tooth."

"I couldn't stop Maxi!" Rhodes said. "And you couldn't have done any better. He's mad."

"Was," Sterling said quietly. "Maxi *was*. Rupe incinerated the corpse this morning. Tell me, Captain Cecil, did you stop little John Lawney from filing Skelton a pair of Acolytes? No, sir. You didn't. Did you stop that sweet little pair of Smiths from entering the Order's protection? No, sir. You didn't. Is Lawney still breathing? Yes, sir. He is. And now Greeves is hovering over his bed like a thirsty mosquito. And Maxi? Right, he's dead. Oh, I'd say you've done everything he's asked of you. If I were a liar. Have you even gained access to Skelton's rooms?"

"They're charm-sealed!" Rhodes said frantically. "And I don't know with what. I need those keys. I'm not equipped to deal with this kind of thing!"

"I agree," Sterling said. "You're not equipped to deal with much of anything, are you, Rhodesy?"

"And what about you? What are you supposed to be doing? According to you, the brats weren't even carrying the tooth. Well, they were, and did you see that hole in Maxi's head? Somebody told them what that tooth could do. If Phoenix comes tonight and Rupe's hidden it . . . if we can't find it . . ."

"I'm doing my part," Sterling said. "And don't you worry your hollow head about it. As for that chip off the old Reaper's Blade—they didn't have it. Sir Roger would have bellowed hell if they did." The sweet smell of pipe tobacco surrounded Dennis as the smoke came up in clouds. "And ask yourself this: Why would Rupe be putting it out so loud that he took the tooth when he knows Phoenix is after it?"

"Because he's a fool and a brute and only happy in a fight."

"Yes, and he'll get one. But Rhodesy, you've never seen war or left a chessboard a winner. He's drawing fire. He's set himself as a decoy. Kitchen money says he doesn't have it."

"What? Then who does? Did he hide it? If we don't find it, Phoenix will kill us both."

"Hush, duckling," Sterling said. "Who else was in the room when Maxi died? Who would know how to use that tooth? Who, better than anyone, can disappear in this place?"

He paused. Rhodes cocked his head. Sterling continued. "If only I had my sidewalk chalks, I'd draw you a picture. Find Nikales, Nolan, the Polygon boy. The thief.

He left the hospital last night and no one has seen him. His pocket will be heavy. You and your clerks search every corner and shadow and stick of this place. Hunt the tunnels, hunt the grounds, hunt the towers. Find him. Seal him. Come fetch me. When we've got him and Rupe and the little Smiths, one of them will have it or point to where it is."

Rhodes stopped his pacing and began cracking his knuckles.

"Now," Sterling said. "Go."

Cecil Rhodes disappeared. The door slammed.

Pipe smoke danced with the wind.

Down on the sloping lawn, two shapes were walking toward the harbor.

Dennis Gilly's heel slipped an inch, and he froze, biting his lip, tasting blood.

"Dennis Gilly," Sterling said. "Apple thief and eavesdropper." Bells jingling, he stepped into view. He didn't look up. His eyes were on Cyrus and Antigone as they crossed the lawns. His hand held his pipe.

Dennis looked at the ledge to his right. It dead-ended in smooth stone. To his left, it dead-ended in smooth stone, but there was a small rainspout—the ladder he used to get up. Climbing higher wouldn't help him. He wanted to cover his eyes, to hold very still and somehow become invisible.

Sterling puffed slowly on his pipe, and the smoke

blew back around his ears. "Come on down, lad. Come have a chat with Big Ben Sterling."

Cyrus filled his lungs with warm wind, beginning to feel more alive. Poor Mrs. Eldridge. In the chapel, her face had been as pale and peaceful as moonlight, but the sight of her had been as violent as a kick to the stomach. The old woman's fingers, empty of rings, had been interlaced. Her white hair had been pushed back from her face and woven into a cobweb-silver braid. She actually looked younger in death.

He glanced at his sister. Seeing Mrs. Eldridge, saying goodbye, had been hard, but somehow easier than not seeing her at all.

The green lawns, the sprawling gray lake, the blue sky walled with rowdy black clouds in the distance—the world around them was beautiful and alive. And they were somehow still alive in it. In this world, in this sun, he could almost believe that he would see Dan again.

Cyrus savored the sun on his face. The wind was muscling through his hair, and the keys were clicking back and forth against his collarbones with each downhill stride. The lightning bug banged against his right thigh. And yesterday's find, forgotten in the chaos—the strange wet ball of Quick Water—was slapping against his left leg while he walked. He looked at Antigone. She looked back. He was turning into a walking collection.

"I don't feel great about this, Cy. Why would anyone be fishing in a storm?"

"It's not a storm," Cyrus said. "Not yet, at least."

For a moment, they were silent, walking in step. And then his sister cleared her throat and coughed.

"Poor Mrs. E," Antigone said. "If she hadn't been helping us . . ."

"Yeah," said Cyrus. "I know."

Antigone looked at him. "Does it make you want to quit?"

Cyrus inhaled. It didn't. And not just because they had nowhere else to go. He shook his head.

"Me neither," said Antigone. "I mean, she died helping us. If we flunk out or whatever after that . . . I almost don't care about getting Skelton's money anymore. Almost. I know we need it."

Cyrus said nothing. His sister was right. But he didn't need any extra motivation, and he couldn't remember the last time he'd given a thought to Skelton's estate. Antigone had known sooner than he had—what they'd learned, what they'd seen, what he'd done in the past three days, all of it had changed who they were. But he knew that now. Collecting tires would mean nothing. Sneaking into his school's gym would be as exciting as sleeping. They could never go back to who they'd been before.

He wasn't leaving Ashtown, not even if it meant studying something.

In front of them, the grass jutted out in a long row of flat-topped mini-plateaus, each one as big as a house. Between these, the slope continued more steeply, down to a long, level stripe of grass—the airstrip. Cyrus and Antigone jogged down. When they reached the airstrip, they stopped and looked back. Dozens of underground hangars were set into the hillside, with the grassy plateaus for roofs. Most of the doors were closed, but a few were open, revealing crowds of pristine vintage planes and clusters of jumpsuited mechanics.

Diana Boone stood beside the nearest one. She was wearing a ragged leather jacket over a jumpsuit, her hands were on her hips, and she was watching four men winch a pale-blue plane with a green underbelly back into a tight space in the small hangar. Beneath the glass cockpit, the plane's name was painted in swooping red letters:

Tick Licker

Frustrated, Diana shook her head and cupped her hands. "Wingtip, Edward!" she yelled. "You'll clip the Bearcat!"

The man at the winch looked up. His gray jumpsuit was spotted with stains.

"Get out of here, Di!" he yelled. "Your Tick's fine.

Leave, or I'll roll all your birds out into the storm and walk away."

Cyrus opened his mouth to yell, but Antigone grabbed his arm and pulled him back around.

"Not now, Cy. No distractions. We're going to the jetty." She dragged him a few steps before he shook her arm loose and kept stride. "And you're twelve," she added.

"Practically thirteen," Cyrus muttered. "And she probably thinks I'm older than you are. I'm taller and less snotty."

Antigone laughed. "Right. You're Captain Wonderful. Dream a big dream." The two of them crossed the airstrip and let gravity lengthen their strides down the slope.

The harbor was full of bobbing sailboats. Sails had been lashed to masts. Smaller motored craft had been lashed into slips along a boardwalk. Some had been cranked up out of the water on metal lifts.

The stone jetty was empty of all but a few shapes. A dripping wet boy and girl were stepping off of it holding a large bucket between them that was splashing madly with something. A woman was running through a crisp routine with two signal flags for the benefit of a distant boat, and then consulting a large pair of binoculars before continuing her gymnastic conversation. At the very end, where wind-swollen lake waves were sending up spray, someone—man or woman—was slumped in a wheelchair with two fishing poles mounted to the hand rests.

"And," said Antigone, "there's our guy."

As they approached, Cyrus could see that the spray was actually reaching the old man. A sopping blanket covered his legs, his chin was tilted forward onto his chest, and his hat had blown off.

Water dripped down his sun-mottled skin and off his beaked nose.

"Is he dead?" Antigone asked.

Cyrus tapped the man on the shoulder. "Hey! You're not gonna catch much in the storm."

"Cyrus . . ." Antigone leaned all the way over the man. A wave washed into the jetty and splintered on the stones. "He's not breathing, Cyrus. He's dead. He is. Call someone!"

"Who's dead?" the man sputtered. "Where? Don't just stand there! Dive in!"

Antigone jumped backward. Exhaling slowly, she closed her eyes for a moment, and then looked up at the sky.

"I'm sorry," Cyrus said. "Mr. Douglas, right? We were worried about you. My sister thought you weren't breathing."

The old man's sparse hair was matted down on his scalp. His skin was the color of spotted greasy cardboard, and his needle eyes hid in the shadows of badly organized coal-and-ash eyebrows. He glared at Cyrus, and then turned to Antigone.

She shook her head. "I'm sorry. You really scared me. Of course you were breathing. I just . . . never mind."

"I wasn't breathing," the old man said. Water dripped from his unevenly stubbled chin. "Hardly ever breathe. Only when I need to talk, or when young bits of skin come rouse me from my diving."

"Your diving?" Cyrus asked. "What do you mean?"

"I mean my diving, you giblet. I was fifty meters down, floating with my bulls, sometime in the summer of fifty-two. They're still down there, wondering where I've got to."

"Right," said Cyrus. "Well, we heard you might be willing to be our free-diving tutor."

"Your what?" the old man asked, squinting. "What summer is this, anyhow? Not fifty-two. Nope. Nope. This is a wheelchair and my hands look half in the grave. I'm no tutor, and never would have been to a pair like you. Scurry on, boyito. Leave me be."

Cyrus's mouth snapped shut, molars grinding.

"What bulls?" Antigone asked, shooting her brother an eye warning. "What did you mean, 'floating with my bulls'?"

"Sharks, lovely." The man showed her his false

teeth. "Bull sharks. Some people have dogs. I had sharks. Keepers didn't take kindly to them. Tried to spear every last one. I cried for a week, and I don't mind saying it." He looked back out over the lake.

Cyrus moved around to face the man. "My name is Cyrus Smith, and this is my sister, Antigone. We have to achieve the 1914 standards for Acolytes—it's a long story. And that means free diving. Can't you help us? Maybe start by telling us what free diving is."

The man sneered.

"Oh, we know what free diving is." Antigone shrugged, trying to seem casual. "If you don't want to help, that's fine. It seems easy. We'll manage."

"Ha!" The man snorted. "The dusky beauty says it's easy. Can you hold your breath for ten minutes? Can you walk on the bottom of this lake in nothing but your skin? I can. I have. I will again."

Cyrus looked at his sister. She crouched beside the wheelchair, staring into the old man's eyes. And then she smiled. "Mr. Douglas, I don't believe you."

The old man laughed. "You think I'm dumb? You think I don't know what you're tryin', girlie? Spray me down with a pretty smile, and then doubt me till I'm itchy? Maybe sixty years ago, that works. Not now. Keep your smilin' to yourself. Now it's all about making a fair trade." He smirked. "I'll tell you what—if you throw me in the lake right now, we got a deal."

Antigone straightened and crossed her arms, taking in the wheelchair and the man's skeleton arms. "No way."

"I'll do it," said Cyrus. "If he sinks, oh well. He wasn't going to help us anyway."

"That's the spirit, lad." The old man grinned. "Be a savage. Do it. Throw me in and I'll help you. My word is gold."

Cyrus stepped forward. Antigone shook her head.

"Come on now!" the old man yelped. "You can't offer a treat like that and not follow through. We have a deal?"

Cyrus spread his legs, bent his knees, and leaned over.

"Cyrus!" Antigone blinked. "You're not really going to—"

The fragile old man rose up in Cyrus's arms, as light as a mannequin.

Antigone jumped forward, but Cyrus had already stepped onto the rocks. A wave washed up around his ankles.

The old man was laughing.

Cyrus heaved. The water leapt.

The blanket swirled on the surface. Llewellyn Douglas was gone.

"Mr. Cyrus! Miss Antigone!" The voice was distant. Lost in the wind.

Antigone stood, motionless, hands over her mouth, eyes on the water.

Cyrus looked back over the jetty, over the harbor, at the lawns and the underground hangars.

A boy in a bowler hat was sprinting toward them, his cape snapping in the wind.

❊ seventeen ❊

LILLY THE BULL

"CYRUS, YOU MURDERED him. Jump in! Find him! Pull him out!"

Cyrus stared back at the gray frothing water. The blanket was clinging to the rocks. There was no sign of Llewellyn.

"He wanted me to," Cyrus said. "He's a free diver. Don't you think he'll be fine?"

"Guys!" Dennis had crossed the airstrip. The wind softened his shouting.

"No, Cyrus. I don't think he'll be fine. Get in there!"

Cyrus took off his jacket, unstrapped and tugged off his boots and socks, and then edged farther down the rocks. "Give him a minute. He'll come up."

Antigone stepped forward and punched the heels of her hands into Cyrus's shoulder blades. Waving his arms, he rocked forward, overbalanced, and slapped into the water, swallowed by an oncoming wave.

Antigone chewed nervously on her fingernail. She was alone in the growing wind, standing in a fading glimmer of sunlight with an empty wheelchair. Suddenly, she dug into her pocket.

Cyrus swallowed cold water. He spat cold water. He felt his muscles and joints tightening as he sank. He felt a wave carrying him back toward the rocks.

Blinking, forcing his inflated lungs to relax, he pulled himself deeper and away from the jetty.

He wasn't going to bob right back up and yell at his sister. Let her wonder. Let her worry. She'd earned it.

Twisting, Cyrus scanned the water for any signs of the old man.

The stone jetty sloped down twenty feet or more until it reached a small, muddy, timber-dotted shelf. Beyond the shelf's edge, deep water became dark water, which became cold, lightless nothing.

Down on the edge of blurry invisibility, Cyrus could just make out a pale shape. Letting out a little of his air, he kicked toward it.

Cyrus could swim. His parents had made sure of it. But this was deeper than he had ever tried to dive. He knew he could hold his breath for one hundred and five seconds before crazy desperation would force him to inhale, and he'd managed to hold his breath for at least that long a few weeks before while scaring a PE teacher and a school nurse.

But he didn't know how long this would take.

As he descended, the pale shape of Llewellyn Douglas became clearer. The old man was swirling in place by the drop-off. And he'd stripped down to his bones, his skin, and a pair of baggy white skivs. He spun in two backflips as easily as a seal—a wrinkly, skeletal, furless seal—and then he shifted, gliding on his back along the shelf's edge.

Spotting Cyrus, he straightened up, laughing bubbles. His false teeth drifted out of his mouth, but he snatched them as they sank and popped them back into his grin.

He pointed up. "Go!"

"Teach us?" Cyrus bubbled, and that was it for his air. He bit his lip and ignored the empty feeling in his chest.

A sparkle of light caught his eye and he looked down. His ball of Quick Water had almost entirely hatched through the fabric of his pocket, and it was erupting with sunlight. Cyrus grabbed at it, but his arms were too slow in the water.

The ball of daylight wobbled free and began to sink. Cyrus flailed while the old man watched. He kicked at it, but the ball parted around his toes and reunited on the other side, wobbling away as it sank like liquid steel, down toward the darkness.

Cyrus hesitated. He needed to be ascending, getting closer to a desperate, gasping breath at the surface. Instead, he dove after the ball. Before he'd gone far, the old man's bony hand closed around his ankle and pulled him back. He poked Cyrus in the stomach and pointed up.

"Go!" he bubbled again. And then, shaking his head, the skeleton in underwear slithered down, moving through the water like an eel.

Cyrus floated up, watching the golden ball disappear beyond the shelf. A moment later, a long, bulky bullet shape with fins rose up from the dark water, cruising toward the old man with lazy tail strokes. It couldn't be a shark. Not in Lake Michigan.

Llewellyn Douglas grabbed on to its dorsal fin and disappeared into the darkness.

Cyrus turned his face up to the surface and surged with every drop of energy he had. His legs and shoulders were out of oxygen. His head drummed, and his vision blurred. And then the surface—air, wind, sun, and gasping lungs.

Sputtering, spitting, wheezing, Cyrus worked to tread water, trying to blink his vision back to normal.

"Cyrus!" Antigone's voice wasn't as close as he would have hoped. "Cyrus! Get over here!"

A little more than a pool's length away, his sister was waving at him from the jetty. Someone in a cape was bouncing beside her.

"Swim, Cyrus!"

His heart was calming. His sizzling lungs were

cooling. Cyrus began crawling toward his eager sister. When he reached the stones, two sets of hands dragged him up out of the water, banging his shins, stubbing his toes, and finally trying to force him to stand.

Cyrus sat down and flopped over, blinking at the sky—the sun blinked back, sliding through the front-running storm clouds before the growing black stampede.

"Cy, stand up." Antigone grabbed at his hands. Cyrus slapped her arms away.

"Mr. Cyrus." Dennis Gilly, breathless, loomed into view. "Something terrible has happened. Will happen. Mr. Sterling's been plotting. Something terrible for sure. He tried to kill me."

Cyrus shut his eyes. "Antigone, I'm waiting for an apology."

"Why? Because I pushed you in? I'm not apologizing. You didn't know if he could swim. Now listen to Dennis. We need to hurry. He overheard something big."

"There was a shark," said Cyrus. "And I'm pretty sure I wasn't hallucinating."

"I know," Antigone said. "I saw it swim by. The old guy rode it, and I've never seen anything more disgusting than that guy in his underwear. I was looking through my half of the Quick Water blob. If you turn it in your hand, you can look in any direction.

It's cool. I'll show you later. Now get up. We need to run. We need to find Nolan before Rhodes and Sterling do."

"What?" Cyrus asked, squinting. "Why do they care about Nolan?"

Dennis leaned forward, and his ribboned bowler hat blocked the sun. "Because they're working for Phoenix, and Nolan has that horrible tooth of Mr. Skelton's—stolen from you—and Mr. Rhodes tried to have Mr. John Horace Lawney killed, and he was there when Mrs. Eldridge was murdered, and there's a plan for something to happen tonight, and Mr. Sterling says they have to get Nolan right away. And you two. And Mr. Greeves. Because one of you will have what they need."

Dennis panted.

Cyrus sat up. "Is this real?" he asked. "Rhodes, sure. But Ben Sterling?"

Dennis inhaled deeply. "Yes! I was sitting on a ledge listening to Misters Sterling and Rhodes talking about it, and when Mr. Rhodes left, I made a noise, and Mr. Sterling noticed and he told me to come down and have a talk, and I told him no and he told me yes and I started humming and pretending not to hear him but he pulls out a little bottle and a tiny dart and he tells me that he was saving it for later but now everyone will think I died of eating a bad apple, and he dipped the dart in the bottle and pulled off the bowl of his pipe and put the dart in the pipe stem, and he was going to shoot me right there."

Cyrus looked at his sister. She nodded. He scrambled up to his bare feet.

"What happened?"

"I jumped," Dennis said. "Off the ledge. Over Sterling. Tumbled in the grass. Hurt my knee, but I came running straight here. We have to find Mr. Nolan and Mr. Greeves."

"I don't believe it." Cyrus flapped his dripping arms and shook his head. "Dennis, I'm sorry, but I can't see Ben Sterling trying to shoot you with a poison dart."

Dennis turned and pointed toward the slope. "I don't lie, Mr. Cyrus. Ask him when he gets here." Five shapes had crossed the airstrip and were striding toward the harbor. Sterling, black-bearded and barrel-chested, led the way on his thin metal legs.

"Run!" Dennis sprinted down the length of the jetty, and the approaching men fanned out, ready to pursue. Turning, Dennis dashed back. "Where? Where do we go? They'll kill us right here. No one's around. No one's here. They've all gone inside. Get a boat. We should sail! I can sail!" Dennis danced in place like he needed a bathroom.

"They would sail after us," Antigone said. "Just

wait, Dennis. They might not hurt us. Anyone in the kitchen could see."

"Mr. Cyrus!" Sterling's voice pierced the wind easily. "I'm afraid our young porter friend isn't well!"

The men reached the base of the jetty. Sterling had brought four surly-looking groundskeepers along with him.

"Dennis Gilly!" Sterling yelled. "Come with us, lad. You've been sniffing the kitchen's whiskey again, and it's time you were sleeping off your visions."

Sterling lumbered half the jetty's length, ear bells dancing in the sun. His apron was gone. His untied and unnetted black beard stuck out stiffly from his jaw. When he moved his arm, Cyrus glimpsed the flash of metal tucked up his sleeve. The four men behind him were keeping their hands out of sight.

"Seems to me," said a quiet voice, "that now would be a great first lesson. Dive in and I'll do the rest."

Cyrus glanced behind him. Off the end of the jetty, barely visible in the waves, Llewellyn Douglas clicked his false teeth.

"Tigs," Cyrus whispered. "Dennis. Follow me. No questions. Just jump in and dive down. Get below the surface." He picked up his jacket and slung it on. He'd ditch it if he had to swim far, but he didn't want to. He glanced at his boots. Too awkward.

"Mr. Cyrus," Dennis said. "I can't—"

"Now!" said Cyrus. He grabbed Dennis by the wrist and turned to grab Antigone. His sister was already gone, kicking in the air above the water.

Cyrus planted his bare foot on the end of the jetty and pushed off. Dennis's weight tugged him backward, his feet swung up, and he landed flat on his back in the water.

Dennis landed on top of him.

Cyrus thrashed, tangled in Dennis. Tangled in cape. And then someone was pulling his arm, pulling him down. Quickly. Smoothly. Something big and dark and rough thumped against his chest. He grabbed on to it with his free arm, and it felt like a tree trunk wrapped in sandpaper—a muscled, swimming tree trunk. The bubbles cleared and Cyrus looked around. The skeleton in underwear had his left arm hooked over one of the big shark's pectoral fins. With his right, he was dragging Cyrus by the wrist. On the other side of the shark, Cyrus glimpsed his sister clutching a fin. Dennis and his cape were dragging from Antigone's ankles.

The shark's tail thumped Cyrus in the ribs, and Llewellyn Douglas tugged him up to the pectoral fin. Cyrus grabbed on, and then the scrawny man threw his arms around the cruising shark's back, slid himself up and forward of the dorsal fin, and then patted the shark's gills.

The tail swept and the shark surged, diving into deep water.

Ben Sterling stood at the end of the jetty, staring at the water. They were kids, brand-new Acolytes. They couldn't have gone far. Dead or alive, they'd be bobbing up soon.

"Big B?" one of the men asked.

"I have some dynamite," said another.

Sterling shook his head. "Get back to hunting the Polygon boy. I'll stay here."

The men turned and began walking off the jetty. "Double time!" Sterling yelled. The men jumped into a jog.

Sterling pushed the fishing-poled wheelchair onto the middle of the jetty and eased himself into it. "Llewellyn Douglas," he said, scanning the waves. "You're down there, too?" After a moment, a smile rustled beneath his beard, and he stood back up. "Old dog," he said quietly. "Old trick."

The wind surged, ringing Ben Sterling's bells and shivering his beard. Chuckling to himself, he hurried off the jetty.

Cyrus felt the water pressure grow as they slid deeper and deeper down the face of the shelf. Suddenly, the shark veered into it, Cyrus's legs dragged across stone, and the last of the light died.

A rock grazed Cyrus's head. His foot. They were

moving through a tunnel. He tucked tight against the shark's body and let himself release most of his air. Dennis was yelling. Bubbling.

Cyrus tried to relax, to forget about what he was doing, to forget about his panicking lungs and his bulging eyes.

The shark thrashed and Cyrus nearly slipped off. They were climbing, winding, ascending.

Time slowed down. Limbs became lead, and then Cyrus felt his foot splash through the surface. He let go of the shark's fin and kicked up into dark, dank air.

Treading water in emptiness, Cyrus wheezed. "Tigs!" he yelled. "Dennis!"

He heard coughing. "Cy . . . help. Dennis—"

Someone threw up.

Cyrus swam toward his sister's voice, but he couldn't tell if he was moving in the right direction—or moving at all. He stopped and bobbed on the surface he couldn't even see, swallowing cool lake water.

"Marco!" he yelled.

"Cyrus . . . it's not . . ."

She wasn't far. Cyrus splashed forward as fast as he could until he slapped something with a stroke.

"Tigs?" Cyrus felt around the body. Dennis's cape. He was still below the surface. From behind, Cyrus got his arms under Dennis's and rocked backward to get the porter's face above the water. The caped body shook, kicked Cyrus in the shin, and then threw up on his hands.

Antigone gasped beside them.

"Tigs, I'm here, I'm here," Cyrus said.

"Dennis was pulling . . . me down." She coughed hard, and then gagged. "I tried, couldn't hold . . . kept sinking."

"I got him," Cyrus said. "You okay? Can you help me keep him up?"

With a sharp clank and a buzzing, flickering explosion, the darkness sizzled into blinding light.

Cyrus closed his eyes against the pain, and then opened them into a squint. The blur solidified. They were bobbing in a pool. High walls were covered with white tiles, cracked and stained and occasionally missing, but glistening beneath a ceiling crowded with caged lights.

The water looked as black as liquid coal, and a large dorsal fin was carving it in slow circles.

"Mr. Douglas!" Cyrus yelled. "Where are you?"

"Over here, boy. Get out and help the cripple."

Antigone sputtered laughter. "Turn, Cy. We're right at the edge. Would suck to drown right here."

Cyrus kicked slowly while Dennis flailed his arms. "Would suck to drown anywhere," he said, spitting water.

Two yards behind him, the pool ended and a tile floor stuck out its lip a foot above the water.

Antigone swam to the wall, boosted her waist up onto the edge, hooked a knee, and rolled out.

When Cyrus reached the wall, he braced himself while Antigone grabbed Dennis's arms and Cyrus heaved the groaning porter up onto the tiles. His wet cape dripped over the edge, and his crushed bowler hat—still tied on—covered his eyes.

Cyrus flopped out of the water and looked around. The room was littered with small wooden crates and old rusted gear on collapsed shelving.

From the other side of the room, Mr. Douglas, pale and dripping, grinned at him. He was sitting with his back against the wall beside a doorway, just beneath a large metal electrical switch. A wet trail on the dirty tile showed where he'd dragged himself across the floor.

"Always hated Benjamin Sterling," the old man said. "Mr. Whispers and Secrets, we used to call him. A plotter and that's that. I won't touch his cooking."

"Who called him that?" Cyrus asked.

"My own self and all my dead brothers. He poisoned my Evelyn ten years back—I don't doubt it—and still he's cooking for the Order." He shook his head. "No-legged liar with a bit of charcoal for a heart."

Cyrus looked at the old man's sagging ribs and skeletal legs. "We need to get you some clothes. Can you stand up?"

"No, I can't stand up. Didn't you bring along my wheelchair?" Llewellyn cackled laughter and then checked his teeth. "And no need for clothes. We'll stay here for a touch, and when Benjamin Filthy Sterling has moved along, Lilly will take us back. Haven't had a swim or a bit of adventure in two ages. Feels like an old friend."

"Who's Lilly?" Antigone asked. She had rolled Dennis onto his belly.

"The last of my bulls," Llewellyn said. "The one the Keepers missed. I raised hundreds of pups in this pool right here. My sweet Lilly was from the final brood—before my legs gave. The biggest I ever bred, too. She's six meters for sure. An ancient lady now—thirty years old—but she still remembers old Llew."

"You want to go back out of here on that shark?" Antigone asked. "Dennis is half dead. I almost drowned. Isn't there another way? What's through that door?"

"Locks and more locks," Llewellyn said. "And stairs and tunnels that lead up to the Crypto wing of the zoo. This was part of it. Been locked for decades—since the Keepers lost control of the collections."

Cyrus glanced at the man's underwear and looked back at his sister. "Tigs, I'm gonna need Dennis's cape over here."

Antigone reached around Dennis and undid his cape. She threw it toward Cyrus, and the heavy, wet cloth slapped to the floor. Then she grabbed at her pockets.

"Cyrus, my Quick Water's gone."

"Already lost mine," Cyrus said. "It doesn't like real water."

"Oh, don't worry." The old man pointed at the pool. "If you dropped it in here, I'm sure Lilly will have eaten it. She's waiting around for a treat like a good little sharklet. Not that I have one for her." He turned to Cyrus. "She bolted your glowing ball right down. Can't blame her—not many twinklings in the deep water."

Cyrus walked to the edge of the pool and watched the big shark carve her circles.

"Pull me over there." Llewellyn rocked in place. "Let's see how much the old girl remembers."

While Dennis, still facedown, moaned and coughed and spat on the tile, Cyrus and Antigone tied the wet cape around Llewellyn's neck like an apron, and then dragged him to the edge of the pool.

Sitting with his feet in the water, the old man stretched his fist out over the surface. Lilly's circles changed. The dorsal did one loop at the far wall and then disappeared.

Llewellyn slapped the tile floor.

"Stand back," he said, and the water exploded.

Eighteen feet of shark flew out of the water and slammed onto the tile floor. A pectoral fin smacked the old man, and he tumbled toward Dennis. Cyrus and Antigone both yelled, jumping back with the heavy spray. Cyrus slipped on the wet tile and landed on his back.

Antigone kept her feet, eyes wide and heart racing. Lilly's yellow eye rolled in its socket, scanning the room.

The old man army-crawled back toward the shark. "Beautiful girl," he said, like he was talking to a puppy. "Look at you . . . lovely Lillith!" The shark's gills flapped, and she swiped the pool with her tail, sending a wave of water up onto Dennis.

Moaning, dripping, Dennis Gilly finally pushed himself up onto his knees and slid back his hat.

His eyes widened and he squealed, scurrying backward into a pile of wooden crates.

Llewellyn stroked the shark's blunt head, cooing and chattering all the time. Then he made a fist and tapped her nose.

"What's in your belly, beautiful girl?" he asked. "What have you been eating to get so big?"

Lilly levered up her head, wrinkling the skin on her dark, thick back. She opened a gaping, cavernous mouth full of teeth, and then, with a noise like ten pigs belching, she regurgitated a huge load of diced fish.

"Good girl!" Llewellyn said, slapping her head. He looked over his shoulder at the shocked kids. "It's one of the first things I taught the pups. You have to monitor diet early on. Only fish for my sharks. People notice if geese and Labradors start getting pulled under."

Looking at the pile, Antigone cringed. "People notice if *people* start getting pulled under. What would you do if there was a foot in there?"

The old man laughed and patted the shark's rippling gills. Lilly began writhing, slapping her fins and wriggling her way back toward the water.

"There wouldn't be. I taught my little girl well. And she knows you now, too. She could smell you across the lake. She'll be a friend to you if you ever need one." He nodded at Cyrus. "Your glowing jelly will be in that pile there. Maybe the girl's, too. Dig around."

Lilly the bull shark tipped over the edge and sent another wave rushing across the tile and swirling through the pile of once-eaten fish.

A clear, gelatinous ball rolled free.

"Pick it up, Cyrus," Antigone said. "I'm not touching that gunk."

Panting in the crates, Dennis pointed at the old man. "I need my cape back."

"No," Cyrus said, glancing at Llewellyn. "No, you don't." He scooped up the Quick Water, squeezed it in half, and tossed a piece to Antigone. He dropped his piece back into his wet pocket. "Mr. Douglas, we're gonna try the doors. I like Lilly fine, but I don't want to do that again. Do you want to come?"

"No," said the old man. "I do not."

"He has to," Antigone said. "He can't go back on the shark alone. How would he get out of the water?"

"I do not have to do anything, young lady. How did I get out of the water here?" Llewellyn shrugged his shoulders free of the cape and raised his Halloween limbs. "I have arms."

"I don't want to come," said Dennis. "And I don't want to go back."

"Don't be dumb, Dennis," said Antigone. "We have to do something."

"I don't know," said Cyrus. "He could survive on Lilly's fish bits for a while."

"Cy . . . I'm not even going to say anything." Antigone walked over to the metal door and banged it open. "Not locked." Reaching around inside, she found a switch. The doorway brightened with a click. "Stairs," she said. "Pick up the old man and come on."

"Don't touch me," Llewellyn said. "I'm your diving tutor, aren't I? Show some respect. Besides, even if the doors to the zoo are unlocked, you don't want to go that way. Those creatures are less than friendly."

"Yeah?" Antigone put her hands on her hips. "What about sharks? When did they become friendly?"

"Lilly came in a litter of thirty and she was the friendliest pup of them all. Always was and always will be. Never a nip from Lilly."

"Um . . ." Cyrus pointed at the black pool. "What about that one?"

Llewellyn squinted at the water. A second dorsal, badly scarred, was tailing behind Lilly's figure eights.

"Well, snicker my doodle," Llewellyn said. "Lilly's found a friend." He laughed, giddy as a birthday boy. "A wild bull! And all this time, I've been thinking she's lonely. I've been sitting out on that jetty worried about my girl."

The old man slid his feet back in the water and rested his chin on his hands, watching the two dorsals swirl.

He sighed, scrunched his wrinkled face, and glanced back at the kids, dabbing his eyes. "If I had a daughter, which I don't, I imagine this is what it would be like seeing her coming down the aisle in white." He pointed at the second dorsal. "You treat her right, you hear me? I'll come in there. I will! I'll come for you."

"Right," said Cyrus. "You're a kook, and we're not going back in there."

"Suit yourselves," Llewellyn said. He took off the cape and threw it at Dennis. "We'll meet again," he said. "If you survive the zoo."

Pushing off the floor, Llewellyn Douglas dropped into the shark pool.

Cyrus looked at his sister, widened his eyes, and shook his head. "He's crazy."

Antigone shrugged. "I don't know. He's pretty unappetizing. He might be fine." She jerked her thumb at the door. "Want to go now, or wait and watch?"

"Now," said Cyrus. "Quick. If he gets chomped, I'll have to jump in."

⇒ eighteen ⇐

ZOO

CYRUS AND ANTIGONE stood in a long hall lined with metal doors. The stairs hadn't been long, but they led to a tangle of hallways. Cyrus and Antigone and a moping Dennis had been wandering for a while, dead-ending in storage rooms full of dry grain or tools or scrap metal cut away from cages.

Dennis had been no help at all.

The floor was grimy, and lightbulbs dotted the ceiling in both directions—only a few of them working. Cyrus scanned the filthy floor and then glanced at the bottom of his bare foot. It looked like it was layered in axle grease.

Antigone pointed down the hallway. "I think we've been down there." She turned around. "But that looks familiar, too."

"It's all the same," Cyrus said. "Maybe the old guy was wrong. There's not a way up out of here."

"Not an option," said Antigone. "I'm not getting back in the water with any sharks." She groaned, shifting uncomfortably. "I hate wet clothes. These pants are starting to chafe, and my feet are blistering."

"Take off your boots," Cyrus said, wiggling his toes and kicking a rotting rag against the wall. "Bare feet are so much better in a place like this."

Antigone turned to Dennis. The drenched porter was carrying his cape in a wad beneath his arm, and he still hadn't untied his crushed bowler hat. He was leaning against a wall, staring at absolutely nothing.

"Dennis," Antigone said. "Please, tell us about this place. You might not think you know anything, but you definitely know more than we do. Anything? Have you heard anything, read anything, dreamed anything?"

"They're going to fire me," Dennis said. "Sterling doesn't need to kill me. I'll be thrown out of Ashtown. Where will I go?"

"Why would you be thrown out?" Cyrus asked. "Sterling's the one who'll be in trouble."

Dennis shook his head. "Who will they believe? Dennis Gilly, failed Acolyte, failed porter? Or Benjamin Sterling? Everyone loves him. He's been the cook for—I don't know how long—since he lost his legs. Greeves will think I'm crazy."

"Well," said Antigone. "We'll tell him you're not crazy."

"How do you know?" Dennis asked. "Maybe I am." He sighed. "I'm not like you two. I had to go into the service corps and now I'll even lose my bed in the porter's dorm. I don't have any family. Where will I go? What state is around Ashtown?"

"Wisconsin," said Cyrus.

"I'll be out in Wisconsin. What do they do in Wisconsin? Nothing I'm good at, I'm sure."

Antigone stepped in front of the damp porter. "Cyrus and I think you're great, Dennis. Don't we, Cy?"

"Sure," said Cyrus.

Dennis looked up and shook his head. "You're both 1914 Acolytes. I wouldn't have made the 1969 standards . . . even if I could have afforded the dues. I just wanted to sail. Who cares about Latin?"

"Not me," said Cyrus. "Not at all."

Antigone nodded at her brother and slowly rolled her hands for him to go on.

Cyrus smiled. "Hey," he said. "How would you like to be a Polygoner, Dennis?"

Antigone dropped her hands, surprised.

Cyrus continued. "If you get kicked out, you can stay with us. We'll hide you. But if you don't get kicked out, you can still be a Polygoner."

Dennis looked at Antigone. She smiled. He turned back to Cyrus.

"Really? Are you just trying to get me to feel better? Are you making something up?"

Cyrus shook his head. "We're not making it up."

He slapped the boxing monkey on his leather shoulder. "That's our symbol or logo or whatever. But there are only two Polygoners right now. Three if we count Nolan. We need more."

"What do I have to do?"

"Well." Cyrus grinned. "You have to help us, and that will mean doing whatever we say."

"Cyrus . . ." Antigone's voice was all warning.

"There are other rules, too," Cyrus said quickly. "But we can explain those later."

Dennis straightened. "Do you really think I'm good enough?"

Cyrus laughed. "What do you think, Tigs? Is he good enough?"

"Dennis Gilly," Antigone said. "You just swam with a shark. How many people do you know who have done that?"

Dennis thought for a moment. "You two and Mr. Douglas."

"Right," said Cyrus. "You're as good as we are. And you like to sail? Are you good at it?"

Dennis nodded solemnly.

"Good," said Cyrus. "Then you can be our sailing tutor, too."

"Mr. Cyrus—"

Cyrus shook his head. "Don't ever call me that again. If you do, we'll kick you out."

Dennis nodded seriously. "Right. I won't. What do Polygoners do?"

"Whatever needs to be done," said Cyrus.

"And right now," Antigone said, "we need to find a way out of here."

Dennis looked in both directions. "But I've never—"

Cyrus raised his hands, and Dennis's mouth clicked shut. "This is the first test, Dennis. We're not going to help you."

Nodding slowly, Dennis squinted down the hall, and then turned and moved to the first metal door. He opened it and walked in.

Gasping, he staggered back out. "Stuff," he said. "Rotting stuff." He pointed down the hall. "I think we should go that way."

"Don't think, Dennis," Cyrus said. "Do. We're following you."

The porter threw his wet cape against the wall. "Wait here," he said, and strode down the hallway, opening doors.

"Cyrus," Antigone whispered. "You're evil."

"What are you talking about? Look at him! He just turned into Napoleon."

"Yeah, but what will he do when he finds out that there's no club? It'll break his heart."

"He won't find out, because there *is* a club—maybe a gang or a full-on league. And we're in charge. Well, technically I'm in charge, but you can be the secretary or something."

"Yeah," said Antigone. "Sure. That'll happen."

"Treasurer?" Cyrus asked. "Or do you want to be the Avengel, like Greeves? You can enforce my proclamations. Or you can just be the mascot. Your call."

"Copresident."

"Ha." Cyrus eyed his sister. "A second ago, you were denying that the league existed, and now you want to muscle in on my leadership?"

"Shut up, Rus, or I'll drop the 'co.'"

"Hey!" Dennis yelled. "I've found a way . . . somewhere."

When Cyrus and Antigone reached him, Dennis was beaming with pride beside an open rusty door. Ancient hay bales had been stacked on one side of the room. On the far wall, a ladder ran straight up to a trapdoor in the ceiling.

"I'll bet it goes up to the feeding rooms behind the cages," Dennis said. He scurried up the ladder and lifted the trap. "At least, I think so. It's a little dark."

"Okay," Cyrus said. "Hop down, Dennis. We'll check it out."

Dennis stared at him. "No. You said this was a test. There are rules. You can't trick me. I always follow rules."

Cyrus opened his mouth and then shut it. He had

nothing to say. Dennis climbed up, wriggled through the trapdoor, and let it bang behind him.

"Terrific," said Antigone. "Dennis always follows rules, and you are now his rule book. Pull the plug now, Cy."

"Pull the plug on this new, amazing Dennis?" Cyrus shook his head and moved out of the way. "Go ahead. Ladies first."

Antigone climbed the ladder, and Cyrus climbed behind her. With each step, leather water dripped out of her boots and onto Cyrus's head.

When she reached the top, she threw open the trap and climbed through.

When Cyrus reached the top, he stuck his head up and into pure reek.

"Oh . . ." He groaned, gagging.

"Get up here, Cy. Plug your nose. I think Dennis passed out."

The room was extremely dim, but Cyrus could just make out his sister's shape. The only light was seeping in through the seams around a heavy door and a smaller, square hatch set into it at head height.

Cyrus stood up and covered his nose. "Did an elephant die? I can taste it."

"It smells like skunk plus last year's fish," Antigone said. She nudged Dennis's crumpled shape with her toe. "What do we do with him?"

"What do we do with *us*?" Cyrus asked.

"No! Leon, down!" A boy's shout echoed through the darkness. "Down!"

A bubbling bellow drowned out the voice. A second later, the floor shook with a crash. Birds shrieked. Unknown animals whooped with excitement.

Cyrus and Antigone jumped to the light-outlined door. Cyrus found a bolt and jerked it back with a loud crack. The heavy metal door swung open into a cage.

The two of them stepped through onto a dry floor dusted with old straw. The walls on each side were gray stone. In front, thick iron bars separated them from a bright and immensely large room lined with cages.

Cyrus walked to the bars and pressed his face between them. Antigone squeezed beside him. The foul-smelling zoo was beautiful, but battered. Marble floors were smeared with filth. Cracked stone columns grew into steel girders, which peaked in Gothic arches, carrying a paned mountain range of skylights that ran the length of the room.

The place was alive with daylight.

Cages lined the walls and mezzanines, but Cyrus didn't look to see how many were full. His eyes were on an armored white shape attempting to run down the middle of the room. It looked part astronaut and part white fire hydrant, rocking forward on thick, awkward limbs.

Chasing it, clattering and clawing, grunting and snapping, was a turtle the size of a van. A tail that looked like a whole crocodile dragged behind it. Clawed, elephant-size feet thumped beneath it, and its long, rocking, spiny shell was the size of a smaller car all by itself.

"Leon!" the white shape shouted, hopping slowly. "Stop!"

The turtle stretched out a wrinkly, scaled head that would have been big on a buffalo and opened a mouth large enough to swallow pumpkins. Its neck sprang forward, and its mouth snapped shut around the white shape's head. It clamped and reclamped, while thick white legs kicked and thick white arms flailed. Then, lifting the shape up off the ground by its head, it began shaking its prey from side to side, banging legs against its spined shell.

"Hey!" Antigone yelled. "Over here! Come over here!"

"What are you doing?" Cyrus asked. He reached for his sister's mouth.

But Leon the turtle had already heard. The thick white chew toy clattered to the floor.

"We have bars," Antigone said. "We'll be fine."

Cyrus looked at the iron in his hands, and then he looked at the turtle as it flared its lopsided nostrils and stepped toward them.

"I don't think these bars have a chance."

The white thing tried to sit up but couldn't. It flopped side to side and managed to roll onto its face. When it looked up, Cyrus blinked. It had two large silver mesh eyes and an upside-down triangle for a mouth.

"What are you doing in here?" it asked. "You better get out fast."

Leon the turtle was approaching slowly. And then he levered open his enormous mouth. A long piece of skin in the back of his throat writhed like a snake.

Cyrus and Antigone took a step back from the bars. When they did, the turtle bellowed, raised its shell off the floor, and thundered forward.

Before it hit the bars, Cyrus and Antigone shot back through the rear door, tripped over Dennis as he sat up, and tumbled into a wall.

The iron bars screamed under the turtle's impact.

So did Dennis.

The bars bent, but they did not break. The turtle twisted his head to the side, hooked a single bar with his beak, and ripped it free.

"That's Leon!" Dennis yelled. "We're going to die!"

A second bar clattered to the floor.

Antigone stood and kicked Dennis. "Get up and start acting like a Polygoner!"

The white shape appeared behind Leon and pointed. "Four doors down!" it yelled. "That way!" And then it lumbered off.

Leon tore two more bars out at once, then he wormed his head through the gap. He needed to show off his bait.

The huge turtle dropped its shell belly to the floor, cranked open its mouth, wrinkling its puckered old-man face, and held very still—all but the attractively wiggly bit of skin.

Cyrus grimaced, watching the turtle's snake-size uvula twist and slither. "That's disgusting."

Antigone grabbed him by the arm and dragged him down the dim hallway behind the cages.

Leon writhed and snapped as they left, banging his shell forward, bending iron.

Four doors down, Cyrus threw another dead bolt and opened the door, and the three of them stepped into another cage. Wooden roosts were mounted to one wall in an enormous tangle. Bones were strewn across the floor. The bars of the cage were not bent and were not merely missing. They had been torn to pieces.

Dennis froze, giggling nervously. Cyrus and Antigone pulled him through the bones, through the fragmented bars, and out into the main room. The three of them stopped and stared.

"Oh my," Antigone said. "Cy, are you seeing this?"

Cyrus nodded. He had no words. Leon the impossible turtle was still grunting and trying to fight his way into the cage, but Cyrus couldn't even be bothered to look at him. The room was much bigger than he'd been able to see through the bars of a cage, and it was not a room. It was a neoclassical indoor jungle. Second- and third-story mezzanines held open cages and palm trees. Vines climbed eighty feet from the floor to the upper peaks of the skylights. At the far end, so distant as to be visible but noiseless, a small waterfall flowed off the upper mezzanine and into a pool. A few long-tailed birds circled high above.

"This was the biggest wing of the zoo," Dennis said quietly. "It's slightly amazing."

"Slightly," said Antigone. "I'd say."

The white astronaut was waiting for them. He glanced back at Leon and up at the birds.

"Cheese, Leon!" it yelled. "Go get your cheese!"

Instantly, the turtle tore its head free and began scraping its way quickly back in the other direction, its tail slithering and its huge spiny back bobbing as it went.

The white shape put club fists on wide hips. "Now maybe you'll tell me how you got in here. Not that it matters. The O of B will have your bags packed in the morning for this. Some of the Keepers don't even want me in here."

"What are you?" Antigone asked.

The white thing reached up and twisted its head counterclockwise until it popped off.

On top of the enormous white body was the small,

red, sweating face of a twelve-year-old boy, wet hair glued to his forehead. "I'm James Axelrotter, zookeeper. You can call me Jax. Who are you?"

"Jax!" Cyrus said. "We needed to find you. We have to get some animal tutoring or something."

The boy scrunched his face. "I don't tutor. And if I did, why would I start with trespassers and rulebreakers?" He glanced up at the birds in profile against the skylights, and then back over his shoulder.

"We can talk about that later," said Antigone. "We need to get out of this place and find Greeves. Right away."

Jax nodded and pointed them toward a distant door at the end of the room. "That is the closest exit. Stay with me." He began waddling, and Cyrus followed him, examining the boy's white suit.

"What are you wearing?"

"An artificial exoskeleton," Jax said, scanning the room while he walked. "Made from more than half a million interwoven and rubberized Golden Orb-weaver webs—among other things. It's the only way I can survive very long in here. This place was the Crypto wing—unusual, bizarre, especially deadly, and supranatural creatures. Construction began after the Civil War. Axelrotters have always overseen it. Leon was one of the first to be housed here."

"But they lost control of the animals," Dennis said. "That's why it's closed."

Jax tried to glare at him over his enormous white shoulder. "They did not *lose* control of the animals. Twenty-four years ago, a Keeper named Edwin Laughlin—Phoenix to everyone now—was inspired by Leon and altered these animals. My grandfather and a number of his staff were killed as a result."

"I don't understand," Cyrus said. "Inspired by Leon? You mean he made the animals big?"

Jax again glanced up, and then turned a full circle as he moved, eyes all over the room. "No. He did not. Though it can have that effect eventually. At first, he modified the personalities—animalities, I guess—of particular animals. Then he exchanged consciousnesses—animal to animal. He ended by modifying and blending animals physically. That is when he was caught. But not before his final phase was executed on more than a few of them—the Leon phase."

Jax looked up and around. "Stay close. I want you alive when I turn you in to Mr. Greeves."

"Terrific," said Antigone. "Right. That's what we want, too."

Cyrus looked over his shoulder. Dennis was huddling quite close to him. "What's the Leon phase?"

"Leon is named after Ponce de León." Jax glanced back. "Spanish explorer. Found the Fountain of Youth in Florida. But it wasn't much of a fountain. It was a murky swamp pool deep in the Everglades. They were even swampier then. Leon is how he knew he had found it."

"Are we joking right now?" Cyrus asked.

Jax shook his head while he walked. "That was five hundred years ago, and Leon was already huge and ancient, snacking on gators. Leon is what happens when an alligator snapping turtle lives in the Swamp of Youth for a few centuries. He'll still be alive after our grandchildren are dead. Ponce told the Order about the huge turtle, and *they* put Leon on the Sage lists and sent Journeymen out to check on him every so often. Then when the swamps were drained off for farming and the fountain was lost, Leon went on the move. He started eating horses on some ranch. That's when the O of B collected him."

"I would never believe any of that," Antigone said. "But I've already seen the turtle. So the Leon phase of the experiments . . ."

Jax sighed. "Transmortality. Nearly immortal animals."

"*Nearly* immortal?" Cyrus asked.

"Not one has died yet," said Jax. "But it's only been two decades. The Sages in the Orbis put all the transmortaled creatures in here, and then they sealed it up. I come in, do my best to clean, and feed them and try to keep everything from going too wild. Not much else I can do."

Something slapped onto the floor behind them.

Cyrus spun around, and Antigone grabbed his arm. Dennis squeaked. Jax swore.

The birds were descending. But they weren't birds.

A fat-bodied red snake slithered toward them, rearing to strike. When it reared, it spread two wings, glistening with white feathers.

Another snake hit the floor. And another.

Jax shoved Cyrus toward the end of the room. "Get to the door! Run! And keep your eyes up!"

Raising his helmet, Jax twisted it back into place. "Now!" he yelled. "Go!" And he lumbered toward the snakes.

Cyrus, Antigone, and Dennis ran.

White wings churned the air above them.

❊ nineteen ❊

BRENDAN

A RED CURLING tail brushed through Cyrus's hair, and the viper dropped to the floor six feet in front of him. Others were dropping farther ahead, closer to the door.

Behind him, Antigone screamed.

Cyrus spun around, nearly colliding with Dennis. The porter veered off, but he didn't stop sprinting.

While Cyrus watched, his sister grabbed a snake by the tail and plucked it out of the air. Swinging it hard, she knocked two others to the ground behind her, hurling her serpent club away as she did.

"Duck!" she yelled at Cyrus.

Turning, Cyrus ducked as another diving viper grazed his ear. He dodged around two on the ground.

"Tigs!" he yelled, slowing.

"Go! I'm right behind you!"

Cyrus's bare heels stopped touching the cold marble floor as his strides lengthened. Ahead of him, a viper coiled and reared to strike, wings spread.

Cyrus didn't turn and he didn't slow down. He

vaulted, launching into the air and spreading his legs as the snake struck.

His shins folded back the white wings. A fang caught in the thigh of his pants, whipping the snake around and spinning it across the dusty floor as he landed.

"Tigs?" he yelled again.

Dennis had reached the door. He was pulling it open. Cyrus was almost there.

"Tigs!" Cyrus broke down his sprint and turned around.

A big, four-legged shape slid out from the shadow of the mezzanine, rumbling a growl like distant drums. Cyrus froze. It was a bear, long-legged, short-faced, and with a body the size of a bull. It was black, but its belly was tiger-striped with white. White rings circled its eyes, and white fangs dangled beneath its heavy upper lip.

Bounding forward, it rose onto its hind legs, towering twice Cyrus's height, swatting at the vipers. The snakes climbed, circling out of the bear's reach.

Cyrus backed toward the door. The bear dropped to all fours and moved toward Cyrus, claws like flamingo beaks clicking as it came. He couldn't see Antigone behind it.

"Antigone!" Cyrus shouted. "Jax!"

Small bells jingled beside him.

"Gone if she's in there, lad," Sterling said. "Wish I'd gotten here sooner, but these legs aren't made for sprinting." The cook patted Cyrus on the shoulder as the bear bellowed, stringing drool from a drooping lip.

"Let's get this door closed and bolted behind us."

"No." Cyrus shook his head. "Tigs!" He stepped forward, but Sterling grabbed his shirt and held him back.

Cyrus wrenched himself free and staggered toward the bear. "Tigs!" he yelled. The big animal crouched, waiting.

Cyrus took a step to one side and braced himself, preparing to run.

"Hold, lad," Sterling said. "You don't have a chance. Ah, well, I hate to do it, may the animal gods forgive me."

Cyrus glanced back. The bearded cook extended a four-barreled gun. The gun belched, and a sphere of white fire corkscrewed forward, erupting into the bear's chest. The animal leapt into the air and then bolted for the cages like an avalanche of smoking fur. But Sterling wasn't done. Firing at the circling vipers, he jingled forward until he stood beside Cyrus, and then, with a quick jerk, he brought the butt of the gun down onto Cyrus's skull.

Antigone was standing beside an open window at the end of a long, curving hallway dotted with closed doors. The window behind her was three stories up. The doors went to . . . she didn't know where.

Her heart was still racing. It hadn't stopped since she'd gotten out of the zoo. Her face was still flushed. Jax had just managed to pull her into a cage. The bars had kept out the bigger animals—the smoking bear and the four-winged vultures—but the snakes . . . A heavy bone had been her only weapon, and her arms ached from swinging. Her hands were blistered. She should have died.

She slipped her Quick Water back into her jacket pocket. It still showed her nothing but darkness.

She'd told Rupert everything. But she didn't care about Sterling. Where was Cyrus? He'd been ahead of her. He had to have made it out. But then where was he? She'd been stuck inside with Jax for almost an hour. Another hour had passed since she'd gotten out and no one had seen Cyrus.

A sick lump of worry sat in her throat. She shivered and slapped her arms, staring out the open window. She wasn't cold. Even with the early storm wind, the air was warping with heat. The storm still hadn't broken, but the sun seemed to be gone for good, swallowed by flickering clouds.

She wanted Cyrus. She wanted Dan. She wanted to sit beside her mother.

Behind her, a door opened and Jax stepped out beside Rupert Greeves. The boy's face was still red, but rings of salt from his sweat had dried onto his cheeks and forehead. His clothes were soaked through, and he held a glass bottle full of water in one hand.

Greeves filled the hall. He scratched his bandaged jaw, eyeing Antigone.

"We need to go back," she said. "Right now. Cyrus and Dennis might still be in there."

Jax shook his head. "I looked everywhere. They're gone."

"What about the fireballs? Who was shooting those?"

"I was busy saving your life at the time," Jax sniffed. "I was unable to locate the source of the fireballs."

"You know," said Antigone, "you don't talk like a twelve-year-old."

"Thank you," said Jax, and he took a swig of water.

Rupert Greeves sighed. "Mr. Axelrotter, you're free to go. I may speak with you again. Miss Smith, the Brendan has asked to see you. Walk with me." His hand closed around her arm.

Rupert led her down the hallway and past the flight of stairs she and Jax had ascended.

After a few bends and a long curve, the hall dead-ended in a white paneled wall. Rupert pushed the paneling in and slid it to the side, revealing what looked like an elevator's strange and distant cousin.

"You didn't see that," he said, "because I wasted time we don't have following protocol, blindfolding you and spinning you around seventy-seven times before leading you here. Remember that if anyone asks." He stepped in.

The sides and floor were brass wire mesh. Two thick cables ran down through holes in the ceiling and out of the floor. There were no buttons—only a large needled dial on one wall and a small lever beneath it.

"I thought we were in a hurry," Rupert said, looking back at Antigone.

She stepped in beside him, and he slid the paneling closed. The needle on the dial bounced. Rupert twisted the casing around it, and then he pulled the lever.

The elevator—and one of the two cables—began to rise smoothly.

After a few moments, the cage bumped and began to climb diagonally. It shifted again, rocking gently as it moved horizontally, finally bumping again and ascending up another vertical shaft.

Antigone didn't say anything. She was staring through the brass mesh, watching the overmortared backside of stone walls creep by, broken up by the occasional boarded-up door.

Rupert glanced at Antigone and then looked back through the ceiling and up the shaft. "Show respect and speak truth. And his name isn't Brendan. That's his title. His name is Oliver Laughlin."

Greeves slid a panel open and stepped out of the elevator.

Antigone held back. "What do I call him? Mr. Laughlin? Mr. The Brendan?"

"Call him sir."

Antigone followed Rupert Greeves down a polished hall with a black-and-white mosaic floor, into a sprawling room dotted with thick carpets and couches. There were no bookshelves. No books. No pictures. Intricately carved beams held up the low ceiling. A wall of paned windows looked down a sloping roof, past a row of titanic stone statues guarding the gutters, and then out over the lake. The glass panes quivered in the wind.

Rupert led Antigone away, around a long table and into the far corner of the room, where two walls of windows met. An old man was lying on a couch, piled beneath blankets. His empty eyes were focused on the ceiling. Two chairs sat across from him. His hair was thin and white, but long, reaching just below his pointed jaw. His skin was blotched and carved with deep creases. He was unshaven and had been for some time.

Beside the window, a boy with a sharp, freckled face stood with his back to the glass and his arms crossed. The boy. The boy from the Galleria, from the picture— the boy who nodded and everyone obeyed.

For a moment, his eyes were on Antigone's, and then he turned to Rupert.

"Go ahead, Mr. Greeves," the boy said. "He will hear you."

Rupert quickly reported what Antigone had told him. Antigone watched the boy's face sharpen and his brow furrow. When he spoke, his voice was crisp.

"Sterling and Rhodes are condemned because of what an Acolyte says that a porter said that he overheard?"

"No," Rupert said. "Not condemned. Not yet. I will speak with them both when they've been found."

The old man on the couch shifted, but his eyes were still on the ceiling. "Phoenix is coming."

Greeves faced him quickly. "Yes, sir. Maybe. But the gates have been strengthened, the guards have been doubled, and the Keepers have been warned. All of my hunters will be out tonight."

The Brendan waved at the chairs in front of him. "Sit."

Rupert nodded Antigone into a chair, and then he sat.

The old man coughed, and then spoke. A rattle in his throat roughened his smooth drawl—like sand in butter. "It has been more than two decades since my brother defied the Order, two years since he last raised his voice to me. He is now ready, and he is unafraid. What of the tooth? What of the Smith children?"

"I have brought one of them with me, sir. Antigone Smith is seated across from you."

The old man sat up quickly, easily, and turned

suddenly sharp, pale-blue eyes on Antigone. The blankets fell onto his lap.

"Miss Smith," he said, taking in her skin, her hair, her hands. She was wrapped in a damp leather jacket, and she still felt undressed.

"My father was an evil man, Miss Smith. My brother Edwin—Phoenix by his own naming—is an evil man. Do you hold them against me?"

Antigone glanced at Rupert for help. Hard creases were set into his dark face. His eyes were on the Brendan.

"Should I?" Antigone asked.

"No," the Brendan said. "But if you are alive tomorrow, perhaps you will. Where is the tooth, Miss Smith? The shard of the serpent's fang, left to you by William Skelton, the thief and liar."

"I don't know where the tooth is," Antigone said. "My brother is missing. We should be looking for him. He has it."

The old man sniffed and ran a bony hand through his long, thin hair. His eyes drifted out of focus. "You are now searching for two brothers. And I dearly wish never to see mine again. But wishing is useless. He is coming, Miss Smith. Tonight. Your time at Ashtown will be short. This Estate nears its end."

Rupert stood, his fists and jaws clenching. The Brendan sighed. "Wait a moment, Greeves. Do not rush off to war so quickly. There is something she should see."

He pointed behind his couch to a half-opened door. "Inside."

Antigone followed Rupert across the room to the door. She glanced back at the boy. His arms were still crossed. His lips were tight.

The door opened into a dim, strange-smelling room. A large bed was crowned with a tangle of rumpled sheets. Bowls of burned-down incense sticks lined a shelf on the headboard in front of small, tarnished metal images.

In front of a closet, Antigone's movie screen had been set up. Her projector sat propped on a stack of books on a small table, positioned and ready. Her two cameras sat in their open cases beside it.

"What's going on?" Antigone jumped forward. "How did these get here? Someone fixed the lenses. They'd melted." She looked at her half-molten projector. "There's no reel. There's nothing to play."

Rupert flipped the switch, and the empty spools began to turn. Light beamed through the air and danced on the screen.

Dan was driving. The wipers were beating silently.

"That's my movie," Antigone said. "Where's it coming from? How is this happening?"

"The lens," Rupert said. "He's trapped it all in the lens."

Antigone crouched to examine her projector. Rupert pulled her back to her feet.

The images jumped.

Dan was lying on a bed. His eyes were closed, his legs and chest were bare. He was thin. Pale. Underfed.

Antigone bit her lip and covered her mouth with her hand. "What's he—"

Dan changed. His shoulders grew. His chest and arms and legs thickened. His legs lengthened in jerks between frames. His hair grew long, and then black, and then blond again. Shaved patches appeared on his scalp. Wires dotted his body and then disappeared. His ribs sprouted a regiment of small muscles. And suddenly, bruises appeared across his body, a bloody laceration above his eyebrow, and a bite mark on his neck. His lips were split, and his left eye was swollen shut. His right eye was open but staring into nothing.

"Is he alive?" Antigone asked. She grabbed Rupert's arm. "What happened? Is he alive?"

Rupert was as stiff and motionless as a statue.

The image jumped. It was one of Antigone's movies again. Cyrus smiling beside his mother's hospital bed. Antigone smiling, brushing her mother's hair, kissing her head.

"No," Antigone said. She shook her head, looking away. But she had to look back.

Her mother was in a different room, and it wasn't

the hospital. Sunlight poured through the window. Curtains were blowing.

Antigone's whole body clenched. Rupert's big arm hardened in her hand.

A tall, thin man with thick black hair stepped in front of the camera. He was wearing a brilliant white suit beneath a dingy and battered lab coat. He looked like the Brendan but much younger. And longer—stretched. He stepped forward and his face filled the frame. Antigone wanted to duck or dive away from his pale eyes.

"The cloak," Rupert said quietly. "Nolan was right."

The image on the screen shook. The projector's lens was vibrating. Somehow, someway, he was speaking. His mouth wasn't moving.

"Smiths," the man said slowly. "I seem to have what is yours, and I believe you have what is mine. But I see no reason for us to quarrel. I'm sure some—friendly—arrangement can be reached to avoid the extremely unpleasant. As for you, my brother Brendan, there can be no arrangement."

Phoenix moved out of the frame.

Antigone's mother had vanished from the bed behind him. A dead blackbird lay on her pillow with wings spread. And then the image jumped to old black-and-white film. Two cowboys pulled guns and fired. German tanks rolled through Paris.

The screen went white, flickered, and then jumped to the beginning. Dan in the car.

Rupert clicked the projector off and walked out of the room. Antigone hurried behind him.

"Miss Smith," the Brendan said quietly. "No one can blame you. Give him the tooth. Save your family if you can. The rest of us may be beyond saving. Greeves, dissolve the Estate immediately. Scatter the members. Go. Leave Phoenix an empty Ashtown. I will wait for execution alone."

Rupert stepped around in front of the Brendan, his chest swelling. He jerked off the old man's blanket and hurled it against the window. Jaw clenching, hands flexing, he looked down at the feeble shape, and his lip curled. "You betray the people beneath you. You betray the people who lived before you. You betray the world the Order serves." His eyes were razors. "Graves will be opened. The Burials will be emptied. A millennium's imprisoned curses will walk free. How long until the nations are on their knees?" He shook his head. "I would rather be the first to die than survive and murder others with my cowardice."

The Brendan's eyes sparked, but the spark died quickly. The old man drooped back into his couch. His eyes found the ceiling.

Greeves looked at the boy. His eyes were wide, his arms uncrossed.

"Come with us now, Oliver, or not at all."

Turning, Rupert strode across the room. The boy, Oliver, jumped to follow him.

Antigone stepped slowly in front of the Brendan. Her body was shaking. Her veins were pumping fear, not blood.

"You're just going to give up? Can't you stop him?" she asked. "Can't you do anything at all?"

"Once upon a time," the old man said quietly. "But no longer. Lie low and the lightning may overlook you. Phoenix will stumble in the end."

Antigone could hardly stand. Blinking, with images of her brother and mother swirling in her head, she made her way to the elevator.

As they descended, she sniffed, fighting nausea. Oliver moved into the far corner.

Rupert stared at the ceiling. When they reached the bottom, he spoke. "Neither of you will mention him. You will say nothing of his nonsense."

He slid the panel open and Antigone stumbled into the hall. Oliver stepped out beside her. With a single angry jerk, Rupert ripped down the elevator's ceiling and reached up into the cables. A long pin came free and rattled to the floor. He stepped out into the hall.

A moment later, the brass cage groaned, slipped, and plummeted. The three of them watched the cables racing, unspooling in the empty shaft.

When the crash came, Greeves slid the panel closed and turned away.

"Oliver," he said. "We have much to prepare, and we must find Mr. Rhodes and Mr. Sterling."

"What about Cyrus?" Antigone asked. "Will you look for him?"

Rupert Greeves, Avengel of the Order of Brendan, stepped back to her, bent down, and looked into her eyes.

"Antigone," he said. His breath smelled like leather. His face was stone. "My blood belongs to the Smiths. I am ready to die for your mother, for your brother, for Cyrus, and for you. I will die before that creature controls even the sewers of Ashtown. Soon I will send some of my hunters in search of your brother. You will follow them. Stay close to me. I must move quickly. Can you do that?"

Antigone nodded. Oliver was looking at her, pale behind his freckles.

A moment later, Greeves was striding away, Oliver at his side. Hurrying behind them, Antigone dug into her jacket pocket.

Her quaking Quick Water glowed faintly on her palm, no longer dark but far from bright. She raised it to her face.

⇥ twenty ⇤

WE ALL FALL DOWN

CYRUS HAD SEEN his sister. He knew he had, but only for a moment, and her features had been hugely warped in fish-eye—she must have been holding the ball close to her face. But it had definitely been her.

That had been hours ago.

At least she was alive. That made bad things better. She wasn't in a bear's stomach or a turtle's stomach or a dozen different viper stomachs.

He would have gotten a longer look if the Quick Water hadn't squirted out of his fingertips. Now it was on the floor, wedged behind the biggest jar of miniature pickles he had ever seen.

The pickle jar was taller than he was, but only because he was tied up and strapped into a chair.

The chair was bolted to the floor in front of a large butcher-block table.

Patricia adjusted her cool body on his neck, and the keys scraped quietly against his collarbone. Once again, Cyrus rocked himself forward in his straps and tried to look at the clear fungus ball he'd dropped. When he'd finally managed to get it out of his pocket, he'd only had a few seconds to look before the guards had come in, untied him, searched him, tied him back up, and left.

Cyrus leaned harder, but he could see nothing. Groaning, he sat back up.

Dennis was tied and lying on his back. There had only been one chair in the enormous pantry. His eyes were wide open and he was watching Cyrus. Occasionally, he grunted. A pot holder had been shoved into his mouth. Cyrus's too, but he'd managed to spit his out.

"Hang in there, D," Cyrus said. "They won't leave us in here forever."

Dennis grunted, widening his terrified eyes.

"That's what you're worried about," Cyrus said. "Right. Me too. I just hope they don't cook us. I don't want to be eaten."

He looked around the crowded shelves. Spices. Grains. Hanging sausages at the other end. An entire wall of garlic. Another of dried peppers. "But why else would we be in here?"

Dennis rocked from side to side, and then rolled onto his face. His hands were tied behind his back. He arched his back and shook his head, fighting the pot holder.

"Go," said Cyrus. "You can do it."

Slow steps thumped on the stairs. Bells jingled.

Big Ben Sterling ducked down through the low

doorway and into the pantry. No hat, no beard net or apron, no sign that he'd been cooking. He was carrying a large glass of something brown.

"Lads," he said, raising the glass. "I drink to you, and to all boats and bridges that have ever been burned." Knocking back half the liquid, he sat on the table in front of Cyrus, banged the glass down, and smacked his lips.

"What are you doing?" Cyrus asked. "What the heck is going on?"

"What is Ben Sterling doing?" the cook asked, massaging his knees. "Why, I'm taking a night off and lying low, Brer Fox. For this last supper, I was nothing but a saucier and prep cook. As for your other question, well, that's outside of Ben's control."

Dennis grunted and bounced on his stomach.

"I'm sorry, Mr. Gilly," Sterling said. "I don't understand."

"Are you going to kill us?" Cyrus asked. "You can have the tooth. That's what you want, isn't it? Let me go and I'll get it for you."

"The tooth, the tooth." The cook drained his glass and licked the rim. "Soon enough, lad."

Cyrus jerked against the straps. The cook watched him without a smile. His eyes were heavy.

"I loved this place," Sterling said. "In its way and mine. Ben Sterling's done right by the Order, but has the

Order done right by Ben Sterling? Tonight it ends, lad. The living have dwelt above the Burials long enough. Let them lay their heads down and be silent."

"Are you drunk?" Cyrus asked. "Do you want the tooth or not?"

Sterling smiled. "You have it, do you? Where would you tuck a thing like that? Your little nook in the Polygon has already been searched. You swallow it? Tell an old cook and I'll believe you."

Cyrus breathed slowly. He could feel the keys against his skin. He could give them away right now, but then what? Sterling wouldn't let him go. What reason would there be to keep him alive?

Sterling continued. "Rupe would like us to believe that he has it. But maybe it's in your sister's hands. There were only so many people in that room when poor Maxi was done in." Sterling shrugged. "When you're all lined up and watching each other's pain, the truth will bubble out." He looked at his empty glass. "But my coin is on little Nikales, Nolan the Thief. He's snake-slippery. Un-dying Nolan. Unaging Nolan. He just sheds his skin and slinks away. He's a dark one, lad."

Cyrus lifted his head. "Let me try to find him," he said. "He'll give the tooth back. He told me I could trust him."

Sterling filled the room with laughter. "You had it hid a moment ago. So Nolan does have it, then? He told you to trust him? And you did, didn't you? And he took the tooth and disappeared. Why does Nolan want it, lad? Would you like to know? It isn't pretty. Nolan wants to die. Nikales was fifteen years of age—a poor Persian boy—when the hero Gilgamesh went diving for the fruit of life. And he found it, too, at the bottom of the Persian Gulf—he plucked it from the lost garden and the living tree. But when he rose from the waves and lay gasping on the beach, the thief saw his chance. He snatched the fruit and fled, eating as he ran. But it wasn't to be so easy. Gilgamesh cursed that boy for a serpent and a thief. Oh, Nikales lived on—even when old Gil cut him down. He remained young, but as an undying serpent. Three thousand years and he still looks to be a lad, unless you stare into his eyes. Three thousand years, that boy has been peeling off his snake skin."

Sterling slapped the table. Then he leaned forward and winked at Cyrus. "Wherever Nolan is, he has that tooth in his hand, a smile on his face, and not a spark of life in him." He paused, tugging his beard. "But maybe not."

Dennis had stopped squirming. He was up on his side, staring at the cook.

Cyrus's heart was racing. "You're working for Phoenix, aren't you?" He kicked his bare ankles against rope. "Did you help him take Dan? Did you want Maxi to kill us?"

The cook shook his head. "Sorry, Mr. Cyrus. Things have gone as things have gone, and Benjamin Sterling will play his part to the end."

"What end?" Cyrus asked.

The cook's face grew suddenly serious. "I am not drunk, Cyrus Smith. Far from it. But tonight . . . I wish I were. I'd remember less in the morning. Goodbye, lad."

"Wait!" Cyrus said. "You knew my dad. You cooked us his favorite meal. You must have liked my parents. Why are you doing this?"

Sterling didn't answer. He was looking at the Quick Water, peeking out from behind the pickle jar. He slid off the table—legs bending beneath him—crouched carefully, and picked it up.

Frustrated, Cyrus banged his head back against the chair. "Please! Just let us go."

Sterling peered into the Quick Water. Sighing, he glanced back at Cyrus. His mouth twitched into a smile, but his eyes were heavy.

"You may look Cataan, lad, but you're a Smith through and through."

Footsteps drummed on the stairs.

Sterling hesitated, but then he nestled the liquid ball into a pile of onions on a crowded shelf and eased quickly away.

Four men tumbled into the pantry.

"Storm or no storm, Greeves or no Greeves, Phoenix

is coming in," one of them said. "Rhodes is ghost-white and pig-sweating. Rupe grilled him good, but he didn't crack. Not yet, at least. Still no sign of Nolan."

"Greeves is bayin' for you, too, Ben," said another. "And he made a scare speech to the whole dining hall. They've gone gun-ready, every last one of them, and they're as edgy as wildcats. He's been in and out of the kitchen."

"Why do you think I'm not in the kitchen?" Sterling asked. "I'll speak with him after his meal. He has been served, hasn't he?"

The men grinned.

"He grabbed something," said the first. "And special deliveries have been made to all the guards. We should have some fun with this pair before the action starts."

Cyrus bit his lip and twisted in his chair to see Sterling. The cook shook his head. "Leave them for Phoenix."

"Why?" All four men were confused.

"Why don't you go watch the show?" said the first man, grinning. "We'll stay and cut off their toes. Shouldn't take too long to learn what they know."

"Get out," Sterling said. "Out! I know orders, and I know what Phoenix wants, and it isn't dead or toeless boys. What there is to get, he'll get, and no one else. Out of my pantry until your heads hold something more than air!"

The four men squeezed quickly up the stairs and a door slammed behind them.

Sterling sniffed loudly and moved over to the shelf beneath the onions. From the shadows in the back, the cook pulled out an old mayonnaise jar. It was full of clear liquid.

"Strong stuff," he said loudly. "Remarkable. If I should ever find myself needing to save a life"—he pulled an eyedropper out of his apron and set it on the jar—"I think I'd use two drops beneath the tongue."

Looking at Cyrus, Sterling curled his own tongue and clicked it behind his teeth. "Farewell, lad. And to your sister, too." He scratched his beard and smiled. His eyes were hollow. "You're right," he said. "I did have a fondness for your father and his bride. Old Billy Bones lived two years running on the road. Don't know if I could do half that, but it might be time to try. It might."

He climbed the stairs. His voice tumbled back down. "You were a good porter, Dennis Gilly! One of the best."

A door opened and shut. Bolts slid.

Cyrus looked at Dennis, again trying to writhe his way to his feet. He looked at the Quick Water, nestled into the onions, and at the mayonnaise jar with the eyedropper. He still had little idea what was happening, but he'd picked up enough, and none of it was good.

"Come on, Tigs," he said. "You can see us. Now find us."

• • •

Antigone heard the clock strike eight—through the trees, through the wind and the rain and the early storm darkness. She looked down at the small, heavy box in her hand. The sides were wooden, but broken up with the mounding backs of smooth brass tubes. On top, black-and-white images shot past on a glass screen, bulging even more than an antique television—like a slice off a crystal ball. Staring into it gave her a headache.

Antigone blinked and shook her head. An hour ago, in the dining hall, she'd listened to Greeves address the Order. But she hadn't stayed to watch the members react. Greeves had hurried her outside, given her the box, attached her to Diana Boone, and disappeared. Supposedly, the box showed her what one of Rupert's flying "hunters" was seeing. But the images moved too fast. She'd barely been able to make out the lake.

When she'd tried her Quick Water, she had seen Cyrus's fingers and thumbs but only briefly. After that glimpse, the Quick Water had only shown distortion, shadow, and dim greenness. Olive green. Pickle green. Forest green?

While the images had flitted through her hands—treetops, tree trunks, odd shapes, and glowing windows—she had searched every trail through the trees between the zoo and the main buildings. She had kicked every bush. Twice. Next, she was going to start looking under individual blades of grass. She didn't care how hard it was raining. She didn't care if her stupid flashlight had died. She didn't care if the black clouds had swallowed the sun and killed the day's last light. She was not going to stop until she had found her brother.

Diana Boone came striding down the path wearing a hooded raincoat. The wind whipped it around her. She carried her own box.

"Tigs!" she yelled, and Antigone flinched. She was soaking wet for the second time in one day, her feet were blistered, her legs were chafed, her soaked leather jacket was lead-heavy. Cyrus was missing, and a psycho had her mother and brother. She didn't want anyone calling her by the name Cyrus had given her.

Diana slowed down and stopped beside her. The wind and the trees were fighting. Somewhere close, a big branch popped free and tumbled to the ground. Trunks groaned.

"I brought you a better coat." Diana held out a large parka shell.

"Too late," Antigone said. "I drowned an hour ago."

"Put it on."

Antigone did. It didn't matter one way or another.

"Gunner's got nothing. And he did a pretty full sweep. He just stopped into the kitchen to grab a bite. You should, too. It would help. As for me, I went to all the entrances and down to the harbor. The hunters haven't turned up anything, no one's seen anything, and believe me, they're looking."

Antigone looked down at her box. Trees warped and flashed. And then she saw two shapes—girls, standing in the rain. A flash was all she needed to recognize herself. She looked up. A shape sliced through the air and the rain above them. Slowing, an enormous dragonfly circled around and paused, staring at Antigone from two compound eyes the size of tennis balls. Two more shapes shot by above it, wings clattering like machine guns. Her dragonfly turned and shot away through the trees. It was the first time she'd managed to see it.

Antigone's mouth was open, but she didn't even taste the rain.

"Rupe raised them, and he has all of them out," Diana said. "One patrolling for every guard, and a couple extra hunting for your brother. But they won't be able to fly much longer in this storm."

Antigone looked back down at her box. "And I see what they see."

Diana leaned over Antigone's shoulder. "It takes a lot of getting used to, especially when you're trying to fly behind them. They have three-sixty vision and they're crazy fast. The translator does what it can, but you're still left guessing a lot."

Diana grabbed Antigone's arm and began pulling

her up the path. "It's time to find Rupe. He might have learned something."

Stepping out of the trees, they met the full force of the wind. The main building of Ashtown loomed on top of the hill, guarded by an unshaken stone regiment of rooftop statues, lit windows eyeing the storm.

Antigone's rain hood snapped up in the wind. It actually did help. She looked at the overly confident, overly nice, overly competent girl beside her.

"What am I going to do?" she asked. "My mom, my brothers . . ."

Diana threw her arm around Antigone's shoulders as they marched up the hill. "You're going to hang in there," she said. "That's what you're going to do. You're a Smith. I'm a Boone. We don't roll over."

A bundled and hooded shape was moving down the hill, carrying a pack on its back. Beneath the swirling raincoat, two rod-thin legs were visible.

Antigone stepped down the hill to follow him.

"Hold on," Diana said. "We'll tell Rupe where he is. He's heading to the harbor." She looked down at the screen in her hand, and then over at Antigone's. "Check your water ball again."

Antigone dug into her pocket. The Quick Water glowed in her hand, but the wind and the rain made it impossible to see anything clearly.

"It's lighter than it was," Antigone said. She tucked

her hand under the bottom of her coat and ducked her face down inside the neck.

A moment later, she popped her head back out. "It's Cyrus. He's tied up. And those might be Dennis's feet!"

She held out the neck of her oversize coat. "Quick! Where are they?"

Diana Boone only needed a second.

"That's Sterling's subpantry," she said, popping her head back out and squinting down the hill at Sterling. "It's under the kitchen floor."

Sterling was slipping on the wet grass, sliding down to the airstrip.

"The guards will stop him," Diana said. "Come on."

With the wind pounding their backs, Antigone and Diana turned up the hill and began to climb.

Benjamin Sterling braced himself and slid, staggered, braced himself, and slid again. The storm was more than just another thunder banger, blowing in off the lake. This was one to remember, and he would remember it.

The boats were bobbing and rocking in the harbor. Spray was washing over the jetty. The two little guard shacks were glowing, but he couldn't see any motion inside. He hadn't expected to.

His bag was heavy, but he hadn't taken as much as he was owed. Just a few trifles from the collections—

things stolen by the Order and then tucked away and forgotten. Some spices. His books of recipes.

How much were two legs worth?

The O of B wouldn't miss any of it. They wouldn't be missing anything. And Phoenix wouldn't notice, either. His eyes would be searching for a different prize.

Sterling stopped. He'd reached the first body. Jenkins. Facedown in the grass. An old guard. A good guard. Sterling stepped over him and continued on. He couldn't walk by the guardhouse. Not without looking in.

He slipped forward. A moment later, he pulled open the door.

Four armed men had fallen into a tangle on the floor. A fifth was facedown on the small table. Guns and flickering dragonfly screens had been useless. All five had been good men. But Phoenix had no use for them, and they had no use for Phoenix.

Guilty meat, guilty bread, a guilty thermos of coffee sat innocently on the table.

Sterling moved on.

Hobbling out on a dock, he stopped at a pretty little teak skiff. It had belonged to Cecil Rhodes. Now it would belong to Benjamin Sterling.

The angry lake and the rushing wind were killers, but the legless cook could only smile at the storm. The wind was an old friend promising freedom. And the seething water was nothing like as dangerous as the North Sea in its winter fits or the Caribbean in a hurricane or the Cape of Storms when the boneyards beneath the cliffs were hungry.

He drew the anchor and unfurled the small sails, tacking starboard, out and around the jetty. Close-hauling the sails, he put his nose as tight to the wind as he could, plowing and bouncing through the heavy freshwater waves.

When his course was steady and his beard was dripping like a loaded sponge, he reached into the deep pocket of his oilskin coat, and he smiled.

A tiny ball of liquid perched on his thick fingertips, glowing—the small ball he'd pinched from Cyrus's Quick Water. Ben Sterling would see what happened. He'd know the end of the story. The kitchen always knows.

Above him, he heard the sound of muffled engines. Green and red lights blinked in the air.

Phoenix was descending.

Nolan sighed. He hadn't eaten all day, his sticky new underskin still stung whenever he moved, and he was hungry. Hungrier looking down on a dining hall full of armed people inhaling their dinners between nervous whispers. Only the monks seemed unaffected by the mood of the place, mounding their plates and talking loudly about judgment and divine protection.

At first, he hadn't fully understood why Rupert had

wanted him to leave the hospital and hide. Now, after a day of playing fox and beagle, he knew perfectly well.

Nolan had watched men hunt for him; he'd tucked himself in dead-end ducts while clumsy groundskeepers stumbled sneezing through the dusty tunnels, searching for Nikales the thief and cursing Sterling. Sterling? The legless cook was right at the center of whatever was unfolding.

As soon as the Smiths had arrived in Ashtown, Nolan had known that Phoenix wouldn't be far behind. He'd had his theories about Phoenix. With the Solomon Keys in hand, creeping through the most sealed of the Sage collections, he'd confirmed them.

He'd found a naked wooden mannequin.

According to an official note pinned to the naked chest, the mannequin should have been wearing the Odyssean Cloak. The cloak, originally a talisman to protect and enhance Odysseus's mind and vitality against the wrath of various gods, had been collected and abused by Keeper John Smith some five hundred years ago, resulting in his Burial.

Thirty years ago, a nameless Sage had added a scribble to the bottom of the card: "Presumed stolen."

Nolan had told Rupert. The long-missing cloak might explain the mind and abilities of Phoenix, but even if it did, what made Mr. Ashes, he couldn't even guess.

Today, he'd crept into the document wing of the Sage

library looking for a stack of old handwritten notes he'd seen once before—transcripts of interviews with a troubled young Acolyte, detailing the horrible experiments his father had performed on him and their various effects on.his body and mind.

He had rolled the transcripts into a tube. The tube protruded from his pocket.

And now he was wedged high in a vent, wondering what doom would fall on Ashtown, sure that whatever had been planned, no bullets could stop it.

Beneath him in the dining hall, glass crashed and silver clattered to the floor. Men and women yelled in surprise and horror as the first diners slipped out of their chairs, twitching where they fell.

Dragging Antigone, Diana Boone quickstepped up the kitchen stoop, past the trash cans, and banged through the door.

The room was in chaos.

Pots were boiling over. Smoke was pouring out of unattended ovens.

The floor was a tangle of bodies. Cooks and waiters and busboys sprawled motionless on cold stone tiles.

Gunner, tall in his long, wet coat, pale and sick, was holding a large revolver in each hand, pointing at the only two cooks still on their feet, and at four surly groundskeepers. His legs were shaking. Little Hillary Drake, the girl from Accounting, was curled up, quivering on the floor beside him.

"Who did it?" Gunner yelled. "Where's Sterling?"

"Gone," said a cook. "He just walked out. Don't shoot. We had nothing—"

"Shut up!" Gunner yelled, and he staggered backward into the island of simmering pots.

He moved the guns to the groundskeepers. "Phoenix's lads, aren't you?" He was slurring. "All of you. Embarrassed you couldn't hack the Order? Well, me too, but I didn't turn to murdering for a clown."

The men didn't say anything. They only had to wait. The tall Texan wouldn't last long.

Dripping, Antigone threw off her coat. "Gunner!" she said. "What's going on?"

Drawing her own revolver, Diana ran across the room and dropped to her knees beside Hillary.

Head lolling, Gunner lowered his shaking arms. Two of the groundskeepers jumped forward, but too soon. Both of Gunner's pistols rose and cracked. Both men tumbled.

Gunner slipped to his knees, his face twitching. "They poisoned the . . . everyone," he said. "Everyone. Greeves warned us. Phoenix . . ." He dropped his left arm to the floor, exhausted. His right hand wavered. "You!" he yelled at the last two groundskeepers. "Did you know?"

The two men breathed slowly, looking at the bodies of their friends, taking in the room.

"Answer me!" Gunner yelled. He fired into the wall behind them.

"Yes!" one of them blurted. "But it wasn't serious. Sterling recruited us. We never knew it would be like this. We didn't know."

Gunner swallowed. "Is Phoenix coming?"

The man nodded and pointed out the wall of rain-rattled windows. Below the dark clouds, blurry but visible, green and red wing lights were blinking. A seaplane was touching down in the rough water.

"He's here," the man said.

"On your faces," Gunner said, and the grounds-keepers dropped to their knees and fell forward. "Antigone . . . tie . . . tie . . . find some rope."

The kitchen door swung open and two laughing men stepped through. "We need a gun! Little Jax is brawling in here, going crazy with some table knives—"

Gunner shot twice and both men dropped, yelping, clutching at their legs.

"Them too," Gunner said. He closed his eyes and fell onto his face.

The unwounded groundskeepers both jumped to their feet, but Diana slid to Gunner's body, raising her own revolver. "Down, ticks. I'm a Boone. From here, I could shoot your rat ears off. Not that I'm aiming for your ears."

The men dropped back onto their bellies. Diana

picked up one of Gunner's pistols and tossed it to Antigone.

"Point at what you want to hit and keep them down."

Shaking, the warm gun heavy in her hands, Antigone aimed at the men, and then at the two white-faced cooks. Diana ducked into the dining hall.

"Jax!" Her voice was still loud through the door. Gunfire was louder. She ducked back through. "Keep pointing, Tigs. Jax is fine, and he's coming this way."

The grate rattled off of the heat tunnel in the wall behind her, and she spun around.

Nolan stepped into the kitchen and looked up at two gun barrels pointed right at him.

The dining hall door burst open and Jax jumped through, red-faced and bleeding. "Jaculus venom!" he yelled. "My vipers! I don't know how Sterling got it, but he did. I built an immunity a long time ago. Where is he?"

"Shoot if you like," Nolan said. "But I was just going to ask the same thing. Where is he?" He squinted out the window. "That's a plane. Sterling doesn't matter. Phoenix is here." He scrunched his face. "And if he's here, we shouldn't be. Where's Greeves? I didn't see him in the hall." He looked around. "Where's Cyrus?"

Antigone's eyes widened. "Cyrus!" she yelled. "Diana, where do I go?"

Backing up, Diana picked up Gunner's second gun

and handed it to Nolan. "Get these four tied up. I still don't trust the cooks." Then she hurried through the room, grabbing Antigone as she went. On the far wall, behind the groundskeepers, Diana slid a bolt and jerked open a little door. Tight stairs twisted down and to the right.

Dennis had managed to worm his way across the floor until his trussed feet were on the pickle jar. But he still hadn't spit out the pot holder.

"Did you hear it that time?" Cyrus asked. "That's a gun. I know it is. How many rounds is that? Who do you think is shooting?"

Dennis grunted and wiggled.

"Sorry," said Cyrus. "I know." He looked back at the Quick Water in the onions. "Come on!" he yelled. "Tigs, I know you're somewhere. I know you can see me. I'm surrounded by spices! Where could I be?"

The door opened. Stairs moaned.

"Hello?" Cyrus said. "Who is it? This room is occupied."

"Cyrus!"

Diana staggered into the room, Antigone pushing from behind.

"Wow," said Diana. "You guys are the lucky ones." She bent down and plucked out Dennis's gag.

The porter sputtered. "Lucky? This is lucky?"

Diana nodded.

"It's terrible upstairs," Antigone said, pulling on Cyrus's straps. "Sterling's poisoned the whole Order. Everybody. The kitchen is full of bodies."

"You didn't even see the dining hall," Diana said. She stopped suddenly, forcing herself to breathe. She looked dizzy. "The Order's gone. Everyone." Her eyes widened and she blinked quickly. Pulling the last ropes off Dennis's wrists, she helped him to his feet.

Cyrus stood up, and Antigone thumped into him with a hug. She was soaking wet.

Cyrus pulled free and picked up the mayonnaise jar and eyedropper, handing them to his sister. "Sterling said to put two drops under the tongue. We were the only ones in here. He was telling us what to do."

"What to do after he poisoned everyone?" Antigone asked. "Why would he do that?"

Cyrus shrugged. "I don't know. Maybe he's not all bad."

His sister's eyebrows shot up.

"Or," said Cyrus, "maybe he is all bad, but he doesn't want to think he is."

"Come on," Diana said. "Back upstairs. We'll ask Jax."

In the kitchen, all four of the thugs had been tied up with apron strings.

Jax had Hillary and Gunner lying on their backs, and his fingers were on the Texan's throat.

Dennis staggered through the kitchen and dropped to his knees beside Hillary.

"His heart's beating," Jax said. "Slowly. Every five seconds or so. With spasms. Hillary is worse, but she's much smaller." He looked up at Diana and the others. "It doesn't take much with a Jaculus Viper, and unlike normal snakes, it doesn't need to be injected. The venom is acidic enough to get into the blood through tissue—skin, stomach lining, anything that has blood in it. It was in the food, so that gives us a little time— they'd all be dead already if it was a direct bite. But there's too many people." He teared up and looked away quickly. "The small ones have thirty minutes. Forty-five if they're lucky. Maybe. I have to get to the zoo, catch a viper, cut it open, drain a gland, and get back. And that might only give me enough for five people." The zookeeper sobbed. "I'll have to pick. I don't want to pick."

"What about this?" Cyrus asked, holding out the jar. "Sterling had it."

Swallowing, James Axelrotter took the jar, twisted off the lid, and sniffed at the contents. Surprised, he snatched the glass eyedropper out of Cyrus's hand. Pinching a dropperful, he raised it to his mouth and dabbed it with his tongue. It hissed. The boy zookeeper flinched, and then laughed. "This is it! I don't know how he got this much, and I don't care."

Jax opened Gunner's mouth and squeezed two drops under his tongue. Then he rolled him onto his face.

"It'll foam," he said. "And they won't come to for a little while. They'll choke if we leave them on their backs. There are hundreds of people and not much time. I'll need help."

He turned to little Hillary Drake, and Dennis opened her mouth.

"Excuse me," Nolan said. "But we can't stay here, and soon enough, we won't be able to do this at all." He pointed at the window. "The plane has landed, Phoenix will be here any minute, and there are other thugs still around to give him a welcome."

"Have any ideas?" Diana squinted at the dark window.

"Maybe," said Nolan. "Almost."

Jax and Dennis rolled Hillary onto her face, and then crawled to the next body—a busboy.

"Whatever we do," Cyrus said, pointing at the four tied-up men, "they shouldn't hear about it."

"Drag them downstairs," Antigone said. She jumped over to Jax. "Give me some," she said. "We need more droppers. I'll start in the dining hall."

Cecil Rhodes sat on his couch, drumming his fingers on his knees, wiping sweat on his sleeve, and then drumming his fingers on his knees. He couldn't stop thinking about what Maxi had done to Mrs. Eldridge in that very room. His eyes kept drifting to the bloodstain on the floor, and then up to his telephone. It was supposed to ring. Any second.

He looked across the room at the muscle who had been assigned to him. The man was working on his teeth with a fingernail.

"Did it really work?" Cecil asked. "What happened?"

The man sighed, examining his hand. "I told you already. They kicked, they screamed, they dropped down dead."

Cecil didn't like the man's eyes. They were cold. And catlike. But they weren't as bad as the gill slits on the sides of his neck. He used to wear a scarf, and Rhodes wished the man would tie it back on. Cecil knew what the man had done as an Explorer. Cecil had served as the O of B's prosecutor at the trial.

The phone rang.

Rhodes jumped forward, nearly knocking it off the desk.

"Hello, sir. Yes, sir. It's done. Just the boy, sir. The girl may be among the poisoned." Rhodes covered the handset and looked up at his guard. "Sterling?"

"No sign of him."

Cecil lifted the phone back up. It was slippery with sweat. "No, sir. We don't know where he has gone. Would you like us to begin moving the bodies? No?

I understand, sir. We will leave them for you to view. Wonderful. Yes, sir."

He hung up and jumped back, like he was shaking off a spider. The man with the gills laughed.

Edwin Ashes-Laughlin-Phoenix rose from his seat and limped forward into the cockpit of his seaplane. One of the pontoons was grinding against the jetty. But he didn't care about the rocking waves or the damage to the plane. He cared about what he could see at the top of the slope, with its windows lit. He cared about a small piece of sharp tooth, and hidden sleepers in their Burials. They were now his.

The men and women of Brendan were dead. The time had come for a Phoenix to rise up out of Ashtown.

Behind him, two unconscious shapes lay motionless on narrow cots, and a red-winged blackbird fluttered and screeched angrily in a cage hanging from the ceiling.

"Shall we bring them?" One of the green twins pulled off his headset.

"No," said Dr. Phoenix. "First, the triumphal entry."

twenty-one

THE SLEEPING MOB

DR. PHOENIX WAS not going to enter Ashtown through a kitchen door. Nor would he make one of his offspring carry an umbrella for him. He had walked, flanked by his two lean sons, all the way up and around to the main lawn. Now, with rain streaming off his long trench coat and his straw hat, he stood at the base of the great stairs, near the wet body of a porter.

He could hear the beating wings of a platoon of giant dragonflies in the darkness behind him. They had grown in number, but there were no guards to see what they saw, and no one to command them to attack.

Climbing the stairs, he approached the huge wooden door, but it whined open before he reached it.

Inside, the glistening mapped floors and the vaulted frescoed ceilings stretched away toward the leather boat on its pedestal. Phoenix inhaled slowly and then sighed. It had been too long.

Cecil Rhodes and twelve others stood in a line with their backs against the wall.

Dr. Phoenix savored the sight. And then, laughing, pulling off his gloves, and shedding his hat and trench, he crossed the threshold into Ashtown. Farther down the hallway, he could see bodies, all facedown, limbs splaying awkwardly, foam dribbling from their mouths—the casualties of his triumph.

"Where is the boy?" he asked Rhodes.

Rhodes cleared his throat and picked at his mustache. "Not exactly sure, sir. Sterling had him. But, as you know, we seem to have lost Sterling."

A gilled man laughed. "Crack team."

Phoenix turned slowly, and then moved down the line until he stood in front of the man. He was much taller than the man was, though far thinner.

"My friend, who gave you those eyes?" he asked, smiling. "Those lovely shark gills?"

The man said nothing. Sweat beaded on his forehead.

"Did you ask to be born, sir? Did you ask for sight, for smell, for ten fingers? No. And yet you were given them. And I have given you more."

The man looked into Phoenix's eyes and flinched, trying to look away but unable to. Panic raced across his face. Phoenix raised his right hand, a long forefinger pressing against his thumb. He snapped, and the man's eyes rolled back in his head. His legs wobbled, and he staggered forward, gasping.

"Your body no longer wants its lungs," Phoenix said. "And gills do need water." The man fell to the floor. "Be comforted," Phoenix continued, smiling. "You are unique. Not many men can drown in air."

While the man kicked, Dr. Phoenix turned back to Cecil. "You are missing nine of the men named to me. Where are they?"

Rhodes licked his lips and shook his head. "I don't know, sir."

Phoenix nodded, filled his lungs, pushed back his black hair with the heels of his hands, and flattened the lapels on his soiled lab coat. "Do please take me to the bodies, to the harvest, to the sweet sunset of the Order's chattel."

"Right," said Rhodes. "Follow me, then."

While they moved down the hall, Rhodes cleared his throat. "About what we discussed, sir," he whispered. "The Brendanship . . . the coup is complete. It might be appropriate for you to tell the others. I will, of course, reiterate my loyalty to you."

Dr. Phoenix stopped and let his head hang. His long arms dangled limp by his sides. His shoulders bobbed with laughter, but when he looked up, his face was a sharp tombstone.

"Mr. Rhodes," he drawled loudly. "You are a traitor to your people, your Order, and your friends. I would not entrust you with my laundry." He moved on.

"When I have need of more betrayals, then I shall have more need of you. Come. I have asked to see the dead, the many you have stung for me."

"I didn't—" Cecil stopped himself. The green twins parted around him, neck gills fluttering, heeling to their master. "But you said . . ."

"There will be no Brendan!" Dr. Phoenix yelled. "No Order, no ranks, no charade of self-importance! Only master and mastered, Mr. Rhodes. I will build a new race, a species apart and above the filth of humanity. Ashtown will be a womb, and you shall be a nursery maid."

The twins followed Dr. Phoenix down the hall and past the boat. The other men trailed behind, some glancing at Cecil, some smiling, some smirking, some hanging their heads.

A minute later, Cecil Rhodes stood alone. He looked back down the hall at the large door still open onto the courtyard, the door leading away from Ashtown, away from what he'd done. Rain spattered on the stone steps, and he could see a porter's feet. Dragonflies darted past the entrance.

Turning away, he ran after Phoenix, rushing past hundreds of damning eyes staring out of photos, past sprawling bodies bearing witness to his crime.

One of the bodies jumped to her feet and kicked him in the stomach.

Breathless, he crumpled to the floor and slid into the wall. His eyes filled with tears, and as he blinked them away, he found himself looking up the barrel of a revolver and into the face of Diana Boone.

The hammer clicked back.

Over her shoulder, the Smith boy appeared. He was holding a small African club.

"God knows I should," Diana said. Her voice was low. A growl. "But I can't waste the bullet."

The boy stepped forward and raised his club. The blow fell.

Cyrus looked down at the limp, unconscious lawyer. Diana was already scanning the hallway.

"That's one," she whispered. "Your sister? Jax? Dennis?"

Cyrus shouldered his club and looked into the Quick Water. His heart was racing. "All down," he said softly. "They saw them coming."

"Good. Watch our backs."

Diana jogged down the hallway toward the big, open front door and a porter's feet, pulling out the small corked bottle Jax had given her as she did.

Looking over his shoulder, Cyrus ran behind, keys jingling against his chest.

The two of them stepped out into the wet wind and flipped the small porter onto his back. Cyrus opened the boy's mouth and lifted his tongue. Diana squeezed two drips off her dropper, and they rolled the boy back onto his face.

Straightening, Diana squinted out into the dark courtyard. "See anyone?"

"Over there," Cyrus said, pointing. "On the path. Two people."

Side by side, they stutter-stepped down the slick stairs, reached the gravel path, and jogged through the stinging rain.

"It's Rupe!" Diana yelled, and she moved into a sprint.

The big man's head and shoulders were off the path, his face in the grass. He was wearing a rain cape, but the hood had fallen back. In one hand, he held a short shotgun. His other fist was clenched around foil-wrapped chicken. A dragonfly screen flickered in the grass. The boy, Oliver, was lying facedown in the gravel.

Antigone's cheek was pressed into the red carpet. She'd put a large man's foot on her head to disguise herself, but there hadn't been much need. The place was strewn with bodies. Young, old, men, women, children, monks. Under tables, on tables, tangled up in tablecloths, buried beneath food, shattered china, and the limbs of dining partners.

So many people and so much silence. Each breath felt like a sneeze in church. The Quick Water had worked. She'd seen the horrible man coming with his people, and she'd shoved Dennis down and whispered at Jax. He hadn't stopped. Not at first. Not until the doors had moved and the two green men had stepped aside for the monster in the bright white suit beneath the soiled lab coat. She stopped her breath and felt her heart quicken.

The cloak. She hoped Nolan was right.

A small crowd had entered behind Phoenix. Don't look closely, she thought. Don't, don't, don't.

The bodies closest to the kitchen were all facedown. The bodies closest to the kitchen were all foaming at the mouth.

The monster in the white coat moved farther into the room, prodding the unconscious dying, grinning from ear to ear.

Suddenly, he stopped and closed his eyes, lifting his face and raising his arms.

"Children of Brendan," he said, falsely somber, "I pardon thee whatever sins thou hast committed—"

He stopped, interrupted by a cough. Lowering his long arms, he squinted around the room. Nolan's voice descended from the ceiling.

"'My name is Edwin Harry Laughlin.'" Lilting, mocking. "'I am sixteen years old and a recent Acolyte in the Order of Brendan, Ashtown. My father's name is Harry Hamilton Laughlin. My mother's name was

Pansy. She died two years ago, after one of my father's experiments.'"

Phoenix's face purpled, and then paled quickly as he collected himself. "It seems we have a wit in the room," he drawled. "Do show yourself now. Or how can I know in which direction to applaud?"

Antigone bit her lip, watching Phoenix's men swivel and search. And then the two identical green men slid forward, creeping smoothly across the bodies like stalking wolves. Their nostrils were flared, and their eyes were on one of the heat vents just beneath the beamed ceiling.

"Shoot him," Phoenix said.

The men drew guns, and a pair of fireballs corkscrewed toward the vent, exploding in the grate.

"Idiots!" Phoenix groaned. "I would prefer if you didn't burn the place. Bullets! Use bullets. And your heads."

The men tucked away their weapons and drew new ones—long-barreled revolvers. The beveled grate bent and puckered as they fired, and the smell of sulfur and gunpowder drifted through the room.

Antigone jerked at each report, but no one was watching. She could see Dennis breathing hard. Jax was inching forward, his jar tucked beneath his arm, dropper in hand. Antigone wanted to yell at him to stop moving. The men were right there. If any of them so much as glanced down, he'd be killed.

The firing stopped. All eyes were on the ruined grate. The silence was brief.

" 'My mother,' " Nolan said, " 'was the sort of sweet, empty-headed thing great men like my father can find themselves burdened with. There were even moments when I loved her. But I hate her Gypsy blood. I hate that it is in me. I want it out. I will get it out. My father tried, and he came close. I will succeed. At least, there are times when I think I will. I dream that I will. But my waking hours are spent in pain. My legs. My mind. Too many blood purifications. Too much electricity. I cannot sleep without nightmares, and when I wake, my bed is swamped with sweat.' "

Dr. Phoenix was a statue, his face bloodless. His eyes unfocused. "You, sir . . . ," he began, but his voice trailed away. His jaw clenched, pulsing. His chest heaved. He was panting now, rolling his head, clenching his fists. Antigone tensed and slid a little farther away. Nolan had wanted Phoenix angry, but why that would make him take off his coat, she didn't understand.

And then, suddenly, the thin man with the black hair raised quivering hands to his shoulders. He tore off the stained white coat and threw it on the ground. His suit coat followed. Antigone blinked. The man's hair was whitening. His nostrils flared, and his shoulders thickened, broadening. Huge hands balled into hairy melon fists. His legs thickened, shortening and bowing out.

Snarling, Phoenix—Mr. Ashes—leapt forward, scrambling over bodies, jerking the guns from his sons' hands.

A gun fired, but not his. Flame flashed out of the vent, and Dr. Phoenix—Mr. Ashes—dropped to his knees. One of the twins fell. The other reached the wall. The firing shifted toward the door, into the crowd.

Yelping, leaving one of their own behind on the floor, the men flooded back into the hall.

Antigone saw Jax pinch two drops into the next mouth, roll over the body quickly, and wriggle on.

Dennis raised his head nervously and then scooched himself forward.

The coat was on the ground. Antigone puffed out her cheeks. It was her turn.

Antigone tucked her little bottle into her jacket pocket. She had a gun in the other, but guns were everywhere. Sliding slowly over a drooling monk, still gripping her Quick Water, she braced herself and prepared to run.

Phoenix rose to his feet, and his back rippled beneath his shirt as he looked up at the vent. Dropping his guns, he splayed and flexed huge fingers. His voice was molasses-thick and just as slow. "I'm not that easy to kill, friend."

"You and me both," said the voice of Nolan. "But the green one there looks hurt."

441

Phoenix moved like a gorilla, knuckling off the ground as he rushed toward the wall beneath the vent. Behind him, one of the wounded twins struggled to his feet. The other stepped out of his way.

Phoenix leapt at the wall and two wrecking-ball fists crashed through the plaster. Leaving his arms in the holes, he pulled himself up off the floor. One fist at a time, he punched grips in the plaster as he climbed.

Antigone's eyes locked on the rumpled white coat. She should have gone already. What was she waiting for? Jax was nodding at her. Dennis, peering through bodies, widened his eyes meaningfully. She had to be fast. Faster than she had ever been in her life.

One of the bodies near the kitchen door moaned loudly, coming to. Another one rolled onto its side. A third struggled to sit up. She'd waited too long. Phoenix's men were peering back in from the hall.

"Go!" Dennis yelled. "Run!"

Antigone scrambled to her feet. Three men jumped forward through the door. Nolan's gun cracked again and they jumped back. Both twins turned.

Antigone's knees were bouncing high. Running through the bodies was like running through Cyrus's pool of tires—tripping, slipping, bouncing off backs, stepping on wrists. Her eyes searched for empty spots of floor and bounced back up to the coat. Jax was high-stepping toward the kitchen. Dennis lagged behind him.

The twins were hesitating, picking their prey from among three runners. The coat was rumpled on the floor halfway between Antigone and the worried crowd in the doorway. Thirty feet. Fifteen.

She heard Phoenix crash back off the wall behind her. Nolan was firing again, trying to cover her.

Antigone slid across a tangle of teenage limbs in white shirts and snatched the coat. Turning toward the kitchen door, she ran like a dog in drifted snow, leaping bodies, popcorning up and down wherever her feet could find the floor. She was the only real target now. She was racing two bleeding green men with golden eyes.

The coat flapped behind her like a flag.

Guns were cracking all around. A bullet ripped through her short hair, and a pair of fireballs swirled over her head and exploded on the wall. Phoenix was roaring. Nolan was yelling. Jax and Dennis were shouting over their shoulders. They reached the door and burst through in front of her.

One of the lean twins was faster than the other. He dove, snagging her ankle.

Twisting at top speed, she fell backward through the kitchen door, slammed onto the floor, and slid headfirst into the island of still-flaming burners.

The kitchen was all stench and burnt food and groaning bodies. Gunner was sitting up with his head in his hands. Jax was sweeping pots off the burners and shouting something. Dennis had tripped over little Hillary Drake and tumbled beneath a table.

Antigone jumped to her feet, dropped her Quick Water on the floor, and jerked her small revolver from her pocket. Closing her eyes tight, she pointed at the door, looked away, and squeezed three times, feeling the gun bark and jump.

Jax had already cleared the pots and turned up the flames. Antigone threw Phoenix's coat across the flickering burners.

A yell as primal as pain itself rose up in the dining hall.

The door flew off its hinges, and the twins entered. Behind them, bellowing in agony, white-haired Edwin Harry Ashes leapt into the room. His right arm was on fire.

Ignoring Antigone, he grabbed the edge of the island and swung up and over it, knocked his coat to the floor, and stamped out its flames.

Jax raised a gun, but Ashes sent him sprawling with the back of his charred and smoking arm. He leapfrogged back over the island easily, crashing to the ground in front of Antigone, staring into her eyes with black rage.

Stammering, stunned, she tried to raise her gun. His left hand closed around Antigone's throat. Bullets hit the floor.

Her breath was gone. She kicked and clawed and

punched. She gasped, her ears ringing as she watched the twins throw Dennis back to the ground. Her vision blurred. The ceiling and walls disappeared.

And then there was nothing. Not whiteness, not blackness—nothing. And she became part of it. Almost. She slipped to an invisible floor.

Things were exploding. More guns. More fire. She didn't like guns. And she wished Cyrus would stop yelling. She was trying to sleep.

Breathing hard, dripping, Cyrus and Diana ran back up the front steps.

"What now?" Cyrus whispered.

"Time for the plane."

"Do we go all the way around?"

Diana shook her head. "Too long."

A few of Phoenix's men were visible down the hallway, peering through a door. Cecil Rhodes was still motionless, a huge knot over his temple. Cyrus hoped he hadn't hit him too hard.

Gunfire.

"What's going on?" Diana glanced down at Cyrus's hand. He held up the Quick Water.

"Shooting at Nolan's vent."

Diana nodded. "We have to hurry." She slid quickly inside and hung close to the wall, the enormous reptile skin above her.

Cyrus had ditched his club next to Greeves. Now he held the little shotgun in his right hand, the Quick Water in his left. He'd wanted the revolver. Diana didn't care what he wanted. She could hit something with a revolver. Anyone could hit something with a shotgun.

The crowd suddenly flooded back into the hallway as Diana and Cyrus ducked around the corner. Diana jogged down the side hallway and around another corner. She forced a door open and slipped inside. The Africa collection. Cyrus hurried in behind her and shut the door.

"Di?" The room was a black hole.

"Over here," Diana said. "Keep well to your left and come straight on."

Something large and breathing bumped into the back of Cyrus's legs. Yelling, he staggered forward and fell. Teeth clacked together.

Air rushed through the room. Teeth didn't clack. They ground and snapped. In the darkness in front of Cyrus, the gold outlines around Sir Roger's eyes began to glow. The skull was on its ear, rocking in place, trying to bite.

Cyrus kicked it hard, skidding it back into the darkness.

The lights flashed on. Frightened, confused, Diana stood at the switch, looking from Cyrus to the big skull.

"I have the Dragon's Tooth," Cyrus said. "Sterling wasn't lying. I have the tooth that killed Roger."

"What?" Diana blinked. "You're serious?" She shook her head. "Don't tell me. We don't have time. Get up and come on."

They ran across the room to a small door set between shelves. Diana opened it, and they stepped into old brooms and mops and buckets.

"Shared closet," she said, and kicked open another door, shattering a brittle jamb.

The next room was lit. Card catalog cabinets taller than houses lined the walls. Flights of spiral stairs on wheels dotted the room. Across from each other, two middle-aged women were facedown on the same desk, a plate of food and a scattered game of chess between them.

"Keepers' Catalog Room," Diana said. "Tough job. Every item and collective holding of the Order is listed in here."

Cyrus set his shotgun and Quick Water on the desk, pinched cheeks and lifted tongues. After the drops, the women's faces went back onto the chessboard.

Diana rushed off to another door.

They crossed a hall, went downstairs into a machinist's shop, upstairs through an old coal-chute door, and out into the rain.

Turning his back to the wind, Cyrus checked his Quick Water again.

Diana was running down the hill.

"Trouble!" Cyrus yelled. "Di!"

She didn't hear him, and he didn't care. Antigone was running in his palm. Cyrus raced alongside the building, dodging window wells and columns. He could see the kitchen's garbage stoop, and he passed beneath the lit wall of windows. He could hear the yelling.

Climbing the stairs on the garbage stoop, Cyrus pulled back the hammers on his shotgun and put his shoulder into the door, forcing his way into mayhem.

A woozy Gunner was on his feet. Jax was down. Dennis was down. Two tall green men stood above them, their eyes on Nolan, bleeding and blackened, as he emerged from a heat tunnel. The kitchen door was off its hinges, and on the other side, dozens of people were trying to lever themselves off the red dining hall carpet.

Cyrus ignored all of it.

A man with gorilla hands was strangling his sister.

"Drop her!" Cyrus yelled.

Snarling, the man threw Antigone to the floor and faced Cyrus. "Smith!" he said, stepping forward. "I drained your father's blood. Your brother and mother. And this"—he kicked at Antigone's crumpled body—"your wretched sister. And you. All of you will die."

Cyrus's gun had two triggers, side by side. He pointed at the man's broad chest and pulled both of them.

Mr. Ashes rolled backward with the blast, and then rose to his feet.

"Right," said Cyrus. "You're one of those."

He dropped the gun and reached for his neck. His fist closed around the keys. Pulling them free of Patricia, he clenched the tooth between his knuckles.

Ready, he raised his fist.

The angry ape of a man froze, and then smiled. His anger drained away, and while the mayhem in the kitchen rumbled on, he picked up his white coat. The right sleeve had burned away up to the elbow.

"Come on!" Cyrus said. "Come fight! Are you scared now?"

As the coat slipped over the man's shoulders, Cyrus watched him change. The veins and creases in his face smoothed. His arctic hair blackened.

He thinned, his body stretching, lengthening.

Dr. Phoenix stepped forward. "Boy," he said. "Your mind is as open to me as was your pitiful brother's, as was your unfortunate mother's. It is as open to me as the sky to the bird, as the sea to the shark. I'm afraid that I must be quite insistent. Give me the tooth and those keys."

Smiling, he held out his unburnt hand.

Cyrus shook his head. "I don't know what you're trying to do, but it's not going to work."

The man reached Cyrus. "The arrangement can still

be friendly. I am no longer Mr. Ashes. I am prepared to show mercy. I will spare your mother. Perhaps even your brother. They are sleeping so peacefully in my plane right now. My sons could bring them in."

Rupert Greeves, eyes rolling and foam dripping down his short beard, staggered into the kitchen on wobbling legs. He was carrying Cyrus's small club.

"Phoenix!" he bellowed. "Your cowards fled." He tried to cross the kitchen, but the twins jumped back, shoulder to shoulder, weapons raised, barrels ready to spit their balls of fire. Nolan stepped beside Greeves.

Dr. Phoenix didn't turn. He smiled at Cyrus.

Give him the tooth, Cyrus thought. No. Hit him in the stomach.

Phoenix shook his head.

Give him the tooth. Cyrus shook his head at his own thoughts. They weren't his thoughts. He looked at Phoenix's temple, gauging the distance.

"No," said Phoenix. "On the tip of an arrow, maybe. Carved into a bullet, perhaps. If only you had thought ahead. Would you like your family to live? Or would you like to be responsible for their deaths?"

Greeves staggered forward, bellowing and swinging his club at the green men. He slipped and hit the ground.

Lunging forward, Cyrus swung for the temple. Phoenix's left hand swallowed his fist easily, but the tooth plunged deep into Phoenix's palm.

Smiling through the pain, Phoenix began to twist Cyrus's grip, levering his hand back, driving him to the floor. Cyrus's breathing stopped. His mind wouldn't let his lungs inflate. His heart was slowing. The key ring bent and began to give. The silver sheath popped loose in his palm.

No. Cyrus tore his fist free and staggered back, still clutching the tooth between his bloody knuckles, his lungs suddenly bursting with air. Phoenix stepped forward calmly.

Cyrus looked at his unconscious sister, at Jax and Dennis rising to their hands and knees, at Rupert and Nolan facing the bleeding green twins and their guns, at Gunner and the waking mob through the doorway in the dining hall. Turning, Cyrus lurched toward the kitchen's back door. He had to lead the hunters away.

Banging out into the wind, Cyrus slipped down the stairs onto the wet grass. Scrambling to his bare feet, he ran along the building.

Phoenix was yelling. Behind Cyrus, the twins slid out of the doorway and into the storm. Cyrus accelerated through the shadows, brushing his shoulder against the wall. And then his shin collided with a hidden bicycle. Shoving the partially separated tooth and keys into his pocket, he grabbed the handlebars, jerked the bike away from the wall, and jumped into the seat. A large umbrella propeller spun in the wind above him.

He didn't have time to worry. He pushed off down the hill, pumping the pedals.

Cyrus gasped as the wind jerked the bike off the ground. He surged up past the first-story windows and back toward the building. The propeller tip sparked on stone and the bike swung, cracking Cyrus's knee hard against the wall. He wasn't flying, he was blowing away like an unleashed kite. The gusting wind pulled him from the wall, spun the bike in a circle, and forced him toward the trees. Below him, the ground was dark. Treetops were jagged silhouettes waiting to swallow him. Pedaling furiously, Cyrus tried to lean and tried to steer, but he was at the wind's mercy.

A fireball swirled past him, and he felt the heat on his wet skin. He watched it dissipate in the wind as it climbed. The wind spun him around. He was facing the harbor but blowing backward. Two more fireballs climbed into the sky in front of him, shredded by the wind high above. Cyrus stood, pumping hard on the swaying pedals, and scanned the ground forty feet below. He could just make out the twins, guns raised.

Jerking hard on the handlebars, Cyrus managed to twist the bike around, getting the harbor and the wind at his back. He was racing toward the main building.

Teeth grinding, Cyrus pumped for elevation as the wind threw him forward.

He was climbing, but not fast enough. Statues loomed

above him along the roofline. A fireball burst on the stone in front of him, blinding him with light. Another rose up in front of him, singeing his face.

It exploded in the umbrella propeller, raining fire, burning skin.

Cyrus didn't stop pedaling as he fell. The bike crashed into the wall and tumbled down the stone face. The wind tore the blackened propeller free and Cyrus slammed into wet earth with the bike on top of him.

Gasping, blinking, he managed to push the bike off. A green-faced man with strange eyes leaned over him. His eyes were golden. Gills fluttered on his neck. His identical brother loomed behind him.

"Take it!" Phoenix yelled in the wind. "Bring it to me!"

Cyrus's breath was gone, and his mouth was filling with blood. He spat and gasped and felt for his pocket, trying to roll onto his side. Wrong pocket. His fingers grazed glass and tingled with electricity. The green man pushed him flat and pressed him down. Long hands groped for his pockets.

"Can't," Cyrus gasped. Gritting his teeth, he gripped the lightning bug cube, tugged it free of his pocket, and slammed it against the twisted metal of the bike frame. Glass shattered. Shards dug into his palm, but the pain was nothing to the roar of electricity that shot up his arm.

Thunder grumbled on the wind.

With his empty hand, Cyrus grabbed at the groping twin's shirt, tugging him down while he raised his electric fist. Green arcs sparked between his knuckles.

A blow slammed into his face, but he didn't let go. A knee crashed into his ribs. Cyrus sputtered, shoving his quivering beetle hand down the man's shirt, just managing to open his throbbing, electricity-petrified fingers, releasing the lightning bug against green skin.

The twin shivered with the current. The storm sky flickered. Too late to get away. Cyrus clamped his eyes shut.

Through his eyelids, the flash was bloody red. Pure heat ripped through his body.

He heard nothing. He knew nothing. All was forgotten.

Someone was slapping his face, even harder than the needling rain. He opened his eyes. Greeves, looking ill. Antigone, worried hands cupped over her mouth. Nolan, with his hand raised for another slap. Instead, he pulled Cyrus to his feet. His bare feet hurt. A lot.

"Where's the tooth?" Nolan asked.

Cyrus shoved cracked and blistered hands into his pockets, but he didn't need to. He felt empty. The tooth's power was gone. The keys were still there, but they and the remaining charms were loose in his pocket. And the key ring, bent and molten, was stuck to the empty silver sheath.

A green man lay in the grass with open, steaming wounds. Cyrus blinked quickly in the wind, remembering the struggle. His eyes wanted to roll back in his head. "They took it. After the lightning. Sorry."

Without a word, Rupert and Nolan began running down the slope.

Antigone threw her arms around her brother's neck. "We're alive," she said. "But Mom. Dan. He still has them. Was he telling the truth? Are they in the plane?" She squeezed her brother hard.

Letting go, she wiped her eyes. "Where is Diana?"

Cyrus looked around. His body felt like Play-Doh. His brain was blistered.

"The plane," he said. "Diana, we . . ." He swallowed. "She's trying to blow up the plane."

Lightning shattered the sky. Thunder washed around them. Down near the airstrip, fireballs corkscrewed back up the slope and over their heads.

Diana Boone reached the airstrip and looked back up at Ashtown. She could see motion in the lit kitchen windows, but Cyrus was gone. She didn't have time to go back. He knew where she was. He could catch up.

The rest of the way to the jetty, she was more cautious. The dragonflies found her—she felt bad for them, slower and battered by the storm—but Phoenix hadn't seemed to feel that his plane needed a guard. Over-confident, she thought. She hoped.

The plane was all the way at the end of the jetty, tied off and facing the shore, grinding its pontoon up and down the rocks as the waves washed in. She'd thought about cutting it loose, but with the wind it would only drift into the harbor. Now she was wishing that she'd paid more attention to her cousin's monotone reci-tations as he worked on her Spitfire. He would have found the fuel line in no time. And, once he'd found it, he would have known what to do with it.

Diana glanced back up. The kitchen door opened. Two tall shapes stepped through. They were looking for something. They didn't have to look long. Spiraling fire-balls climbed into the sky.

Diana's mouth fell open. Cyrus was trying to fly away. In this storm. Pulling her gun, she began to run back down the jetty. She paused. She had her own job to do. She'd have to do it quick.

She turned back to the plane. The water was rough, too rough for any sane pilot to attempt a takeoff. But it had been too rough for any sane pilot to attempt a land-ing. And the wind would give the plane extra lift.

She had no time. None. And no plan. Bright, erupt-ing fireworks continued up by the main building. She couldn't let herself watch.

Diana looked at the gun in her hand. She had five rounds. She looked at the plane's grinding pontoon. Three steel braces attached it to the main fuselage. They were pipes, and they weren't very thick.

Scrambling down the rocks and through the spray, Diana hopped onto the pontoon. Pulling the hammer back on her revolver, she aimed down at where the forward brace attached to the pontoon. She fired.

A hole appeared in the metal.

Up the hill, lightning forked to the ground. The thunder washed around her, fading quickly in the wind.

Diana fired into the brace two more times, and then twice up into the plane's engine for good luck.

She heard guns. Two tall shapes were coming down the hill. Phoenix was retreating, but where was Cyrus? Shapes were rushing out the kitchen door, and she saw muzzle flashes. A fireball swirled back up the hill but fell short, erupting into a hurricane of sparks in the wet grass. Another painted white flame across the face of Ashtown.

Diana moved down the jetty. Her gun was empty. The shapes at the top of the hill were huddling over something.

Two shapes were retreating across the airstrip. They'd be at the jetty soon. Pursuit had begun. Gunfire. White flame swirled back up the hill in reply.

Lightning struck again, but behind her, over the

water. Diana covered her ears against the thunder and backed toward the plane. She didn't want to be in the water with lightning falling, but she didn't have much choice.

The two tall men reached the jetty—Phoenix with one green man.

Diana hopped onto the pontoon and slipped off quietly, treading water beneath the plane. She could hear yelling, but her ears were ringing from thunder and her own gunshots. The wind and waves swallowed the rest.

Fuel dripped into the water around her.

The twin dropped to his knees on the jetty, and white fire swirled back at invisible enemies. Phoenix jumped into the plane.

Spitting water, Diana wished she hadn't emptied her gun.

A moment later, the engine sputtered to life. Diana closed her eyes against the propeller's battering breath and wished she could cover her ears.

Cyrus stood panting in the rain beside his sister. His face was singed and blistered. Rupert Greeves and Nolan stood beside them, their clothes smoking. The guns were all empty, and every time they took a step forward, another fireball bowled up the hill, exploding in the grass while the wind whipped the flames around them.

"Cyrus," Antigone said. "We have to get them. We can't let him do this."

Cyrus said nothing. Blinking away the rain, his eyes bounced between the plane and the man guarding the jetty.

The plane's engine started. The propeller was growling, ready to pull, ready to climb. Lights were on in the cockpit. It hadn't blown up. Where was Diana?

Tensing, he inched forward. Greeves dropped a heavy hand onto his shoulder, holding him back.

Cyrus bit his lip, tasting blood. If his brother and mother were really on that plane, he couldn't watch them leave, not with that man, not into a storm. He didn't have a choice. Dying would be better than watching.

A dragonfly whipped by overhead.

Rupert watched it go, then he raised two fingers to his mouth and whistled long and sharp.

Cyrus dashed down the hill.

The first fireball seemed to come in slow motion. He dropped onto the wet grass and slid through its sparks. Hopping up, he had three strides before the next one exploded at his feet.

He jumped as high as he could, flailing his arms, kicking through the heat, overbalancing as he came down. The crash became a roll, and he was up again and running.

A wave of dragonflies streaked above him. Nolan came up beside him.

The screaming pitch of the seaplane's engine climbed, and it rocked away from the jetty, beginning to turn around in the harbor, preparing to fight the wind. The man on the jetty was finally retreating to the plane, running fluidly, spraying fire over his shoulder. A fireball exploded around a ship's mast. Three others drifted away into the trees. The dragonflies were on him now, and he swung at them as he ran. At the end of the jetty, he launched himself easily through the air, landed on the plane's moving pontoon, grabbed the wing, and swung himself up through the open door.

The dragonflies veered away.

Cyrus reached the wet stone. His mouth opened and his tongue crawled out as he pumped forward, every tired muscle firing, his limbs screaming as he sprinted the long stone curve. Nolan was falling behind. Rain stung. Legs burned. None of it mattered.

The plane had completely turned. It was just off the end of the jetty. The engine shrieked at the wind, and it began to pull away.

One second. Two seconds. Three.

Cyrus planted his left foot on the end of the jetty and threw himself out into the air.

He smacked into the tail and tried to hang on, his

hands slipping down the wet metal, peeling open his lightning-blistered palms. And then the plane hit its first wave and shook Cyrus off. Dropping to the water, he grabbed for the pontoon, just managing to hook his left arm around the rear brace.

The plane was picking up speed, bouncing, slamming into each wave, dragging him on his back, nosing him under into the force of a waterfall, skipping him across the top like a stone.

The pontoon smashed into a wave and rose above the water.

Cyrus's torso rose with it. His waist was free. His legs slapped into the next wave. The force jerked him loose and sent him rolling across the rough surface. Above him, free of the water and accelerating into a climb, the plane burst into flames.

Sputtering but still conscious, Cyrus watched the plane as it dropped, trying to touch back down against the windblown waves.

With a snap, the first whitecap ripped off a pontoon and sent it cartwheeling across the surface. The plane's nose smashed into the water. Its tail rose and fell forward in a somersault.

Metal creaked and sighed. Flames trickled out onto the water.

Cyrus tried to swim toward the wreckage, but the wind was too strong for his weakened arms, and the chop of the water was too big, driving him back toward the distant shore.

Filling his tired lungs to bursting, he dove, pulling himself below the moving surface.

Ten feet down, he started kicking forward. He could hear the groaning metal of the plane all around him. He had no sense of direction, no energy in his limbs, and no possible chance of reaching the wreckage.

But he couldn't stop. Not now.

A large shape rose up beneath him. Sandpaper skin against his hands. A vertical fin. He grabbed on, and Lilly the bull—he hoped—surged forward through the darkness.

The popping and creaking grew louder. Before long, the orange dance of fire lit the surface above him.

He patted the shark and let go, kicking up toward the inverted cockpit.

Both doors were open.

The submerged cockpit was empty.

Cyrus slid through a door and pulled himself back toward the rear of the plane and up into an air pocket.

Dan was sitting on the plane's ceiling, bleeding from his forehead, cradling his mother in his lap. His blond hair had been cropped close to his scalp. His eyes were frantic and confused. He was much bigger.

"Cy!" he yelled. "What are you doing here? What's going on?"

. . .

Antigone watched Cyrus and Nolan run, and her teeth drew blood from her fingers when Cyrus jumped.

She saw the plane drag her brother into darkness. She saw the fire and the tumbling crash. She raced after Greeves as he ran down to the docks, and she jumped into his metal shell of a boat while he jerked the cord on the motor.

Nolan was standing on the end of the jetty, watching the lake's churning surface burn. Diana climbed up the rocks beside him and sat, covering her mouth in shock.

Antigone grabbed on to the heaving prow, and the boat surged and chopped its way out into the lake. Her mind was numb. Water stung her unblinking face. Wind and rain tore at her hair. Distant lightning and approaching flames seared their brightness on her staring eyes. The burning plane was sinking—the last three people she loved were sinking with it.

Rupert circled the wreckage and circled again, tightening his loops, passing through islands of flame. Finally, cutting the engine, he jerked his shirt over his head and prepared to dive.

Antigone grabbed his arm.

Antigone was the one who heard her brother—her *brothers*—calling out her name from the oily water. She was the one who spotted the three shapes in the darkness. And when Rupert had lifted her mother's limp, dripping body from the waves, and a muscled, confused Dan had swallowed her in a hug, and Cyrus had emptied his gut of lake water and lay gasping at her feet, when the boat had finally turned its nose back to Ashtown, she was the one who held her mother's head in her lap, rocking with the heaving waves, stroking dripping white hair, looking at her battered and bleeding brothers, mixing hot tears with the rain.

A mile to the east of the sinking plane, Lilly the bull found something strange. Two somethings. She could smell them. She could feel their vibrations in the water running down her skin. One of them was a people. He smelled like a people, looked like a people, and moved like a people. She mustn't eat the people or taste the people or be seen by the people.

But the other was not a people. Parts of it smelled people, but more of it was like dog and monkey and . . . vile tiger shark. It had gills. She could feel the gills vibrating as it swam. It was not slapping the water like people. It was slithering through it, dragging the people on its back.

She needed to know what this new thing was. And, for a shark, there is only one way to be sure.

After trial, after hardship and horror, even after the darkest night, the Earth still turns. The sun still burns, though its light may discover many changes. When the morning sun rose into blue sky over the freshwater sea that is Lake Michigan, when its light kissed the stone walls and towers and windows of Ashtown, the chapel held twelve bodies in need of graves—eleven members and staff of the Order of Brendan who had not survived the night. One who had been murdered in the office of Cecil Rhodes.

Rupert Greeves stood beside them, his brow furrowed, his hands crossed, studying the faces of those he had lost. Five of his guards. A man and a woman, newly engaged, both cooks. A smiling Keeper. A monk. A wrinkled Sage. A young Acolyte. And Eleanor Elizabeth Eldridge. Alone, Rupert had already uttered blessings over each of them.

Jax had wept over each of those he had not reached in time, and he had paced every corner of Ashtown with his antivenin until Rupert had forced him to bed.

Rupert himself had not slept, and it would be a long time before he did. There were too many things to do, and the list wouldn't stop scrolling in his head.

Cecil Rhodes was missing. The other captured traitors were in containment, waiting for Rupert's arrival.

The young Oliver Laughlin was comatose.

Wisconsin authorities were waiting for his call about a reported plane crash.

An elevator needed fixing. The Brendan—soon to resign, no doubt—was probably hungry.

The O of B had lost its cook, but that wouldn't stop people from wanting breakfast. He hoped everybody liked French toast, because that's all he knew how to make.

Phoenix had the tooth.

Rupert dragged a heavy hand down his jaw and through his pointed beard. He didn't even like to think about what that meant—old images, scars on his memory, flickered past, and he was again digging graves for the misshapen and disfigured remains hidden by a younger Phoenix in the walls and floors of Ashtown. His own brother's body . . .

Rupert closed his eyes. He was going to need help from the other Estates. And he would have to train up help for himself within Ashtown. He opened his eyes, staring straight ahead. The future was invisibly dark, but to Rupert Greeves, it smelled like war.

He looked down at the row of bodies in their open boxes. Twelve dead in two days.

Sighing, Rupert Greeves turned and left the chapel. Everything else could wait until he'd been to the hospital.

John Horace Lawney was sitting up in his bed when Rupert arrived, carrying a large envelope under his arm. Gunner was snoring in the bed behind his uncle.

"Horace," said Rupert, nodding.

"Greeves," said Lawney.

The two of them looked at the row of beds.

Daniel Smith. Katie Smith. Antigone Smith. Cyrus Smith.

Diana Boone was curled up with a blanket on the floor. Nolan was hunched over, snoring in a chair by the window. Breeze-rustled curtains dragged through his hair. A slightly frayed red-winged blackbird hopped on the sill behind him.

Groaning, Daniel Smith opened his eyes and stretched his thick, bruised arms above his bandaged head.

"Mr. Smith?" Rupert asked.

Daniel opened his eyes. "Mr. Greeves!" He sat up carefully. "Are you here, too? I mean, were you there last night? In the boat. That part seemed like a dream. I didn't know why you would be here. Don't you live in California? You know, in the house? Sorry, I'm really foggy right now. Good to see you, though. It's been a long time."

"Likewise," Rupert said. "I have something for you. And I wish I'd given it to you sooner." He handed Daniel the envelope. "If you recall, I bought it from you furnished. Since that time, no one has set foot inside it. I owe you an explanation, and at some point, I intend to give you one. But for now, this will have to do."

When he'd gone, Horace stood up and shuffled over to Daniel's bed.

"What is it?"

Daniel dropped the papers onto his lap. "It's the deed," he said. "To our old house in California."

With hot eyes, Daniel Smith looked down the line of beds, and he laughed.

❧ twenty-two ❧

NEW YEAR'S EVE

Cyrus Smith rapped his knuckles on the table and slowly rolled his head. His right leg was bouncing. A notebook was open in front of him, a pen was in his hand, and a large leather-bound volume faced him on a small stand.

He stared at the window. The world outside was white. Snowflakes were drifting on the sill.

A clock was ticking. Worse, across the table, an hourglass was busily draining its sand.

Beside the hourglass, Nolan was tipping back in his chair, yawning and slowly peeling the skin off his forefinger like he was taking off a sock.

"Do you mind?" Cyrus asked. Nolan set the finger skin upright on the table. It was only missing the fingernail.

"I got a splinter," Nolan said. "That's it. This is what happens when I get a splinter."

"Lame sauce," said Cyrus. "On the other hand, you don't die."

"Shut up and do your Latin. This is your third time

taking this test, Cyrus. No more chances. You can't sluff it again."

"Yeah, yeah," Cyrus said. "I passed that Creole thing this morning, didn't I?"

"You did. But this isn't a 'Creole thing.' It's Latin. And you have to pass it, too." Nolan slammed his chair down. "Get to work, Cy. Seriously. You have to finish this time. After all you've been through and all you've learned, I don't want you kicked out over Latin."

"Rupe wouldn't really do that," Cyrus said.

Nolan laughed. "Rupert Greeves? Cyrus, please. You know he would. He'd have to. And you've still got your Medicinal and Occult exams later. Both long ones. Did you finish with Jax already?"

Nodding and scrunching his lips, Cyrus turned back to his Latin.

The distant sound of steel on steel crept into the room. A crowd oohed and aahed.

Cyrus tried to ignore it. He was supposed to be there, watching Antigone's Weaponry exam with Greeves. He glanced at the hourglass, and then at the dead language in the dead book in front of him.

A red-winged blackbird landed on the snow-drifted windowsill.

Why were there so many distractions?

A piece of skin shaped exactly like a nose drifted across the table.

• • •

Breathing hard behind her wire mask, trying to stand tall, Antigone walked back to the weapon table. The Galleria was full to overflowing. She scanned the faces. Clumps of girls and boys in long white trousers and white sweaters—black symbols patched onto cable-knit chests. Men in jackets. Nervous women. Even the fat-faced monk who had once attacked her in the dining hall. The Galleria had been full for Cyrus's exam, too, but he'd passed Weaponry two months ago, even before she'd passed Linguistics.

"Saber!" Rupert yelled. "One adversary!"

Her last one. She'd done well enough with the foil. Not so well with the dagger. But saber was her worst—the most tiring and the most painful of the fencing blades. Slashing was harder for her than touching with a point.

Setting down her dagger, she picked up the heavier blade and returned to the starting position. The crowd was silent, all except for Dan. He was whistling like a football fan—not exactly in keeping with O of B decorum. Adjusting her mask, she patted the symbol embroidered onto her own chest. Cyrus's leather jacket had chosen it for them. A boxing monkey inside a shield—the symbol of the Polygoners.

A thick Journeyman walked out in his white suit and wire mask, taking his position across from Antigone.

"Dice him, Tigs!" That wasn't Dan. Cyrus had

arrived. She almost smiled. For good or ill, his Latin exam was over.

The signal came, and sabers clashed.

Diana Boone stood in her large Eskimo coat, bouncing in the snow and rubbing her hands together. The airstrip was clear of drifts—for now—and the old Bristol Scout biplane sputtered beside her, idling, remaining warm until Antigone arrived.

Poor girl. Diana didn't know who had it worse. Cyrus was spending his day moving from dry paper test to dry paper test, while Antigone's day was a trial of physical endurance. Lifesaving and resuscitation, the gun range, fencing, and now her first solo flight—and in a canvas-bodied museum piece, too. How either of them could fit it all into a day, she didn't know. But the year was dying. By midnight, one way or another, they would no longer be Acolytes.

Diana heard the crowd before she saw it. Rupert Greeves, hatless, snowflakes tangling in his pointed black beard, was walking between Cyrus and Antigone, followed by the many spectators eager to see the testing of the outlaw Polygoners.

Antigone was still in her fencing suit. She walked straight to Diana and gave her a hug.

"Whatever happens," she said, "thanks for everything."

Diana nodded. "You ready?"

"I have to be, don't I?"

"She's ready," Cyrus said. "You should have seen her with the saber. Carved through two Journeymen. It took an Explorer to bring her down." He gave his sister a boost and watched her climb into the open cockpit.

Once seated, Antigone brushed back her short hair before pulling on her cap and goggles. "Cy-Rusty there didn't do too bad, either!" she yelled above the engine. "He actually finished a Latin translation."

"Without strangling Nolan," Cyrus said. "That's the impressive part. We'll see if I passed."

Antigone wrapped a long white scarf around her face. The crowd stepped back, and the old World War I biplane sputtered and bounced down the snowy airstrip. Slowly, perfectly, effortlessly, the plane rose into the air and climbed out over the icy lake, a hillful of people whistling and whooping as it did.

Cyrus raised his Quick Water and waited. His sister's bundled face, the sprawling lake, the tail of the plane, Ashtown—all of it appeared in the palm of his hand, bent and warped in glorious fish-eye. Cyrus smiled at Antigone, and then scrunched his lips and flared his nostrils, knowing she could see his clownish face.

For a moment, and only a moment, the image in his

hand flickered. Cyrus blinked, and he was again looking at Antigone. But in that brief flash, he was almost certain that he'd seen a black beard, an ear, and a wobbling golden bell.

That night, New Year's Eve, the new cook put out his best spread yet—and it wasn't any good. But no one cared. Snow was falling while the old year died, and fireplaces were roaring in every room in Ashtown.

Cyrus and Antigone Smith sat on an empty bed. Dan sat between them. Their mother, still lost in peaceful dreams, slept on the bed in front of them.

"I'm proud of you two," Dan said. He slapped their knees, and then pulled them in tight. "You did it. And I think it's good that you're staying. We'll still be together a lot."

"And I'm glad you're starting school," Antigone said. "Get rid of your lazy ways."

"Right," said Cyrus. "California is good for that. Can we go eat? I did Latin today, so I'm starving."

Antigone started to stand, but Dan pulled her back down. His once-blue eyes had been darkening over the past few months, and his pupils seemed to bulge a little . . . vertical. The Order hadn't been willing to let him leave at first. They'd poked and prodded and tested and observed until they'd been sure that he was fine—that his mind was undamaged and that he was, well, who he thought he was. But that didn't mean that Antigone was used to his eyes. She didn't mind his new height or the size of his shoulders or the shape of his teeth or his quick bursts of strength when he picked her up or squeezed her. He was more than healthy, and that made her happy. But she missed the blue sparkle when he smiled.

Dan cleared his throat. "Just one more thing I need to tell you. Not a big deal, but I thought you'd be interested."

"And . . . ," said Cyrus.

"I sold the Archer."

"What?" Antigone asked. "How? Who would buy it?"

"Well, it's not like I was asking a lot for it, and it does have a certain truck-stop beauty."

"Who?" asked Cyrus. He felt a strange tug inside him, a tug he knew well. This was another goodbye. Another piece of him gone. But he didn't mind. Not this time.

"Pat and Pat. They're fixing it up. The pool, too. And they'll move their diner in. I threw in the waffle maker."

Laughing, three Smiths stood. Three Smiths bent and kissed their mother on the head, and as they left the room in each other's warmth, outside the window, a red-winged blackbird sang.

In the dining hall, the men and women of the Order mingled, laughed, and occasionally shouted. But one table—a round table in a corner beneath a battered and bullet-pocked vent—was especially rowdy. People called them the Polygoners, but only three of them were actually members of the O of B.

Dennis Gilly, sailing instructor, was explaining the origins of certain rules to Nolan, who was telling a joke to little Hillary Drake from Accounting, who didn't get it but was laughing anyway. Jax, the twelve-year-old zookeeper, was singing a song he'd written about turtles. Gunner, too tall for his chair, was joining in whenever the chorus came around, but was refusing to sing the right words. Daniel Smith was emptying a third plate. Diana Boone was telling Antigone an old family story. Cyrus had been interrupting to show them both tricks with bread. Oliver Laughlin, the boy, sat quietly smiling with his arms crossed beneath a boxing monkey on his chest.

Laughing, Cyrus leaned back and watched the circle of faces around him. He'd been late to this already very late celebratory dinner—he'd had a Latin test to sink through the ice off the end of the jetty.

But his chair had been waiting for him. He looked at his sister, his brother, at Diana and Dennis. In the end, he would say goodbye to them all, or they would say goodbye to him. Life would pass. They would all find their ends. But not now. Not yet. For now, they were alive. Together. And that was enough.

Rupert Greeves and John Horace Lawney walked up to the table.

"Excuse me," said Horace. "And a happy New Year to you all."

When the replies had died down, he continued, adjusting half-moon glasses on his nose. "Mr. Cyrus Smith and Miss Antigone Smith, Mr. Rupert Greeves, the appropriately appointed Avengel of the Order of Brendan, informs me that you have completed the requirements established at your presentation this past summer, and have met the standards for Acolytes, 1914."

"Huzzah for the Polygoners!" Jax yelled, raising an empty milk glass.

"Quite," said Horace.

"I know Latin!" Cyrus yelled.

"*Not* quite," said Nolan.

Horace plowed on through the laughter. "As the representative of one William Cyrus Skelton, Keeper, now deceased, it is my duty to inform you that, in the eyes of the Order of Brendan, you are now—finally—considered to be Mr. Skelton's full, complete, and uncontested heirs. Barring, of course, any specific exclusions in Mr. Skelton's Last Will and Testament."

The table went silent. Horace peered at Cyrus over his glasses.

"Well," said Cyrus, "what do we get?"

"That," said Rupert, eyeing Horace, "is between you and the Order. And as the New Year has now arrived, I am here to invite you to join me in my office for an unsealing of the documents and a formal reading of the will."

Cyrus and Antigone stood up and pushed back their chairs.

Antigone waved to the group. "We'll be right back."

"No," said Horace, laughing. "I don't think you will. This should take some time."

Beside a quiet country road outside of Oconomowoc, Wisconsin, not too far west of the frozen freshwater sea called Lake Michigan, there is a lady on a pole. She stands as silent and pale as the snow falling around her, crowning her head, chilling her extended arm.

Behind her, the Red Baron slept in a bed of snow beside an enormous bulldozer. Beneath her, an old green pickup idled. A large woman leaned against its hood.

A man, as big and bearded as a musk ox, came hustling toward her. He was holding a silver box and switch, dragging an electrical cord behind him.

He put his arm around his wife. She put her arm around her husband. The two of them looked up at the Pale Lady.

And then the New Year erupted with life, with silent, slow-falling flakes of wealth. Snow became golden. Darkness crept away.

Cyrus gripped the worn leather on the arms of his chair and glanced at his sister sitting next to him. She tucked back her short black hair and bit her lower lip. Across the top of the large desk, John Horace Lawney adjusted his half-moon glasses. Rupert Greeves stood behind him, arms crossed.

The little lawyer set a blue glass brick the size of a shoe box on top of his desk. Dust ghosted off its sides. Cyrus leaned forward. It wasn't glass all the way through. It was some kind of package wrapped in glass. Heavy folds met on the top beneath a large black seal.

"Will the Avengel please break the seal?" Horace asked, leaning back in his seat. Rupert stepped forward, sliding a gold ring onto his finger. Clenching his fist, he dealt the center of the seal a quick, crisp blow. The glass cracked through the corners. Horace delicately peeled the pieces away like giant petals.

An ebony box sat amid the shards.

Horace opened it and leaned forward, peering beneath the hinged lid through his half-lenses. Cyrus held his breath as the little lawyer lifted out the contents one at a time. First, a creased and folded hand-drawn map of Mongolia. Second, an apple core the color of leather. Third, a little booklet called *How to Breed Your Leatherbacks.* Fourth, a folded rice-paper sphere for a Chinese lantern, wrapped in a protective oilcloth. The lawyer expanded it carefully until it sat on his desk in front of Cyrus and Antigone, a little larger than a classroom globe. A map of the world had been crudely drawn on its yellowing paper, and the oceans were filled with ink scrawlings in a language even Rupert didn't recognize. Also in the box, a tiny bamboo tray full of hardened oil with a candlewick.

While Cyrus and Antigone watched, Horace attached it to the bottom of the paper globe and lit the wick.

The room glowed orange. Cyrus glanced at his sister. Map shadows striped her surprised face. Moments later, the sphere floated gently into the air, spinning slowly. "Right," said Cyrus.

"So . . . ," said Antigone.

Rupert Greeves laughed. "Horace, I think you'd better read them the will."

EPILOGUE

IN A COLD, dark room, Dr. Phoenix sat at his desk, chewing thoughts, digesting dreams. A smooth black tooth chilled his one remaining palm. His soiled white coat had only one full arm, and so did he. Despite every spell and charm and oily medicine, the other hand had drifted away. In ash.

Smiths. He hated all Smiths.

He ran a finger across the tip of the Reaper's Blade. He had done much with it already. He had planted many seeds. Soon the harvest would come.

This would be a year the world would remember.

Five minutes later, Phoenix stepped down a flight of tight stairs and pulled open a heavy metal door. Frozen air flowed out around his crippled legs, and he hobbled in, passing between stacks of long metal boxes, each with a glass door in its side. Naked shapes were visible behind them.

Finally, he stopped, breathing hard, puffing vapor.

Behind a glass door, three boxes up from the floor,

lay the lifeless body of a tall man with blond hair. His puckered bullet wounds were pale. His dead lips and ears and eyelids were blue. His name was written in ink on a small card attached to the glass.

LAWRENCE JOHN SMITH

END OF BOOK ONE

Obsecro **ut** haec recites: Jam incipio calcare orbem terrarum, colere agrestia, **jugum** injicere maribus quemadmodum antea fecit frater meus, sanctus Brendanus. Nec prae timore avertam gradum ab umbris nec mea lumina a luce. Secundum imperia Procuratorum me geram, nec quicquam secretum ab Sagis habebo. Sint stellae mihi duces et Dominus me servet semper. Ceterum, in Bibliotheca inhaustu abstinebo fumorum.

❧ GRATITUDE ❧

Kate Klimo and Mallory Loehr
for eyes, words, and belief

Meg O'Brien for laughter

Dennis M., Joe E., and the rest of the sixth floor
for batting cleanup

Ellice Lee for my new uniform

Heather Linn for every little thing

Rory, Lucia, Ameera, Seamus, and Marisol
for being (and test-driving large portions of this
in their own bedtime adventures)

❧ ABOUT THE AUTHOR ❧

N. D. WILSON is the bestselling author of the 100 Cupboards series and *Leepike Ridge*. Once, in the fourth grade, he split his buddy's arrow while shooting at a mattress from twenty yards. Now, he writes at the top of a tall, skinny house, where he lives with a blue-eyed girl he stole from the ocean, their five young explorers, two tortoises, and one snake. For more information, please visit AshtownBurials.com.

Read on for an exciting excerpt from

Ashtown Burials II:
THE DROWNED VAULT

RUPERT POINTED his light at a smooth spot on the wall
of the underwater cave. Cyrus swam forward, blinking
in the clear freshwater.

The stone had been carved with a long inscription.
At the top, Cyrus recognized the Tri-Dracul crest of the
Smiths. He traced the inscription with his fingers.

RIP

Captain John Smith
Sometime Governour of Virginia
Blood Avenger of the Order of Brendan
Who Buried his bodie the 21st of June 1631
Here lyes one conquered, that hath conquered Kings,
And did divide from Draculs three
Their heads and lives in chivalry.
But what avils his Conquests, now he lyes

Interr'd in earth, a Prey to Worms and Flyes?
O may his soul in sweet Elysium sleep,
Until the Keeper that all Souls doth keep,
Return to Judgement, and after thence,
With angels make his Recompense.
Wake him not, lest he wake.

Cyrus looked at Rupert with wide eyes. *Seriously?* Rupert nodded and tapped Cyrus's neck, where he kept Patricia and her keys, then floated forward and pointed to the *him* in *Wake him not*. Cyrus blasted bubbles out of his nose and then focused. The *i* was actually a keyhole. His throat tightened. He'd entered a Burial before, and it hadn't been pleasant.

Cyrus reached up and slid Patricia off his neck. The keys, suddenly visible, dropped through the water into his hand, and silver Patricia coiled around his wrist, swallowed her tail, and disappeared. In the water, the strange Solomon Keys had taken their natural shape. The gold one was long and heavy, with a triangle at its head, a circle in the middle, and a square at the foot. It was clearly too big for the hole. Cyrus fingered the smaller silver one—simple, slender, smooth, and sharp, like a miniature corkscrewing scimitar. Trying not to think about what he was doing, he slid the key into the hole.

He turned it.

Silence. And then grinding. The inscribed slab fell slowly toward him. Cyrus jerked out the key and kicked away. The cave echoed like the inside of a drum when the slab hit the bottom, but Cyrus didn't notice. He was staring at the hole in the stone wall. Something was floating out of it. Seaweed? It was uncurling out of the darkness, slowly drifting across the floor of the cave.

A tangle floated in front of Cyrus. He touched it, rubbing it between his fingers. It was hair. Four hundred years' worth of hair.

Rupert handed one of his long knives to Cyrus, and then swam straight into the tomb's narrow tunnel.

For an hour or more, Cyrus hung behind Rupert, collecting mussels that the big man pushed back between his legs and kicking them toward the cave. The hacked-off hair had to be shuttled all the way back. And even then, it somehow managed to drift down and tangle around Cyrus's face.

Finally, Rupert swam all the way out of the tunnel, handed off the spotlight, and gestured for Cyrus to lead.

Cyrus kicked forward.

The chamber at the end of the tunnel was small, but the ceiling rose into a dark vault. Cyrus drifted up, pushing through the hair with his spotlight and knife until he reached the middle of the room.

Below him, the slow storm of hair parted, and he was looking down at the body of a man, floating just above a stone table. The man's face was calm but creased with scars where it wasn't hidden by his beard. His limbs were chained to cannonballs, and the heavy chains kept him floating only inches above the table. He wore a breastplate that had tarnished black, and a long blue coat with blackened metal buttons. Tall boots had been removed and tucked beneath his floating legs. Long, corkscrewing fingernails dangled from his hands, bent against the floor, and ran up the walls. More nails twisted and tangled up from his toes, but Cyrus was focused on the face. He'd even forgotten the hair.

It was like looking at an uncle he had never known. It could even be his father, if his father had lived to see another decade. He had his father's brow, a slightly larger version of his father's nose. The same shoulders. The right height. Rupert nudged Cyrus, and the two of them descended.

Cyrus floated directly above his sleeping ancestor, face to face with him. He wasn't sure how to process it. But he knew what he had to do. He set the spotlight on the Captain's chest, and started with the beard.